# Immortality

## Armed To The Teeth

By

Paul J. Kearns

ISBN:9781739784461

For Carrie, Quinn, and Erin.

This book is a work of fiction. All names, characters, locations, and incidents are either a product of the Author's imagination or are used fictitiously. Any resemblance to actual events, locations, or persons, living, dead or undead, or immortal is purely coincidental.



Any mentions of members of the armed forces in this book are done so with the utmost respect to the people who have and still do serve in the military. Thank you for your service.

Content Warning:
Death, severe injury detail, graphic gore, torture, emotional abuse,

**Acknowledgements**:

Thank you to Carrie, Quinn, and Erin for all your love and support.

Thank you to my Mum, Dad for bringing me up right, for teaching me that I can shape my own future, and teaching me to go and get what I want from life.

Thank you to Noel and Sam for the ongoing support and for believing in me.

Thank you to Louise Croft for all your help.

Thank you to all my extended family for being there when we have needed you most and for being amazing.

Thank you to all my friends, you know who you are and know I love you.

To Mr. Roberts, my former English teacher at Little lever secondary school as it was back then, thank you for being a great teacher and encouraging me to continue writing fiction.

Email Paul:
PJKauthor@hotmail.com

**Other books by Paul J Kearns:**
The Hunted and other Twisted Tales.

Special Operations vampire Elimination Unit

Beasts of Immortality Book 1: Blood and Purpose

**You can find Paul J Kearns on social media.**
Facebook:
https://m.facebook.com/PJKearnsAuthor/
Instagram:
https://www.instagram.com/pauljkearnsauthor/
Twitter:
www.twitter.com/pjkearnsauthor

## Chapter 1.

Andra stood and looked out from the hole in the building that had been the window of Alex's apartment. The town beyond was lit up by the street lights. In the distance she saw the blue lights of multiple police vehicles headed in their direction.

"Palmer, Davis, I want the remains of that body collected and taken down to the van. Hussain, use the hand vac to collect a sample of the ashes from the carpet. I want to know who died here. Mc'Ready, find the casings from the shots we heard. Hughes, White, go downstairs, disperse any crowd that may be forming, and get the van. The police will be here in five minutes. I want to be gone before they get here," Andra barked.

They all got on with the tasks that Andra set for them. She picked up the weapons the vampires had used, while Mc'Ready searched, and Hussain got to work with the vac. Hughes and White escorted Palmer and Davis down the stairs as they carried the solidified remains into the lift and then out of the front door. Davis opened the rear door of the van, and Palmer threw what was left of Blanc down next to Blur, who was wrapped in chains.

"What the fuck is that?" he said.

"It's all that's left of your friend," said Davis.

"What the fuck?! Get it away from me! Get that thing away from me!" he screamed as he wiggled in an attempt to move away from the husk.

"Someone put something in his mouth to shut him

up," said Andra as she approached them.

"How about a bullet?" said Palmer.

Andra looked at him and smiled. "Tempting but I need him alive. He's the only one who knows what really happened," said Andra.

Blur continued to scream.

"Just shut the idiot up. He's pissing me off," said Andra.

Palmer pulled a clove from his pocket and pushed it into Blur's screaming mouth. He tried to shout around it until Davis pinned his head to the floor of the van with the sole of her boot and pressed the Barrel of her Barretta into his temple.

"Shut the fuck up, or I'll shut you up permanently," she said.

With that he went completely silent.

Hussain and Mc'Ready came down and joined them. Andra then ushered them all back into the van. Four minutes had passed from Andra giving the orders. By the time the police arrived a minute later, there was no sign the team had even been there.

They drove around for a while in an attempt to track Alex after he leapt from the apartment. Despite his huge size there was no sign of him. After a few hours Andra reluctantly instructed White to return to base. He drove back across the dark town as the horizon was beginning to brighten with the promise of a new day's sun. He drove into the warehouse through the security measures and down into the garage. When he had pulled into a parking space and applied the handbrake they all climbed out.

"Palmer, Hughes. Take the prisoner to a holding cell. Don't hurt him. We're not animals like these pieces of shit. White, Davis, Hussain and Mc'Ready. Take the body, the ashes and the weapons to the science department. I want to know what the hell happened to that vampire and I want D.N.A. scans done on the ashes. I want to know who they were. I want prints and D.N.A. pulled from the weapons too. I want to know if any of the vamps we have records of were involved with this. Then all of you go get some rest it's been a long night. You were all great," said Andra.

## Chapter 2.

Alex woke up feeling groggy as if he had been drinking heavily. He was sprawled naked on a cold, hard, concrete floor. The air smelt strange here. It was a human smell, like sweat and skin, of fear and desperation. There was another smell mixed in with it. A smell only known by those who have experienced it. The smell of blood, old and new. The smell of exertion and excreta. The smell of vampires. His eyes moved under their lids, then he slowly opened them. The room was dark, musty and unkempt. Rubbish and clothes were strewn all over the floor and piled up in corners.

'Oh shit,' he thought as he sat up and stretched. 'Where the hell am I?'

He looked around, this definitely wasn't his apartment. It looked like a basement with pipes that ran along the ceiling and damp running down the filthy concrete walls. He was suddenly aware of his nakedness. He looked at the clothes around him to see if any of them were his. He took hold of a scrap of material and picked it up. As he did it began to unravel. Something fell from it and onto the floor. It looked like the hand of a mannequin. He reached out and upon picking it up he realised it was more than that. It was tough like boot leather and as he turned it in his hands he was shocked to see fingerprints and fingernails. He was more shocked by his urge to bite into it.

The extraordinary events of the previous night slowly came back to him. He had visions of Vincent showing at his door after so many years. He remembered being bitten by Vincent, then watching his brother turn to ash and fall apart. Tears welled in his eyes and streamed down his face. He remembered the vampires breaking into his apartment, and the pain of them beating him as he began to transform. He also remembered their screams as he began to eat them.

A noise from behind him brought him back to his present situation. He spun around and got to his feet in one movement. Before him stood a tall steel cage. A man inside scampered to the back when he realised Alex was looking at him. His clothes and skin were covered in grime and blood. Alex approached the cage and the man, who was now cowering in the corner, began to scream.

"Please, don't hurt me. Please, don't...don't hurt me!"

"I'm not going to hurt you," said Alex.

He picked up a pair of trousers, searched for the label, saw that they were the correct size and pulled them on.

"Please don't hurt me!" said the man again in a howl.

"Look, I promise, I'm not going to hurt you. What's your name?" said Alex.

The man looked up and his eyes met Alex's. Tears streamed down his face that was a picture of absolute terror.

"I'm Alex. And you are?" said Alex in a calm tone.

The man's expression softened. "I…I, I'm Steven,"

he said.

"Why do you think I'm going to hurt you?" said Alex.

"I saw you. I, I saw what you did to them. I…I saw what you did. You tore them apart! You ate them! You were a monster. You ate these people! Then...then...then you changed. You changed into you as you are now. Then you lay down and went asleep! Like it never happened! Oh god I'm losing my mind!" yelled Steven.

"Steven. Please calm down. You're not losing your mind. Things just got a bit weird and you saw some things that you shouldn't have," said Alex gently.

"Weird? You ate those people. You fucking ate them!" said Steven.

"Do you know what those people were? Do you know why you're here?" said Alex.

Steven slowly shook his head with a sad smile.

"I was in a bar. This woman bought me a drink, we danced a little and the next thing I knew I woke up here. Shortly after you burst in and tore them all to bits. I don't know what is going on," he said as tears rolled down his face.

"She was a vampire. They brought you here as food," said Alex.

"A vampire? Just my luck. I knew I shouldn't have trusted her," said Steven.

"You believe me that easily?" said Alex.

"Mate, you were a fuckin' monster a few hours ago and I watched you change into a man. I haven't taken my eyes off you since. Right now vampires aren't that high on the list of things I'm willing to believe," said Steven.

Alex smiled, and Steven smiled back.

"I'm gonna let you out as no one else knows you're here. You can't tell anyone what happened though. You can't tell anyone what you saw," said Alex.

"Yes, I won't tell anyone. I just want to go home," said Steven.

"Hold on. I'll find something to open the door," said Alex.

He took hold of the padlock that secured the door and looked at the keyhole thoughtfully. He gave it what he thought was a gentle pull. The metal loop stretched, then snapped like it was made of soft plastic. The two men looked at each other, they were both amazed by his strength. He opened the door and Steven hesitated for a moment but then stepped passed him and out of the cage.

"Can I just ask you one thing?" said Steven.

"Yes, go ahead," said Alex.

"If they were vampires, what the hell are you?" said Steven.

"I'm the one who's going to destroy them. Go home, Steven. Don't tell anyone about me or the vampires. Don't give me a reason to have to come and find you," said Alex.

Steven nodded nervously and ran off into the early morning light. Alex smiled to himself. He knew Steven wouldn't tell anyone. No one would believe him anyway.

He had left a trail of devastation when he had

smashed his way into the building. The vampires wouldn't have even expected an attack anything like the one that had happened to them. He had no idea how many of them had been here but the place was empty. Their screams flooded back into his mind. With Alex's transformation, the tides had turned. Vampires were no longer top of the food chain and that terrified them. He knew they would fight with everything they had to survive.

As he made his way out of the building he found a t-shirt and slipped it on. He now realised he was in an old derelict mill about a mile from his apartment.

As he walked home he passed a bus stop. It had a clock that read 'Sat 13th – 7.20.' A man at the bus stop on the other side of the road shouted.

"Nice costume, mate. Halloweens not till next month."

Alex assumed that he was referring to his torn clothes and messy hair. So he smiled and kept on walking. As he continued on his journey he received strange looks from the few people he saw but ignored them and kept on walking. After about twenty minutes he arrived on the street across from his apartment block. The building was cordoned off and surrounded by emergency services vehicles. He looked up at the huge hole he had made when he leapt from his apartment the night before. He could see people examining the edge of the hole. There was no way he was going up there to announce himself as the resident without speaking to Andra first.

He kept on walking and soon he reached the

warehouse base. The soldier at the gate stepped out of his cabin and looked at Alex with the same confused look the other people had. He then raised his gun and pointed it at Alex.

"Alex, stop right there," he said.

"Moses, what the hell? Why are you pointing your gun at me? I've known you for fourteen years," said Alex.

"I have strict orders from Lieutenant Colonel Hudson to stop you on sight," said Moses with his gun still trained on Alex. He clicked his radio. "Ma'am, Alex has just arrived."

"Keep him there. I'll be up in a minute. What does he look like?" Andra's voice crackled through the radio.

"He looks like Alex, Ma'am, but…well…different. It's better if you come and see for yourself, Ma'am," said Moses.

"Ok, I'm on my way," said Andra.

A few moments later Andra stepped through the warehouse's main door dressed in a suit and approached them. She was accompanied by three guards all armed with AA12 automatic shotguns.

"Stand still, Alex. Place your hands above your head," said Andra.

She walked over and fixed him with a hard stare. She placed a hand on his wrist, turned him around, and cuffed his hands behind his back.

"What the hell is this Andra? You know me. Why am I being treated like an enemy?" said Alex.

"We just have to make sure you're not a danger to us. Make sure you're still on our side," she said.

“Of course I am. I don’t know how you would even doubt me,” said Alex.

He moved his arms and easily broke out of the restraints. The three soldiers quickly raised their guns to aim at his head.

“Wow! Hold on lads,” he said and raised his hands.

“Look, Alex, we’re doing this for our own safety. Speaking of which, it’s not safe to talk out here. We're taking you to secure room five. If you begin to change we won’t hesitate to put you down. Do you understand?” she said.

“Ok, ok. Yeah, I’ll cooperate?” said Alex.

“Until you can prove otherwise we will need to treat you as a possible threat,” she said in a cold tone.

The guards escorted him into the building.

## Chapter 3.

07.50.

Saltorg was sat in his office in the Manchester branch of Medicyber Technologies. He and Dienco had started the business in the early 1830s as Salt and Enco's Medical supplies. They had changed the name many times and started up many offshoot businesses over the last one hundred and ninety years. Those offshoots were now deeply rooted in almost every area of the medical industry.

Lately, this building had been completely overhauled with clean rooms, floating rooms, top of the range computers, networks and all new equipment. Their business was at the forefront of 3D printed artificial limbs powered by microprocessors, and nanoengines. Their experimental artificial organs were groundbreaking. All outward aspects of the company gave the impression that they were concerned with the betterment of human health and welfare. Any signs that it was secretly run by vampires, who were working to improve their abilities and UV resistance were extremely well hidden. Their darkest secrets were only known by the vampire hierarchy.

He was looking over some figures on his computer when his phone rang. He took it out of his pocket. The screen displayed Dr. Revitska's name. He swiped the green button and put the phone to his ear.

"Hello doctor," he said.

"Hello Mr Saltorg. I…er…I have bad news. Vincent Austin escaped last night," said Revitska

"He escaped?! How the hell did this happen? You better have an extremely good excuse, Bodvik!" said Saltorg.

"We suspect he broke out of his cell with the aid of a renegade vampire. Unfortunately, our CCTV was scrambled during the escape. Somehow he and this renegade killed fifty guards. They were unstoppable. It was a massacre," said Revitska.

"I am utterly disappointed with you. This is horrendous news. Which renegade vampire did this?" said Saltorg.

"From what the few witnesses who survived have said, we suspect she is a traitor named Sapora. She has been waging a personal war against our kind since her master, an American Elder named Boltat, cast her and her apprentice out for breaking the Lycanthrope peace treaty," said Revitska.

"I have heard of her. I didn't know she had made her way over here," said Saltorg.

"Nor did I, sir," said Revitska.

"I want her found. I want her corpse presented to me by the end of this week," said Saltorg.

"Begging your pardon, sir, but we have more pressing issues at this present moment," said Revitska.

"What on earth do you mean?" said Saltorg.

"There is also good news, sir. I personally surgically implanted a tracker chip into the base of Vincent's skull. It was to monitor vital organs…but it also monitored his location," said Revitska,

"I'm listening," said Saltorg.

"It was damaged in the escape so his vital signs are unknown but it is still transmitting his location. He stopped at an address in Oxfordshire early in this morning. Google Maps shows it to be residential apartments. I sent a team from a local base to track him just after he stopped. I have not heard back from them so I assume the worst. I believe he could have met up with his brother there. He has since moved to another location. It's a guarded warehouse not far from the apartment building, sir. An old warehouse that I believe has been converted into a military training centre. I suspect that this could be the location of Andra's private army and headquarters. It's just a hunch but I think we should investigate," said Revitska.

"Doctor, you are brilliant. To fit him with a transmitter was a stroke of genius. It's unfortunate those soldiers had to be sacrificed but he may have led lead us straight to that bitch," said Saltorg.

"I know it has worked to our advantage but I'm a little sad that he has escaped. I enjoyed torturing him," said Revitska.

"You're a sick bastard, doc, but I'm glad you're our sick bastard. I want to move in as soon as possible. When can you have your soldiers ready?" said Saltorg.

"I can provide one hundred and ten soldiers. That's all I have left after the escape. They are all ready to go. We all want to catch those bastards," said Revitska.

"Ok, have them ready to move as soon as possible. I want to attack as just after sunset. I'm taking charge of this operation so tell your soldiers are now under my command effective immediately," said Saltorg.

"Very well, sir. I'll see you soon, sir," said Revitska.

"Will you be coming with us, Dr?" said Saltorg.

"Yes, sir. It has been a long time but you may remember we first met when you fought alongside Attila the Hun," said Revitska.

"Yes. I remember, we have fought some fine battles together haven't we," said Saltorg.

"We have indeed, sir," said Revitska.

"Tomorrow we will be celebrating another fine victory," said Saltorg.

"Yes we will, Mr Saltorg. I'll see you soon," said Revitska.

Saltorg ended the call and selected another number from his contacts and made a video call. It rang for a moment then a huge face filled the screen.

The vampirism had changed Dienco. He was eight feet tall with an incredibly heavily built stature. His long hair and beard were thick and in rope-like braids. His skin was thick, tough and pale.

"Hello Mr Dienco," said Saltorg.

"Ah, Mr Saltorg! How are you, my brother?" bellowed Dienco in a deep, gruff voice. His accent was still Germanic as he was the only one of the Children of the Blood who still lived in the land that had become Germany.

"I have news. The brothers of the prophecy may

be together again. I am leading a small army to their location to destroy them once and for all," said Saltorg.

"What do you mean, dear brother?" said Dienco.

"Erm…Vincent has escaped," said Saltorg.

"What?! How can that be?! I thought Dr Revitska had him held in a secure location. I'll pull that little fool in two!" roared Dienco.

"Calm yourself, brother. The good Doctor took the liberty of implanting a tracker in Vincent's neck long before the escape. In his eagerness Vincent may have led us straight to his brother and Andra," said Saltorg.

"Well then, I do apologise. That is fantastic news. When do you intend to attack them?" said Dienco.

"As soon as possible," said Saltorg.

"I can send you some soldiers if you need," said Dienco.

"In all honesty that is why I called you. Some of your best soldiers would be greatly appreciated," said Saltorg.

"Very well. I have three hundred Blutesser Soldiers prepped and ready. They are in London. I'll have them sent to your location of choice when you need them. I can get you another five hundred ready in a week's time. They are at your disposal," said Dienco

"Thank you, brother. With the urgency of the situation the three hundred will be very much appreciated. The location is in Oxford so we'll travel down to them. I want to perform a coordinated attack," said Saltorg.

"They are ready now. All you need to do is tell my associate, Mr Goss, the location. I have a plane that can deliver a cargo of soldiers anywhere in half an hour. I, unfortunately, will not be able to get to England for at least two maybe three days, so I wish you well in this battle," said Dienco.

"Thank you, Dienco. With your soldiers I know we'll win. No human has ever taken up arms against me and lived. What chance do a handful of veterans stand?" said Saltorg.

Dienco roared with laughter.

"I will see you when your hands are wet with their blood," he said.

## Chapter 4.

Alex sat in a small grey concrete room with a two-way mirror and 'Secure Room Five' stencilled on the wall. He rested his elbows on the steel table in the middle of the room and held his head in his hands. He had been waiting like this for over thirty minutes. There was a click of the lock and the door burst open. Andra strode in and slammed the door behind her. She threw the table into the wall, lifted him up under his arms and kicked the chair from under him. She stood him on his feet and stared at him. Her eyes were cold and hard.

"What the hell is this all about Andra? Asking me if I'm a danger? Asking my loyalty?" said Alex.

"Well, are you?!" said Andra.

"Yes! Why wouldn't I be?" he snapped.

"Have you looked in a mirror or seen your reflection?" she said.

"No. What are you talking about?" said Alex.

"Look at yourself," she said as she turned him to face the mirror. His jaw dropped and his heart sank. He stood and stared at his reflection in the mirror. Physically, it was him but it was wrong. His skin was deathly pale and his eyes were bright but looked hard like glass. He forced himself to bare his teeth and fell back against the wall. His canines and lateral incisors were long and sharp.

"What the fuck?! I have fangs? I look like a...like a..." he stammered in shock.

"You look like a fucking vampire," she said.

"Yes, but…but how the...what the fuck? How do I

look like a vampire?" he said.
Andra's eyes never left him and she leaned in close.

"You look like a vampire," she sniffed him. "You smell like a vampire. After all I taught you. All these years of looking after you. You go and get bitten by a fucking vampire!"

"I'm not a vampire!" he said.

"No? Then what fuck are you?!" she said.

"I don't know. You saw me last night. Did I look like a vampire to you?!" he said.

"You remember that?" she said.

"How could I not? It was one of the worst nights of my life!" he said.

"Tell me what happened. None of this is making sense," she said.

"Vincent came back," he said

"Vincent came back?" she said furrowing her brow.

"Yes, he came back. He explained to fulfil the prophecy he had to bite me," he said.

"And you let him?!" she said with a look of horror,

"Not straight away. He explained everything to me. They had tortured him for years but he had never given us up. He told me how he had escaped with the aid of a rogue vampire, he had to drink vampire blood to get the strength to escape. He bit me and moments later he…he died in my arms. The vampire blood gave him strength but it killed him too." Tears welled in his eyes. "I still trusted in him, even after all the years that had passed. He was my identical twin brother. I…I don't expect you to understand. After he died a gang of vampires broke in. I couldn't stop them. I tried, honestly I did but the transformation had already begun. I'll never forget the pain of them attacking me. If Vincent hadn't bitten me I would be dead. The transformation was even worse. It felt like every nerve in my body was on fire and being torn apart at the same time. You probably know how that feels."

Andra nodded her head. He continued to speak. "I killed one of the vampires while I was changing, pulled the fucker in two, or near enough. The other two I…I ate them. I don't know what came over me, just this urge to eat them, and so I did," he said.

"I'm so sorry Alex. I…I didn't know Vincent was dead."

She was suddenly overcome with the longing to hold him, to comfort him but she needed to stay in control of the situation.

"And now I'm being treated like your enemy. You always said there must be something more to me. Now there is and this is how you treat me?" he said.

"I'm sorry if you feel you are being treated harshly, Alex, but the thing you changed into… I need to know we can trust you when you're in that form. You were so strong. If you decided to attack us none of us could've stopped you; not even me. I need to know that you are on our side and that you can control yourself. Can you control the change, or is it similar to a form of lycanthropy? Do you need certain conditions or can you change at will? How long can you stay in that form? An hour? Two hours? Or a day?"

"I don't know. I have only changed once and I woke up this morning in a vampire den about two miles from here. I don't remember changing back. It must have happened when I passed out. I do know I'm a lot stronger in this form than I was before, but I don't know if I can just change at will. To answer your question though, I am still Alex Austin and I am still loyal to you and the S.O.V.E.U. The vampires are my only enemy, and it would seem they are a food source too," he said with a half-smile.

She looked at him and her eyes softened slightly.

"I need you to try to change. I need to run some tests and try and figure out what you are now. I need answers to my questions," she said.

"Now?" said Alex.

"Yes now. Try and imagine the change or think about vampires. When we found you, you were still eating one of your attackers. We have brought what was left back to the lab," she said.

"You have it here?" he said.

"Yes. We're still running tests on it to try and establish how you did it. I mean the vamp should have burned up but something about the new you makes them kind of, dry out," she said.

"I can't explain that. I get the weirdest urge to bite them," he said.

"What's it, erm, what does it taste like?" she said eyeing him curiously.

"It's kind of like eating crispy bacon. It tastes kind of similar too," he said.

"I'm both amazed and revolted at the same time,"

she said.
They both smiled at each other for the first time in this interaction.

"Ok, ok. Come on, focus. See if you can bring on the change," she said.

Alex closed his eyes and tried to focus on the physical change. He thought about the blood pumping through his body but nothing happened. He tried to make himself angry but nothing happened. He thought about the vampires attacking him, Vincent, his parents, and his grandparents but besides a raised heartbeat and an urge for revenge, nothing much happened. So, he thought about biting chunks out of vampires and found he began to salivate. It was an odd realisation that his brain was now hardwired to think of them as food. He would never have dreamed he could think about vampires like that. He had always thought of them as the enemy, but to think of them as sustenance, that was something new. A feeling of controlled anger grew in his stomach. Something akin to rage but with a purpose and similar to an adrenaline rush. He felt his muscles begin to itch and ache, but nothing more. He opened one eye and looked around but he was still mostly human.

"Anything?" said Andra.

"Hold on, I think I've got something," he replied as he looked at her with his open eye.

He thought about vampires as his enemy and as his food. The fire in his belly returned and the adrenaline began to flow again. The hunger grew and the burning sensation grew in his muscles. His body started to ache and he felt his skin pucker as though he was covered in goosebumps. Blood rushed to his muscles and they bulged under his flesh. His bones ached like the growing pains he had experienced in his youth. He opened his eyes and could see his body changing. He let out a cry, it was the perfect blend of pain and anger. Andra's jaw hung loose as she stared up at him in awe while he continued to grow. His face began to distort as his bone and muscle structures elongated and shifted. Everything about him was changing and the pain was immense. The first time had been pure agony but this time he found he could almost bear it. He cried out again, and as the sound emanated from his changing throat it became a roar. His teeth moved to accommodate the serrated, shark-like teeth. His skin thickened and became scaled. With that the transformation was complete. He felt energised and capable. He felt power course through every fibre of every muscle in his body. The first time his body had driven itself. He knew from that experience he was strong enough to tear down walls and kill vampires with his bare hands, but what would be the limits of this new body? He felt a sense of anticipation and couldn't wait to test out this new form. He looked at Andra and she looked back at him in awe.

"Incredible. How do you feel?" she said.

He moved his lips and rocked his jaw. His whole face was completely different in size and shape different now. His long snout and long teeth seemed like they would impede speech. His jaw hinged at the back of his skull which allowed him to open his mouth incredibly wide. He could still slide it left to right though. He could also change the shape of his tongue. This helped him change the sounds of his growls. He experimented with this and soon found that he could speak in a similar fashion to when he was in his human form.

"Uh…I…feel amazing… It's like…walking…all my life…and suddenly finding…I can run," he said. His voice was so deep Andra could feel it vibrating the air around her.

"It's good to know you can speak in this form," she said.

"I know. Turning in circles and pointing at things with my snout like a dog would have got old fast," he said.

"How long can you stay like this?" she said.

"I don't know. I think it was about five hours this morning but I don't know if that's just because I fell asleep," he said.

"Ok, can you change back?" she said.

"I've only just changed. Can't I go and have some fun in the training gym?" he said.

"No. We need to see if you have full control of this new body of yours," she said.

"Yes ma'am. I'll have a go,"

He forced himself to stop thinking about vampires but nothing happened. He tried thinking of happy memories but he remained in the same form. So, he tried thinking about returning to his human form but there was still no change. He closed his eyes again and took a few minutes focusing his mind. He realised Andra had spent the last twenty years training him to condition his mind and body to do exactly what he wanted them to do. This was the reason for all that training. He relaxed, slowed his heartbeat and focused his mind on changing. He felt his muscles relax as their fibres shrunk. His bones ached again and his limbs began to return to their usual lengths. He was becoming lighter but his strength was also returning to its usual level. He opened his eyes, which had returned to their hazel colour, and looked around him. He fell to his hands and knees and after a few moments he was human again. He stayed there on his hands and knees, panting and sweating like a person who had just run a marathon.

"That was amazing. How did you do it? How do you feel?" said Andra excitedly.

"I just…used, the training…you had taught me," he wheezed. "I focused…my mind...and body on...changing. And fucking knackered is how I feel," he said.

He turned over and lay on the floor. She casually placed a square black bag over his crotch.

"Do you need to rest or anything to eat?"

"I just need to lie down for a minute. I've already eaten this morning." he smiled.

She rolled her eyes and smiled.

"I meant food like a bacon sandwich or cereal, not vampire flesh," she said.

"No, I'm ok thanks," he said.

"You have to use my quarters. Your quarters were turned into a dorm room after you moved out," she

said.

"That's fair enough," she said.

"But don't laugh at my furniture. I may not be human anymore but I still like my creature comforts. And don't go poking through my things," she said.

"Ok, don't worry I won't laugh or nosey around. Can you please get me some clothes? I think I might have to get some stretchy pants if I'm gonna keep changing," he said.

"There is a pair of black pants and a t-shirt in the bag," she said.

He looked down, took hold of the black square and opened it. As he was pulling on the shirt the intercom clicked on.

"Andra, this is the science department. We've got some things you need to look at ASAP," said Fletcher.

"Ok I'll be there in a minute," said Andra.

She turned and walked over to Alex who was now dressed. She then grabbed him and hugged him tight.

"I'm glad you're ok. I really am so sorry about Vincent. You always knew he hadn't abandoned you and you were right. I was wrong and for that I'm sorry," she said

"Thank you, Andra. I love you," said Alex with tears in his eyes.

"I love you too. Now go and get some rest," she said.

She kissed him lightly on the forehead and walked out of the door.

## Chapter 5.

It was 9.00 when Alex opened the door to Andra's quarters. He walked in and had a look around. She had amassed a small collection of antique suits of armour. Each was housed in a glass case similar to displays in a museum. Among them were a suit of tortoiseshell samurai armour, a suit of hammered steel English armour from the Tudor era, and a perfectly preserved Roman Empire era leather breastplate. He wondered among them in awe. She also had an array of weapons that spanned human history and from around the world. An ancient Japanese Katanas was in the same display case as an ancient Greek Xiphos sword, and a Roman Gladius sword. Another case held a Scottish steel Claymore and Japanese Odachi. Mounted along one wall was a Morning Star, a flail from Europe, a Nordic steel battle axe, and a Zulu Iklwa spear. Some of these weapons were almost as old as Andra herself. He assumed some of them could have only been obtained by her actually using them in battle. They should have degraded but she had kept them all as near to their original condition as possible. He continued the walk through the quarters. As he did, he wondered what she was talking about when she told him not to laugh at the decoration. He continued and walked into the next room. It was decorated like a Victorian-style sitting room. There were all sorts of board games including old board games from around the world that were well used. In the corner sat an old television set that looked like it was from the 1960's. The thick layer of dust on it showed that it was hardly used. He still didn't see anything to laugh at. Tiredness suddenly overcame him but he had to open a few doors before he found the bedroom. He barely noticed the pink duvet cover and the fluffy cushions as he slumped onto the bed and lapsed into a deep sleep.

Andra arrived at the science lab at around the same time. She walked past a centrifuge spinning test tubes that held samples of the ashes that had been found. A bank of computer screens showed readouts and 3D models of DNA, molecules and images from a series of microscopes. The head scientist, Dr. Fletcher, called her over to an autopsy table that held the mutilated vampire body. The head, shoulders, and both arms were gone. The organs within the torso were dried up and had a texture similar to papier-mache.

"Ma'am. Thank you for coming down here so promptly," said Dr. Fletcher.

"What have you got for me?" she said.

"We have run tests on the ashes you brought in earlier and the results are very interesting. We've also taken samples from these remains and have some results from them too. I've never seen anything like them," he said.

He was a tall man in his late forties with thin rimmed glasses and a shaven head.

"What have you found?" said Andra.

"Well, we took samples from the remains here and here," he said as pointed to the areas of the body where it had been bitten and torn away. "There was a strange substance around the wounds and bite marks. We took samples and tested them. The results show it is Alex's saliva. So assumed that it would be somewhere between human and vampire. According to the results, it's neither," he said.

"What do you mean, neither?" she said.

"It is Alex's saliva but, erm, well, it's something else. The chromosomes that are usually present in humans, that essentially make him human, well ma'am, they simply aren't there," he said.

"So what is he?" she said.

"He's more like you, but whereas you have some human D.N.A., he doesn't. He has parts that determine his appearance, his behaviour, and his intelligence. But, he's not human. For all intents and purposes he is a new species. An entirely new species. The saliva contains some very specific enzymes. They are what have caused the hypercoagulation in these remains and probably every other vampire he bites. They work in a similar way to rattlesnake venom but I've never known these specific enzymes to be produced in nature. They cause human blood to coagulate hundreds of times faster than any snake venom. So in a vampire that reaction causes something akin to petrification. This vampire should have burned up but the enzymes stopped the process, allowing Alex to feed on her at will. It's lucky that you interrupted him when you did or we wouldn't know any of this," said Fletcher.

“I’ve seen him change into his new form and then change back. He’s amazing,” she said.

“Yes ma’am, he is. The vampires have finally fallen a rung in the food chain. They have been trying to prevent this since their inception. They’ll be shitting themselves when they find out about him. We have the only one of them who knows about him. I would like to run some tests on him with this enzyme,” he said.

“What are you proposing doctor?” she said.

“I’m curious as to whether the enzymes could be weaponised,” he said.

“You have my permission. Do whatever you need to do. What results did you get from the ashes?” she said.

“You may want to sit down ma’am,” he said.

“Why?” she said.

“The ashes belong to two vampires. One of whom is of Diencoian and Giladian offspring,” he said.

“And the other is Vincent?” she said.

“Yes ma’am. How did you know?” he said.

Andra folded her arm, looked at the floor and lightly nodded her head.

“Alex told me. Vincent is the one who turned him. He said he had drank vampire blood. Apparently, it gave him the strength to escape his captors but eventually killed him,” she said.

“Well, that makes more sense. The other vampire died from the chemical destabilisation caused by being killed. The consistency of Vincent’s remains is consistent with instantaneous complete cellular apoptosis. In layman’s terms, every cell in his body died at the more or less at the same moment. He died as close to a natural death as a vampire can get. There's something else too. We found this in the ashes," said Fletcher and held up a sealable plastic bag. It contained a tiny silver spherical object no larger than a pin head.

"Let me see that," said Andra as she took it from him.

She looked at it and her eyes widened as she realised what it was.

"Oh shit. This is a fucking tracker chip," she ran to the intercom and pressed to button. "I want everyone on high alert. Our location is compromised. This base is now on lockdown. An attack is imminent. We bunker down and make a stand. That is an order. Arm yourselves, armour up, and check your weapons. More info and orders are to follow."

She walked back to the doctor.

"That's a transmitter chip? It's the smallest one I've ever seen. Should we destroy it?" he said.

"The intelligence I have received from my informants showed their scientists were experimenting with nanotech but I didn't know they had actually built anything that worked. Don't destroy it. If they lose the transmission they will know we're onto them. They must have been tracking Vincent. That's how they got to Alex's apartment so fast. I assume they'll be monitoring the feed. Our position is probably already known by now, but they don't know that we know. So we will be ready for them," she said.

"What if we were to send it out in a car with a driver?" he said.

"Vincent wouldn't be moving at this time and we don't have any cars with blacked out windows. They don't know that we know their coming, so, we stand and fight. Trust me, we have the ace up our sleeve that I have been waiting a long time to be able to use. How long is it since you shot a gun, doctor?" she said.

"I practice three times a week, ma'am. I'm ready if you need me to fight," he said.

"Good, I may need you to. Be ready for my call," she said.

With that, she left.

Twenty minutes later she had gathered her attack team and her Sergeants in the conference room. They talked for an hour and formulated a plan. When they were ready she pushed the talk button on the intercom.

"Hello. I want everyone's attention. As you know our location is compromised and I'm expecting an attack at dusk. I assume the vampires don't know that we've found their transmitter so we will be ready for them. Every piece of body armour, every weapon, and all the ammunition needs to be checked. There are two hundred of us so I'm going to split us all into five groups. There will be eight soldiers posted at the main entrance armed with silver gas grenade launchers, C7A2s, and RPGs. They are the first line of defence. They will take out approaching vehicles, launch silver gas into the ground-based vamps then retreat back inside. The next layer of defence will be made up of sixty soldiers and me. The vampires with probably focus their attack on weak spots around the main entrance. If they breach the base and we can't hold them off we will fall back to the next floor. There, a group of fifty soldiers will be defending the intelligence department, and another fifty will be defending the science department. If these posts are overrun you will fall back to the next floor and help the thirty soldiers posted there to guard Alex. I have reasons to believe he is the main target. They will most probably turn up in high numbers but we will be ready for them. This is the plan, your superiors will give you your orders. Listen to them and we will get through this," she said.

Andra looked at her watch. It was now 15.32 and she realised Alex was still asleep. She walked into her quarters and looked around for him. She found him slumped on the bed still in his clothes and still lay in the same position I which he had fallen onto the bed. She sat down next to him.

"Alex. Allleeex. Wake up, sleepy head," she said in a sing-song way.

He stirred but didn't wake.

"Hey, come on wake up!" she said.

He slowly opened his eyes.

"Uh, Andra? What time is it?" he said.

"It's three thirty two in the afternoon," she said.

"I've been asleep for six and a half hours? Why did no one wake me?" he said.

"I thought you could use the sleep. By the way, we're going to have visitors," she said.

"Who?" he said.

"A shit load of vampires," she said.

"What? How?" he said.

"We found a tracker chip in Vincent's ashes. It must have been how they found your apartment so easily. The bastards used him. I should have checked the ashes before we brought them back here, but we were in a rush," she said.

"The fucking bastards. What's the plan?" he said.

"The whole base is locked down. All the soldiers are prepped and ready. All that training we've been doing. Well, it looks like it's going to start to pay off," she said.

"Ok. What am I doing?" he said.

"I want you deep in the base on the training level. You're the biggest threat to them and they will attack you on sight so you're going to be protected," she said.

"Oh come on Andra. I'm ready," he said.

"Maybe so, but we don't know your limitations yet. That and I don't want you going all monster and hurting or killing my soldiers instead of the vampires in the process. They're only human. They're the people we're trying to save by fighting the vampires," she said and looked him square in the eyes.

"Ok Andra," he said with a sigh.

"Am I making myself clear?" she said.

"Yes, Ma'am. Loud and clear," he said.

She patted her hand on his shoulder, then stood up

and walked to the door.

"Come on now. I want to refresh on some techniques before they get here," she said.

"Ok, Andra. Nice cushions by the way," he said with a smile.

"I thought I told you no laughing," she said.

"Ok," he said and pressed his lips together to suppress a laugh.

"I'm not apposed disciplining you, you know," he said.

"Ooh, kinky," he said in a laugh.

"Shut up and come on," she said with a smile.
He got up from the bed and they walked together to the training room.

## Chapter 6.

Saltorg sat in one of four Chinook helicopters that flew en route from his MediCyber office in Manchester to the MediCyber HQ in Birmingham. There he was to rendezvous with Dr Revitska who would be ready and waiting with his one hundred and ten soldiers.

The four helicopters descended towards the building and landed in the huge courtyard. The wreckage of the burnt out van had been removed and the window Vincent had punched out had been covered with a plywood panel.

The helicopter's rotor blades wound down with a rhythmical thump. Saltorg stepped out from the cargo bay door and ran the short distance to a small door within a pair of wide sliding doors. It was opened just as he got to it and then closed immediately after he had stepped through it.

He stood six feet and seven inches tall. His straight, grey hair just about reached his shoulders. His eyes were deep blue with a brow that gave him a constantly angry expression. His hair had been grey when he had been turned by Ruhsarr and he almost looked the same; only his height and build had altered slightly. In his human life he had been a mage. After he had become a vampire he turned his attention to alchemy. As the years moved on he had taken a keen interest in science. His appearance had hardly changed because he had been performing most of his experiments on himself. Through the use of a cocktail of potions, medicine, and surgery he had stopped most of the mutation effects of vampirism on his body and his D.N.A. It was he who had discovered that because of their rapid healing abilities vampires take very well to implant surgery. Like the transmitter that had been implanted in Vincent.

He now stood in a large room where all the soldiers and their equipment were awaiting his arrival. Infront of them stood Dr. Revitska. Saltorg approached him with a broad smile. The doctor was dressed all in black body armour and a balaclava rolled up showing his face.

"Hello, Doctor. Are you and the soldiers ready to go?" said Saltorg.

"Yes sir. We are all prepped and ready for battle. Would you like to inspect the soldiers to make sure they meet your approval, sir?" said Revitska

"Yes, I will. Thank you, Dr," said Saltorg.

He stepped toward the soldiers who were stood to attention in eleven lines of ten. He walked up and down between them checking their armour and posture. They were good, healthy vampires. One or two looked a little out of shape but that wouldn't matter once they were alongside Dienco's soldiers. He addressed them with all the force of a drill Sergeant.

"Ok, it's still daylight out there so make sure you're fully covered. Are you all ready to attack Vincent and his brother?" he said.

"Sir! Yes sir!" they all said in unison.

"This will not be an easy fight. The enemy are trained soldiers. They are only human but they can still kill you if you lower your guard. Is that understood?" he said.

"Sir! Yes sir!" said the soldiers again.

"Ok. Let's move out. Go!" said Saltorg.

The wide doors were opened and the soldiers ran out in their lines and boarded the helicopters.

"Maybe we'll get that purple bitch too," said Dr Revitska.

"Don't underestimate her. I've seen the trail of devastation she can wake. She doesn't take prisoners, doctor. Come on let's go," said Saltorg slapping the Dr on the back.

The flight to London took half an hour. The clock in the helicopter read 16.07 when the helicopters landed in a small private airfield that housed Dienco's soldier training facility. It was three miles west of the capital city. It had once been a World War Two airfield, but Dienco had converted, and extended it. There were now four floors, each the size of four football pitches and all underground. Saltorg, Dr Revitska and the soldiers disembarked the helicopters and filed into the wide entrance of the base. When they were all inside a man approached them. He was dressed in a black suit with a matching shirt and tie.

"Hello, Mr. Saltorg. I'm Mr Goss. Mr Dienco informed me of your arrival. How was your flight?" he said.

"It was ok. I'm used to travelling in more comfort, but we're here now. That is the most important thing," said Saltorg.

"Indeed, sir. The Soldiers you ordered are ready

to go. May I introduce you to Sergeant Lake. He is the soldiers' acting superior," said Goss.

"Thank you, Mr. Goss," said Saltorg.

As the MediCyber soldiers arranged themselves into their formation, Saltorg and Sergeant Lake spoke.

"Good day, Mr Saltorg. The three hundred troops you requested are downstairs and awaiting your orders," said Lake.

"Very good. Thank you, Sergeant. Have the soldiers been briefed on the attack strategy?" said Saltorg.

"No. Not yet, sir. We've been awaiting your arrival. They are on the training level," said Lake.

"Not yet? We are about to lead an assault on the only legitimate threat to our species and the soldiers have not been briefed on the strategy?! I need them brought up to this level and ready for inspection the mission brief A.S.A.P.," said Saltorg.

"Yes, sir, Very well, sir," said Sergeant Lake.

"Is there anything we can get for you in the meantime?" said Goss.

"There is. My soldiers need refreshments, and some require a smoking break," said Saltorg.

"Ok, sir. I'll have the staff prepare your refreshments, and there is a ventilated breakroom on this floor where you and your troops can relax," said Goss and went to see to Saltorg's requests.

"It's the least you can do. Lake, why are you still standing here? Go, round up those soldiers. That is an order," said Saltorg.

"Yes, sir," said Lake and stepped away in a hurry.

Half an hour later Saltorg was stood in front of four hundred and ten troopers. They all talked and laughed amongst themselves.

"Face front! Attention!" said Saltorg.

The soldiers all fell silent, snapped their heads forward to face him, and stood to attention. His voice carried effortlessly through the room and the vampires could all hear him clearly. He laid down his plan of attack. The drop zone, the entry and the attack pattern when they had gained access. All his plans were based on the assumption that they were not expected.

Everyone was then given four hours to rest, train or play sports and games. At nine pm all the Blutesser soldiers stopped what they were doing and checked every piece of equipment they had. Every gun was checked and checked again. They weren't just vampire soldiers. They were highly trained fighting machines. The MediCyber soldiers followed their lead and fell in line.

"Look at them. Andra and the twins aren't going to know what hit them. I can't wait to tell Lord Ruhsarr that the prophecy has been averted," said Saltorg to Revitska as a huge smile played across his face.

"How are we going to transport them all? Do we have enough helicopters?" said Dr Revitska.

"We don't need the chinooks. We only need one plane," said Sergeant Lake.

"One plane?!" Exclaimed the Revitska.

"It's one hell of a plane. One of Mr Dienco's own designs. The Hulington 47, also known as Hell's Gates," said Lake.

At 22.00., just after the sun had set, the soldiers filed out of the building onto the runway. In front of them stood the enormous plane. It was similar in size to a Boeing 747 with a flat, wide body. The jet engines had suppressors that reduced the noise to little more than that of a car engine. They all filed onto the plane via the four doors in the left side of the vehicle. As Dr Revitska sat down in his chair he noticed that it didn't have a lap belt but shoulder restraints, similar to that of a roller coaster. He also noticed each chair was also housed in its own semi-partitioned cubical. The floor of each cubical had grooves along their edges, and one edge had a hinge. His heart thumped in his chest while all the soldiers sat down and attached all their equipment to themselves. The pilot's voice came over the tannoy.

"Attention. We'll be setting off in five minutes. Please make yourselves comfortable. We'll be flying at an altitude of ten thousand feet. We are ten minutes from our destination. Upon arrival, we'll circle and drop to one thousand feet. There we will hit go zone. You'll have a twenty second descent so remember your training. A warning will sound upon approach so be ready before we reach the go zone. Ok, we'll see you back here before sunrise tomorrow."

The tannoy clicked off and the engines roared to life. The plane began to move and taxied onto the runway. A few minutes later the plane increased in speed pushing the occupants into their chairs. Moments later it was hurtling down the runway before taking to the sky.

*

Andra watched the sun go down then turned and walked back into the base. The front entrance was sealed behind her. Only one narrow access door was open so the eight soldiers outside could fall back. All the soldiers were in their positions. The tension in the air was tangible and no one said a word. The soldiers were all nervous but ready.

*

"Ten thousand feet above the go zone and starting our descent," said the pilot over the tannoy as the plane began to bank and descend.

“Eight thousand feet.”
The air breaks opened and the plane began to descend faster.

“Six thousand feet…five…four...three...two. Approaching one thousand feet in three, two, one. We are in the go zone. We are in the go zone!”
The shoulder restraints raised up and the underside of each passenger’s compartment fell open like trapdoors along the hinges that Revitska had noticed before. They swung down on the hinges and locked open. The seat of the chair folded down parallel with its backrest and four hundred and ten vampires dropped from the plane. Now in freefall, they adjusted themselves into an evenly spaced formation. Then a quarter of them pulled their arms and legs in and fell faster. The rest put their arms and legs out to make their body area as large as possible and slowed their descent.

*

On the ground, the eight human soldiers were watching the roads. One of them heard something above them. He looked up and saw the silhouette of a huge plane flying at low altitude above them. He flipped down the night-vision goggles on his helmet and saw hundreds of little silhouettes falling towards them.

“Targets coming from directly above!” he said to

the others.

"Firing," said another as he aimed his rocket launcher at the silhouettes. The RPG flew up as the vampires came down. They moved their bodies and dodged the projectile until one of them caught it with his face. The explosion tore him to bits. The others around him were thrown slightly off course by the blast but kept falling. The other soldiers fired RPGs into the vampire horde, killing a few more of them. The soldier who had raised the alarm lifted his rocket launcher again but before he could pull the trigger a vampire landed on its feet in front of him with a bang. As it straightened up the soldier reached for his knife but the vampire grabbed him and snapped his neck. Before it could drop the soldier his partner pushed the barrel of his shotgun into its eye and shot it dead. More vampires were landing. The soldiers were shooting silver gas and bullets into the group but their numbers were increased by the second. Some of the vampires were burning up but most of them quickly pulled on gas masks. In a stroke of bad luck the wind began to pick up and the gas dissipated as fast as it was being deployed. The noise of the vampires landing on the concrete ground was becoming a rain of thunderous drums. They were closing in on the base on mass.

"Fall back," said one of the soldiers.

The soldiers moved back as a group, shooting at the

horde and trying to hit targets. But the vampires were weaving around faster than the soldiers could aim. The last soldier flipped his rifle into full auto and began emptying the magazine into the horde. A few vampires burned up, but his efforts were hardly making a dent. The plan was to get in and close the door. He shouted "Falling back," but as he set one foot inside the warehouse a bullet tore through his right arm. Another ripped open the thigh of his left leg. He stumbled but before he fell three more tore through his chest. He lay in the doorway spluttering. The soldiers who were already inside moved to pull him in but a vampire grabbed him and dragged him back outside. There was a strange stillness among them for a moment. As they moved to shut the door it was forced open and twenty vampires filed in at high speed. They all moved in different directions. Across the ground, along the walls, and up across the ceiling.

"Breach!" shouted a voice.

"Contact!" shouted another.

The sound of automatic gunfire echoed around the room but the vampires moving at an incredible speed. Andra shot three of them dead, then jumped up and ran at one of them with her Katanas unsheathed. They were causing a diversion of which the goal was unclear until one of them ran for the door controls. It leapt at them and pressed the open button. Andra charged at him but he smashed the control panel before her blade sliced him in two. The sounds of metal sliding against metal and the hiss of pistons rang out as the heavy door began to open.

"Everybody get into cover. Shoot in controlled bursts. Make them count," she said as the door lifted slowly. The soldiers shot at the legs of the vampires who in turn were shooting back under the door. Some of them started pulling the barrier up. Soon there were forty of them pulling whilst others defended them. The screech of tearing metal came from the door. It slid up rattling and scraping in its runners, and the vampires flooded in like a tidal wave of bullets and fangs. The two sides were engaged in a vicious gun battle for fifteen minutes but it soon became clear that the vampires were overrunning the humans.

Andra was slicing off heads and limbs and splitting torsos but her efforts were making little difference. The vampire numbers were just too many. A vampire bit into a soldier's neck and drained right in front of her. She sliced off the back of its head and ordered the soldiers to fall back. The thirty remaining soldiers retreated into the deeper levels of the base.

They reached the science and the intelligence level that was separated into two areas. Each half the size of a football pitch. The group split between these two areas. The plan was to bottle neck the vampires coming from the stairs and attack from the two angles. This worked for a while and a number of vampires were killed. But soon they were using their speed and numbers to outmanoeuvre and outgun the humans. Hordes of them ran up the walls and across the ceiling before dropping onto the soldiers, whilst the rest of them were providing covering fire. Andra was looking out for strategic targets as well as attacking any vampire she came across. She noticed a tall vampire who looked familiar.

As she watched him she saw bullets hit him but they had no effect as he was healing almost instantly. He walked up to soldiers and pushed the palm of his hand against their chests. Blood spouted from their mouths before they fell to the floor.

She ran and leapt at him swinging a katana at his head. Without even looking at her, he raised his arm and the blade deflected off his forearm. Her other blade was close behind the first, but he deflected this one too. She jumped up and kicked him in the chest. As he stumbled back she leapt forward and stabbed at his chest. The blade stopped before hitting his heart as if something was in its path. He knocked the blade away and threw his hand out at her with his palm flat towards her torso. She pushed his arm aside as a one foot long spike shot out of his palm. She swung a sword up through his chin. This move should have split his face in two, but again, there was something hard under his flesh. His balaclava fell away as his head flew back. He brought his head back down to face her again and she glimpsed the shimmer of metal under the wound as it healed. She realised why she recognised his face but she had not seen him for thousands of years.

"I have hydraulic rams graphed to the bones in my arms, titanium shielding of all my vital organs and subdermal micromesh Kevlar armour. I've upgraded myself beyond your abilities?" said Saltorg.

"I'll find a way to kill you," said Andra.

"Good luck with that," he said as he blocked more of her attacks. He stepped forward and stabbed her in the shoulder with his left arm spike.

"I'm going to find those little freaks of yours, and I'm going to take their heads," he said.

"Good luck with that," said Andra with a smirk. She pushed him back and thrust her blade into his chest with all her strength. It punctured his flesh and she twisted the blade before pulling out. He stumbled back and cried out in pain and anger. She and the guards were fighting for all they were worth but try as they might the vampires were getting past them.

Alex's voice came over her headset:

"They're getting in down here. We're holding them off but we're gonna need some help. There are hundreds of them."

"Shit! They're trying to divide us. We're dying up here. We'll try and fall back,"
she said.

"What are the orders, Ma'am?" shouted Hussain over the gunfire.

Andra looked back towards the entrance down to this floor. The direction they had come in. There were hardly any vampires there.

"We're gonna back up the way we came. Make it look like we're running away," she said.

Hussain looked at her as if she were mad.

"I beg your pardon, Ma'am? I'm not leaving all our soldiers down there to be slaughtered."

"We're not leaving them. We're blocking them in," said Andra.

The orders spread to all the soldiers to return up to the front door. They made a run for it taking out any vampires who stood in their path. Most of the vampires were making their way to the lower levels now anyway and leaving the path clear for the soldiers.

"There running, Sir," said Sergeant Lake.

"Let them go. Alex and Vincent are downstairs.

They're our main targets," said Saltorg.

Only seventy-five soldiers regrouped near the front entrance.

"Ok, soldiers, find some cover. Hughes, Mc'Ready, get that door closed. The rest of us are going to guard this exit. They got in here, but not a single one of those bastards is getting out," Andra said.

"What's the plan, Ma'am?" said Davis.

"Something I should have done from the start," Andra said.

She hailed Alex on his headset.

"Alex. You there?" she said.

"Yes, Ma'am," he said as gunfire crackled all around him.

"Do your thing," she said.

"Are you sure, Ma'am? What about all the other soldiers?" he said.

"There won't be any other soldiers if you don't. We're trying to get the outer door closed again up here. We're gonna block them in," she said.

"Ok Ma'am. Be ready for them coming back your way. I'll send the soldiers here back up towards you first," he said.

"Ok. See you soon," she said.

"See you on the other side," he said.

Alex pulled the headset out of his ear, turned to Fletcher and the soldiers surrounding him.

"Give me some cover. When it starts I want you all to get back up top to Andra through the emergency escape staircases."

"When what starts?" said Fletcher.

"This," said Alex pulling off his shirt.

His shoulders wrenched back then forward and began to widen. He threw his head back and roared as he began to change shape.

"Ok, people. Give Alex some cover!" said Fletcher.

The soldiers shot at the vampires in controlled bursts. Alex's muscles and bones grew and writhed under his skin. His legs lengthened and his trousers ripped. The bones of his skull crunched as they grew and changed shape. Huge, serrated teeth erupted from his gums and pushed his human ones aside. His roar shook the air around him as his skin thickened and hardened into scales. The vampires were flooding in through the doors on the other side of the room and pouring from the air vents. Alex looked at them around him. He could see and hear the blood being pumped around their bodies by their hearts; human and vampire alike. Though, the human hearts beat faster and harder than those of the vampires. He could see the difference in body temperature between the two species. He could smell the cordite and the oil from the guns. He could smell the fabric cleaner from their clothes, the polish and dirt from their boots. He could smell the sweat from the human soldiers as opposed to the distinct lack of any body odour from the vampires. He could smell the blood on the vampire's breaths, and a hunger grew in him. He leapt high over the soldiers and landed among the vampires. They were all shooting at him, but the bullets flattened against his body and fell to the floor. He bit at them tearing off chunks and swallowing them. An arm here, a head there. The rest of their bodies were solidifying into macabre, mutilated statues. Others he was just tearing to pieces. Plunging his claws through their chests and tearing them in two. The vampires kept coming, but he was unstoppable. They threw their full force against him but he was a force of nature. In droves, they started to panic and run. In all their training and combat they had never faced anything like this. They were used to being the stronger more aggressive beings. This thing, this beast was beyond anything any of them had ever faced.

"Get back up to the top and help Andra," Alex said to Fletcher and the other soldiers.

They fell back and started to exit the room via emergency staircases. Alex tore apart any vampires who tried to follow. The room was quickly filling with vampire husks and ash.

Saltorg and Revitska came running down the stairs as some of their soldiers were trying to run up and away from the marauding beast in the training room.

"What the hell are you doing? Get back in there at once! They're only a bunch of humans," said Saltorg.

Some of the vampires remembered their mission and followed him back towards the fight. As Saltorg walked into the room a burning vampire hit the floor at his feet and exploded in a cloud of ash. Over the crowd of his soldiers he could see a huge beast wading through the crowd and dismembering vampires with ease.

"Oh shit. What the fuck is that?!" he said.

"Don't fear, sir. I have a poisoned knife. This shall be over in a moment," said Revitska.

Not wanting to disappoint his boss and trying to prove his worth in battle once again. He ran at the beast leapt over all the troops and landed on Alex's back.

"No! Revitska!" said Saltorg.

The tip of the doctor's knife stuck in one of the scales on Alex's lower back. He turned and looked at the little vampire.

"Revitska?" he said in a low, mean growl.

He then seized the doctor by his throat, held him up to his face and stared at him.

"You tortured my brother for twenty three years," he said.

Revitska's eyes grew wide as he realised who this beast was and the implications of his existence. Urine ran down his leg and splashed on the floor.

"Please, oh lord, save me." whimpered Revitska.

"When I see you Lord he's gonna die too," growled Alex. Then bit off the doctor's arms, tore off his legs, and threw him to the floor. The doctor's screams turn to a croak as his throat dried up.

"What have you done you dull minded beast?!" said Saltorg.

He ran over and knelt next to Revitska, only to find that his friend was nothing more than a husk.

"A beast, yes. Dull minded? Absolutely not," growled Alex.

Saltorg stood and punched him across the snout. It was a punch that could have crushed a vampire's skull. Alex just looked back at him and then thrust his fist into the face of this tall vampire. The force sent him flying back across the room. He landed on his back, then flipped over and leapt back towards the beast using his vampire speed. He was caught by the throat in mid-air. He choked and gasped realising what had happened. A huge fist impacted his face repeatedly. He put his hand out and shot the spike into the arm that was holding him. Alex roared and shook the vampire loose. Saltorg was flung across the room and landed hard on his left side. He pulled himself to his feet and popped his shoulder back into place and then his nose and jaw. Alex was ripping more vampires apart when Saltorg landed on his back and started stabbing him in the head. Alex reached up, grabbed him and threw him to the floor.

"Who the hell are you?" he said.

"I'm Saltorg. One of the four children of the blood. Mage, scientist, surgeon and leader of these vampires. I assume you are the bastard Andra took in. Tell me, where is your brother?"

"Andra had to take me in because arseholes like you killed my family. As you might be able to deduce from me looking like this, Vincent is dead, as you soon will be. When I'm finished with you I'm going for your boss, Ruhsarr," said Alex.

A feeling of dread fell over Saltorg. He had never been in a fight he couldn't win. Despite his internal dread he kept up the external show of bravado. He had to fight Alex for honour. He had to fight to show that he did not give in, even in the face of adversity. Even when threatened with death. His composure was flawless.

"So the prophecy has begun. Though you will not complete it," said Saltorg.

He lunged at the beast and stabbed him over and over in the stomach. Alex roared in pain and swung a hand at Saltorg. He ducked and spun out and around Alex so he was behind him. He then plunged both spikes into his back. Again Alex swung his arms around clawing for him. Saltorg went to move but a hand caught him by the forearm. Alex dragged him around in front so they were facing each other and lifted him off the floor; looking at him and then at his hand. Saltorg fired the spike out of his palm and Alex tightened his grip. The bones of Saltorg's arm along with the hydraulic system inside cracked and popped as they were crushed. Alex took hold of the spike and pulled. The hydraulics and most of Saltorg's hand came with it. He then dropped the screaming vampire, who crumpled to the floor; blood pouring from the wound. Moments later his arm started to heal and he stood up still holding it. He looked and Alex and grinned despite the pain and being spattered with his own blood.

"You can't win this. Ruhsarr is too strong," He said.

"None of you can stop me. Your lord is doomed," said Alex.

"He's your lord too. He made you. He bit your whore mother. She used to work for me. I pointed her out to him. He would have killed her if he hadn't been interrupted. His bite made you and Vincent what you are. At least Vincent was a pure blood, you are just an abomination who should have been cut from your filthy mother's womb!" said Saltorg.

"Yeah, that's gonna do it," said Alex.
He punched the vampire across the mouth then grabbed his head, pushed him down, and ground his face against the concrete.

"Your lord is a fucking idiot. He knew the prophecy yet, he still bit a pregnant woman. In making me, he killed you all," said Alex.

"You can't kill me. I have metal plated organs," said Saltorg.
He reached up with his good arm and the spike shot out, stabbing Alex in the eye. Alex jumped back with a screaming roar as his punctured eye dangled in ruins before it began to grow back. Again, Saltorg thrust out his hand, palm first, but Alex dodged the spike this time. Saltorg spun, slashing wildly at Alex with the tip of the spike but he missed again. Seeing a brief pause in Saltorg's flailing attack Alex caught the arm and bore down on his grip.

"No! No!" screamed Saltorg.
He kicked and trashed to no avail. Alex grabbed Saltorg by the chest with his other hand and plucked the vampire's arm off at the elbow. As simple as snapping the claw from a crab.

"You bastard. You fucking monster!" screamed Saltorg.
He kicked Alex in the face with all his strength and the beast dropped him. He landed and slowly he

pushed himself up with his remaining hand.

“My lord will kill you, and your bitch, Andra. He will kill you and end your feeble bloodline. You will be reunited with your pathetic mother and father in hell,” said Saltorg.

“I’ve had enough of your shit. I’m gonna crush you,” said Alex.

He grabbed Saltorg by the head and slammed his skull into the floor repeatedly. Despite this the vampire still struggled, so he lifted him from the floor and swung him by the neck like a rag doll. He charged through the vampires, ploughing them aside, and at full pace he slammed Saltorg’s head into the wall. Pulled him away and smash his head back into the wall over and over until he heard his skull crack. He held Saltorg up and looked at him. His eyes were staring wildly and the left side of his head was dented in. He opened his mouth and in a whisper of defiance said,

“You will lose.”

Alex put the Saltorg’s head into his mouth and bit down. His teeth shrieked as they slid across, then punctured through the titanium coated bone like carving knives through an aluminium can. He crunched the head into a pulp and swallowed it. As the body hardened into a husk he bit and chomped and it swallowed it all down.

The vampire soldiers had watched in horror as

this beast ate their leader. What they had witnessed was supposed to be impossible. He was one of the Children of the Blood, the 'true immortals.' One of the unkillable had just been killed. Everything these vampires knew had just been turned on its head. They began to back away from Alex. A few of them turned and pushed their way through the crowd. Moments later they all turned on mass and ran in abject terror.

Something happened to Alex now that he didn't expect. His mind was flooded with images, memories of places he had never been, and people he had never met. Thoughts as both a human and as a vampire with thoughts and knowledge of mage work, mechanical and digital engineering. All subjects that he had never learnt. It became clear these were the neural contents of Saltorg's mind. Then he saw the location of another member of the Children of the Blood; a woman. She was tall and attractive, yet monstrous and deadly. Her name was Gilad. He could sense her in the world and he realised, she could sense him too. He saw her panic, just like the vampires fleeing him now were panicking.

They ran from him in frantic horror and he gave chase. Tearing apart the stragglers as he herded them up the stairs towards the front doors. One hundred and thirty of them ran wildly and unknowingly towards the trap Andra had set for them. Some of them were shooting back at Alex as he forced them to keep moving through the carpark level and up the tunnel to the front entrance.

Andra could hear the rumble of hundreds of running feet and shouts of fear before she saw them approaching. The horde of frantic vampires were running up the corridor.

"Open fire!" she said.

The soldiers launched a hail of bullets, RPGs and grenades at the vampires. They fell in droves, burning and tripping over each other.

A vampire turned and ran but Alex snatched him up by the shoulder as he tried to dodge past. The vampire pulled the pins from two grenades and held them against the huge hand. The blast tore him apart and destroyed Alex's hand in the process.

Alex roared in pain and clutched at his ruined arm. A few of the vampires shot everything they had at him hoping that their bullets would do some damage that he was injured. Their hope dwindled as they watched in terror and awe. Bones grew from the shattered stumps, muscles stretched and attached themselves to the new bones, and flesh wrapped itself over his palm and fingers. He had never been badly injured before and he was amazed at the speed at which his body healed. Andra had seem what had happened and smiled when she

realised he was fine.
The vampires knew they were merely stalling their fate. Talking quickly among themselves, trying to figure a way out. They threw all their remaining grenades in the direction of Andra and the soldiers.

"Down!" she ordered.

The soldiers dropped behind cover. The grenades were exploding at different rates. Shrapnel was ripping through their defences leaving some dead, while others were injured and screaming in pain.

"Stay down!" said Andra.

She leapt out of cover and ran at the vampires. Their bullets ripped at her clothes and flesh grenades exploded around her but she kept moving and healing. She threw her head back, and her nose and jaw began to change shape as they extended and shifted beneath her flesh.

Alex turned and clamped his new hand down onto the closest vampire's head, crushing it like a man squeezing an orange. He saw Andra charging towards the vampires on the other side of the crowd. Her face had transformed into a snout. He knew what that meant and his lips curled into a smile.

She took a deep breath and then spat out a thirty foot long fireball into the writhing mass of vampires. They screamed and howled as their flesh burned and exploded. Burning embers filled the air but she kept spewing her fire all over them. The flames hit Alex and just buffeted around him. He pushed forwards thrashing his fists this way and that. They shattered easily as his huge hands punched through their charred remains. Through the chaos he saw Andra draw another breath.

"They're all gone Andra. They're all dead. We did it," he said.

"They are?" she said in a hoarse voice.

"Yes," he said.

"Yes! Take that, you bastards!" She shouted and then laughed.

As she got close to him, he saw her face was like his. A long extended snout with serrated teeth and a forked tongue. It changed back to its usual state as she ran towards him. She leapt at him and he caught her. She kissed him on the nose and then playfully punched him across the snout.

"We're badass, vampire killing motherfuckers!" she roared.

"Fuckin' A," he said and smiled.

She hugged him tight.

"I've never actually seen you do that before," he said.

"The fire?" she said.

"Yes," he said.

"It's not something I can do all the time. Just when I need it most," she said.

"It's cool as fuck," he said.

"I know," she said with a smug smile. "You're not the only one with tricks."

"We make a great team," he said.

"You know it, big man," she said. Her mood of joy and excitement quickly lost its vigour. "Talking about team, we have to help our soldiers."

"I sent as many back as I could from downstairs. How many survived?" he said.

"Seventy six, I estimate. We have to help them. Those bastards hit us so fucking hard. We have a lot of injured, a lot walking wounded, fewer dead than I predicted, but still more than I would have wanted," she said.

"I can't help but feel responsible," said Alex. "If it wasn't for me being here those soldiers would still be alive."

Andra's expression softened.

"If it hadn't been for you, all of us would have died," she said.

"If I hadn't come here none of you would have died," he said.

"Alex, this is war. It's been going on for thousands of years. All of these soldier's lives have been affected by vampires in one way or another. They would have joined the S.O.V.E.U. if you had been with us or not. They gave their lives for something they believed in. You can't blame yourself. Blame Ruhsarr and all the other vampires.

These soldier's deaths are not on you," she said. Alex looked into her eyes and saw sincerity there.

"Ok. Let's go and help them," he said.

They walked back up the tunnel to the entrance and began helping the soldiers. They dressed wounds and helped others to the infirmary.

## Chapter 7.

They spent the next day with the uninjured soldiers searching for any surviving survivors or any straggling vampires. They found a few soldiers but no vampires. They also collected the bodies of the dead soldiers and placed them into body bags. It was depressing work but it needed to be done. Lastly, they collected up all the husks of the vampires who Alex had bitten. There weren't many but the ones they did find managed to fill a large refrigerated storage container.

"Do you think you bit enough of them?" said Mc'Ready as she swung the container door shut.

"They should just about be enough for a midnight snack," he said with a smile.

She looked at him and laughed.

Andra scanned the clock with her tired eyes. It was 2.30 in the morning. They had done all they could that day. She and Alex were now sat talking at a table in the mess hall.

"Did you see the guy with the spikes in his arms?" said Andra.

"Yes. He was like a tank. He was a pompous cunt too," he said.

"Yes, he was. I recognised his face, but I don't recall his name," she said.

"He said he was named Saltorg. Claimed to be one of the four children of the blood," he said.

"Saltorg. Yes, I remember now. He was still a smug twat after all these years. Do you remember me telling you about the four vampires Ruhsarr picked to give the dragon's blood?" she said.

"Yes, I do," she said.

"He was one of them. I assume you fought him," she said.

"I did. I beat the shit out of him but he was tough as old boots. I had to smash his head in to beat him. He had metal around his skull, you know. It still wasn't enough to stop me but it was fucking impressive. Something really weird happened when I ate his brain. It's like I absorbed all this information from him. Like, I don't know, a cerebral download I suppose," he said.

Andra wrinkled up her nose.

"Really? That's kind of disgusting but also really interesting. What did you learn?" she said.

"Like you said, he was a smug twat all his life. He was an incredible scientist. He could have done some good in the world if he wasn't a selfish old vampire. He was very proud of those hydraulic spikes he had in his arms. He wasn't too happy when I pulled one of them out." He smiled.

"Eww. I can bet he wasn't. Anything else?" she said.

"I think I might know where the next vampire is too," he said with a smile.

"Really? That's great. Are you going to share?" she said.

"I might. What's it worth?" he said.

"Your life," she said with a smile. "But seriously, who and where are they?"

"A female named Gilad. I saw she was in Paris, but as I got the information about her I think she sensed me too. She made plans to go to Manhattan, New York. I don't think that she knows that I can still sense her," said Alex.

"Gilad. She's dangerous. I've never fought her myself, but I do know she runs a lot of clubs and owns a lot of dangerous people. She has a glamour," she said.

"A glamour?" said Alex.

"She has the ability to control both humans and vampires alike using merely her voice. It's a form of psychic manipulation. Vincent was investigating her before he was abducted. I'll inform my spies in New York to keep an eye out for her arriving," she said.

"And us? What are we doing?" he said

"We're going to have to relocate. This safe house is compromised. I'll leave a small group of soldiers here to protect it and keep away the riff raff; thieves, urban explorers and the like. Other than that it will be kept online at an automated level as a decoy," she said.

"When do we go?" he said.

"We'll let the soldiers sleep for now. Then we'll move in the morning after the sun has risen. I'll see if there are any of the soldiers who want to volunteer to stay here. Failing that I'll come up with the group. The wounded survivors have already been sent to a local army hospital," she said.

"I'm not feeling tired. Is there anything we can do?" he said.

"What do you have in mind?" she said.

"Is there anything that needs doing before the move?" he said.

"We could pack the heavy equipment we will be taking from this place. It all needs to go into crates and then into storage containers to be transported," she said.

"I was thinking something fun," he said.

"It will be fun. We will make it fun. Besides, it needs doing. We have the strength to move it all faster and with more ease than any of the soldiers. Also, if we wait for them to wake up it will be tomorrow afternoon before we can start to transport it. You need to learn to manage your time wisely Alex. Just because you might live forever doesn't mean you can leave things until later all the time," she said

"You need to learn to have more fun," he said with a grin.
She cocked her head to the side and gave him a 'fuck you' smile.

"Ok. Next time we have some spare time we'll do something fun," she said.

"Ok, it's a deal," he said.

"Come on. Stop whining and let's get this done," he said.
They labelled the crates and then filled them with exercise equipment, computers, laboratory apparatus, weaponry and tactical equipment.

"Hey Alex…Alex," she said.

"Yeah?" he said, as he carried a crate into a storage container.

"I spy with my little eye something beginning with M," she said.

"Really, you want to play I spy?" he said.

"Yes. Come on, it'll be fun and help the time pass. Also, it keeps your observational skills sharp," she said.

"Ok, ok. Go on, ask me again," he said.

"I spy with little eye something beginning with M," she said.

"Er, monitor," said Alex as he carried a crate full of computer equipment into the storage container.

"No," she said.

"Mattress," he said as he looked at some bedding.

"No," she said.

"M16," he said, pointing at a crate of weaponry.

"Nah," she said.

"Microscope," he said looking, at a crate of scientific apparatus.

"Come on Alex!" she said laughing.

"What then?" he said.

"You give up?" she said.

"Yes, I give up," he said.

"Magnesium lightbulbs," she said with a smile.

"Huh? Yeah, because they are completely obvious," he said.

"Yeah, the room would be dark without them," she said.

"Yeah, but…" he said.

"Is this game too advanced for you?" she said sarcastically.

"No, I just want to play something else is all," he said.

"Because you're losing?" she said.

"No," he said.

"Whatever you say, loser," she said.

He rolled his eyes and shook his head.

"Come on, Andra. Can we just play something else?" he said.

"Of course we can, loser. What do you want to play?" she said.

"How about the quiet game?" he said holding up a

roll of tape with a cheeky smile on his face.

"I'd like to see you try," she said.

"Don't test me," he said.

She laughed and pulled a face at him. He smiled and shook his head again.

"I've got a great one for you, how about who am I?" he said.

"How do we play that?" she said.

"I think of a person, like an actor or a singer or someone like that. A celebrity of some kind, and you have to ask questions like: Are they alive? What gender they are? Are they in action films? That sort of thing. I can only answer yes or no until you have enough information to guess who the person is," he said.

"Ok. Sounds fun. You go first," she said.

"Ok, got one," he said.

"Right. Are they alive?" she said.

"Yes," said Alex…

They were still playing games, filling the crates and putting them in the storage containers when the soldiers started to wake up at 7.00.

"Good morning Ma'am. Good morning, Alex," said Fletcher as he approached them.

"Good morning, doctor," they both said.

"The soldiers and I can help you finish up here," he said.

"No need, we're done. The containers just need loading onto the lorries and transporting to the next base," she said.

"You've packed everything?" he said with a look of amazement.

"Yes. It's all ready to go," she said.

"Ok, Ma'am. Where are the lorries taking them to?" said Fletcher.

"Newcastle. I have informed the base there to be ready for our arrival. Can you two handle that? I have some things to sort out," she said.

"Yes, Ma'am," Alex and Fletcher said.

Andra walked into her office, picked up the phone and began making calls. Alex, and Fletcher ushered the lorries into the building two at a time and helped the drivers load up the storage containers. Alex pretended to just be an average human. It would cause the drivers to ask too many questions if he used his real strength. He couldn't risk a video of him getting out into the wrong hands. He just acted like a normal soldier. Two hours later the lorries were all loaded up. Andra called Alex and Fletcher into her office.

"The soldiers who are too injured to work again have been pensioned off with two years full pay bonuses. The families of the soldiers who died have be given five years full pay and full pension. The soldiers who are injured but will fully recover will have full pay for six months. Fletcher, I'm entrusting you to oversee the transportation of the personnel and the equipment to the base in Newcastle, leaving immediately. Alex, Round up my personal attack team," she said.

"Yes, Ma'am," said Fletcher and stood up and attended to his duties.

"Are we going to New York?" said Alex.

"Yes. My spies have contacted me. Gilad's private plane landed at a small airfield this morning at 0200 their time, 0700 our time. An armoured car took her and her entourage to 'The Nocturnal Club', a metal club she owns. They are all still there," she said.

"What the plan, boss?" said Alex.

"Our plane takes off at 1030. We'll land at 13.30 their time. It'll take us another hour to reach our accommodation. We'll let the soldiers rest, then tomorrow, make our move. Get my team and be ready to go for 0930," she said.

"Yes, Ma'am," he said.

## Chapter 8.

Alex walked to the mess hall. Davis, Hughes, Palmer, Hussain, Mc'Ready and White stood to attention and saluted him as he walked into the room. Alex saluted back to them.

"At ease, soldiers," he said.

Palmer stepped forward.

"Sir, on behalf of us all. Our friends died last night. We're angry, in fact, we are pissed off, sir. But thanks to you we survived. If it wasn't for you we all would have died. We're ready to lay down our lives if you ask it of us. To follow you wherever and into whatever battles you may lead us," he said.

They all saluted him again, and Alex saluted them in return. Palmer smiled and stepped back into the group who formed themselves into a line and stood to attention. He nodded and smiled weakly. Inside, he still felt that some of this was his fault. He pushed the thought away, and his smile grew. He knew Vincent had done the right thing in biting him. He understood what his brother had sacrificed, and that chance he had now would affect a lot more lives than just his.

"Thank you, all of you. I am honoured to be held in such high esteem by you all. I promise I will do whatever it takes to destroy the Tyrannical reign of Ruhsarr. I also will do my best to keep you all alive.

I know you all have your reasons for being here, you too know mine. Together we will win this fight. The men and women who fell last night will not be forgotten, nor will they die in vain. They will be celebrated when we liberate mankind from this ancient enemy," he said.

"Sir, Yes sir!" they all said in unison.

"The attack last night was orchestrated by a vampire called Saltorg. He was one of Ruhsarr's top vampires. A group who go by the name 'Children of the Blood.' When I killed him last night I received information as to the whereabouts of the next vampire. They are in New York City, and so that is where our next mission location. I expect it will be an urban combat situation. Andra will fill us in on the mission brief during the flight which is in twenty minutes. Get your equipment and personal effects together and be ready to go in five minutes.

"Yes, sir," they all said.

Five minutes later they were all in the garage and stood beside the armoured van that would take them to the airfield. Besides the eight of them in this huge garage, the entire base was empty. The other soldiers had already left.

Andra stood in front of them. She was dressed in a grey woollen, pinstriped suit, with no tie and the top button of her shirt unfastened.

"Alex has already informed you that we're going

to New York. Our accommodation will be one of our safe houses there. It looks like a small hotel, hence the smart casual attire. Anyone seeing us coming off the plane or going into bases will just think we're civies. You will have time to change clothes on the plane. Once there we will meet up with the North American department of the S.O.V.E.U. They know the prophesised vampire killer is alive, but they don't know he is among our numbers, and I want it to stay that way for the time being. Our plane leaves in fifteen minutes so we best pull our finger out," she said.

With that she ushered them into the van and drove out of the bases. Only stopping so Andra could get out and locked the door and gates before they left.

At the airfield they boarded the small private jet and took off without a hitch.

## Chapter 9.

Gilad's plane had touched down at a private airfield in the Northern of Manhattan at 2.00. There was a car already waiting there to take her to her club. She arrived at the 'The Nocturnal Club' at two thirty. She was now in her office watching the activity in the club on a bank of CCTV monitors. The drum beats and blistering guitar riffs of metal music vibrated and pulsed through the club. A mosh pit raged in the middle of the dance floor. The people pushed and barged into one and other. They were all laughing and having a great time. A man fell but was immediately helped up by the others. She watched with a smile on her face. She loved metalheads. Their energy and enthusiasm were infectious. They were fun and crazy and their blood was infused with adrenaline. In one of the booths at the back of the club a man bit into the neck of a woman.

"For fucks sake," said Gilad as she clicked the button on a walkie-talkie.

"Gerry. Hugh is feeding again in the booths near the back. Go and tell that fucking idiot to take that shit to the back room," she said.

She no longer had a European accent. She had purposefully lost it and found she could mimic any language, accent, and speech pattern after hearing it once. This had helped throughout history when people had been suspicious of foreigners.

"Ok, boss. That guy is becoming a real pain in the arse," said Gerry into his headset.

Gerry was Gilad's right hand man. She had turned him into a vampire one thousand five hundred years ago when she had barely beaten him in an axe fight in Norway. He was the toughest human she had ever fought and she couldn't bear to let him die. So, instead of letting him succumb to his wounds she had turned him. She trusted him above all others and knew that he was more than capable of running all her clubs this side of the Atlantic while she was elsewhere in the world.

The six foot eight inch Norse warrior strode through the club, parting the crowds with ease. He grabbed Hugh by the shoulder and lifted him out of his seat.

"Get your fucking hands…" When Hugh realised who had grabbed him his bravado fell away. "Oh sorry, Gerry. What do you want sir?"

"Take this in the back. You know there's a strict no feeding policy in the front of the club. And don't you dare drain her. She dies, you die. Got it?" said Gerry.

"I'm gonna ask Gilad about this," said Hugh.

"Gilad is watching you on the CCTV. She told me to inform you again of club policy. Also, I run this place with her confidence. This is the second time you've been caught feeding in the front. If this happens a third time, you're barred," said Gerry.

"You think you're so high and mighty," said Hugh.

"Or, I could just tear your fucking head off right here! Take this shit in the back! Don't you ever question me or my authority in here, you little prick!" said Gerry.

“Ok…I…I’m sorry. I’m taking her in the back,” said Hugh.
He helped the girl up and carried her to the corridor at the back of the club that was guarded by two mean looking bouncers. It led to a dimly lit room and the door was kept closed for good reason. There were people lying around on sofas and mattresses with vampires feeding on them. No self-respecting vampire would want to blow the cover of their entire species for the price of a cheap snack. In addition to the security on the doors, the police who checked the club were vampires too. The rest of the night went without a hitch.

*

Later, after the patrons had all left, Gerry was upstairs in Gilad’s office while the staff were locking up.

“It’s always nice to see you, m’lady. You know your visits are always appreciated and more than welcome. But, when you turn up in the middle of the night with armed guards…” said Gerry.

“What am I doing here?” said Gilad.

“Yes,” said Gerry.

“Last night I had a vision. Saltorg, my brother, one of the Children of the Blood was killed violently. In five thousand years none of us have ever been killed, but something literally tore him limb from limb,” she said.

“Fuck me! It must have been someone tough. Saltorg had armoured himself with implants,” he said.

“Yep, and this thing still managed to kill him,”

she said.

"I don't mean to cause offence, M'lady, but this proves that you and the Children of the Blood aren't indestructible. You should draw an army together and take this enemy down," she said.

"Saltorg had an army, it didn't seem to make any difference. This thing didn't just kill him, it ate him," she said.

"Oh shit. Could that would mean the prophecy is true!" he said.

"Yes it could, but that's what I saw. In the vision the beast that ate him was huge like Ruhsarr. Vampires were dying all around them, some stood like statues. They seemed dead but they didn't burn. I saw the beast and for a brief moment it saw me too. I don't know if it saw where I was but at that point the vision ended. I left as soon as I could after that," she said.

"Have you told Ruhsarr and Dienco about this?" he said.

"Of course. I contacted them both on the flight. I would have contacted Jorshean too but I don't know where she is anymore. She is still alive but she travelled beyond my reach. I can no longer sense her location," she said.

"What are we going to do? Is that thing going follow you here?" he said.

"I don't know. It saw me but I don't know for how long. It might have only been able to see for that moment, it might be able to see me now. I have no idea," she said.

"Oh great! That's just fucking perfect, Gilad.

You've put all of us here in danger," he said.
She stood up from her chair and strode towards Gerry causing him to back up to the wall. When her face was inches from his she spoke in a stern tone.

"We are all already in fucking danger, also, don't forget whom you address! If this is the prophecy and if that thing fulfils its purpose we're all dead! You, me, all the vampires who were in this club tonight, Ruhsarr, everyone. So me being here is the very fucking least of your problems, Gerry!" she said.

"Please forgive me, M'lady. I forgot my place. So, what do we do? What is our next course of action?" he bowed his head as he spoke to her.

"We carry on a normal, like we're not expecting anything to happen. We open the clubs, we serve the customers and we let the regulars into the back room. And, if we see anything suspicious we jump on it. We jump right on fucking top of it and we crush it," she said.

"Yes, M'lady," he said.
She grabbed him in a tight hug and then slapped him on the shoulders.

"Look, this thing won't kill us. We're vampires, we won't let it. We will beat this thing," she said.

"Yes we will, m'lady," he said.

"Now go get some sleep. I have to rest it's been a long night," she said.

"M'lady," said Gerry.
He bowed his head to her and left her to go to his room.

She walked out of her office and into her

bedroom. She stood in the on suite bathroom, unclipped the corset from her waist and slipped it off. She unzipped her dress and turned to look at her back in the mirror. The skin of her shoulder blades and back was pale and as firm as the day she was turned. Beneath this flawless surface dwelt a vile beast. As violent, dangerous, and merciless as Ruhsarr himself. Unlike the other Children of the Blood, her vampirism made her beautiful on the outside but inside she had been changed dramatically. She slipped off her dress and walked back into her bedroom. In the centre stood a pole from floor to ceiling. On to which a human had been chained by her servants. She strode over to the man and held him by the shoulders.

"Do you find me beautiful?" she whispered.

The man didn't reply but his lower lip quivered.

"I said, do you find me beautiful?!" she snarled.

"Yes ma'am," said the man in a whimper with tears in his eyes.

"Of course you do," she said with a smile.

She pulled his head to one side and opened her mouth. A large spike emerged from under her tongue. It extended out from her mouth and a proboscis slid from the end of the spike. She thrust it into the artery in his neck and blood flowed through it down her throat to her stomach. When her thirst had been sated she extracted the spike and it returned to its place under her tongue. She released the man and the wound in his neck closed up. He began to writhe and cry out as sharp teeth forced their way up from his gums.

She lay herself down in her coffin. It was not necessary but she had always liked the gothic aesthetic. As the top closed down there was a hiss as it sealed shut and was filled with cooled air. Outside this room her guards stood to attention. She was perfectly capable of protecting herself but she liked that she could manipulate people beyond their will to defend her.

## Chapter 10

Across New York the sun rose and a new day began. People left their homes and commuted to work as coffee shops prepared for the morning rush. The Earth turned and soon it was midday. At 13.30 US Eastern standard time, the small private jet landed safely at an airfield just outside Manhattan. Alex and the others exited the plane as a van with blacked out windows pulled up next to it. The driver got out and helped them with their luggage while they took their seats in the vehicle. Once they were all seated Andra got off the plane and quickly climbed in too. The driver then got back in behind the wheel and started the engine.

"Hello and welcome to New York City. It's a pleasure having you all here, and I hope your trip is successful," he said.

"Thank you. I'm sure it will be," said Andra.

They drove away from the airfield and through the city to their destination.

They arrived at the Smyth Hotel at 14.30 and drove to a parking area at the back of the building. Andra quickly exited the vehicle and was let into the building through the rear entrance by a woman who looked to be in her early sixties. The others brought in the luggage. Andra then introduced them to this woman.

"Everyone, this is Mrs. Barlow. She is the owner of the Smyth hotel. She is also S.O.V.E.U." said Andra.

"Hello, it's a pleasure to have you all here. Please

follow me," said Mrs Barlow.
She then led them all up to the top floor.
It was a large open plan room that took up the entire top floor. Mrs Barlow showed them around.

"You have a view of the city from the north windows. As you can see, we have made up eight beds for you. You have a full kitchen and living areas. If I may direct your attention to the fireplace," she said.
She reached under the top area of it and pressed a hidden button. The fireplace slid back and then aside revealing a staircase.

"This way, please," she said and they followed her up to the attic.

On a large table in the middle of the room there were computers and laptop docks.

"All the computers have physical Ethernet connections for better security. The wall mounted screens are also connected so you can display your monitor screen directly onto them. We have up to date scientific and medical equipment that can be supplied to you upon request. I hope this meets your specifications, Ma'am," said Mrs Barlow to Andra.

"Yes, this is amazing. I see you used my funds wisely," said Andra.

"Yes, thank you, Ma'am. Your donations were very generous. I'll leave you all to set up now. If you need anything just call the front desk," said Mrs Barlow.
With that she left.

Andra turned to the group.

"Ok. We're looking for everything we can find on

The Nocturnal Club. It's a metal bar here in the city. I want blueprints, building permissions, records of building work, renovations. That kind of thing. I want to know who works there and how long they have worked there. I want to know the patrons who frequent the establishment. The company that supply the alcohol. The security measures they have in place. If police ever check the bar, and if they do I want the name of those officers. I want to know the ply of the paper in the toilets and if rats shit in the back alleyway; everything. So come on, chop, chop, let's have it," said Andra.

They all set to work and scoured the internet including some high security military sites.

By the late afternoon they had found everything they could about the place. They studied the blueprints and learned all the exits, the club opening and closing times, the name manager, who the bouncers were, the names of all the bar staff, the DJs, the alcohol suppliers, and the names of the frequent customers.

"Wow! They have some serious security measures around this place," said Mc'Ready.

"What have you found?" said Andra.

"Automated sniper sentinels on the surrounding buildings, Ma'am," said Mc'Ready.

"Automated sentinels? Fucking hell. Who are they expecting?" said White.

"Us," said Andra.

She looked at the pictures and the blueprints of the sentinel gun and read the specifications.

"Could you hack that?" she said to Mc'Ready.

"Yes, I can't see why not, ma'am. It looks military grade but there are ways into everything," said Mc'Ready.

"Ok, do the research and find what you need then you, Alex, and White are going on a little field trip," said Andra.

"Yes ma'am," said Mc'Ready.

She got to work on it straight away and was excited by the prospect of hacking something. She hadn't had much chance to do any since she had joined the S.O.V.E.U. so this was a chance to use her special skills.

Ten minutes later she had the hack software she needed downloaded onto her phone.

"Ready to go, Ma'am," she said.

"Ok, put on some casual clothes and so you look like tourists and head out to the location. I want those guns out of action ASAP or we'll have to cancel tomorrow night's fun and games," said Andra.

"Why tourists, Ma'am?" said White.

"Because tourists wander into places they're not supposed to. They carry cameras, accessories and other equipment so people are less suspicious of them," said Andra.

"They also get mugged more than other people," said White.

"Oh come on. We're S.O.V.E.U. We kill vampires for a living. What are a couple of muggers in comparison?" said Mc'Ready.

"That's the attitude. We're badass motherfuckers,

so act like it. You need to go now. We only have five hours left until they open the bar for the night. There is a garage at the back of the building. Take one of the cars," said Andra.

"Yes, ma'am," they all said.

Alex led them down to the garage. Inside were three cars. He took a pair of keys from the hooks on the wall and passed them to White. He pressed the unlock button on the key and the lights flashed on the first car. They all got in and Alex typed the address into the sat nav as White started the engine.

After thirty minutes of driving through the city they passed The Nocturnal Club. They continued driving and parked in a public car park three streets away. They stepped out of the car and chatted casually as they walked back in the direction of the bar. As they walked White took photos of Alex and Mc'Ready infront of the surrounding buildings to sell their disguises and appear as genuine tourists. Soon they could see the bar in the distance.

"What now?" said White.

"We need to get on the roof of these surrounding buildings and find those guns," said Mc'Ready.

"I have a plan. Let's find a back alley," said Alex. They walked around a building, down an alley and around the corner. Down this alley two men were beating up another man. Alex looked at them as one of the men looked up and left his friend to beat up their victim.

"What the fuck are you staring at, bitch?" he said.

"Hey, man. We don't want any trouble," said Alex.

"Well, too late, mother fucker. You found it," said the mugger.

"I told you we shouldn't have dressed as tourists," said White.

"Just leave us to our business and we'll leave you to yours," said Alex.

"Oh, hell no, English boy. Y'all in my city now. Those cameras look mighty expensive. I bet you got phones and wallets too. Pass 'em over," he said.

"Can't do that, man," said Alex.

"Mother fucker, you wanna bleed? Hand that shit over," said the man as he pulled out a knife.

Alex instantly stepped into a defensive stance.

"Oh, you think you're Bruce Lee or some shit. Let's see how you handle this?" said the man.

He stepped forward jabbing the knife at Alex who dodged to the left. He grabbed the man's wrist, put the palm of his other hand on the back of the man's shoulder, and forced him face down onto the ground. He twisted the man's wrist causing it to pop. He took the knife, snapped it in his hands and threw the parts aside.

"You broke my fucking hand!" whimpered the man.

"It's dislocated. Consider yourself lucky I didn't crack your skull," said Alex.

"The fuck are you, man?" he said.

"Someone who ain't got time for your shit. You shouldn't have got in my way," he said as he pulled the man up by his good arm. "If I see you again I'll kill you. Now fuck off."

"Ok, man. I'm gone. You ain't ever gonna see me

again, man... I mean sir," said the man.
He ran off and dragged his friend away with him.

"What happened," said his friend.

"We outta here man. Those guys ain't playin'," said the man.

"Come on, we can fuck those bitches up," said his friend.

"That guy just broke my arm and my knife with his bare hands and didn't break a sweat. Whatever they doing here, we ain't gonna stop 'em," he said.

"What about this piece o' shit?" said his friend of the man they had been beating.

"Man, fuck that guy. Leave him to them," he said.
With that they both ran. When they had gone the man on the floor dragged himself, painful and bloodied, to his feet.

"Thank you. You just saved my life," he said.

"You're welcome, now can you move along, please sir," said Alex.

"Are you like the CIA or FBI? You're British though so I guess you're MI5, right?" said the bloody man.

"I said move along," said Alex.

"I've never met anyone British before," said the bloody man.
Alex's upper lips curled as he took a step towards him. Something zipped past him and hit the man who fell to the floor unconscious a moment later. Alex turned to see Mc'Ready holding a tranquiliser gun.

"Thanks, Mc'Ready. He was starting to piss me off," he said.

"No problem, sir. Had to be done, he wouldn't take a hint," she said.

"Wait, you've had that all the time. You could have used it on that other guy. Saved me popping his wrist," he said.

"I could, but he needed taking down a peg," she said.

"That's true," he said.

"So, what's your plan, sir? Are we going up the fire escape?" said White.

"Nope, that will take too long," said Alex.

"Huh?" said White.

"Come here, huddle together and hold on tight. It's a bit like a reverse bungee," said Alex.

They huddled together and held on to Alex.

"What are you going to do?" said Mc'Ready.

"Trust me, I do it all the time. Try not to scream," said Alex

He bent his legs and jumped as hard as he could. As they flew upwards parallel to the building White had his eyes shut while Mc'Ready's eyes were wide with fear and exhilaration. They came down and landed on top of the building.

A man in a guard's uniform was walking across the rooftop facing away from them. He approached a panel set into the rooftop. It was four feet wide and seven feet long. He played with a remote control in his hand while he walked.

"Target sighted, Mc'Ready?" said Alex.

"Aye, sir," she replied.

"Shoot him in the arse," said White.

Alex and Mc'Ready looked at him and smiled.

Mc'Ready composed herself, aimed at the guard's left buttock and squeezed the trigger.

"Ahh! What the fuuuaaa?" cried the guard as the dart hit him.

He then stumbled back and forth like a cartoon drunk and then fell down.

"Mc'Ready, grab that remote and let's get these guns sorted," said Alex.

"What about him?" said White.

"Oh yeah. How long will he be out?" said Alex.

"About fifteen minutes," said Mc'Ready.

"We can't leave him here to wake up. He will go back to Gilad and blow our cover," said Alex.

"Tie him to the fire escape," said White.

"I have an idea. We take him with us and keep him unconscious. When we have done the last gun let him wake up and tell him he passed out," said Mc'Ready.

"It's the best idea we've got," said Alex.

He took the remote control from the guard's belt and passed it to Mc'Ready. It was like a TV remote with fewer buttons. She walked to the panel and pressed a button with 'maintenance' written above it. The panel slid open and the sentinel gun rose horizontally out of it on an articulated arm. It locked into position then stood completely still. She examined the gun and found the removable panel that covered the USB socket. She found it and plugged her phone in via a USB cable. She then used the hack software to access the gun's control system. It allowed her to easily bypass the firewall and all other security protocols. She found the ammunition counter and used the software to trick the gun's CPU to register that the magazine was always full. She then looked at the remote. There was a button with 'mag release' written on it. She pressed it and a box under the gun barrel disconnected. She took hold of it with both hands and slid it forwards. It came away and fell to the rooftop with a heavy thump. The bullets unwound from it in a bullet chain that was fed into the gun. Alex pulled the firing arm back and uncocked the gun. Mc'Ready pulled the chain out free. Alex opened the box, picked it up and emptied it onto the rooftop. He passed it to Mc'Ready and she slid the magazine box back into place until it clicked. She then pressed the 'maintenance' button on the control and the gun lowered back down and the panel slid shut. Alex picked up the bullet chain, coiled it up and threw it all onto the next rooftop. He turned to White who was watching the guard.

"You two ready?" he said.

"Yeah, I am. He's still out," said White.

"Good," said Alex.

He picked the man up and slung him over his shoulder.

"Right let's go. How many more of these guns are there?" said Alex.

"Three more, sir," said Mc'Ready.

"How are we getting down, sir?" said White.

"We not going down. We're going across. Come on, put your arms around me and hold on tight.

They held on to Alex as he took a running jump and leapt to the next building. It was higher but he made it seem effortless. He ran across this rooftop and leapt down to the next one. They searched the next two rooftops before they found the next gun. Mc'Ready pressed the maintenance button on the remote then repeated the process of hacking the gun. The security guard started to come around a little so Mc'Ready shot him with the tranquiliser again. They continued and hacked the last two guns. They held on to Alex again as he jumped down to the back alley of the last building.

"Yeah, still don't like that," said White.

"I like it," said Mc'Ready as she smiled at Alex. Alex placed the security guard on the ground with his back propped up against the building. Mc'Ready put the remote control back in his utility belt and slapped him lightly on the face. His eyes twitched and he started to come round. He then groaned as his eyes and he looked at her.

"Hey, buddy. Are you ok?" she said.

"Er…um... W-where am I? Who are you?" he said.

"We were walking down the alley when you climbed down the fire escape. You came stumbling towards us saying something about the heat and then you went all white and collapsed," she said.

"I did?" he said.

He sat up straight and looked around. He wretched and he put his head between his knees but didn't vomit.

"Wow. Take it easy, mate," said Alex.

"You gave us quite a scare. Do you want us to call for an ambulance?" said Mc'Ready.

"No, er, no thank you. My workplace is just down the block," he said.
"Are you sure?" she said.
"Er, yes Ma'am. Thank you so much, but I should be going now," he said as he got to his feet, still feeling slightly light headed.
"It wouldn't be any trouble for us to drive you there," said Alex.
"No, really, sir. I really should get back to work."
"Ok, sir. Be careful then," said Mc'Ready.
"I will, Ma'am. Thank you for all your help."
"Bye," they all said.
"Bye," he said.
He staggered back to the street and then back to the club.
"Ok, let's get back to the base," said Alex.
"Aye, sir," said Mc'Ready and White.
And they made their way back to the car.

By the time the security guard reached The Nocturnal Club he was starting to feel better. He opened the door and stepped inside. In the shadowy area behind the bar where the sun's rays didn't reach, Gerry was checking stock and replenishing the fridges and spirits.
"I've checked all the guns, sir," said the guard.
"Ok. Thanks for that," said Gerry as he turned to look at the man. "Are you ok?"
"Yes, sir. Why do you ask?" said the guard.
"You look a bit pale, even by human standards," said Gerry.
"I feel a little light headed. It's hotter than Satan's

butt crack out there. I'm probably dehydrated," said the guard.

"Here, have a drink and take a seat for a minute. It'll make you feel better," said Gerry as he poured the man a glass of water.

"Thank you, sir," said the guard as he sat on a stool at the bar.

He picked up the glass and began to gulp the water down.

"Woah, slow down, my friend. Just sip at it," said Gerry.

"Oh, ok, sir," said the guard and drank the water slower.

## Chapter 11.

White drove the car back into the garage at the safe house and parked in the same space they had taken it from. Just before he shut off the engine he looked at the clock and saw that it was just after 19.00. He returned the keys to their hook, and the three of them walked up the stairs and into their room.

"How did it go?" said Andra.

"All done. We've hacked all four guns and removed all the ammunition. Thanks to Mc'Ready," said Alex as he looked at her and smiled.

"Did you have any trouble?" said Andra.

"We had to scare off some muggers and tranquilise a security guard who was patrolling the guns, but other than that it all went real smooth," said Alex.

"Good, that's what I like to hear," said Andra.

"How's everything going, here?" said Alex.

"We have all the info we need. We just need to plan the attack," said Andra.

"Ok, shall we get started then," said Alex.

"Yep," said Andra. "Alright you 'orrible lot, gather round."

They gathered around one of the screens. The original blueprints, building permission plans, photos of the bar staff, the bouncers, the management and a picture of Gilad all showed on the screens with their corresponding information underneath. Andra took a laser pointer from her pocket and shone it at the photo of a beautiful woman.

"This specimen is Gilad. She is the main target of this operation and has a mean streak a mile wide. Alex, she is your primary target. If you need to take out other vampires to get to her do so, but don't waste time if you have her in your sights. No one else is to attack her. The reason, she is stronger, deadlier, and faster than your average vamp. Intelligence has evidence of her possessing an ability that can only be described as teleportation. She is able to move short distances in an instant. She also has the ability to control both vampires and humans alike merely by speaking to them. So, as you, Alex, are neither hopefully this ability will have no effect on you. But we don't know that for sure, so don't listen to anything she says. The rest of you, be very careful if you encounter her," said Andra.

She then pointed to the next photo.

"This is Gerrimark, often referred to as Gerry. He's an ancient Norse vampire, he's tall and very strong. His assumes the manager and head doorman roles. If any of you get chance to take him down, do it. He and Gilad have connections with some of the key players in gang violence, drug dealing and human trafficking all across North America. Mostly because Gilad controls some of the head crime bosses on this continent. So, it might get a bit rough out there tomorrow night," she said.

"Why are we going in tomorrow night? Why don't we strike tonight?" said Davis.

"They don't know we are here but they suspect

we might be. If they are expecting an attack it will be tonight. If we wait until tomorrow they may lower their guard a little. They will always be expecting us but even as little as a day may plant a doubt in their minds," said Andra.

"So we're playing mind games?" said Davis.

"Yes, just a little psychological 'fuck you'. Now, the bar staff and bouncers are a mix of humans and vampires, so, this is the plan. Alex, you go in the front door in human form. When you're inside, make a scene. Anything you like, just don't go monster straight away. White, you take a snipping position on this rooftop to the west," Andra said, as she spoke she pointed to positions on the map. "From there you'll be able to cover both front and rear exits. Mc'Ready, you make your way to this position. There you'll find a terminal. From there you'll be able to shut down all communications. Our radios have anti-jammers so we'll still be able to talk, but for them, if it's anything more high tech than smoke signals I want it shut down. Hussain, Hughes, Palmer, Davis and I will approach from the rear. Once White has dispatched any guards in that position, Davis, you blow the door. That is when we gatecrash the party. Once inside the four of you will subdue any human occupants with tranquiliser darts. Each dart will subdue the target for at least two hours. All vampires are to be dispatched with deadly force. Alex, that is your cue to do your thing. When Gilad is dead her hold over humans and vampires will cease. I don't know what will happen to them, but hopefully they will suffer no ill effects.

In any case, we'll pull out and come straight back here and lay low until sunrise. Then we can leave and no one will know we were ever here. Is that clear?" said Andra.

"Yes Ma'am," they all said.

"Any questions?" she said.

No one spoke.

"Ok. You can all have the rest of the night off. Have some fun in New York City. Ok, dismissed" she said.

"Thank you, ma'am," they said.

They all walked away except Andra, Alex and Mc'Ready.

"Hey, we're all gonna go out and get something to eat and then for a few drinks. You two want to come with us?" said Mc'Ready.

"We'll catch up with you. I need to talk to Andra about something," said Alex.

"Ok, see you later," she said and followed the others.

"What do you want to talk about?" said Andra when Mc'Ready was out of earshot.

"You think I can do this?" he said hesitantly.

"Yes, I do," she said and took his hand in hers. "Alex, you're a strong and capable soldier. You're also one of the most powerful beings on this planet. You can do this, Alex. I believe in you. What is making you doubt yourself?" she said.

"Vincent was investigating Gilad when he was captured. I don't know. I'm just worried something might go wrong," he said.

"It might go a little different than planned but we

can handle whatever happens. We killed over four hundred vampires last night. Put your worries to rest soldier," she said.

He looked at her and smiled.

"Is that an order, ma'am?" he said.

"Yes, it is. Now, go and have fun," she said.

"Thank you, ma'am, I will," he turned to walk away but then turned back to her. "I'm hungry but not for the food they're going to get. You want to come with me?" he said.

"Yes, it'll be fun to have a run across the modern rooftops of this city. It's been a long while since I was last here. It'll be more fun than what I had planned anyway," she said.

"What were you gonna do?" he said.

"Just watch TV," she said.

"Oh yeah, gonna put on something spicy while you're all alone," said Alex with a smirk.

"No, but what's wrong with that if I was? You got something against me getting my spicy on?" she said.

"No, there's nothing wrong with that," he said.

"Good. There is nothing wrong with an older woman getting her jiggy with herself," she said.

He rolled his eyes and said, "I'm going to push you off the roof."

"Hey, you started this," she said with a laugh.

He walked over to one of the skylights and opened it.

"After you," he said.

She climbed out onto the roof and looked around.

He climbed up after her and whistled as he looked

over the rooftops.

“That is an incredible skyline. No wonder they set Spider-Man here,” said Alex.

She looked at him and smiled.

“Amazing isn’t it,” she said and looked around for a moment. “Come on lets go.”

They ran and leapt across to the next building.

## Chapter 12.

The other members of the S.O.V.E.U. were out in Manhattan and having a great time. They got yellow taxi cabs and went looking at some of the local tourist attractions and monuments. Later they went to a bar and grill where they all had meals and drinks.

On the rooftops, Alex and Andra were having fun and running fast. There were no people to get close because of the height of the skyline so instead they were racing. They were calling out features on the buildings and seeing who could reach them first. As night fell Alex began the hunt. The city was thick with the scent of vampires everywhere they went so he realised it would be easy pickings. He just needed to find a quiet place to hunt.

Soon he found a road with a low bridge and rooftop from which he could watch the people walking along the pavement. He and Andra were lay on a rooftop and soon a woman walked down the road. Unbeknown to her, she was being followed and hunted by a male vampire. Andra leaned over to Alex.

"How are you going to get him?" she said.

"She is going to have to walk under that bridge further down the road. That is where he will strike. So, that's where I'll strike. I'll make him realise what it's like to be the victim," he said.

"You're going to have to get down there. They'll be at the bridge soon. You don't want to be following him you will scare him off."

"Don't worry I've got it all planned. You just stay here and keep my place warm. I'll be back before you know it," he said with a smile.

He got to his feet, took his clothes off and put them into his backpack. He ran to the edge of the building at high speed and leapt off. He sailed through the night air in a long, low arch, and landed on the other side of the bridge. He then dropped down to the road, transformed, climbed up into a shadow alcove of the bridge, and waited.

The woman, sensing that she was being followed, started to walk faster as she approached the bridge. She looked over her shoulder as she passed under it and broke into a run. Anticipating this, the vampire leapt on her, taking her down to the ground. He opened his mouth with the intention of biting into the back of her neck. He was salivating at the thought of quenching his thirst on her blood. As his fangs were inches from her flesh a hand reached out from the darkness. The fingers wrapped around his head and he was lifted up away from the woman. She rolled over onto her back and saw the man's limbs failing as he was hauled into the shadows by an enormous clawed hand.

"Run!" a deep voice rumbled from the darkness. She jumped up and ran, needing no more provocation.

"What are you?" wailed the vampire.

"Hungry," growled Alex.

He bit into the vampire's shoulder, waited for his flesh to harden, and then ate him. He finished and returned to his spot next to Andra and dressed.

"Did she see you?" she said.
"Only my hand. She ran like hell," said Alex.
"Can't say I blame her," she said.
"Do you think she will tell anyone?" he said.
"Nah, even if she did who would believe her," she said.
"Ok, two more and I will have satisfied my hunger," he said.
"Let's go then," she said.
They continued to traverse the City rooftops until he spotted two vampires chasing a one man into a dark alley. They moved until they were stood on edge of the rooftop of a building and looked down into the alley.
"Run all you like, man. It won't do you any good," said one of the vampires.
"Yeah, we're gonna get you," laughed the other.
Alex undressed again, stood on the edge of the roof, then stepped out into thin air and dropped to the alley below. He had completed his transformation as he fell and landed on one of the vampires. The impact crumpled the vampire to the ground. Alex bit into the back of the vampire's head. He then pulled and tore it away from the body. He flicked his head back and dropped the skull deeper into his open maw crunched it into pieces before swallowing it. He quickly bit off and swallowed chunks of its body until it was gone. The other vampire turned back and saw this huge beast swallowing a foot. He turned and began to run but Alex leapt on him and jumped away taking him to the rooftop. There he ate the vampire, biting off

chunks, crunching and then swallowing them. The potential human victim was left running from nothing until he turned and realised he was safe.

Andra found Alex as he finished eating the vampire.

"Are you satisfied now?" she said.

"Yep, that hit the spot," he said as he rubbed his stomach.

She looked at him with a smile.

"Are you ok?" said Alex.

"Yeah, yes. It's just, uhm. I've waited a long time for you. Everyone other immortal I know is an enemy. You're the only one I know who is an alley; a friend. I've watched you grow from a boy into a man and now an immortal being like me. We've both lost everything but now, here we are. For the first time in a long time I feel hopeful," she said.

"Me too. We are our own little family," he said.

She tapped the side of her fist against his shoulder and turned her face away.

"Are you crying?" he said.

"No," she said and quickly whipped her eyes. "Let's go and find the others."

"Yeah, let's go," he said and slapped his palm against her back.

"Lead the way," she said with a smile.

He set off running and she followed close on his heels.

## Chapter 13.

The Nocturnal Club opened it front doors at 21.00. and began to let the customers in. The beer was flowing, the music was loud, customers were dancing, and in the back, vampires were feeding. The security was tighter than it had ever been. Eight guards were on the front doors and four on the back. Throughout the club there were twelve extra bouncers. They were walking amongst the customers looking for anything suspicious. Gilad slowly walked through the club. She however was not looking for danger, she was hunting. She found what she was looking for in a young handsome man. He was in his mid-twenties, tall and muscular with long, brown hair. Exactly what she was looking for. She liked to think they looked like the warriors. She watched him from afar for a moment before she approached him. She wrapped her arms around him and looked deep into his eyes. She made small talk with him as her mind slithered into his skull, wrapped around his mind and took hold. In that moment he was powerless against her.

"Follow me. I want you, I need you," she whispered aloud words filled with telepathic energy.

These words sunk into his brain, embedding themselves like fish hooks.

"Yes M'lady," his mind said.

He couldn't help but follow her as she guided him through the club and upstairs to her office. She stopped in the middle of the room with her back to him. He walked up to her and gently placed his hands on her hips. She turned to face him and wrapped her arms around him. He looked into her eyes and leaned in. She leaned in too and slowly opened her mouth. Her hold on him grew firmer, one hand held the back of his head and her other arm gripped him by the shoulders. He had been moving in to kiss her but she forced his head to the side. Her tongue lifted up the spike shot out from beneath it and plunged it into his neck. She bled him nearly dry but stopped just before he slipped into the embrace of death. She wanted to keep him so he was no good to her dead. She held onto him with her inhuman strength as he began to shake and convulse. His limbs pounded her body but she was immovable, his jaw clenched tight, and his eyes rolled back. He yelled out in pain, the life drained from him, and he was still.

She lifted his lifeless body from the floor, then carried him into another room. There she placed him in her coffin where he would awake later. Some vampires were woken into their new life alone in fear and confusion. He would wake in her arms and know that Gilad was his queen and he would protect her with his life.

The night didn't bring the attack from the beast in the vision that Gilad had expected. She felt a little disappointed by this. She wanted vengeance for Saltorg's murder. To smear the beast's blood as a warning to all who would even think of defying her.

Just before the sun rose at dawn to end the night, she opened the lid of her coffin and climbed in with her new man-toy just as he began to wake up. They had rough, loveless but lustful sex. To her, the act of sex had become little more than a means to an end. Just another way to assert her control over the people she kept and assure their loyalty to her. She enjoyed it but it was tinged with an empty sadness. In her heart she knew it would never be the same as the happiness she had felt with her sweetheart. She had memories with them, but their name and face had been swept away by the flow and ebb of time. It was so long ago now that it almost seemed like a dream.

*

Alex's phone rang in his pocket. He took it out, "Mc'Ready" was written on the screen. He slid his finger across the answer button and pressed the speaker button.

"Hello?" he said.

"Hi, Alex. We're in a bar called The Keg Room. It's on West 36$^{th}$ Street," Mc'Ready said.

"Ok. We'll be there soon," he said.

"See you in a bit," she said.

Alex hung up his and put his phone back in his pocket. He and Andra set off across the rooftops and arrived on a building across from the bar ten minutes later.

"I can't come in with you, Alex. I will draw too much attention. I'll go back to the base and see you all there later," said Andra.

"Ok. I'll make sure they don't stay too late. Big

day tomorrow," he said.

"Go and have fun," she said.

"Ok," said Alex and dropped off the edge of the building to the alley below.

He crossed the road to the bar and pulled open the door. He was hit by the music and chatter of the customers. The smell of hot food and beer hooked him in by the nostrils and drew him in. Mc'Ready waved at him from across the room.

"Alex, over here," she said.

Mc'Ready, Davis and Hussain were sat around a table while Palmer and Hughes were playing pool. White was at the bar buying a round of drinks.

"So, what did you get up to?" said Davis to Alex as he sat down.

"I was hunting vampires," said Alex.

"Why? We're supposed to be taking the night off," said Hussain.

"I know, but I was hungry," he said.

"Oh yes. Sorry, I forgot about that," said Hussain.

"So, did you find any?" said Mc'Ready.

"Yes, I caught three," he said, patting his stomach. "They were stalking a woman and a man, so I saved some lives, too."

Mc'Ready smiled when he said that.

"So, can you eat normal food too, or does it have to be vamp meat?" said White as he set the tray of drinks down on the table.

"I can still eat normal food, but it doesn't give me the nutrients I get from a vampire," he said.

"It seems weird talking about someone eating vampires. No offence to you, Alex. It's just that they're usually the ones doing the eating," said Hussain.

"The tables have turned and now they're on my menu. I'll eat every single one of them if I have to," he said.

"You should save some space for tomorrow. It's gonna be like an all you can eat," said White, with a big smile on his face.

"I can't wait," said Alex as he rubbed his hands together.

They all laughed.

The night went well and they all had a great time. Knowing that they had work to do the next day they all decided they should call it a night at midnight and made their way back to the safe house.

Though they had been drinking most of them were only tipsy and all were in good spirits. They got up to the room and found Andra sat watching the TV.

"Hello, Andra. I'm drunk," said Davis.

"I can see that," said Andra.

Davis stumbled around and Laughed as White held her up with an arm around her.

"Not all of us are," said Hussain.

"Yep, Zarv doesn't drink and I can't get drunk anymore," said Alex.

"This instant healing isn't as much fun as it's made out to be," said Andra.

"Nope. It would be great for winning drinking games, other than that I might as well have been drinking lemonade," he said.

"You all have a good time then?" said Andra.
"Yep. New York is great. I'll have to bring my family here when I get some leave," said Hughes.
"We visited the Empire State Building, went for a meal and then for a few drinks. It was a good night," said Palmer.
White was trying to help Davis up off the floor but they were both as drunk as each other. When he finally helped her up she grabbed him and hugged him.
"I've never really talked with this man till this morning, but we had a great time together. He can drink just as much I can," said Davis.
They looked at each other and fell about laughing.
Mc'Ready was in the kitchen making peanut butter on toast.
"Anyone want a brew?" she called.
"Yes please," said four of them.
They all sat around and watched TV for a while as they ate their toast and drank their tea. At around 1.00. Andra stood up.
"Ok, soldiers. I'm going to get some rest. I suggest you do the same," she said.
"Good night, Ma'am," they all said.
Over the next half hour they all went to bed until there was just Alex and Mc'Ready left. They were talking as she played with her long red hair.
"So what brought you to the S.O.V.E.U.?" said Alex.
"That's a long story," she said.
"I have time to listen," he said.
"Ok. I was on a mission in Brazil. It was supposed

to be quick and easy. An in and out job, you know. We were a four person unit specialised in target elimination. The lucky contestant that day was a wannabe warlord in the weapons trafficking game. He was holed up in this big old manor house but his security were more interested in playing poker than doing their job. That is what intelligence told us anyway, said they were hired goons. All about the money, you know. So, I hacked the electricity, knocked out the power and we went in quiet and hard. The plan was simple and it was going like clockwork. Harris, our shooter walked into the target's office and put a bullet in his head. That should have been the last of it. We were going down this big spiral staircase when the guy we had just eliminated dropped down the next to the stairs and caught the bannister. Somehow he had survived being shot point-fucking-blank through the cranium. He grabbed West by the neck and shook him like a doll, snapping his neck. He then pulled himself onto the stairs and tore Simmons to pieces. Harris and I emptied a full magazine each into him and he just took it all. He grabbed Harris by the neck and pulled his throat out. I switched to my Remi, blew off both his feet and he fell to the floor, screaming. He lashed out at me, so, I shot off both his arms and I pointed the gun in his face. The motherfucker bit the end of the barrel. I tried to pull it free but he was crushing the end so I pulled the trigger and blew his head off. At the time I didn't know how he could be so tough," she frowned and shook her head. "My unit was gone. We had completed sixteen missions together. I would have trusted any one of them with my life and that fucker had just wiped them out. I was all alone in there and still had to make my way out. His goons were a lot more threatening now. It was now obvious that they had set a nice trap for us. I ran through that place like the devil himself was chasing me. Fuck, he might as well have been. I figured out if I cooked flash bangs for seven seconds before I threw them the vamps couldn't get far enough away from them. So I used them to burn my way out of there. Eventually, I made it to the extraction point in one piece; physically anyway. Mentally that shit took its toll. I had a few choice words for those fucking idiots in Intelligence when I got back to base, I can tell you. The next day I had a word with my Captain and he told me about the S.O.V.E.U. I handed in my transfer papers that same day," she said.

"Man, I'm sorry about your team," said Alex.

"We've all lost people, but we're going to avenge them all, right?" said Mc'Ready.

"Yes, we are," he said.

"Ok, Alex, I'm gonna have to call it a night," she said.

"Me too. Good night, Mc'Ready," he said.

"Call me Lucy," she said.

"Good night, Lucy," he said with a smile.

She hugged him then stood up and went to bed.

## Chapter 14.

Monday 4th August.

The air was still. and the sun shone brightly through the French doors as Alex woke up. He looked at the doors and saw they were slightly open. He got up, slipped on a T-shirt and went to investigate. The air was filled with the sound of traffic and people busily commuting to work. Andra was stood on the balcony sipping a cup of coffee from a cardboard cup with a twin-tailed mermaid on the side.

"Good morning," he said.

"Good morning, bedhead," she said with a smile. He rubbed a hand over his hair in an attempt to flatten it down only for it to bounce back up.

"How did you get that? I thought you didn't want people seeing you?" he said.

"I nipped in round the back. I part-own the company," she said.

"You mean you part-own the shop," he said.

"The company, I invest. You know when you hear about shadow partners in companies. That's me. Coffee is big business," she said.

"I never knew you invested your money," he said.

"Well, you do now," she said.

"How much of it?" he said.

"I'm not telling you," she said.

"Come on. Quarter of it…half?" he said.

"I'm not at liberty to disclose my financial affairs with you. The financial interests of my partners are legally protected by international laws," she said.

"Yeah, ok," he said with a smile.
She didn't smile back, not even a smirk.

"You're serious aren't you," he said.

"Yes, a lot of it is locked up in the S.O.V.E.U. and other secret military ventures. Where do you think all the cool shit comes from? It doesn't just fall out of the sky," she said.

"Ok, sorry, ma'am. Can we change the subject? I feel we have set off on the wrong footing. You said last night that it has been a while since you were here. When was the last time?" he said.

"The last time?" she thought for a moment. "It was 1992, in the summer. This entire city has changed since then, this entire world has changed. The only thing that seems to stay the same is me. I feel like an observer sometimes, like I'm not really here. The thing people don't realise about immortality is that you can still sense the passing of time," she said.

She looked out across the city, and Alex noticed a look in her eyes, like she could literally see the world changing.

"How does that make you feel?" he said.

"Old. It makes me feel old," she said.

"Do you ever wonder what death would be like?" he said.

She looked him right in the eye so intensely he almost looked away, but then her face softened, and she smiled warmly.

"No. I've been alive so long I don't know what death could possibly hold for me. I'm so old even the religions and gods I used to believe in are dead.

You'll understand someday," she said.

Just then, Hussain popped her head around the door, her hair sticking out of a loosely tied ponytail.

"Oh, sorry. I didn't realise it was you. I just saw the door open and heard voices," she said.

"It's ok. We had just finished talking hadn't we, Alex."

"Yes, yes we had. I should go and have a shower," he said.

He squeezed in past Hussain and went to the bathroom.

By 10.30 the rest of the group were up and dressed. Davis and White went out to get the breakfasts while the rest gathered in the attic. Alex, Hussain, Hughes and Palmer were stripping and cleaning the weapons. Mc'Ready was preparing her laptop and phone with all the software they would need. Andra was making some phone calls to her spies and looking over the attack plan again. At 11.00 Davis and White returned with huge sandwiches for everyone. They all sat down and as they ate they talked together. They spoke about the night before, about the past, about their families and their hopes for the future. They all imagined the possibility of a future without vampires. Alex knew it was a lot of pressure but they all assured him he could deliver that future. It was what they all hoped for and he felt in his heart that he could do what they asked of him. They trained in the gym under the hotel, watched some films, trained some more and had some more to eat.

At 20.00 Andra talked them through the plan of

attack again. For three hours they discussed every scenario, working out ways of dealing with every little possible problem. Finally, Andra looked at the clock.

"Ok people, 23.00. Check your weapons one last time. Get suited and booted. We know what we have to do. So, let's do what we do best," she said.

"Yes, Ma'am," they said.

"Fucking A!" she said.

They all did one last weapons check and put on their combat gear. Hughes, Davis White, Palmer, and Hussain were dressed in black tactical body armour and black balaclavas. They wore night vision goggles that were attached by head mounts and clicked into an upright position for the time being. Alex who dressed in casual clothes and Mc'Ready was dressed as a communications technician. They all lined up infront of Andra and stood to attention.

"Ok unit, down to the garage," said Andra. They all made their way down the back stairs and climbed into the van with Davis in the driver's seat.

"Move out," said Andra.

"Ma'am," she said as she put the van in gear and drove out from under the safehouse. As they travelled through the city the adrenaline was running high but none of them let it show. The only signs were little ticks. Palmer's knee bounced, White clicked his knuckles, and Hussain flexed her neck from right to left. Hughes had his eyes closed in a light meditation, and Alex flicked through videos of the inside of the club on his phone.

Mc'Ready tapped away on the keyboard of her computer, and Andra sat so still she could have been carved from solid marble.

Eventually, Davis pulled the van over and parked at the side of the road.

"We're here," she said.

"Mc'Ready, you're up. Hack in and await my command," said Andra as she slid open the side door.

"Yes Ma'am," said Mc'Ready.

She got out of the van and walked casually to the communications terminal. Davis drove the van to the next destination which was an alley a few streets away from the club. She pulled over and parked.

"Alex and White. You know where you need to be. Take your positions and await my command," said Andra,

"Yes Ma'am," they both said and got out of the van.

"Alex, the code phrase to go ahead is: 'So it begins'. If for any reason we need to abort the phrase is: 'No Go.' Got that?" she said.

"Loud and clear ma'am," said Alex.

"See you on the other side," said Andra.

Alex and White walked east towards the club. They turned down another back alley and found the rear of the building with the best view of the target building. They both looked around. When they were sure no one was watching them White jumped onto Alex's back and they leapt fifty feet up onto the building's rooftop.

"Ok, set up you post, and happy hunting," said

Alex.

"Same to you, man. Get that bitch," said White. He held out a fist, Alex held out his fist, and they tapped their knuckles together in a fist bump. White then ducked down and walked to the edge of the building with a clear view of the side of the club. Alex ran in the opposite direction and dropped back down to the street below. When he landed he straitened his clothes and hair. On the rooftop White opened his gun case, assembled his AS50 sniper rifle and adjusted its sights until he had the perfect view of both the front and rear exits.

The van drove to an alley a street away from the club and parked. Andra, Davis, Hussain, Hughes and Palmer got out and moved to their pre-discussed position and awaited Alex's word. The automated sniper sentinels raised up from their resting position and into their firing positions. Their firing hammers clicked rapidly, but without bullets, they were completely harmless

At the front of the building, Alex joined the queue to enter the club. He had to wait for twenty minutes so he started a conversation with some vampires who were also waiting.

"Is it always this busy?" he said.

"Yes, it's busy like this most nights, but there seems to be a lot more security tonight," said one of them.

"Oh really. You know why?" he said.

"I'm not sure. I heard Gilad is back," she said.

"Who's Gilad?" said Alex.

"Seriously, you don't know who Gilad is?" she

said.

"Yes seriously. I'm new to all of this. I was only made two months ago. I'm just here visiting a friend. He told me to visit this place while I'm here," he said.

"Gilad is one of the oldest and coolest vampires in the world. They say no man can resist her. I've only ever seen her once and she is the most beautiful woman I have ever seen," she said.

"Really. I'll have to keep an eye out for her," he said.

"I love your accent. Where are you from?" she said.

"Manchester, England," he said.

"Oh yeah? That's interesting. I live here in New York, I've always wanted to visit Europe though," she said.

"You should. You'd love it," he said.

"Sorry, where are my manners? I'm Beth, and this is Helen," she said.

"Hi!" said Helen, with a huge smile on her face.

"What's your name?" said Beth.

"I'm Tod," said Alex and extended his hand.

"It's a pleasure to meet you, Tod," said Beth and shook his hand.

Helen eagerly shook his hand too.

By now they had reached the front of the queue. The doorman moved aside and let two men and Beth and Helen into the club. He then stepped infront of Alex and fixed him with a steely glare.

"We'll see you inside," said Beth

"Yes, see you in there," he said.

"Hello," he said and smiled at the short stocky doorman, but the man just stared back at him. After a minute or two the doorman stepped aside and let Alex and a few other people in. He paid the entry fee and walked into the club.

On the rooftop, White watched Alex enter the club, and clicked his radio.
"Eyes to Brain. The Wolf is among the sheep, over," he said.
"Copy that, over. Brain to Ears. Be ready for my signal, over," said Andra
"Copy, over," said Mc'Ready.

In the club, the humans outnumbered the vampires two to one. Alex walked to the bar and waited to be served. He looked around for a moment and liked what he saw. The gothic décor and vibrant atmosphere really appealed to him. It was a shame that it belonged to vampires. He knew he had to focus on the task at hand and was reminded of his mission to blend in when bartender looked at him.
"Double rum and coke, please," he said.
A few moments later they placed his drink on the bar and held out a card reader. Alex paid took his drink as Lamb of God's 'Broken Hands' finished blasting out of the speakers. Helen ran over, took him by the hand and led him onto the dance floor as 'Bodies' by Drowning Pool began to play. She stomped her feet and headbanged to the beat. Alex joined in but his ability to sense the presence of

Gilad was distracting him.

Upstairs she sensed his presence too and ran to the bank of CCTV monitors. She recognised him straight away but not as Alex. She thought she was looking at Vincent. Even with his short hair and despite the fact she had not seen Vincent since she had given him to Saltorg. Dienco had informed her that Vincent had escaped and she knew Saltorg had gone to find him. She had sensed Saltorg's death at the hands of the beast from her vision. Adrenaline ran through her veins and her thoughts ran through her mind.

'He is in my club now. But that's not part of the prophecy. Vincent isn't the beast. This must be the brother, he is the beast. The fucking beast is in my club right now!'

She clicked the button on her microphone.

"Gerry! He's here! He fucking here!!" she screamed down the microphone.

"Who is?" said Gerry.

"The beast, the fucking beast from my vision. He's in the club right now. He's on the dance floor!" she said.

"Where, M'lady. I don't see a beast," said Gerry.

"He's Vincent's twin. He looks identical, except he has short hair," said Gilad.

Gerry walked towards the dance floor and caught a glimpse of Alex. He remembered Gilad making such a big deal of catching Vincent that the face was burned into his mind.

"I see him M'lady. What do you want me to do?" he said.

"Kill him. Don't let him change. Don't let him get to me!" she screamed.

The fear in her voice was abundantly clear.

"Yes, M'lady," he said.

He clicked the button on his radio.

"Door staff, lock this place down. No one enters, no one leaves. Everyone who's inside, get to the dance floor right now," he said.

From all areas of the club the security guards moved in on Alex. He looked away from Helen and saw them coming.

"So it begins," he said.

Outside Andra heard him over her radio.

"Copy that," she said. "Mc'Ready, Kill it. White be ready to clear our path. Davis, pop the door, Unit, move out,"

Mc'Ready pressed enter on her computer. The program ran and scrambled all cell phone signals in the local area. Davis ran towards to door, shaping a small square of C4 plastic explosive as she did. She was six feet away when it swung open and two doormen stepped out. She planted her feet against the concrete and slid to a halt. They both looked at her, bared their fangs and hissed.

Inside Alex grabbed Helen, spun around then turned so she was behind him and he was facing towards Gerry. The giant vampire growled and flexed his muscles. Alex ran at him and threw a flying punch. His fist connected with Gerry's head knocking him back into the crowd of people. At the same time Gerry swung his arm and knocked Alex aside. He fell into some people but quickly got to his feet. One of the doormen lunged at Alex but he caught this vampire and threw him over his shoulder onto the dance floor. He landed heavily. Alex twisted his arm, snapping it at the elbow and bones burst through the flesh. Alex thrust the bone through the vampire's chest into his heart. He thrashed as he burned up, sending his ash all across the smooth floor. People screamed backed away as far as they could. Door men were attacking Alex from all directions. He was fighting them off, breaking arms, wrists and noses but the vampire's bones healed rapidly. He saw Gerry striding towards him. He spun and kicked a vampire in the jaw, snapping their neck. He ran at Gerry and punched him in the face, the side of the head, and in the stomach. Gerry took the hits without even flinching. He lunged forward and grappled with Alex. Then turned fast trying to cause Alex to lose his balance but it didn't work. He punched Alex in the stomach repeatedly. The hits were taking their toll and Alex could feel his legs beginning to wobble. He caught Gerry's arm and twisted, pushed him back and uppercut him hard to the jaw. It was enough to make him step back for a moment. Alex jumped and stomped his foot down into Gerry's right knee. The bones snapped so loud it could be heard over the music. Gerry stumbled back and tried to keep his balance. Alex stepped in for the next attack but Gerry he grabbed him by the head and butted him twice. Alex's vision blurred and his head spun. His transformation began automatically as a self defence mechanism. He grabbed Gerry by the throat as his hands, arms and shoulders grew. His shirt ripped away as his back widened and he roared in pain. His head and face changed shape as the bones moved under his flesh. His feet tore through of his boots and his legs grew longer. Gerry punched and kicked against him but within ten seconds Alex was well over nine feet tall. His hand was still around Gerry's neck. The vampire flailed his arms and scratched at the hand but all his efforts were in vain. Alex looked at him through eyes that were becoming dark and reptilian. He growled and Gerry felt it reverberate through his body. A stream of urine ran down his leg. Alex pulled Gerry closer and bit into his head. He tried to scream but the beast's huge jaws were clamped around his face. He felt the teeth slicing through his scalp and under his jaw. A burning sensation ran waves all over his skin. He could hear people scream all around him as his joints fused and his flesh stiffened. The last thing he felt was the horrendous pain of his skull collapsing under the immense pressure of the beast's jaws.

Alex pulled Gerry away and tore most of the destroyed skull from the solidifying body and swallowed it. He threw out his arms, swung the headless body around and roared at the little vampires. Doormen and customers alike ran from him in shock and fear. Suddenly they all stopped and stood still, they turned around to look at him. Their faces were devoid of any expression. One by one a handful of them ran at him and launched into an emotionless attack; then the entire crowd charged.

Outside: Davis drew two machetes and attacked the doormen. They were dodging every swing of her blades. Despite all her efforts and skills she couldn't seem to hit them. One of them grabbed her by the throat and squeezed so hard she could feel the pressure building in her head and began to see stars. With quick thinking she swung her legs back and then forward with all the strength she muster. Andra was moving to step out from her position and was running towards her teammate. She heard the almost imperceptible pop of a silenced rifle and a bullet slicing the air. Inches from Davis' face, the vampire's head exploded. Skull fragments and brain matter flew out from one side. Davis' legs smashed into the vampire's groin and up through his body as he burned up. She fell to the floor and landed on her back as his arms broke apart. The remaining vampire looked in the direction the bullet had come from as another bullet tore a hole between his eyes. He stumbled back but his knees collapsed and he shattered into ash as he hit the ground. Davis got to her feet and looked over up the where White was positioned with his rifle. Through his scope he saw her blow him a kiss, then point the index finger of her outstretched arm at him and move her thumb, imitating the hammer of a gun.

"Anytime, babe," He said into his radio mic.

"Fuckin' A," she replied.

She then took the C4 from her pocket, moulded it into shape again, and then pushed it around the door lock. She pushed a five second detonator into it, ran to cover and put her hands against her ears. There was a pop as the lock was blown out and the door swung open.

"Go, go, go!" said Andra. "Remember, tranquilise the humans but leave the vampires to me and Alex unless you have no other option."

She and the soldiers ran into the building, followed by Davis who closed the door behind them. Inside Andra ran into the back room. To their surprise the room was empty. There was blood, drinks and drugs spilt across the floor as though everyone had left in a hurry. They moved further into the building and though the music was loud they could hear roars and screams coming from the main bar room. As they moved into this larger room they could see both humans and vampires alike swarming around the huge beastly form of Alex in the centre of the dance floor.

He was pushing aside the humans and grabbing the vampires. He took one, bit into its head, then tore it from the body before he crunched in his jaws and swallowed it. He then threw aside the manikin-like husk. He did this repeatedly.

Andra, Hussain, Hughes, Palmer and Davis walked with guns drawn through the piles of partially eaten husks that were strewn across the floor. Hussain shot Hughes a look that was partially shock but mostly awe. He returned to look then Andra gave a hand signal to engage the targets.

Soon the humans were stumbling and falling to the floor after being shot with the fast acting tranquiliser darts. Part of the swarm turned and rushed at Andra and the unit. She hacked apart and shot any vampires that tried to attack the soldiers.

It was becoming clear that the vampire numbers were beginning to dwindle. They started to retreat from Alex only to find Andra and the soldiers on the other side. They huddled in the middle ground and found they had no place to hide. The soldiers continued to dart the humans with incredible efficiency. All at once as if controlled by one mind the vampires split into two groups and ran to either side of the room. They crawled up the walls and swarmed across the ceiling towards one doorway. Andra shot at them, killing some, but the rest didn't stop. They just manoeuvred around the burning ash corpses as they fell and kept moving.

"They're retreating to the basement, to Gilad," said Alex.

"Ok, go get her. We'll finish up here and stop anyone else getting in," said Andra.

Alex grunted in approval and gave chase.
He followed the vampires down the stairs. They all swarmed through the basement doorway, but before Alex could reach it a thick, heavy, metal door slammed shut and blocked his path. He ran headlong at it but heavy locking bolts slid into place with a 'thunk' before could get to it.

Years before Gilad had all the inner walls in the basement covered with six inch thick steel plate for just such an occasion. Her thinking behind this was she could close that door and nothing could get in. She could then wait safely inside until whatever was outside gave up or was eliminated by someone coming to her assistance.

Alex drew back his fist and punched the door. Even with all his strength he only left a shallow dent. He began to pummel it with both fists and the centre of the door dented inwards but not enough to break the bolts. He concentrated his attack on the top corner, hammering at it relentlessly. Eventually, it buckled inwards, and there were audible pops as the locking bolts around the area snapped. He put his hand against the top of the door and as he pushed against it. Soon it began to give way. It bent inwards and he could fit his fingers through, and then his whole hand. Panicked shouts came from the other side. Something heavy hit his hand and he quickly pulled his arm back. A face appeared at the gap and shouted profanities. Alex shot his hand through and grabbed it. He then proceeded to pull the vampire's head through to his side of the door. The vampire screamed and Alex could feel him resisting. With a growl he pulled harder. The vampire's bones snapped and his flesh tore as his entire body passed through a hole that was too small for him to fit through. The vampires on the other side of the door screamed as blood and viscera coated the ceiling and walls infront of them. Alex bit into the vampire's face and then ate the entire husk. He then hammered his fists against the area below the corner he had opened and more of the bolts popped. None of the vampires dared approach the door after witnessing the fate of their colleague. Alex began to throw his full body weight against the door. On the fifth attempt the final bolts gave way and the steel screamed as he bent the door wide open. He strode in like he owned the place. A huge number of vampires gathered in the corridor to stand in his way and tell him otherwise. They all watched his every move as he made his entrance. They raised their guns in unison and shot at him. The bullets hit their target but couldn't pierce Alex's scaled flesh and he just kept moving. He reached them and tore into the mass of bodies, ripping off body parts and shattering bones. They were unsuccessful in their attempts to hold him back. The distinctive buzz Gau-19B minigun started up and the crowd parted. Alex was hit with hundreds of 50 calibre rounds. The continuous barrage of bullets punctured his scales and he roared in pain. He put his arms up to protect his face and charged in the direction the bullets were coming from. He collided with the gun and it's barer and kept running until he heard a bloody splat as he crashed into a wall. He stood up straight and lowered his arms. On the wall infront of him were the crushed remains of a vampire. The horde of vampires attacked him but were little more than an annoyance. He tore them apart like a man pushing through dense foliage. Soon he reached a door behind which he could hear a woman screaming and roaring. He threw his shoulder against this door in the same way he had the previous one and after the third attempt the locks broke and it swung inwards.

He lowered his head and stepped through the doorway.

The room was lit entirely by oil lamps and smelt like grease. Gilad stood at the back of this shadowy room. Between her and Alex stood twenty of her personal armoured guards. Alex stood and looked at them and they looked at him. He smiled, blasted a rasping breath through his teeth then charged into them. In an explosion of movement they launched into their attack. They hacked at him with swords and axes. The blades cut into his limbs and pulled away scales and chunks of flesh. They were causing him damage, but his strength, accelerated healing and armoured flesh outmatched their weaponry. In spite of this they wouldn't and couldn't give up. Alex was tearing them apart but they were under Gilad's control and she was more than willing to give their lives to protect her own. Soon there was only one left, the man-toy Gilad had made the night before. She watched in horror as Alex picked him up, tore him in two at the waist, and cast him aside. She backed away growling and hissing.

"Just me and you now, Gilad," said Alex.

"The beauty versus the beast," she said mockingly.

"I hope you put up more of a fight than your brother," said Alex.

"You'll pay for what you did to Saltorg," she screamed.

"He kept my brother prisoner for over twenty years and had him tortured every single day. Your brother got exactly what he deserved. I was just defending my colleagues. And not wanting to seem petty, but he did attack us first," said Alex with a grin.

Her face twisted into a snarl and she ran at him. She leapt onto him and slashed at his face with her fingernails as they turned into claws. She manoeuvred herself in the air and landed her feet against his chest. He attempted to grab her but she slashed at both his wrists as she back flipped away from him. He let out a roar of pain and anger as blood poured from the wounds. They were healing as he ran at her. She was already moving and front flipped towards the far wall. As she passed into the shadows that played across its surface and vanished. Alex was close behind and slammed his fists against the wall. For a moment he stood confused as to what had just happened. She appeared from the shadows above him and landed on his back. She dug her claws into the top of his head and ripped at the flesh but it was too thick for her to break through. What marks she did leave healed almost as soon as they were made. He reached up, snatched her arm and threw her to the floor.

"Nice trick you've got there, but you'll have to try harder," he said.

He raised his foot to stomp on her but she rolled away and was on her feet. She ran into another shadow and was gone. She appeared to his left and slashed at his abdomen as she ran past him. She disappeared into another shadow then appeared infront of him and slashed his throat. Blood spilt down his chest just before the wound closed. He swung his arm for her but she fell back and disappeared. She landed on his shoulders and dug her claws under the edge of a scale on his neck and started trying to pry it away. He grabbed her shoulder and squeezed. He felt her bones pop between his fingers but she wiggled free and leapt into the shadows.

"I'm getting tired of this shit!" he roared.

Her laughter echoed around the room. He strode across the room looking for something he could use to his advantage and came across some unlit lamps. He grabbed handfuls and threw them against the walls, shattering them and coating the surfaces with the oil. He picked up a lit lamp and when she reappeared he threw it against the wall. The flames licked up and across the walls and within seconds every vertical surface was on fire. She spun around in a state of terror.

"No shadows, no escape. Got you," Growled Alex.

Gilad roared as black and brown scales grew all over her flesh. Her brow became a deep furrow, horns grew from the top of her head and her mouth widened. Long, sharp fangs burst from her gums, her shoulders became loose and her arms flailed like wild, writhing snakes.

"You have me trapped, but I'm not going out without a fight!" she said.

"A fight? I thought you'd never ask," he said.

She jumped on him and one of her arms wrapped around his snout. With her other arm, she slashed at the flesh of his abdomen. The skin was slightly thinner here and her claws cut through the skin and muscle. She forced her hand into his belly. He felt her finger clench deep inside him and she began to pull out a handful of his intestines. As she tried to disembowel him he took hold of her around the waist and slid her coiled arm from his face. Still, she tore at his innards. He hammered his other fist down on top of her head and slammed her into the floor. While she lay there dazed he untangled her hand from his intestines and pushed them back into his body. As the wound healed she fought against his grip and slipped free. She flicked out her left arm in an attempt to wrap it around his neck but he caught it. This arm wrapped around his and she dug her claws into his bicep. With his other hand he grabbed her shoulder as tight as he could. She wrapped her free arm around his hand and tried to pull it away from her. They were both now entwined with one and other and neither could escape. He lunged his head at her but she dodged his snapping jaws. She spun him around and forced his back against the burning wall. He growled and pushed back. They jostled like this for a moment. She opened her mouth and raised her tongue. The long spike of the proboscis extended out and jabbed at his face. He turned his face away and it punctured the flesh of his cheek. He snapped his head back to face her and caught her jaw with his snout. Her teeth bit through the proboscis and blood poured form her mouth. While she was dazed he swept her legs from under her. They fell to the floor and he landed on top of her. He pinned her legs down with his feet and stood up. He took hold of her shoulders and pulled. She unravelled her arms from his and clawed at his face and eyes, but he continued to pull. She screamed as her shoulder joints popped out and the flesh of her arms stretched. With one more heave the flesh and tendons ripped and her arms separated from her body. He threw them aside where they coiled and squirmed around themselves like dying snakes. He knelt down on her and took his head in his hands. Her jaw was healed and she spat and screamed at him. As he looked at her he saw a mix of anger and fear in her eyes.

"Fucking choke on me, you cunt!" she screamed. This last word was drawn out with every last ounce of her defiance.

He opened his mouth and bit into her face. She writhed against his grip but he held her in a tight grip. She screamed and roared as her flesh solidified. Then his teeth cut through her head and swallowed whole chunks of her dry flesh. Then he tore away parts of her torso until there was only her lower half remaining. His hunger was satiated, suddenly a spurt of memories shot through his brain like shards of a TV screen. He saw her past as a human working at the market. He saw Ruhsarr destroying market stalls before taking her life and turning her. He saw Ruhsarr attack a blonde haired woman and leave her for dead. He saw Ruhsarr fight with a dragon. Then he saw her drinking the dragon's blood, watched as it fuelled her inhumanity, her cruelty and her rise to power. He saw her sister, Jorshean, the next member of the

Children of the Blood. A seven foot tall beast, with thick deep green and brown scaled skin. Her long brown hair was matted, and woven with flowers and feathers. She was in a heavy, humid forest and perched on a large wooden tree stump. Her flesh camouflaged her to the environment and surrounding her were the dead and drained bodies of humans. They lay among chainsaws and axes and the felled trunks of trees. Her location came not from Gilad but directly from Jorshean, because of the blood connection. She opened her dark green eyes, looked at him and smiled. He got a warm, kind feeling from her. Not at all like the fear he'd sensed from Gilad. This took him by surprise and he stood for a few moments in a dazed awe at what he had just seen. Suddenly the vision pulled away and he saw she was deep in the rain forests of Peru. Then he snapped out of it and realised he was still surrounded by fire in Gilad's room. He searched around the basement as he changed back into his human form. He found a fire extinguisher, put out the flames and returned to Andra and the others upstairs.

"How did it go?" said Andra as she passed him a package of clothes.
They talked as he dressed.

"As you can attain from my presence I beat her, but she was tough, really fucking tough. She could teleport by passing through shadows," said Alex.

"Wow. I've heard of vampires moving so fast they appeared to teleport but not genuine teleportation," she said.

"This was the real deal. She went in one shadow and came out of another," he said.

"What did you do?" she said.

"It was ideal for her down there with sparse lighting and lots of shadows. So, I set to whole fucking room on fire. Without the shadows she had to face me head on. She tried to disembowel me at one point," he said.

"Fucking hell. I'm glad she is finally dead. She was always an evil bitch. Did you get any information from her?" she said

"Yes, I know the location of her sister, Jorshean. It would have been nice to know how she did that teleportation thing, but I doubt she would have told me. Even if we hadn't been enemies," he said.

"Yeah, that could be useful. You're right though. She wouldn't have let anyone else know. She kept the power for herself. Anyhow, we need to focus on finding Jorshean," she said.

"She's in the rain forests of Peru feeding on lumberjacks," he said.

"That would explain why no one has seen her for a long time," she said.

"She's dug in deep. There might be no direct access by road. Looks like we will have a long journey ahead of us. It'll take weeks to get to Peru and then hike into the rainforest," he said.

"We'll figure out how we're going to play this next round when we get back to the safe house," she clicked her radio mic and spoke into it. "Everyone back to the van! White, Mc'Ready pack up. We're leaving."

They made their way out of the back of the building. The streets were eerily quiet as everyone except Alex climbed back into the van.

"You pick up Mc'Ready, I'll get White. We'll meet you back where you dropped us off," he said.

"Ok, see you in two," said Andra.

She slid the door shut and the van sped off. Alex ran back to the building where he had left White and jumped up to the roof.

"Hey dude. You get her?" said White.

"Yes I got her," said Alex.

"Was she as beautiful as the spies said?" asked White.

"Yes she was, but then I pissed her off and she went all monster and tried to kill me," said Alex.

"Yeah, I can imagine people tend to get a bit shitty when you try to eat them," White said with a smile.

This caused Alex to laugh.

"So, how many kills you get?" he said.

"Some of the doormen, a few of fleeing customers and a couple of crooked cops. Oh, I helped Davis by shooting two doormen too. Headshots all round. You can never be too generous with the headshots," said White.

"That's true. Lead in the head, make 'em dead. Nice work helping Davis too," said Alex.

"Thanks. Just a day in the life of a sniper extraordinaire and his enormous weapon," said White.

"Boasting about the size of your gun again?" said

Alex.

"The size helps but the size doesn't matter if you don't know how to use it. I usually use my charm and wit too," said White.

"You have charm and wit?" said Alex.

"Yeah, yeah fuck off. Anyway, I need my skills, you can just fall back on being a super soldier," said White.

"What are you talking about?" said Alex.

"You seriously haven't noticed the way Mc'Ready looks at you?" said White.

"Mc'Ready? We're just friends," said Alex

"Yeah, ok. It's a good job you got big muscles because that brain of yours gets jealous when it sees a peanut," said White.

"Piss off, dickhead. Really, Mc'Ready, I haven't notice," said Alex with a smile.

"Ok, don't let it go to your head, Romeo," said White.

"Whose jealous now?" said Alex.

"I'm not jealous. Don't get me wrong, Mc'Ready is nice and all but personally I couldn't date anyone in the business. Too much familiarity, too much danger. You know what I mean?" said White.

"I hear that. Anyway, we need to get going. You packed?" said Alex.

"Yes, I'm almost done. Just got to lock the case," said White as he clicked the locks. "Let's get the fuck out of Dodge."

They ran to the edge of the building, Alex grabbed White around the waist, held him under one arm and jumped over the side. White screamed all the way down to the ground.

"Fucks sake, Alex! Tell me you're gonna do some crazy shit like that. You scared the shite out of me," said White.

"Where's the fun in that?" said Alex while laughing.

They walked down to the end of the alley and the van pulled up infront of them.

Davis slid the door open and they both climbed in.

## Chapter 15.

It was half past one in the morning when they arrived back at the safe house. They were all tired and weary except Alex.

"Are you ok?" said Andra.

"Yeah, I feel great. Why do you ask?" he said.

"You seem a bit twitchy," she said.

"I do feel a bit hyper. I think it's got something to do with eating all that vampire flesh. It feels like I've drunk too much coffee," he said.

"Well, you certainly ate your fill," she said with a smile.

"Yep. Yes, I did," he said and smiled back at her. She turned to the rest of the group who were all changing out of their combat gear.

"We have until sunrise. You can use that time to sleep or we can let our hair down and celebrate."

"Celebrate," they all called.

"Ok, there are two cases of beer and some bottles of Jack in the kitchenette. You all worked really hard tonight. Now, let off some steam. You've all earned it," she said.

Palmer and Hughes came back from the kitchenette with beers, whiskey and bottles of cola and passed them around until everyone had a drink in their hand.

"Raise your glass if you're a badass vampire killin' motherfucker!" said Davis.

They all raised their glasses and cheered.

"Fuckin A! Let's get fucked up!" said White.

Andra raised a glass of whiskey. They all knocked

their cans and classes together, then drank, danced and sang.

Two hours later Andra had slipped away to make a few phone calls to ensure they had a safe passage out of New York. Davis and White danced together. Palmer acted as the referee between Hughes with Hussain sat on his shoulders and Alex with Mc'Ready sat on his shoulders as they danced and mock charged at each other in a drunken joust. Hughes went down to one knee.

"What the fuck? Are you proposing to him?" said Hussain.

"It's not a fair contest. I'm drunk but this shit doesn't affect him," said Hughes.

"That's no excuse. Giddy up, horsey!" she said.

"You should have thought about that when you were pouring drinks down my throat earlier," said Hughes.

"You weren't complaining then, I don't want to hear your excuses now. On your feet soldier," said Hussain.

Hughes tried to stand but fell back down to his knees. "I'm done," he said as he put his hands down in front of him.

Hussain jumped off just before he rolled onto his side. She stood over him as he rolled onto his back.

"I think that means we win," said Alex.

"Your horse has gone lame. You might need to put him down," said Mc'Ready.

"Come on, Haystack. Let's go and sit down," said Hussain as she reached her hand out to Hughes.

He took it and she helped pull him to his feet.

“Thanks, partner,” he said as he towered over her.
“Anytime,” she said and slapped his elbow.

They had all expended what energy they had left and so, they sat in a circle of furniture.

Sunrise came soon after. Andra came back into the room at quarter past four and found most of them asleep. Davis had her head lay on White’s chest as they sprawled on a sofa. Hussain was lying in a bed with Hughes lying on the floor next to her. Palmer was sat upright with his head down and his arms crossed over his chest. Alex and Mc’Ready lying on a bed side by side but facing away from each other.

“Ok, get up, soldiers! Get up! I want to see movement! I want to see equipment being packed,” Andra shouted.

With a collective groan they all began to shift about and get up. With the exception of Alex and Hussain, they were all still drunk.

“Come on, I gave you a choice. You did this to yourselves. You can sleep on the plane in a while but right now, we are moving out!” said Andra.

They were all quiet as they collected their belongings and made their way down to the van. Once inside though they talked and laughed about the night before.

Alex was the only one who wasn’t tired or drunk so he drove them to the same airfield that they had arrived at two days before. The soldier at the gate directed them to the runway where their plane was waiting for them. They climbed out of the van and straight onto the plane; some more gingerly than others. Once they were all aboard and had stowed their gear the plane taxied down the runway and took off.

*

At around the same time, the humans left in the club were just starting to wake up. In a state of confusion most of them just put it down to intoxication. Some of them questioned each other as to why they were all lying on the floor. Others got up and stumbled away to other places or just went home. Two of the remaining staff members set about looking for Gerry and the other managers. All they found was dust. One of them rang the police. Soon an investigation was underway. Unfortunately for them, one of the phone calls Andra had made earlier was to ensure that any investigation would go absolutely nowhere.

## Chapter 16.

After six hours in the air, the plane came in to land on the runway of a small airfield. There was a small single storey building with a short control tower on its roof to one side and a wide hanger at the far end. The walls of the building were beige like the surrounding desert landscape. Where the plane had stopped there was a long wall of tinted glass windows. As the door opened, they all disembarked the plane the difference in temperature hit them immediately.

"Erm Ma'am, where are we?" said Mc'Ready.

"We're definitely not in England. It must be forty degrees centigrade out here," said White.

"It is thirty-six degrees, we are in California, southeast of The Death Valley National Park. And this," Andra said as she nodded towards the building. "Is the Aeronautics Research Facility; officially anyway. It's owned by the Donaldson Family and has a mysterious old world benefactor, namely me."

"Why are we here?" said Hughes.

"We're here to meet a friend of mine," Andra said as looked at her wristwatch, a black and orange Timex Ironman Indiglo that she had owned for many years. "And we are right on time."

A door in the glass wall of the building opened and a tall, square man stepped through it. As he approached them they could see that He was in great physical health despite appearing to be in his late seventies. He was dressed in a shirt, tie, and khaki shorts. He wore a pair of aviator sunglasses and was nearly completely bald under his Stetson hat.

"Hello, friends. Welcome to Death Valley, or near enough. I hope you like it warm because it's hotter than the devil's ball sack out here," he said in an affluent English accent.

Andra walked up to him and hugged him tight.

"Henry. I've not seen you for so long," She said.

"Not so tight, dear. I'm not as sturdy as I once was," he said.

"Oh crap, I'm sorry," she said and released him. "I don't know my own strength sometimes."

"Don't worry yourself. It's lovely to see you," he said.

"How long has it been?" she said.

"Seven years. I was in my seventies when I last saw you. A mere slip of a lad," he said jovially.

Andra laughed, "Oh Henry, I have missed you."

"I've missed you too. We have lots to catch up on," he said.

He turned to Alex and shook him by the hand.

"Who's this young chap?" he said.

"This is Alex, Alex Austin," said Andra.

"Ah Alex, of course. I have heard a lot about you. Andra told me you were on your way to becoming a formidable ally of ours. I've heard the stories of your role in this war that is now in motion for the vast majority of my life. The prophesised destroyer of vampires. I always hoped I would have the opportunity to meet the one who adopted the role. It is a heavy burden to bear. One that I would not wish on anyone. Andra says you are worthy to carry it though. I trust her judgement as she and my family have been friends for generations. Henry Donaldson, at your service, sir. My father would have been extremely delighted to know you are finally among our ranks," he said.

"I'm happy to meet you too, Mr Donaldson," said Alex.

"Please call me Henry. So, how exactly do you do away with those vampire fiends?" said Henry.

"I transform into my other form, then when I bite them and they solidify due to an enzyme in my saliva. When that is done I eat them," said Alex.

"You eat them? Oh, jolly good, very interesting. I will be intrigued to see this transformation if you would be willing to show me," said Henry.

"Yes of course. Later on some time," said Alex.

"Marvellous," said Henry.

He turned his attention to everyone else.

"Please excuse me. Where are my manners?"

He shook everyone else by the hand.

"Please come into the building. It's air conditioned and we can plan the next phase of your mission. This way please," he said.

He guided them into the building. It was small with a few comfy looking chairs, a coffee machine and toilets. The air control tower took up most of the space. It didn't look anything like a research building. Henry led them to a door marked 'maintenance' and ushered them all inside. This room was just large enough to fit them all and besides a mop and bucket, it was empty. Henry stepped in after them and closed the door. A pinhole camera within the door itself read his cornea and the entire room began to descend. After what must have been fifty feet the room come lift came to a halt. Henry opened the door and led them out into the ultra-modern research laboratory. Large brushed metal support beams ran down the walls and were crisscrossed with smaller, support bars. There were glass dividers that separated the offices and laboratories. Every flat surface was white and clean. It all made for a professional and focused workspace.

"Welcome to my aeronautical research facility. All started by my grandfather, Leonard Donaldson one hundred and ten years ago and funded by our lovely Andra Hudson here. Over eight decades ago our primary research became the biological understanding and deconstruction of the vampiric race. We also have a pioneering wing in the studies of information technology and more recently artificial intelligence and cyber neurological technology," said Henry.

As they walked deeper into the structure they could see that was constructed from high grade materials. Henry continued to speak.

"We also have a weapons and ballistics development wing, a physical training and health wing, and of course living quarters for all onsite staff. If there is anything you need there is a high certainty we have it."

"We'll need computers with military grade firewalled internet access, one of the planes with long distance flight capability and equipment for traversing a rainforest environment," said Andra.

"Yes, yes. That won't be a problem," said Henry.

"We all need food too," said Palmer.

"Of course. I'm sure you're all quite hungry after your flight. I've already informed the kitchen staff that we will be having guests. They will provide you with all the food and refreshments you require," said Henry with a smile.

As he escorted them through the building they passed offices and laboratories where people were working busily. Soon they arrived at a conference room with a semi-circle of comfortable chairs around a large, glass table.

"Please take a seat and make yourselves comfortable," said Henry.

He walked over to the table and tapped the top of it. A rotating, red circle appeared in mid-air above it. There was a collective gasp from the group and Henry turned to face them with a pleased smile.

"Wow! Is that a hologram?" said Mc'Ready. "I have heard they're being trialled but didn't know there were any up and running."

"Yes, we call it the Holographic Interactive Projection Interface, or HIPI for short because, like you, most people say things along the lines of 'Wow' and 'Cool' when they first see it. I'm not being derogatory. I was the same when I first saw one running. We've run these through many prototypes and developmental stages for the past ten years," said Henry.

"Do you get them from an outside producer?" said

Mc'Ready.

"No my dear, we are the producers. These are all built in-house," he said.

Mc'Ready turned to Andra with a look of astonishment on her face.

"The company I work for make these and I didn't know about it?"

"Well, I supply the funds for this research centre and they develop the tech. It's all a bit complicated but yes in a way I suppose. They're in their late stages of development. Another year and these will replace monitors," said Andra.

"Can I ask how it works?" said Mc'Ready to Henry.

"Well the actual technology is patented and awaiting some other patents, but basically photons are energised and then fired directly at each other from above and below. When they collide they emit light. That light can be seen as the images. When you put your finger into that image it interrupts the stream of photons and the computer recognises that as an interaction and reacts accordingly, like this," he said. He poked his finger into the circle and lines branched off from it with the words 'Home', 'Menu', 'Settings', and 'Search' at the end of each line to form an options tree. Henry pointed to 'Menu' and the first selection of words disappeared and were replaced with more lines and words. 'Home', 'User Files', 'Internet', 'Communications', 'Pictures', 'Music', 'Movies', 'Computer', and 'Search'. He pointed to 'Communications'. This current selection of words again disappeared. More new words appeared in the air labelling the areas of the facility. He pointed at 'Kitchen'. A screen formed in the air. A man in chef's clothing appeared on the screen. The image was crystal clear.

"Hello, Mr Donaldson. How can I help you?" he said.

"Can we have nine meals for me and our guests please, Patrick," said Henry.

"Anything specific, sir," said Patrick.

"Let me see. What is today's special?" said Henry.

"Poached sea bass, sir," said Patrick.

"Oh yes, that sounds wonderful. We're in conference room A1," said Henry.

"Ok, sir. They will be brought to you in around twenty minutes," said Patrick.

"Thank you, Patrick," said Henry.

"You're welcome, sir," said Patrick.

The screen shrunk and vanished. Henry pointed at Home and the first set of words appeared again.

"What do you need to look at?" he said to Andra.

"Living world," she said.

He pointed at 'Search' and a search box appeared with a keyboard floating underneath it. She stepped up to the image and with a confident ease that she was familiar with this technology she typed in 'Living world'. A screen appeared with the words 'This site is a protected military site. Please show or enter identity access code.' She took her military identity badge from her pocket and placed it on the glass table. A white circle appeared around it, which then turned green. The words 'Welcome Lieutenant

Colonel Andra Hudson. Please enter the location you wish to view,' appeared. She typed in 'Peru, South America'. The screen showed a satellite view of Peru. Andra pointed to 'show on full screen' and the image took up the whole display.

"Is this a CGI representation of the earth using real time updated internet feeds?" said Alex.

"No, this is a live video feed from orbiting satellites," said Andra.

"This is real?" he said with a stunned look.

"Yes. This is Peru as it's happening, right now. I'm controlling the satellite camera. Now what is Jorshean's location?"

"Is this legal? I mean you could spy into people's gardens and stuff with this," he said.

"All the things we do and you're worried about whether this is legal?" she said.

"No, but, you know, you could see if people were sunbathing in their garden," he said.

"You can see the weave in clothing and identify people by their fingerprints with this. Fortunately, we have bigger troubles than accidentally seeing Mrs Jones at number forty-two while she is sunbathing topless. Yes, it could be used for spying but the only thing we use it for is monitoring weather systems. Now where is the Jorshean? I want to check what the weather is like there," she said with a wink.

"North-East, along the Amazon river in the rainforest. Towards the border of Brazil."

Andra put her put both her palms towards the image

and moved them apart and the map zoomed in. She then swept one hand across the image until she found roughly the area and then moved aside.

"Alex, your turn. See if you can find the exact location," she said.

He moved to stand where she had been and then moved his hand slowly across the image. It moved effortlessly with his hands. In his mind he could see her. It took him about fifteen minutes of searching and zooming in. Finally, he found the area. Still large but a lot smaller than Andra had left. It was an area of deep rainforest, with a tributary river of the Amazon running through it and a small clearing caused by deforestation.

"She's in there," said Alex.

"Can you be a bit more precise," said Andra.

He looked at the image and zoomed in closer. All they could see was leaves on the canopy of the trees.

"That is where I suspect she will be now, sleeping out of the sun," said Alex

He zoomed out, moved the image to the nearby area of deforestation and zoomed in. There on the ground, where he had seen them in the vision, lay the bodies of five men. Their throats had been ripped out and there were some strange footprints around them, but barely any spilt blood.

"Yep, that is definitely a vampire attack. Time to work out our plan of attack," said Andra.

Mc'Ready was already typing on her mobile. Pulling up information on the area, the local government, local populations, and indigenous animal species.

"Zoom back out to the place you had the screen a moment ago," said Andra.

Alex did as she asked. The screen showed the mass of trees again.

"That's no good for planning our attack. Erm, ok. Change the view to show land gradients. We won't know the exact terrain but we will know what the approach might be like," she said.

"If we come in at this angle and this angle," said Hughes pointing at the screen. "We could perform a pincer movement."

"We form a circle around the area while Alex moves in. If she gets past him we could deploy flashbang to disorientate her and give away her location," said Hussain.

"We're going to need to stick together. We'll move in pairs and then form up and provide Alex with suppressing fire," said White.

"Look, we can't go in all guns blazing on this one. We can't find plans or maps for the ground level, down there it's all unexplored jungle. Personally, I think it should just be me who goes in. She will know I'm coming anyway. If we are all there she will pick you all off one by one. She not only has a physical advantage, she will have the element of surprise. That is her home, she will the know landscape and all its secrets. She obviously not only living in there but thriving. If we all go in we run the risk of one or more of us getting hurt or catching some sort of disease. It will be better if I go alone. There is nothing in there except Jorshean that has a chance of hurting me. Us all going as a whole team will slow me down. No offence to you all, I just don't want to put you at risk of getting ill or injured," said Alex.

"I agree, but you're not going alone. I'm going with you, I've been in many jungles and rainforests in my time. You could use my knowledge," said Andra.

"What's our role in this mission, ma'am?" said Palmer.

"You are all going to get some much deserved R&R," said Andra.

"If that's what you think is best Ma'am," said Davis.

"It is, you will all benefit from a few days well-earned downtime. We've had an incredibly busy few days. Henry, can find my employees some temporary quarters for the next few days?" said Andra.

"Of course Andra. I have already had the V.I.P. quarters cleaned and made up in expectation of your requirement. They're in the eastern side of the facility. They have king size beds, their own on suite bathrooms, internet access, TVs, gaming consoles and access to the V.I.P. gym, spa and bar," he said.

"That sounds perfect," said Andra.

"Yep that'll do me," said White with a grin.

There was a knock on the door. Henry answered it and a man in a suit pushed in a trolley with plates of poached sea bass, vegetables, and assorted side dishes.

"Yeah, time to eat," said Hughes.

"And not a moment too soon. I'm famished," said Palmer.

"I'll leave the cart here, Mr Donaldson. When you have finished please let us know and I will return to collect it along with your crockery and utensils. Ladies and Gentlemen, I hope you all enjoy your meal," said the man.

He turned and walked out of the room.

"Ladies and gentlemen? He obviously doesn't know who we are," said Davis, with a grin.

"Hey! I'm a lady. I'm a lady who kicks vampire arse," said Hussain with a smile.

They all laughed as they sat down to eat their food. When they had finished, Henry called the man back. He collected the plates, knives and forks and then brought in pots of tea and coffee and boxes of biscuits. They thanked him and he left.

"I was thinking, we could fly over the jungle and parachute out a few miles away from her location," said Alex.

He dunked a digestive biscuit into his cup of tea and lightly tapped it on the edge of his cup. He raised it to his mouth but just before he could bite it the end fell off into his cup with a splash.

"Ah crap," he said.

"I don't know. We don't know the area. I say we should assess it from here. There seems to be a lot of deforestation nearby which could possibly be illegal. There could be loggers and poachers on the ground. I can't guarantee their safety if they were to see us," said Andra.

"You could just tranquilise them if you run into any," said Mc'Ready.

"It's a good idea but I still couldn't guarantee their safety. They might get eaten by indigenous predators in the area," she Andra.

"Then they probably shouldn't have been there in the first place. If they're logging and poaching illegally they must know that there will be inherent dangers. You can't save every single human, Andra," said Mc'Ready.

"I know that, Mc'Ready, but if the reason they can't escape is through my doing then I would be to blame," said Andra.

"But they're breaking laws, international laws that have been put in place by international governmental unions. If they were hurt would it not just be classed as collateral damage?" said Mc'Ready.

"Mc'Ready, my job is to eliminate the vampire threat to the human race. I cannot incur collateral damage. Not as a job specification nor from a moral standpoint. I will not knowingly let one human die through my actions, no matter how many international laws they are breaking. I know in other military forces some collateral is accepted but we are the S.O.V.E.U. We are a target specific elite enterprise. Not one human gets hurt! Is that understood?!" said Andra.

"Yes Ma'am," said Mc'Ready. "Loud and clear."

"We need a solution that has as few casualties as possible," said Andra.

"You could go in at night. I'm sure those loggers

and poachers aren't gonna be working in the dark. A lot of wild predators are semi-nocturnal anyway," said White.

"That's true. We could parachute in at night then hike along the river and find her location," said Alex.

"That sounds like the beginnings of a plan to me. What happens after that?" said Andra.

"We sneak into her territory at sunrise. We chase away the loggers who might be there and while she sleeps I'll go for her. It sounds easy but as with most things, if it seems too good to be true it usually is. There is something that has been playing on my mind. When I ate Gilad I got a vision of Jorshean and she smiled at me. It wasn't a sinister smile, if anything it was friendly. Like, she had been waiting for me. As if she was happy to see me," said Alex.

"It could be a trap," said Hughes.

"It feels like a trap. She could have all sorts of nasty shit waiting for me," said Alex.

"We should go in and observe her for a day or two then. See where she goes and what she does," said Andra.

"Ok. We fly over at a low altitude and jump out three miles from the site. Head to the river, deploy the boats and travel along it and get as close to her territory as we can. We leave to boats and hike deep into her territory as we can, then take cover in the canopy of the trees. We track her movements and behaviours and when we know what we're dealing with we make our move. How does that sound?" said Alex.

"Couldn't have planned it better myself," said Andra with a broad smile.

"Will you need special equipment for ascending the trees?" said Henry.

"Dude, this guy can jump about one hundred and fifty feet straight up. I've seen him do it," said White.

"Oh I do not doubt it if he is anything like Andra here," said Henry.

"Neither of us will need climbing equipment, but we will need a hide for when we're in the trees. Camouflage clothing would be a good idea too," said Alex.

"That won't be a problem. Tell you what, you can take two of our inflatable, camouflage boats. They look like dead wood, you lie down in it and it looks like a pile of old branches. You can see out but they can't see you," said Henry.

"That would be excellent. We could use some of those," said Alex.

"Ok. Just hold on a moment," said Henry. He stepped up to HIPI and clicked a few things and brought up an equipment inventory. "Just select the items you will require and they will be packaged and ready to go with you on the plane," said Henry

"Thank you," said Andra.

She began selecting the most essential Items.

"What time will you need to depart?" said Henry.

"We'll leave tomorrow afternoon at around 1400 hours. That way we should get there for about 0030 hours. That should give us more than enough time to get the boats ready and float downriver. But tonight would you be so kind as to let us enjoy your excellent hospitality?" said Andra.

Henry smiled. "Of course, you are all welcome here. If you would all follow me, I'll show you to your accommodation," said Henry.

He then led them through the facility. After five minutes walking they arrived in a large area. There were reclining chairs gathered around a pool, a spa area, massage tables, a sauna, a hot tub and everything else you would find in a top end spa.

"Welcome to the V.I.P. lounge. There is a gym, bar, kitchen and the mess hall is downstairs. All our equipment and staff are at your disposal. There is no one staying here right now so please pick one of the rooms that surround this area. They are all carpeted and the bed sheets are all genuine Egyptian linens. I hope you enjoy your stay with us," said Henry.

"Will you join us at some point for a chat? You know, a bit of catching up. It's been a long time since I last saw you and now the business is out of the way I would love to talk with you." said Andra with pleading eyes.

Henry took her hand in his and gave it a gentle squeeze.

"I have some matters to attend to first but when I'm finished I'll be happy to talk with you. You are, after all, my oldest friend. I finish at five so I'll come and join you then," he said with a warm smile.

"We'll see you then," said Andra and smiled back at him.

He turned and walked away.

"Well, I'm going for a swim," said Alex.

"And that hot tub has my name all over it," said White.

"Can I join you?" said Davis.

"My dear. I'd be honoured if you would join me," he said as he bowed and held out his hand.

"You're such a knob," she giggled.

He stuck out his elbow and they linked arms, then walked off to the changing rooms.

"I'm going to have a massage. I'm aching all over," said Hussain.

"Yeah, I feel achy too. A massage sounds wonderful," said Mc'Ready as she looked at the handsome masseuse.

"Dibs on him," said Hussain with a laugh as she ran ahead of Mc'Ready.

Hughes looked at Palmer with a smile on his face.

"Bar?" he said.

"Bar," Agreed Palmer.

Andra joined Alex for a swim. She slid effortlessly through the water as her scales reduced the amount of water resistance over her body.

Later, while the others went down to the bar, Andra and Alex spoke with Henry in one of the spare rooms.

"Now, my dear, what would you like to talk about?" said Henry.

"The general things. How are you? How's the kids and grandchildren?" said Andra.

"They are all very well. Sophia has been a little ill lately, but nothing too terrible. Her dementia is getting worse but I have the best doctors I can afford caring for her," said Henry.

"I'm sorry to hear that," said Andra.

"Thank you. It's an awful shame to see her mind deteriorate so fast but it's just one of those thing. We're dealing with it as it happens, horrible as it is. Jenny and Stephen are both well, still working in their fields of medical sciences. Anthony and Sandra have separated though. Such a shame. I like Sandra but they have their reasons, and it's an amicable separation. Two of the grandkids, Andrew and Amelia are attending university and Harrison is an electric car designer at one of the large manufacturers, the name escapes me right now. And me, I am well. I have medication for the gout now and I'm trying to lower my cholesterol, but for an eighty-five year old man I can't complain. How have you been?" he said.

"I'm ok. Some good things, some bad. We were recently attacked by Saltorg and his private army. We lost a lot of good soldiers. Fine people, just, wiped out," said Andra.

"The horrors of war, my dear. It never gets any easier to accept loss," said Henry with a sympathetic smile.

"That's true," said Andra with a frown.

"What happened to Saltorg?" said Henry.

"Alex eliminated him," said Andra.

"Good. I always hated that bastard," said Henry as his face grew stern He was the complete waste of a brilliant mind. The scientific advances he could have made would have been astounding, but he was hell bent on focusing in the complete wrong direction," said Henry.

"I said the same thing. He was a true genius. He could have changed the world. We eliminated Gilad last night, too," said Alex.

"Good. You seem to be making good progress. Is it with these newfound abilities that you are doing the eliminating? Because these are high stakes vampires you have taken out of the picture. These elder ones, The Children of the Blood. Are you sure these abilities are reliable? They know what your presence on the Earth means. They'll throw everything they have at you when you turn up at their homes. Dienco has an entire army at his disposal. He'll sacrifice every single one of them to the fight if it keeps you from getting to him and his children," said Henry.

"Yes, it's because of my new abilities I able to eliminate them. It's only been five days but due to Andra preparing and training me for this my whole life, I know how to use my body to optimal effect. She has taught me about Dienco and his family. I know a momentous battle lies ahead of us but I have no choice in the matter. There is only one direction I can go against the vampire horde and that is through. I've had a long time to come to terms with what I am and what it means to just about everyone on this planet. The transformation part is still something new but I'm getting used to it," said Alex.

"Ah yes, that's right. You transform don't you. What does the change feel like?" said Henry.

"The first time it was incredibly painful. Vincent knew that biting me would unlock my abilities but he didn't know what would happen. When it began I was trying to fight it even though it couldn't be stopped. I mean, I had been told I would become this vampire hunter but I didn't realise I would change so dramatically. It's still uncomfortable but not anywhere near as painful," said Alex.

"Vincent, you brother. Andra has told me all about him and your family. Please allow me to express my grief at the fate of your family. They were all extremely brave. Without their heroism you would not be here today," said Henry.

"Thank you, Henry. I am very proud of them," said Alex.

"You are welcome. May I request a demonstration of your transformation that they have made possible?" said Henry.

"Yes, sure. Can I ask a question first?" said Alex.

"You may?" said Henry.

"How did your family get into the business of vampire hunting?" said Alex.

"My great grandfather was Leonard Donaldson. His family made their fortune when they began breeding and selling thoroughbred horses in 1850. When he was thirty five, in 1871, he and his brother, Arthur, started an investment bank. Five years later Arthur was killed by a vampire. Leonard caught the wretch in the act and killed them. Arthur's half of the business was passed to Leonard so he sold the bank and invested three quarters of the money into the manufacture of weaponry and the invention of new armaments. He then spent his spare time hunting and killing as many vampires as he could find. Vowing to wipe the vampire scourge from the Earth. That is when he met our lovely Andra," said Henry.

"That's right, I was stalking a gang of vampires and observing them from the rooftop of a workhouse late one night. I was waiting for them to get close enough to ambush them. In a flash Leonard leapt out from a hiding place and killed two of them in a heartbeat. I was as shocked as the vampires. He swung his blade toward another but they dodged and knocked him to the floor. I dropped down and killed the last three. Leonard, thinking I was also a vampire, began to attack me. I dodged or blocked every attack he made; but barely. Realising I wasn't merely a vampire he turned and ran before I could talk to him. I began following him but it took two more attempts to get him to talk to me. And even then I had to chase him for a mile and a half and knock him down. The first thing he said was 'If you're going to eat me just get it over and done with you bastard'. I nearly laughed, but then I saw how defiant he was. He was an incredibly brave man. In the years following our first encounter we formed a company that would later become the S.O.V.E.U." said Andra.

"Yes, he was a great inventor too. He developed weapons primarily for the killing of vampires. Those weapons have gone on to be integrated into modern weaponry. In the early 80s my family invested heavily in computer technology on my advice. That just about brings us to date. With you we are stepping into a new era. With your unique abilities my great grandfather's vow will come to fruition. My father always spoke of the possibility of you. A prophesised stroke of fate. I must admit I once thought that someone like you was just a tale of hope they told to keep our spirits up. Would you be so kind as to allow me to see you in your other form?" said Henry.

"Yes," said Alex.

"You can change behind the room divider. It will give you some privacy," said Henry as he pointed across the room.

Alex stood up walked across the room, unfolded the large panels and stood behind it. He then undressed and folded his clothes. Only the top of his head showed above it. He focused his mind and felt his body begin the transformation. As he grew more of his body rose from behind the divider until he had to stoop his head. His chest and upper abdomen were visible as the dark scales formed from his flesh and then hardened to form his natural armour. Henry's eyes widened and his jaw dropped as he watched the process in awe.

"My boy, you are amazing. I have waited my entire life for you to make your appearance and you do not disappoint," he said.

"Thank you," said Alex in his low, rumbling growl.

"You should see him fighting," said Andra with a smile.

"I bet those bastards don't know what's hit them.

I'd love to see you take them down a peg or two. Can I take a photo of you for the records? I document everything you see. All this will be important one day. You mark my words," said Henry.

"Erm…Ok, But don't put it online. I wouldn't want it to leak and spoil the surprise for all the vampires," said Alex.

"Don't worry about that. Our records aren't online said Henry. Andra would you mind standing next to him to give the image some perspective?" said Henry.

Andra walked over, stood next to Alex and put her hand up on his shoulder. Henry then took a few photos and looked at them.

"Perfect," he said.

"Can I?" said Alex pointing at the divider.

"Oh yes, by all means," said Henry.

Alex stepped back behind the room divider and a few moments later was able to put his clothes back on. Henry then showed them both the photos.

"Wow. I didn't realise I was so big," said Alex.

"That's why the vampires are scared of you," said Andra.

"Tell me more about this enzyme in your saliva," said Henry.

"Fletcher says it's a pro-coagulant. It makes the flesh and blood of any vampire I bite solidify. Turns them into a kind of husk that I can then eat," said Alex.

"That is fascinating. So it works similar to snake venom in blood, making it clot at an accelerated rate?" said Henry.

"Yes, it's largely the same process and because the blood is instrumental in inhibiting cell degeneration in the vampire's bodies it solidifies their flesh too," said Alex.

"How wonderful, well, not for the vampires but for us it's the one up we've needed. You will save a lot of human lives, young man," said Henry with an enthusiastic smile.

They spoke together for another hour and decided to see how the others were getting on. They made their way down to the bar where they found Mc'Ready playing a drinking game with the others. She had her hands behind her back and was trying to drink one of three shots of whiskey that were lined up on the bar.

"What's the game?" said Andra.

"Lucy has to drink the shots but she isn't allowed to touch the glasses with her hand or drop any of them. If she does she is out. Palmer is already out, he's sat over there. He's only allowed to drink the cheap wine for the rest of the night," said Davis and pointed to the table in the corner. At that moment the shot glass slipped from Mc'Ready's mouth and bounced off the bar.

"Ah shit!" she said.

"Oooh," exclaimed the rest of the group.

"And you're out. Go sit with Palmer on the loser's table. No more expensive liquor for you," said Davis.

Mc'Ready smiled as she trudged to the table and sat down next to Palmer who poured her a glass of wine.

"It's not the good stuff but certainly ain't bad. Beggars can't be choosers, right?" he said.

"I ain't complaining," said Mc'Ready.

"Do you want to play?" said Davis to Andra, Alex and Henry.

"No thanks. I'm not drinking tonight," said Alex.

"Me neither," said Andra.

"I'm a little too old to play drinking games these days, my dear, but will have a glass of the single malt though, please," said Henry.

The bartender smiled and poured whiskey into a glass.

"A little more please," he said.

She poured until Henry raised his hand.

"Thank you, my dear," he said.

He picked up the half-full glass. At the end of the game Hughes was announced as the winner. Andra and Alex went to their rooms and left the group to their fun.

## Chapter 17.

The sun was high in the Californian sky as most of the group were waking up.

"Oh my head," were the first words to leave Mc'Ready's mouth as she opened her eyes.

Hughes sat up in his room, slowly rubbed the sleep from his eyes, and then lay back down again.

"Ugh, totally grim," he muttered to himself.

Alex and Andra had been in the gym since seven. They had completed a cardio workout, weight training, and were now sparing in the dojo.

"Right, young 'un. All disciplines, no holds barred," said Andra.

She had gotten used to being the fastest, and strongest person in the room. But Alex was proving that he was just as fast and strong; even in his human form.

Upstairs Davis, and Mc'Ready were both walking towards the breakfast bar at the same time. Both were in the dressing gowns that were provided in their rooms.

"Hey, a woman of my own excellent taste in fashion," said Davis as she rubbed her forehead.

Mc'Ready smirked.

"I think I look how you feel," she said.

"Yes, it was fun last night. It got a bit wild there. You told Alex how you feel about him," said Davis.

"Ah, crap. Me and my big mouth," said Mc'Ready.

"Hey, don't worry, I think he likes you too. There is no point keeping quiet in this line of work. You never know how long we might have. You know that, we've all lost people," said Davis.

They each drew out a tall stool from the side of the bar and sat down. A tall slim waiter walked out from the kitchen area and stood behind the bar.

"Good morning ladies, what can I get you?" he said.

"Something nice and fatty and lots of water," said Davis.

"Bacon and pancakes with syrup and a hot pot of coffee each," he suggested.

"Oh yeah, that sounds amazing," said Mc'Ready.

"Coming right up," he said with a smile and went back to the kitchen to prepare their order.

Hussain came over and sat down.

"Today is gonna be a lazy day. No rushing around for me la, la, la," she sang out of key as she took her seat.

"Please stop Zarv," said Mc'Ready.

"Hey, it's not my fault you two are hungover," said Hussain.

"Seriously, I won't be responsible for my actions if you keep singing," said Mc'Ready.

"Ooooh grouchy," said Hussain and leaned in inches from Mc'Ready's ear and sang. "La, la, la."

A punch headed straight for Alex's face but he ducked aside and caught Andra's hand. He pulled her towards him and swept her legs from under her. He took hold of her throat as she was in the air and was about to slam her to the floor. She grabbed his wrist used her momentum and swung her legs up his back. She then wrapped her legs on each side of his head and hooked her ankles under his chin. With all her strength she swung her legs back, pulling his head with so much force that he was taken off his feet and they both landed on the ground. His head slammed into the mats but he rolled over until he was in a kneeling position. He then stood up still holding on to her. As he stood up he lifted her up with him. She put her hand on the back of his head, placed her feet on his chest and pushed away as she released his head. She catapulted herself away from him, flipped through the air and landed on her feet. He ran at her and kicked towards her head but she knocked him aside. He landed on his other foot and swung another kick at her. She caught his leg but he then jumped and kicked towards her jaw. She released his foot and whipped her head back. His foot missed her jaw by an inch and he turned himself in the air then landed on his feet. He spun around to face her and raised his guard.

"Wow! Time out, time out," she said.

Alex stood down and smiled at her.

"Good workout, eh?" he said.

"Oh yes. It's great being able to spar with someone who can keep up with me. Come on let's get some breakfast," she said.

They finished up, showered and headed back upstairs. They walked into the bar area to find Davis and Mc'Ready eating their breakfast. Hussain was sat next to them eating a plate of chopped mango and melon. Mc'Ready gasped and was suddenly very interested in her food.

“Andra, Zarv is torturing us,” said Davis sticking out her bottom lip.

“What on earth are you doing to them?” said Andra.

“I’m just singing, ma’am,” she said with a sly smile. “It’s too lovely a morning not too.”

“Singing while we have hangovers,” said Davis.

“Oh my, gosh! If that’s all it takes to torture you let’s hope you never get taken hostage,” said Andra.

“It’s ok for you. You don’t get hangovers,” said Mc’Ready.

“And no one made you drink so much,” said Andra.

“Touché, Ma’am. Touché,” said Mc’Ready.

They both laughed.

Mc’Ready became a little nervous as Alex took a seat beside her.

“Are you not having breakfast?” he said to Andra.

“I’ll come and get something later,” she said.

She turned and walked back to her room.

“Can I get you anything, sir?” said the bartender.

“Water, please,” said Alex.

“Of course, sir,” said the bartender.

He took a glass from a rack filled it with water and placed it on a napkin upon the bar.

“Thank you,” said Alex.

“You’re welcome, sir.”

The bartender turned and walked towards the kitchen and busied himself with other chores.

Davis looked Hussain in the eyes like she was trying to make a psychic connection with her.

“Come on, Zarv. Show me that funny video you

were telling me about last night"

"What video?" said Hussain.

Davis opened her eyes wide and gave her a hard stare.

"Oh...oh yeah, that video," said Hussain.

They both jumped down from their stools and quickly walked away, leaving Alex and Mc'Ready alone together. There was a long silence in which time Alex sipped his water. He then took it upon himself to break this silence and release its tension.

"So, you drank a lot last night?" he said.

"I'm so sorry about what I said. I must have been so embarrassing," she said with a wince.

"It's ok. You don't need to apologise. It wasn't embarrassing. We were just talking. All you said is that you have feelings for me," he said as reassuringly as he could.

"Oh, that's all? I'm so embarrassed," she said.

"Why, what's wrong? Is it me, because I'm not fully human? I understand if it makes you uncomfortable," he said.

"No...No! Alex, it's not that. It's just all of this. I promised myself that I wouldn't get involved with anyone at work and here I am, telling you I have feelings for you," she said.

"It's ok. I like you too, Lucy. I have since I first met you. I've just, never had the guts to tell you," he said.

She smiled.

"Alex, the destroyer of vampires hasn't got the guts to speak to me? Come on, pull the other one," she said.

“Seriously, no kidding. I think you’re amazing. You’re so smart and funny. It doesn’t complicate things that we met at work. I know we’re so busy at the moment with all of this but when this is all over I’d love to spend some time with you,” he said.

“That would be great. I’d love to spend time with you too. Just as people and not as soldiers,” she said.

“Or as the destroyer of vampires. Talking about that, I’m sorry but I need to go and do my thing. Andra and I will be flying out soon. I need to speak to her before we set off. We can talk more when I get back… if that’s ok with you,” he said.

“Yes. I’d like that, and thank you,” she said.

“What for?” he said.

“For not making things weird,” she said with a smile.

“Don’t worry about it,” he said and smiled back. He leaned in and kissed her on the cheek then turned and walked towards Andra’s room. They smiled at each other and he was halfway across the room before they broke eye contact, but she still watched him until he went through the door.

## Chapter 18.

Alex knocked on Andra's door before entering the room. She was sorting through some personal possessions she was taking with her. In her fingers she held a small ancient looking knife blade. She turned it in a firm but gentle grip.

"What's that?" he said.

"It's the knife my father gave to me. It was a present for my eighth birthday when he decided I was old enough to how to slaughter the animals. He was a blacksmith of sorts. Back then people had to be a jack of all trades. The quality of his knives and tools was particularly good. Besides raising animals for food produce and clothing, tools were what he sold and traded. He made this one especially for me. It once had a bone handle but that has disintegrated over the years; over the millennia," she said with a wistful look in her eye. "I keep it to remind myself that I once had a father. It's literally all I have left of him. Everything else is gone, like the handle, even his bones will be dust now."

Tears rose in her eyes before one fell to her cheek and rolled down her scaled face. She quickly wiped it away. "I'm sorry," she said and forced a smile.

"It's ok. You're allowed to cry," said Alex and put his arm around her shoulder.

"I've heard people say they can't remember their parent's faces after they have died. I remember everything about my father when I tried to talk to him after I had been changed. I remember his face turned from anger to fear, and horror as he realised who I was. I remember his voice and the names he called me: vile, disgusting, abomination. I remember the pain of both his words and the bailing fork he stabbed deep into my chest. The way he stumbled back and scrambled away when I pulled it free and the wounds closed before his eyes. I remember my mother's cries as he forced me to leave by slashing at me with a sickle. I needed my family at that time but instead I never saw them again. I blame Ruhsarr for that and I will never forgive him for all he took from me."

Tears flowed down her face now and she didn't try to hide it. She knew Alex understood what she felt.

"You must have some good memories of him?" said Alex.

"Yes, I remember him playing with us in the fields, dancing with my mother whenever they had chance, teaching me to milk the cows and run the pigs into the pen, singing us to sleep and kissing us good night with his big itchy beard. I have fond memories of him," she smiled.

"Try to remember those and let the bad ones go. I know that is easier said than done," he said

"I do try. Hopefully, those memories will fade when Ruhsarr is dead," she said.

"I hope they do. You deserve some freedom," he said.

"What do you remember about your dad?" she said.

"I remember him being big and strong. I was so young when he died. I know my memories of him are different to those of other people. You know, the way you know someone as a child compared to how you know them as an adult," he said.

"He was a good man. I didn't know him until after your mother died so I can't tell you if that changed him as a person; but I know it must have done. I mean, how could it not? He'd talk about her anytime he was given the chance. He'd tell you stories of how they met, the day they got married, and when they bought their first house. He said when she found out she was pregnant with you she was over the moon. It tore him apart that she never got to hold you. I saw him break down and cry sometimes but never infront of you two. He talked about her with such fondness that you could tell he loved her completely.  When I saved him he took on his new role of a protector and not a just father. I mean a father should protect his kid but he was more than just that. His commitment was like no one else I have ever met. Except you and Vincent, you take after him in that sense. He absorbed everything I could teach him. He was willing to and ultimately did give his life to protect you. It's because of him that you were alive when Vincent got to you. He wasn't always serious though. He loved to tell jokes and play with you just to hear you laugh. He was a lovely man. The day you were born was the day the love of his life died. That must have been tough, it would have broken lesser people but your dad was made of stern stuff. I see him in you, you look a lot like him. You stand like him and move like him too. You should be very proud to have had him as a father," she said.

He smiled as a tear fell to his cheek and rolled down his face before he caught it.

"I am," he said.

She grabbed him and hugged him.

"Come on, let's go," she said as she slapped his shoulders and then dried her eyes. "We have things to sort out."

"Yep, we need to make sure we have all we need. Wouldn't want to get there and find we're missing something," he said.

At that moment Henry walked into the room.

"It's nearly twelve o'clock. Are you both ready to go?" he said.

"I just need to me get my bag," said Alex.

He walked to his room and shouldered his backpack. When he returned Andra was closing the door to her room and was talking to Henry.

"Of course, you have time to speak to your soldiers and then we have to make our way to the hanger. In my experience pilots do not like to be delayed," said Henry.

"Yes, I understand their sentiments," said Andra.

They walked back into the lounge area and the others were sat around looking at Hughes who was telling a story about a barracks he was on with Palmer.

"We can hear talking coming from this dorm that is supposed to be empty. As we walked in I said, 'Is this the one that is supposed to be haunted? And he says, 'Fuck off,' we had been in there for a few minutes and it was obvious that there was nobody in there. So, I sneak off into this room and it was so dark I couldn't even see my hand in front of my face. I can hear him saying, 'Hughes, Hughes? Where the fuck are you man?' Thinking on my feet, I stand against the far wall and hold my torch under my chin. I see him stop at the door and peer in. That's when I flick on the torch and scream like, 'AAAAGGGHHH!' And he damn near shit himself."

The group laughed hysterically.

"You got me that time, man. I'll give you that one," said Palmer with a laugh.

Alex walked over and they all stood up and gathered around him.

"Hey. We're going down to the hangar now to prepare for the mission. So we'll see you all in a few days," said Alex.

They all stood up and saluted him.

"Good luck sir," said Palmer.

"Yeah! Kick her fuckin' ass," said Davis.

"Look after yourself," said Mc'Ready and hugged him.

White came over and shook Alex's hand and hugged him in the same movement.

"Do us proud, buddy," he said.

He then hugged Andra too.

"Look after yourself too, Ma'am," he said.

"I will," she said and smiled.

Hussain hugged them both.

"Put a bullet in her from me," she said.

Hughes saluted and shook their hands.

"I hope the mission goes without a hitch and you return safe and well. Beware of leopards. A friend of mine was in Peru a few years ago. He said their perfectly adapted to their environment. Really quiet but really fast, and strong too," he said.

"Thanks for the advice. We'll keep that in mind," said Andra.

Henry then escorted the two of them through the facility. The scientists, technicians and office staff took notice and watched them pass by. They walked down a long corridor that was twenty feet in both height and width. At the end was a lift that was just as big. Its huge doors slid open as they approached. Once they stepped inside the doors slid shut. As the lift began to ascend Alex looked around the huge cavernous space. He had never seen a lift this size. It was easily thirty feet in length.

"Am I allowed to ask why this lift is so big?" he said.

"It's for transporting the components parts from here to the surface where they can then be assembled," said Henry.

The lift came to a halt and there was an audible click as the huge breaks locked into place and took the weight of the lift. The doors slowly slid open and they stepped out into an aircraft-hanger. Technicians and mechanics were working on several planes. Each had HIPI that showed the internal structures of the planes with a real-time readout of the pending maintenance. Angle grinders and welding apparatus sent sparks and arcs of light from different areas of the planes. Pneumatic ratchets sounded off all around the place.

Henry escorted them to the far end of the hanger

that housed a small cargo plane that was painted deep green.

"This is your plane, Phantom Lightning. She has long distance flight capacity as you requested. You could get all the way around the earth on one charge. Obviously, she has had some modifications. Three inch sheet steel on the underside and with the electric engines she runs as silently as a plane her size can. All your equipment is over here in the crate waiting to be checked by you and then I'll have it all loaded on board," said Henry.

"It's electric?" said Alex.

"Yes. We've installed our new cobalt free power cells and latest electric engines into a previously fuel driven plane," said Henry.

"How does it all work?" said Alex.

"They're based on the same electromagnetism concepts as most electric engines but they're almost forty times more efficient," said Henry.

"That's incredible," said Alex.

"Yes, our staff are at the top of their game," said Henry.

Andra opened the five foot by five foot crate. Inside there were bundles of mountaineering ropes, pulleys, snap hook, D-rings, a high hide, water canteens, mess tins, a machete and sharpening stone, a travel stove and solid paraffin fuel, binoculars, a night vision scope, a set of two-way radios, two sleeping bags, two pairs of camouflage clothing, two inflatable canoes, awes and two one and a half feet long circular packages of material fibreglass folding poles. Andra took one of them from the crate and looked at it with a puzzled look on her face.

"Ah, that's the camouflage canoe cover I was telling you about. If you take it out of the material bag it'll open automatically like a pop up tent. It has hooks for attaching it to the canoe," said Henry.

Andra unzipped the pack and it opened just like he said it would. He placed it on the floor and smiled.

"That's incredible. It looks real, I mean, really real," she said.

Alex looked at it with a look of admiration; like a child with a new toy.

"It's taken us a long time to get it to look this realistic and be a functional piece of equipment. If you twist it and fold it flattens just like a tent," said Henry.

Alex tried it a few times and it worked every time.

"That's so cool," He said with a smile.

He then slipped it back into its bag and placed it in the crate. He took out the night vision scopes and passed them to Henry.

"We won't need those," he said.

"Neither of you?" said Henry.

"Nope. We can see in the dark," said Alex.

He closed the top of the crate and bent down to grab it.

"Please be careful," said Henry.

Alex lifted the crate up without even straining and then moved it onto his shoulder,

"Sorry, were you saying something?" he said.

"I was going to tell you the crate is heavy but it looks like you have it under control," said Henry.

Alex smiled at him, then carried it onto the plane and set it down. The technicians looked at him with a look of awe and disbelief. Then three of them struggled to push the crate into place, strap it down and attach a parachute to it. He then walked back off the plane to Andra and Henry. A man approached them, he had a short beard and greying hair under a Sacramento River Cats baseball cap. He wore a button up shirt and blue jeans.

"Andra, Alex this is T.J. I have chosen him to be your pilot," said Henry.

"Hello T.J." said Andra and Alex.

"Hello, ma'am. Hello sir," he said and shook their hands.

He looked at Andra with a curious expression and they quickly looked away when he saw that she had noticed.

"I do apologise, ma'am," he said.

"It's ok. I don't mind you looking. I was attacked may years ago by the Lord of the vampires. It changed me to how I look now," she said.

"You were attacked by Ruhsarr? Wow. You are lucky to be alive, even more so not to be a vampire, ma'am. I was only looking because you have an extraordinary beauty, ma'am. If it is ok me saying so," said T.J.

"Yes, it's ok. Thank you T.J." she said and smiled at him.

"Can I ask you about your experience as a pilot? I assume you are highly qualified if Henry has chosen you personally?" said Andra.

"Of course, ma'am. I started out flying the duster

on my dad's farm at the age of thirteen, I flew in the US Air Force for fifteen years, I flew as a commercial airline pilot for twelve years, and I've been test flying the electric engine planes here for the last four years. If it has wings, ma'am, I can fly it," he said.

"Impressive," said Andra.

"If you would like to go over the plan with me I'll tell you what I think," he said.

"Yes, of course. With your experience I'm sure it won't be anything you can't handle," she said.

"Thank you kindly, Ma'am," said T.J.

They sat in the cargo bay of the plane and went over everything twice.

"The flight will take ten hours. The manoeuvre leading up until when you both exit the plane will take twenty minutes from starting our descent to the drop zone. I'll give you the signal when we start our descent and another when we're in the drop zone. Is that ok with you?" said T.J.

"That is perfect," said Andra.

It was 13.00. by the time their plans were all in place. T.J. went around the plane to make the final checks and then climbed into the cockpit. Andra and Alex checked their equipment and weapons. As they were travelling light Alex had his katana, a Desert Eagle and an M60. Andra had her monk's spade, an AK47 and an AA12 automatic shotgun.

"Ready when you are," said T.J. through the cockpit door into the cargo bay.

Andra stuck her head through the doorway.

"Ready," she said.

They stowed the guns in their weapon cases, sat down in chairs situated just behind the cockpit and fastened their seatbelts. The Hanger doors were opened and T.J. started the engines and released the wheel brakes. The plane rolled out of the doors and out onto the airfield.

"This is T.J. requesting clearance to take off."

"This is air control. T.J. You're clear to take off when you're ready," said a voice over the radio.

"Thank you air control," said T.J.

The plane taxied onto the runway as T.J. manoeuvred it into the correct position. He slowly slid the throttle up to full power causing the engines to whirr to full speed. The plane quietly accelerated and sped down the tarmac before climbing skyward.

## Chapter 19.

They had been in the air for three hours and the plane was being buffeted around by turbulence and high altitude winds. They were flying at forty-five thousand feet to avoid commercial air traffic.

Alex was sat in his chair with his arms folded, his head down, his eyes closed in an attempt to sleep.

"Eye spy with my little eye something beginning with C," said Andra.

Alex opened one eye, looked at her, and then sat up.

"Erm, Cargo plane?" he said.

"No," said Andra.

"Crate?" he said.

"No," she said.

"Camouflage?"

"Nope."

"Then I don't know, and I'm trying to sleep."

"Come on, just play."

"Andra, you're one of the oldest living being on this planet travelling to hunt another of the oldest living beings on the planet, who is highly adapted to her environment. An environment that only one of us has experienced. Don't you think we should focus a bit?" he said.

"I was alive before this game was invented, so just humour me and play," she said.

"Ok, cargo net?"

"Bastard," she said.

Alex looked up at her and smiled.

"Right, this one'll stump you. I spy with my little eye something beginning with B," he said.

They played for another ten minutes then Alex fished around in his pocket and pulled out a deck of cards.

"Yes. Good lad!" she said.

She pulled over a crate to act as a table.

"What are we playing? Poker, Blackjack, Snap," he said with a smirk.

"I was always good at poker but it's been a while, so might be a little rusty," she said

"Don't worry, I'll walk you through the first round, refresh your memory," he said.

"Are you good?" she said.

"I thought I was. I played against Mc'Ready a few weeks ago. She said she was so-so at poker. Kicked my arse," he said as he shuffled the cards, dealt and then set the remainder on the box.

"She's a lovely girl, our Lucy," she said and looked him in the eyes.

"I know. She's a lot of fun," he said with a little smile.

"She likes you, you know. You can tell by the way she looks at you."

"I know. She told me last night. We're going to spend some time together when this is all over."

"That's great. I'm glad you're trying to have something of a normal life," she said.

He sorted his cards out and shifted awkwardly in his chair.

"Bad hand?" smiled Andra.

"No, it's just, well, what's the point in spending time with her? I'm not human anymore. I know I look like I am, but I'm not. She is though," he said.

"Your point is?" she said and gave him a quizzical look.

"I don't want to be blunt, but there will come a day when she dies. If and only if anything happens between us, eventually, I'll have to watch yet another person I love die," he said.

"What about the great times you could have together? Are you saying it's not worth loving people because their mortality is fragile?" said Andra.

"No, I mean. It's a natural process that life is followed by death, but not for the likes of us. She'd be gone and I'd be left on my own, heartbroken yet again."

"Oh, Alex. Their lives are fleeting but that is the beauty of them. People don't live forever so you have to love them while you can. Each one of them is different and precious. I had to learn that lesson the hard way a long time ago too," she said.

"So you have loved people since you were changed?" he said.

"Yes, of course. I've had a few lovers in the past five thousand years. This immortal life is long and agonising if you try to live it alone. I tried, thought I could make it by myself but it's not possible. You just have to appreciate them while you can," she smiled.

Her mind raced with great warriors fallen in battle and people who had lived incredible lives. Lives that she had been part of. All people she had loved.

"Thank you, Andra. I'll talk to her when we get back," he said and smiled.

She smiled back at him.
"Three nines and a ten," she said and placed her cards on the box.
"Ooh man, what could beat that? A Kings flush possibly," he said and threw his cards down.
"You twat," she said with a smile as she picked the cards up, shuffled and dealt them "We should play for something?"
"What like?" he said.
"My respect," she smiled.
The next five hours were passed by with more card games, reading, and some sparing.

At 22.50 T.J. turned and spoke.
"Ok, twenty minutes. We're beginning our descent. Please make all final checks to your equipment now. It'll be a steep descent so things might get a little choppy,"
"Roger that. Thank you, T.J." said Andra.
The plane began to descend faster than Alex expected and he nearly slid off his chair. They ran through the final checks, making sure everything was locked, zipped, and sealed properly while trying to stop things from floating around. As they put on their parachutes the plane went through some heavy turbulence. Everything that wasn't strapped down was thrown around.
"Sorry, can't help this. We're going through pockets of rising air," said T.J.
"It's ok, you'll have a game of fifty-two card pick up to play later on," said Andra.
"Good job it's my favourite game," he said with a

laugh.
The plane was coming down fast when he started to pull up.

"Five thousand feet," he said.

"Ok, Alex. Clear your mind and focus only on this moment. Nothing else matters but getting this right," she said.

"Yes Ma'am," he said.

"Four thousand feet," said T.J.

Andra and Alex checked each other's parachutes.

"Three thousand feet," said TJ.

"As soon as we're clear of the plane pull your chute. It'll just slow your initial fall. We'll still be coming in fast when we hit the ground but it will be better than with no chute at all," said Andra.

"Two thousand," said T.J. "One thousand." He began counting down the hundreds. "Nine hundred... eight…seven…six."

The plane levelled out, the rear cargo door lowered and locked into place. They could see the canopy of the forest zipping by below them.

"Five hundred feet. You're clear to go. I repeat you are clear to go," said T.J.

"Try to aim for a clearing," said Andra.

They unstrapped the crate and pushed it out of the back of the plane. Its chute unravelled and opened as it fell. They quickly jumped out after it and opened their chutes like Andra had said. Their fall was slowed slightly but in an ungainly manner. The plane pulled up and soared away as they quickly approached the trees. Seconds later they were coming down into the higher branches. Andra's chute got caught but she quickly detached it from her harness and caught onto a branch. Pulling herself up to stand on it. She looked around and saw Alex was dangling from a branch by his chute with a one hundred and eighty foot drop below him. He swung his legs back and forth and used his momentum as he tried to reach a nearby branch.

"Detach your chute as you swing forward. Your momentum will carry you," she said.

He threw out his arm and reached for a branch as he detached his chute. He caught the branch and pulled himself up. He looked at her and winked.

"Ok, let's go," he said.

They jumped from one branch to the next until they reached the crate. Alex took the weight of it while Andra detached its chute.

"Right, how do we get this down there without breaking it?" He said.

"We could use the ropes and pulleys," she said.

"We could if we want to take all night. I was thinking we could tie it to my back, and then I'll climb down," he said.

"Yes, that is a good idea. We don't want to draw attention to ourselves," she said.

"We just dropped out of a plane and crashed into the trees," he said.

"Would you have preferred hiking for a week," she said with a grin.

"No," he said.

"Then zip it," she said with a smile.

"I'll give you zip it," he said.

"What does that mean?" she said.

"I have no idea," he said with a smile.
She smiled at him in return.

"Come on. Let's concentrate on this," she said.
He opened the crate, took out a bundle of rope, unravelled it, and tied it around the top of the crate. He then sat down on the branch with his back to it and Andra tied the rope to his parachute harness until it was securely attached to him. She helped him to his feet.

"After you," she said.

He began to climb down through the branches choosing his path keeping in mind that he had the crate strapped to his back. She gave him a head start and then followed him. The climb down was made more difficult as they disturbed roosting birds who angrily flapped their wings before taking off, and lizards who scampered aimlessly out of their path. They had to rethink many of their handholds as some of the branches were moist and slippery with moss and lichens in places. They reached the last of the branches and had to climb down the trunk. Alex's hands slipped a couple of times on the bark and he tore away a few handfuls in an attempt to keep his grip. After five minutes they reached the undergrowth. Everything was damp with condensation. It was another fifteen feet to the ground but the root base of the tree splayed out making the descent somewhat easier. They were in almost complete darkness as none of the moonlight penetrated the dense under-foliage but their eyes adjusted and they could both see perfectly well in the low light. Animals and insects of all kinds called to each other. Mating calls, warnings and threats rang out into the dense night forest air. As they stepped onto the ground Alex shook his hands, and then wiped them on his trousers. All the animal noise stopped as a deathly silence fell over the entire area.

"What happened?" he whispered.

"We're the higher predators here. The wildlife can sense that," she said.

"Wow. Does that always happen?"

"Yes. It can sometimes be useful in places like this. If there are any large predators we can hear them before they get too close. Now, we have much to do," she said.

He bent down and rested the crate on the ground and unclipped his parachute harness. He untied the rope from around it and coiled it back up into a bundle. Andra pulled open the crate and sorted the canoes, their camouflage, and all the smaller items into two holdalls. The High hide was in its own bag with shoulder straps. Alex picked it up and put it on his back. Andra passed him a bag with his share of the crate's content, and he picked up his weapons case.

"Ready?" he said.

"Yes," she said.

She picked up her holdall and case and they made their way through the forest. It was only half a mile to the river but it was tough going through the thick foliage and trees they had to push and weave their way through, but they made steady progress.

Eventually, they came to the river bank. Here the

pale moonlight easily found its way to the water here as the river was nearly a quarter of a mile wide. They took the canoes from their holdalls and inflated them until they were solid using a duel action hand pump. They placed them at the water's edge, loaded their equipment into them and attached the camouflage covers. Alex picked off any insects from his body that had hitched a ride. He heard swearing and looked over to Andra as she flicked a leach aside.

"I fucking hate all things that suck blood," she snarled.

She put her oar together, pushed her boat away from the bank, out into deeper water while effortlessly stepping in and sitting down. He did the same but his boat rocked from side to side making him look sloppy compared to her graceful entrance. They only really had to use the oars to keep a straight line as the current did most of the work carrying them downriver. Fish, disturbed by the passing boats, splashed their tails through the water's surface in protest. They ranged from small to enormous in a vast array of species.

"We should have brought fishing rods," said Alex.

"Why, we could just reach in and grab them," said Andra.

In the distance they saw lights and heard the voices of men talking and laughing. They lay back in their canoes and pulled the covers over the tops. As they floated by they counted eight men who were carrying guns and weapons. It was clear they were poachers. A few of them saw the two piles of driftwood that floated by but being none the wiser they merely continued their conversations. The two boats passed at a painfully slow pace. When they were finally clear of these humans they pushed back the covers and looked back behind them. They saw the poachers get into a pickup truck and drive along a dirt path. Their human eyes were not able to see the two figures sat in the boats as they were shrouded in near complete darkness. Alex and Andra looked at each other.

"That was close," she whispered.

"Yeah, we better keep our eyes peeled from now on. At least we can tell Henry his equipment works," he said.

The current continued to carry them ever further downriver for another hour. Alex fished around in his bag and pulled out the GPS tracker. The screen showed a map with their location and at the top the longitude and latitude coordinates.

"Another half mile," he said.

The river wound and turned its way down towards the Amazon as caimans hauled themselves out of the water. Turtles and fish swam away in a hurry as they passed by. Alex kept one eye on the GPS tracker as the numbers got closer to the coordinates that they needed.

"Somewhere round here is perfect," he said.

"Head towards that tree with its roots in the water," she said.

Alex looked at the bank and saw the tree that she pointed out. It was huge, at least two hundred feet, and stood high above the canopy of the other trees.

Its incredibly wide trunk stood partially over the water with its roots twisted and coiled into the river. They were exposed where the earth had been washed away between them.

"That will be a good reference point on our way back," he said.

"I know," she said with a smug smile.

They rowed their canoes to the water's edge and pulled them up onto the shore.

"Push the boats into the roots of the tree and put the covers over. They'll look like driftwood that has been snagged on the roots."

"Nice, hidden in plain sight," he said.

"Exactly," she grinned.

They took their weapons and equipment from the canoes and then pushed them to the tree. Once they were in place they tied a rope to the front of one canoe passed it around a few of the roots, tied it to the front of the other canoe and let them float on the water. They looked just like clusters of old branches. The effect was flawless.

Alex strapped his katana to his back, loaded a magazine into his Desert Eagle and slid it into his hip holster. He looked over at Andra as she slid a drum magazine into her into her AA12 and strapped it into place.

"Ready?" she said.

Alex pulled a map from his pocket and looked at both it and the GPS tracker. He picked up the high hide, put it on his back and picked up his bags.

"Yep, let's go. We need to hike about three miles to the northeast," he said.

They set off walking into the forest. At first the undergrowth was light but soon became dense and humid. Andra's monk's spade made easy work of hacking a path through foliage and the vines. Animals ran and scrabbled away from them as they went. For about an hour it was tough going. For every three steps they took forward they took two back. Eventually, they came to a clearing with a small pool of water at its centre. They both stopped and stood perfectly still. Crouched to the left of the pool was a leopard. It tore at the belly of a deer that it had brought down a few minutes earlier. It lifted its head a little, flicked out its tongue and licked the blood from its nose. It let out a low, rumbling growl. Andra took a step forward and bared her teeth. The Leopard hissed and bared its teeth. Andra's jaws jutted out, her face grew into a snout and a deep threatening growl rose from her throat. The leopard stood up straight, took the carcass in its jaws, heaved it up as high as it could and dragged it off into the forest. They walked across the clearing and past the pool. Alex looked at her with an impressed expression on his face as he followed her lead.

They hacked and walked their way deeper into the forest. The air grew dense and more humid again and there were a lot of little pools. Some were small enough to step over but some they had had no choice but to walk around. They were walking up a shallow ridge with Andra leading the way. Suddenly Alex lost his footing and his legs slipped sideways from under him. Before he knew it he was sliding down the side of the ridge. He tried to stop himself but the ground was saturated with water and came away in his hands. He ended up in a deep pool of muddy water. Andra was slowly and carefully following him down the ridge and trying to avoid slipping. She stood on the water's edge next to the groove he had calved. He sat up, shook the water from his head and turned to look at her.

"What are you like? And you wanted to come here alone?" she said with a smile on her face.

"I meant to do that. All part of my great plan," he said.

As he spoke her eyes moved to something infront of him and the smile fell from her face. He turned to see what she was looking at and saw the wide, scaly snout and dome eyes of an enormous anaconda. It lunged forward and bit into his face around the jaw. He grabbed it with both hands as it turned him around and began to coil itself around him. His arms were pinned to his chest with his hands under his chin as it constricted around him. Andra leapt from the river bank and landed in the water beside them. The snake turned him round more and more. It squeezed as he breathed out and he felt his ribs pop as they snapped under the pressure. He felt his hips grind and cried out in pain as his pelvis buckled and then snapped. Andra took hold of the snake's body and tried to pull it off him but its strength was immense and it stayed where it was. Alex breathed out and he felt the snake loosen momentarily. Before it could tighten its grip he pushed with all his might and slipped out his right arm. He grabbed its head as it tightened around his chest. He tried to pull its mouth from his jaw but it bit down harder and its teeth tore his skin. He tightened his grip around its throat and it released its bite for a moment. He hoped it would realise he was stronger than it had anticipated and let him go, but it was unwilling to release its catch. It forced its head towards him and bit into his face again. Alex squeezed his hand into a fist and crushed its skull. The coils of the body spasmed and trashed, twisting over itself for a moment then became limp and the animal fell away from him. He collapsed into the water and began to sink but Andra hooked him under the arms and dragged him to the side. He sucked in a deep breath as his ribs clicked back into place. Then, using Andra for support, he pulled himself to his feet. His legs shook with pain as his pelvis shifted back into its correct position and the bones knitted themselves back together.

"Are you ok?" she said.

"Yeah, just give me a minute," he said.

"Why didn't you change?" she said

"I didn't get chance," he said.

He bent down and touched his toes and his back popped into place. He stood up straight and rotated his shoulders.

"Ready when you are?" she said and gestured with her hand for him to take the lead.

"Yeah, let's see what else I can get attacked by," he said sarcastically. "I thought you said we are the higher predators out here. That thing didn't give fuck."

"Man, come on. That was a fucking huge anaconda. An animal that size doesn't have any natural predators. It wasn't remotely scared of us," she said.

He took the GPS tracker from his pocket only to find that it had been crushed. Andra passed hers to him. He looked at it.

"This way," he said and began walking.

They continued deeper into the forest for another two hours. Soon the sun began to rise over the horizon. Here in the forest, besides the rays of light broke in through little gaps in the canopy and undergrowth, it remained dark. They walked along the side of a deep valley as the Amazon River thundered at the bottom of a ravine three miles East of them. Suddenly Alex stopped and stood perfectly still. Andra turned and looked at him. He had an expression similar to that of confusion on his face and his eyes searched the landscape.

"What is it?" she said.

"I can feel her. She's close by," he said.

He began to walk with purpose reminding Andra of a bloodhound following a scent. He was looking from left to right as he reached the valley top. Andra followed him as he strode through the forest until they came to a rocky outcrop. There was a small opening at the base of it no more than three feet high.

"She is in there," he said.

He put down his bags and took the high hide from his shoulder. He then bent down to climb into it when Andra put a hand on his shoulder.

"Yes?" he said looking back at her.

"Don't go in there. You don't know how deep the tunnels might go. You could be lost in there for days. We should put up the high hide and wait, otherwise, what was the point in bringing it all this way? She will be easier to track out here in the open," she said.

He turned his head and looked into the cave.

"We're so close, we could finish this now and be on our way back tonight," he said.

"Listen to me, Alex. I watched the rise and fall of the Roman Empire. They thought their Empire would last forever and the Emperors believed their power was given to them by their gods. They became complacent thinking they could never lose that power. They paid dearly for their ignorance," she said.

He looked up at her.

"Don't become complacent, Alex," she continued. "Use the powers you have wisely and never take them for granted. If you do you are setting yourself up for a fall."

He knew she was right. He looked into the darkness of the tunnels, the type of darkness that suggested it was miles deep. That wasn't a problem. He could see in the dark. The problem was the maze of tunnels that could be down there, and knowing a vampire hideout, would be down there.

"Let's get the hide up," he said as he looked up at her and smiled.

They slid the poles of the high hide into to sleeves

in the material counterpart and slotted them together inside exactly like a tent. It formed a seven foot by seven foot cube that was almost completely enclosed except for a window in the front and a zip-up door in the back. Andra passed a rope with a three-hundred kg weight capacity through a loop on the top of the hide, while Alex placed a rollout floor into the bottom to form a rigid platform. They set up a circuit of lowlight cameras connected wirelessly to a tablet. Alex placed this and their bags and equipment inside the hide. Andra took hold of the end of the rope and jumped as high as she could upwards into the canopy. She landed on a branch, threw the rope over the branch above her and hauled the hide up from the forest floor until she was happy with its position. She then tied the rope to the branch she stood on. She dropped down, landed on a lower branch, and looped the rope around it. Finally, she tied the end through a loop on the underside of the hide to prevent the whole thing from swinging too much. Alex climbed the trunk of the tree, joined her in the high hide, and they prepared for a long day of watching and waiting.

As the sun passed over head they talked about the past, things that had happened to them on raids, stories people had told them, and stories they had read on the internet. They listened to music, played games, read books and watched the local wildlife. Howler monkeys roared and the chainsaws rumbled in the distance.

"There are loggers over there," said Andra.

"Shall we go and give them a bit of a scare?" he

suggested with a smile.

"Maybe, when we've completed the mission," she said with a sly smirk.

**Chapter 20.**

A private jet landed on the same airfield just outside London where Saltorg had taken the Blutesser troopers from just a few days before. It was 21.00., the sun was low in the sky and it would soon kiss the horizon. The plane taxied down to one of the hangers and manoeuvred into it. The doors opened and a set of stairs unfolded towards the tarmac, a flight attendant stepped out, descended the stairs and stood to the side of them.

"This way my lord," she said in a jovial 'happy to help' tone.

The huge shape of Dienco bent down, squeezed through the door, and stepped out onto the stairs. He was joined on the tarmac by his two sons Tuhak, Helden, and his daughter Sesire. They had all been born to him by his wife Yutsi who had stayed in Germany. They were tall and strong with long black hair like their parents but none of them were as tall as Dienco. The dragon blood had continued to alter his DNA over the millennia and made him into a beast; even by vampire standards. He stood nearly eight feet tall, with an enormous muscular build.

They walked through an enclosed tunnel with no windows designed especially for vampires that led directly from the hanger to the main building.

"Come on, move your arses! I want to talk to Sergeant Lake right now!" Roared Dienco.

"Father, calm down, we have arrived. I'm sure we

will get to speak with your employees very soon," said Sesire.

"I didn't just sit in a flying metal tube for the best part of two hours to wait calmly to speak to people," he said.

He strode off down the tunnel and his children followed him. When he reached the reception area he marched up to Mr Goss who stood up from his chair behind the desk.

"Hello, Mr Dienco. How may I ..."

Dienco cut him off midsentence.

"Where is my brother, Saltorg!? Where is Sergeant Lake!? Has anyone returned yet!?" Roared Dienco.

"They-they-they-haven't come back yet, my Lord," stammered Mr Goss in an extremely nervous manner.

"Nobody!?" said Dienco.

"N-n-n-not yet, my Lord."

"Where is the pilot who airdropped them!? Do you have the coordinates for where they were dropped!?" said Dienco.

"He-he-he's not-not here right now my lord. I can radio for him for you, my Lord. H-he knows where they were dropped, m-my Lord."

"Please contact him and tell him we need him here as soon as possible," said Sesire as she stepped infront of her father.

The man hands shook as he picked up the phone.

"Relax. My father is angry because he fears that

they may have met their deaths. Just take a breath," said Sesire reassuringly.
The man took a deep breath and searched through the phone's contacts until he found the number he was looking for.

"Johnson, I need you to return the airfield as A.S.A.P. We have Mr Dienco here. He needs your assistance," said Mr Goss.

"Ok, on my way. I'll be there within the hour," said Johnson.

"See father, all that shouting for nothing," said Sesire.

"Well, he better hurry back then. I need to know where he dropped them. I've had no communication with Saltorg since he ordered soldiers for the attack two days ago," said Dienco.

"You should have known he would need our help in a fight. Taking on Andra and her minions might have been too much for them," said Helden.

Dienco placed his hand on Helden's shoulder and squeezed it hard until his son winced in pain.

"Do not speak derogatively about Saltorg's battle abilities. You weren't there in the ancient times. He has proven himself many times," said Dienco.

Half an hour later, Johnson arrived at the airfield outside London. He drove up to the control tower and parked his car. He then walked inside and Dienco walked up to him.

"Johnson, finally you have decided to turn up," he

said.

"My Lord, I apologise for my lateness. I got here as soon as I could, my Lord," said Johnson.

"Tell me where you dropped Saltorg and the Blutesser soldiers," said Dienco.

"Yes My Lord, Saltorg said it was an S.O.V.E.U. outpost in Oxfordshire. I remember the coordinates. I can take you there but we'll have to go by helicopter because of the location. There is nowhere to land a plane," said Johnson.

"How soon can we go?" said Dienco.

"As soon as you wish, my lord," said Johnson.

"I want to go now. I fear Saltorg may be in trouble," said Dienco.

"Very well, my Lord. I will have to fuel and check the helicopter first. It'll take around thirty minutes."

"You have thirty minutes, no more!" said Dienco.

Exactly thirty minutes later the helicopter was ready to go. Dienco, Tuhak, Helden and Sesire climbed in the aboard. The rotor blades got up to speed and they took off.

By 23.45 Jonson had the helicopter held in a hover above the warehouse base.

"We're here, my Lord," he said.

"Good, bring us down, we'll jump out and approach on foot. Set the helicopter down after we enter the building and stay in contact. I don't know how long this will take. We may need an immediate evacuation," said Dienco.

"Yes, my lord," said Johnson.

He brought the helicopter to two hundred feet and the four vampires jumped out.

Four soldiers were standing guard at points along the fence. The attack came swift and sudden and was executed with extreme precision. All of the guards heard the helicopter but didn't see the shapes falling from directly above them. The four vampires landed then struck the guards across the face just hard enough to knock them unconscious. They then met at the front entrance of the base carrying or dragging a guard each.

"I think I hit mine a bit too hard," laughed Tuhak. He held up a man whose face was bruised but his head swung loosely on his neck.

"No matter, they're not going to last much longer anyway," said Helden with a smirk.

"Cut the chatter. We need to get into the building. Do any of them have keys or cards," said Dienco. They checked the pockets and all found a pass card which they all waved over the scanner at the door to no avail. They all pushed and kicked against the door and even tried sliding it but it didn't move.

"Hold on," said Tuhak inspecting the door. "It's welded shut. We're not going to move it," said Tuhak.

"Any other ideas then?" said Sesire.

They all looked around for a minute and Helden found the narrow access door. He put his foot against it and pushed. It gave a little but not enough, so he kicked at it but still held.

"Step aside," said Dienco.

He waved the soldier he was still holding around infront of it. There was a hiss and the door slid open.

"Always be observant, son. Sometimes brawn isn't the answer," he said.

"They must have implants," said Tuhak.

"Yes or maybe bio-scanners," said Dienco.

He stepped inside followed by the others. It was quiet and dark in the building. Only a few spotlights shone through the darkness of the descending tunnel. A voice broke the silence from the end of the tunnel.

"Breach!"

Dienco peered through the darkness and saw a figure knelt down with something held on their shoulder.

"Firing," said the voice in a strangely calm tone.

"Down! Get down!" said Dienco.

They all dropped to the floor and got into what cover they could as an RPG hissed its way up the tunnel and exploded as it hit the huge entrance door.

"The crazy bastards are firing RPGs in here?" said Tuhak.

"We're obviously not welcome," said Helden.

"Saltorg, my brother. I hope you didn't suffer," whispered Dienco as he realised the now obvious fate of his fallen kin.

Move in," he said.
Bullets ricocheted all around them as they ran. Moments later Dienco snatched the rocket launcher out of the soldier's hands. He watched in shock which quickly turned to fear as Dienco broke the gun in two.
"Naughty," said the vampire and cast the pieces aside.
The four of them dodged every bullet that was fired at them and disarmed eight soldiers of all their weapons, side-arms and knives.
"You'll never take me alive!" shouted a soldier. He pulled the pin from a grenade and held it above his head. With a heavy swing of her arm Sesire slapped the device. It sailed up the tunnel towards the door where it exploded out of range. The soldier cried out, holding his forearm at the point where the broken bones had punctured the skin, and his hand flopped around loosely.
"Have we got any more heroes?" she asked but received no answers. "As I thought," she said.
"Restrain them," said Dienco.
The vampires dragged the soldiers to the floor and bound their wrist, elbows, knees, and ankles with zip ties.
"First of all, I am Dienco. Master of the armies of Lord Ruhsarr. I am going to ask you some questions and I want answers. It is now obvious that Saltorg and the soldiers he brought with him to attack this base were defeated, as they are now not here, and

not answering any communications," said Dienco.

"Yeah, he's dead! They're all fucking dead. They got their arses kicked, mate," said one of the soldiers.

The other soldiers laughed and jeered defiantly.

To have his brother's demise mocked with such flippancy angered Dienco, but he knew the soldiers were trying to get a reaction from him.

"Ok. I'll ask you a question. Where are Andra, Vincent and Alex?" said Dienco.

The room was silent and no one answered.

"Tell me and you can all go home to your families." he said.

There was still no response from the soldiers.

"Don't you want to go home to your families?" he said.

"Oh, do fuck off. We're ain't gonna tell you anything," said another soldier.

A boot smashed across the side of his face. Tuhak stood over the soldier's quivering body as a pool of blood expanded out from Their broken face.

"I wouldn't annoy Tuhak. He doesn't like humans," said Dienco.

"My brother was killed by a human," said Tuhak.

"I watched my mother get torn apart by vampires when I was seven years old, so cry me a fucking river," spat another soldier.

Tuhak picked the soldier up by his throat.

"I'm going to enjoy draining you of all your blood," he said.

“Sorry, I don't kiss on a first date,” smirked the soldier.

He held the soldier right up to his face and growled.

“Bring him here,” said Dienco.

Tuhak carried the soldier over to Dienco and held him out. Dienco took him by the ankle and let him quickly drop, then swing as he held him up like a fish.

“What is your name?”

“Taylor,” said the soldier.

“Well, Taylor. I'm going to use you as leverage,” he whispered. “Now, tell me where Andra and the others are,”

“No,” said the soldiers collectively.

“So be it,” said Dienco.

He placed his thumb on Taylor’s ankle above his fingers and pushed. There was a sickening crack as the bones broke and Taylor screamed.

“Where are they?” said Dienco.

Nobody answered.

He took the next ankle and broke it in the same way. Again Taylor screamed.

“Don't tell ‘em. Don't tell 'em,” he spluttered.

“His knees are next,” said Dienco.

He adjusted his grip on the man placing one hand around Taylor’s thigh and the other on his calf.

“Tell me and all his pain will stop. You can all just go home.”

The guards held their silence. Dienco snapped Taylor’s knee as easily a human could snap a twig.

Taylor howled in pain.

"Tell me!" Roared Dienco.

Still silence.

Taylor's other knee was broken.

"Don't tell!" he sobbed.

"You're making me do this!" said Dienco.

One of the soldiers had tears rolling down his face now. Dienco looked him right in the eyes.

"All you have to do is speak. You can stop your friend's pain. Just tell me where Andra is," said Dienco in a reassuring tone.

"No, Jones! He's a liar! He'll kill us all," cried Taylor.

Jones looked away and Dienco broke Taylor's elbow. Again the man screamed.

"Ok! Ok, Ok I'll...I'll tell you. Just please, stop hurting him," said Jones, who was openly weeping now.

"Good, tell me what I want to know and you will all be free," smiled Dienco.

"No. Don't you dare! Don't you fucking dare!" said Taylor.

Dienco put his hand over Taylor's mouth.

"Tell me or I'll break his neck," said Dienco in an angry tone.

"They're in a warehouse base, like this one, in Newcastle upon Tyne. About four miles from the city centre. A place called Hartside Industrial Estate. Please stop," pleaded Jones.

"See, that's all we needed," said Dienco.

The soldiers gave each other knowing looks. They knew their colleague was sending the vampires to a well-stocked and heavily armed base full of soldiers.

"Kill them," said Dienco, flatly.

"But you said..." cried Jones.

"I'm a vampire, you're a human. What did you really expect?" said Dienco.

He threw Taylor to Tuhak. His son caught the man, tore out his throat, and dropped him to the floor to bleed out.

"Your mother deserved it," he said and spat out the blood from his mouth.

The other vampires tore into the necks of the other guards and dropped them.

Dienco stood over Jones.

"Leave this one alive. I despise traitors," he said. He then bit into the neck of the guard beside him.

They left Jones tied up and screaming in the underground base as the blood of his dying colleagues formed a pool that surrounded and grew ever closer to him.

Dienco closed the access door and radioed Johnson in the helicopter.

Two minutes later he was hovering above them and coming down to pick them up. They climbed aboard and they took off.

"We need to get to Newcastle as soon as possible," said Dienco.

"We'll need to go back to base and fuel up, my

Lord. Newcastle is around 250 miles away. It'll be a two to three hour flight," said Johnson.

"Very well," said Dienco.

An hour later the helicopter was refuelled and ready. Johnson radioed the lounge area.

"My lords, M'lady. Your transportation is ready and waiting on the airfield," said Mr Goss.

"Thank you," smiled Dienco.

They made quick checks on their guns and weapons with Dienco still preferring his huge battle axe. They walked out to the helicopter and climbed aboard.

"Welcome back. All ready?" said Johnson.

"Yes. Take us up," said Helden.

Two hours later they were approaching Newcastle.

"Where's the base, Lords?" said Johnson.

"It's in an industrial estate called Heartlands. Do you know where that is?" said Dienco.

"I can find it, sir," said Jonson and tapped on his sat-nav. "We're nearly there. I'll begin our descent," said Johnson.

He brought the helicopter down to one thousand feet. They swept the area looking down on the city. Tuhak and Sesire were looking at the ground below on monitors connected to infrared and heat cameras that were built into the underside of the helicopter. They approached the bank of warehouses one of them gave off a heat signature much higher than the ones surrounding it.

“There, the one in the middle,” said Tuhak, his voice full of excitement.

The pilot hovered over it.

“Number twelve according to the sat-nav,” said Johnson.

“You are sure?” said Dienco.

“Yes, father. Definitely, it’s much hotter than the others,” said Sesire.

“Ok, Johnson, bring us down. Do you want to join us in this fight?” said Dienco.

“It would be an honour, my Lord,” said Johnson, swelling with pride.

“Good man. Land in front of the warehouse then. In fact, shoot out the front door out. No point making a subtle entrance and it will be a nice surprise for them too,” said Dienco.

Johnson flicked open a red arming switch on the helicopter’s joystick, squeezed the trigger underneath it and launched a small missile directly into the centre of the doors. They were blown inwards in a cloud of metal and concrete that left a gaping hole where it had once been. As Johnson landed the helicopter the others were already running through the smoke and rubble into a building full of humans who were unprepared for such a swift and brutal attack.

## Chapter 21.

Andra and Alex had whiled away the rest of the day until the sun finally sank beyond the horizon. Alex was asleep until Andra shook him awake.

"Wha-what?" he stammered.

She put her finger to her lips signalling for him to be quiet.

"Something's stirring up the wildlife," she whispered.

The animals outside the hide didn't know that Alex and Andra were there, so they sang and growled and called.

He checked the tablet and switched through the selection of images relayed by the cameras. In five of the images flying insects buzzed around and some small animals crawled in and around plants, trees and clearings. In the image from the camera pointed at the mouth of the cave he could see something stirring in the darkness. He passed the tablet to Andra, stood up and slowly and looked out of the opening in the side of the hide. He stared down at the opening of the cave. Suddenly all the animals around them stopped making any sound and it became eerily quiet. On the tablet Andra saw the saw the image of a long, dark green, scaly snout emerged from the cave, and the nostrils snorted at the air. An exhaled breath rasped through the teeth and then the whole head emerged closely followed by the long, wiry arms, and strong shoulders. Matted black hair hung down from the head. From his vantage point Alex could see that the hair ran all the way down the spine. On the tablet Andra could see the fingers splayed out over the ground and there were a long, black claws at the end of each scaly digit. The whole being emerged from the hole with its body parallel to the forest floor. The back legs rotated further at the hip than any human legs could with the thighs at an almost horizontal angle to the ground. The knees bent and the ankles were rotated so that the feet were flat against the ground. A long, thick tail trailed behind the body and it moved in a similar fashion to a komodo dragon. Its entire body was covered in the same dark green scales. Unlike the small scales that encompassed Andra's body, these were thick, heavy scales, akin to that of a crocodile. They watched as it snorted at the air and looked up into the trees. As Andra watched the tablet the beast launched itself forward and the screen went black. She switched through the images and found there were now only five. She took out a small notepad and wrote a message.

'Is that her?' she wrote and showed it to Alex.
He nodded.

'She destroyed a camera,' she wrote.
Alex took out a pad and pen of his own.

'She knows I'm here but doesn't know where. She's different than she was in my vision. She looked human. She's adapted to this environment.' He wrote and showed her.

'She knows they're our cameras?' she wrote.
He replied with a shrug.
They looked back down to the ground and Jorshean was gone.

‘Where is she?’ she wrote.

‘Don’t know. Keep eyes open,’ he wrote.

Andra looked at the tablet, they saw the plants infront of one of the cameras move and then the screen went blank. She switched to the next image showed a tree, it shook and again the screen went blank. There was one last screen that quickly went blank too.

‘She definitely knows,’ Andra wrote.

Alex looked down towards the ground. He saw a flash of movement and the outline of flexing limbs but there was no sound. He sensed she was close, really close just as the branch above them creaked. Suddenly the rope to the top of the hide broke. Alex and Andra yelled as their world dropped, then flipped. They and all their equipment fell to the top of the now upside down hide. They swung wildly among the branches of the tree. There was an impact on the inverted underside of the hide, knocking the platform from the frame. It landed on them and rolled up. A hole was torn in the material of the hide by long, black claws. The long green snout they had seen on the video tore the hole wider as it pushed through the material. A strange duel layered roar, both high and low pitched at the same time, erupted from its larynx. Andra and Alex raised their guns and squeezed the triggers. Bullets tore at Jorshean’s flesh sending her reeling back with hisses and growls. She saw the rope, slashed it, and the hide dropped. Alex and Andra grabbed for their bags and weapons as everything was thrown into freefall. Everything seemed weightless for a moment, then they hit the forest floor hard and lay there, battered and confused. They got to their feet and worked their limbs. Their bones crunched and popped back into place. Alex grabbed the material of the hide and tore it open. He stepped out and Jorshean landed gracefully a few feet from him.

She stood up on her hind legs and stared at him. And he stared right back at her.

"Jorshean. Looks like we have found each other," he said.

Her face clicked as the bones reshaped themselves. Her snout shrank back into a more human face, her torso shortened, and he arms changed in proportion. She almost looked human but was still covered in those thick scales. She looked a lot more like she had in Alex's vision.

"Be gone. Leave this place. Tell Ruhsarr he is my lord no more. I refuse to return to your human world," hissed Jorshean.

Andra stood up still covered by the remains of the hide.

"Stop fucking chatting and grab her!" she said. Alex stepped forward and raised his hands.

"Leave me be," said Jorshean taking a few steps back.

She then turned and sprinted off into the forest. Alex watched for a second, shocked by her speed. He then ran after her before she could disappear into the undergrowth.

Jorshean weaved around trees, vaulted over fallen trunks, and dodged past tree branches in her attempt to lose Alex. He was keeping pace with her though, so she smashed through the undergrowth, littering the air with splintered wood and debris. He held up his arm to protect his eyes but then had to pull splinters from his arms as he ran. She leapt high into the trees and grabbed a branch. She swung under it like a trapeze artist then let go, launching herself higher into the tree canopy. Alex tried to do the same but the branch snapped and he tumbled back to the ground. He tucked up his legs and rolled then was back on his feet. He continued to chase her from the ground. When he regained his momentum he jumped, and launched himself into the trees. He leapt from branch to branch but she was still getting away from him despite him moving as fast as he could.

She moved in a strange manner. Sprinting along tree limbs, leaping to catch a branch and swinging underneath it with one hand before releasing it and catching a branch with her other hand. Swinging from that branch, landing on her feet, leaping and vaulting over a branch with one hand. Landing on her feet running from branch to branch on all fours then swinging under and vaulting over more branches. The closest comparison he could make was a trapeze artist free-runner with the agility of a monkey.

He stretched out his arms as he leapt for a branch and allowed his body to begin to change. His shoulders burst through his clothing, followed by his arms and legs. As he ran through the tree canopy his head and body changed and he lost his balance. He slammed into a tree trunk and fell towards the ground. He crashed into the trunk of another tree where he grabbed and scrapped at the bark. He dug his claws in and tore grooves in its woody flesh. By the he stopped he was on the ground. He ran to another tree and quickly climbed the trunk. He leapt to another tree and was soon chasing Jorshean through the canopy. She looked back and saw he was gaining on her.

"Jorshean!" he roared.

His shout was so loud it broke the night air like a clap of thunder.

Andra heard it and smiled to herself. Jorshean had been a horrific and cruel vampire. She had caused the death of many of Andra's friends over thousands of years then one day, four hundred years ago, she had simply vanished. Almost everyone who had seen her since was now either dead or in no fit state to talk about their encounter. This scourge of mankind was finally getting her comeuppance.

Alex was on Jorshean's tail. She swung under a branch and catapulted herself up into the higher layers of the tree canopy. Alex smashed through branches sending wood, leaves, and insects flying in all directions. He found himself falling and scrabbled to grip a branch but tore away any he got hold of. As he fell out of the canopy he threw out an arm and caught hold of a tree trunk and pulled his body towards it. He slammed his feet against the trunk and grabbed it with both hands. He slid down the tree for some distance before coming to a standstill. He started to climb back up as fast as he could.

Continuing to make it look easy, Jorshean landed higher up in the trees and ran. She realised she wasn't being followed and slowed down a little. Suddenly the tree shook and the huge shape of Alex exploded through the foliage. She turned and ran but he was right behind her. She caught a branch, landed on it, planted her feet and launched herself off it in another direction. A second later Alex smashed through branches and slammed into a tree trunk. Anger burned like a raging fire in his chest as he struggled to change direction. But soon he was right behind her again. He reached a hand out for her tail but she back flipped over him. As she sailed over his head she kicked out her feet and struck him on the top of his head. He stumbled, lost his footing, and fell from the branch he was on. His huge mass crashed against a lower branch but he managed to grip onto it. He stopped and looked behind him in an attempt to locate her. She landed on a branch about twenty feet above him. He wanted to thrash and rage but he stopped, controlled his anger, and focused it as Andra had taught him. He set off running in the same direction as Jorshean, but not up to her level. She ran and changed direction at high speed using all the tricks she knew, but Alex still kept up. She leapt and caught the branch of a tree and Alex leapt towards the same tree. He tucked his head to the left and hit the trunk with all his weight in a rugby tackle. The trunk was no match for his body and it exploded outwards in a shower of splinters and bark. The tree above him leaned wildly then fell at the point of impact. Creaking and wailing as the fibres of trunk screamed and tore apart under its own weight. It smashed violently through its neighbouring trees, rolling and twisting as it went. Alex saw Jorshean hanging on to a branch, a grimace of shock on her face. He threw himself at her and she let go of the branch but he was too fast and hurtled towards her. As his body crashed into hers he wrapped his arms around her and they fell together. He opened his huge mouth and looked into her eyes. He was expecting to see the same fear in those eyes as he had seen in Saltorg and Gilad. But as she looked at those horrendous teeth in his powerful jaw she did something he did not expect. She placed her hands on his face and the strangest thing happened. All the anger that raged with him dissipated. He closed his mouth and realised she was hugging him. He rolled himself in the air and braced himself for impact. The top of the tree smashed into the ground throwing out a cloud of splinters and soil. He landed on his feet a short distance away. She leaned back away from him and smiled.

"Place me on the ground, please? I will not run, I have no desire to fight you," she said.

He hesitated to let her go. He was confused as he was expecting to be getting bitten and scratched by now.

"I promise," she said.

He put her down and she looked up at him.

"Is it you? I assume you are the one who inhabited my thoughts, am I correct?" she said.

"Yes. I saw you in a vision too. Why did you smile at me?" he said.

"I have been awaiting your arrival for so many years," she said.

"Then why did you run from me?" he said.

"I know who you are now. When I attacked your box in the tree I just assumed you were sent by Ruhsarr. He has been trying to bring me back for me for many a year now. He has sent others in the past and I have killed them all. I refuse to return to Europe, I will not live that way again. I was stricken with horror when I saw you, you look and move like a vampire so I ran. When you changed I realised you could be the one afflicted by the prophecy," she said.

"I'm sorry about that. I just thought you knew I could change form," he said.

As he spoke he returned to his human form. She smiled as she watched him.

"There is no need for an apology," she said.

"Can I ask you why you don't want to fight me? All other vampires I have met have wanted to kill me," he said.

"I have no desire to fight you because I have no desire to survive our encounter. This existence was forced upon me. I have wanted for the prophecy to be true for so many years," she said.

"You mean you want me to end your life?" he said quizzically.

"Yes, I know. It must seem strange to you. You are so young, but it is the truth. Immortal life sounds so enthralling to mortals. Yes, live forever, never fall ill and never be encumbered by the inconveniences of death. But the realities of this never ending existence, they take their toll. I have committed heinous crimes. I once massacred an entire city. I drained the blood of as many humans as I could. Those I could not drink from I impaled by the dozen on iron rods and then roast them alive over bonfires. I did all that merely for my own entertainment. Hundreds of people died because I was drunk on power and wanted to alleviate my excruciating boredom. I take no pride in my actions of the past. I am a monster and I am cursed to walk this earth forever more. I want to die and trust me it's not for a lack of trying," she sat down on the stump of the dead tree and rested her elbows on her knees. "I have tried everything I can think of. I have shot myself in the head, and stabbed myself through the heart with blades made from every substance I thought should kill me. Silver, gold, wood, salt, iron. Nothing worked. I have set myself ablaze, blown myself up with every incendiary substance I could find. I have tried to decapitate myself on many occasions; it really hurts. I have bled myself dry. I have been crushed flat in a hydraulic press but still, I got better. I have drank poisoned blood, dead blood and vampire blood. Every time I heal faster than I can be hurt. I stood out all day in the desert sun and my scales just grew thicker until I was solid like a statue. I have even thrown myself into a volcano. All that happened was that the lava melted the outer layers of my flesh, and I healed faster than it could burn me. My only choice was to haul myself out. I wanted an end, not eternal agony. That is the reason I'm scaled this way. My body has taken it upon itself to protect itself from myself in the most extreme way."

"I thought all those things were supposed to destroy vampires?" said Alex.

"As did I, but seemingly suicide is not an option for me. Even the trees which seemed eternal in my human life will shed their mortal coil, but not me. You are my only option; my only hope. I have turned my back on the world, on what I am, but these horrific memories have burrowed happy little homes for themselves in my mind and it is from those homes they torture me, and will do so for eternity," she said.

"What if it doesn't work? I mean, if everything else hasn't worked my bite may not work either," he said.

"Hopefully that is not the case," she said.

"But if it doesn't you could come back with me and Andra. You would be able to help me find Dienco and Ruhsarr. Help us stop him and maybe Ruhsarr's death will free you. You have an incredible wealth of knowledge that would give me an insight into the inner workings of higher levels of vampire society," he said.

"That is a wonderful offer but you forget, I have no intention of returning to the civilised world. Neither with you nor anyone else. I do not intend to offend you, but I have had my fill of being a blight on this earth. Also as I remember Andra doesn't much like me. The knowledge you will gain by ingesting my flesh will give you more information than I ever could put into words. You will have the location of Dienco and I will have the death I have craved for so long. Promise me you will put an end to the shadow my kind has cast across this world," she said.

"I promise you, I will," he said.

She stood up and watched as he changed into the beast again. He picked her up and held her in his arms.

"I'll make it quick," he said.

"There are some who would request you take your time," she said and nodded towards the treeline where Andra stood watching. He looked over then to her and then back to Jorshean.

"Do you wish I had fought you?" she said.

"Believe me, this is one of the hardest fights I have ever fought," he said with a forced smile.

"What do you think will happen to me? Will I go to some form of afterlife?" she said.

"To be honest, I don't know," he said.

She smiled. "It does not matter. Anything is better than this, even nothing. Release me." she said.

He opened his jaws, placed his teeth on her head and for a moment he hesitated.

"Please," she whispered.

He bit down hard and fast and felt her skull crack between his teeth. Blood poured down her cheeks, her scales began to thicken, her claws grew and she racked them over his skin. Then she was still and her body began to harden into a husk. He bit into her and ate her flesh as fast as he could; not stopping to think about it.

His mind swam with Jorshean's thoughts and memories of the past. A huge flying beast landing on a village she had lived in. Sicking pain as the monster tore into her neck and the agony of life flooding back into her as the vampirism snaked and coursed its way through her body. Horrifying memories of her laughing and mocking the tortured screams of a mother as she tore her dead baby apart; then draining the blood of the mother too. Alex fell to his knees and wretched. More images raced through his mind of her singlehandedly sacking entire towns, and indiscriminately killing the whole population. Slaughtering families in their homes, buildings full of praying people, and streets full of men, women, and children; laughing as she chased them. Laughing as they ran, and fell, and trampled over each other trying to get away from her. He then felt her fear, sadness, and regret as she experienced a crisis of conscience. Her realisation that she had become a monster, mad with power. He saw all the ships had been on and all the travelling she had done in an attempt to hide away from the world. He felt all she had suffered as she tried in vain, over and over again, to end her life and release herself from this self-made hell. He then saw himself through her eyes, he looked like an angel in the guise of a monster. The memories ended and another vision began. A large landmass he recognised as Europe. It zoomed in on Germany, then closer on a city, and even closer until he was looking at an old, rectangular fortress with a tall modern brick tower built within its outer walls. Inside the tower upon a thrown sat a huge ancient vampire. He talked and laughed with three other vampires. Their laughter died and he looked around as he sensed Alex's presence. He focused and they made eye contact. The vampire shuddered with a fear that turned to anger. He turned back to the other vampires and barked at them.

"Dienco!" growled Alex.

And the vision ended.

He stayed knelt for a moment before slowly opening his eyes. He looked around, re-associated himself with his surroundings and got to his feet. He walked over to Andra. She looked at him and smiled.

"Why are you smiling?" he said.

"I'm proud of you. You could have used all the rage you have inside, for what she and her kind have done to you, to exact revenge. Instead, you chose compassion and understanding," she said.

"You heard our conversation?" he said.

"Yes. I've been stood here long enough," she said.

"I almost did use my rage. She did something to me when she put her hands on my face. All my rage evaporated," he said.

"She used to use a similar trick to turn her foes against each other. Looks like she learned how to use it to incite compassion instead of anger," she said.

"Well, it worked on me. She was so sad, so broken up about what she had done in the past.

Most vampires don't care but then I saw what she had done. I'm not surprised she didn't want to live anymore. What happened to her? What made her grow a conscience?" he said.

"No one knows for sure. It was rumoured that she was looking for an ancient treasure. In that rumour she found something and was cursed by it. All I know for certain is my spies saw her sailing west at night from the coast of Denmark in 1612. After that there was no solid evidence of her location until today," she said.

"Really? That is interesting. I wouldn't mind having a look in her cave. Imagine all the things that could be in there. Unfortunately, we don't have time for that type of exploration. In the vision I saw what I assume is Dienco. He knows we are coming so I intend to pay him a visit as soon as possible," he said.

Andra had a look of disappointment on her face.

"What? You want to have a look in the cave, don't you," he said.

"Well, we are here now and it's not easy to get here. It's not like we can come here on a whim. We'll go in for an hour; no more. Document what's in there and then we'll go, she said.

"Ok, you're the boss," he said.

They made their way back to the cave.

"After you," he said and gestured with an open hand to the cave mouth.

Andra stuck her head in and had a look around. She then crawled in and began to move deeper into the space. Alex then followed her in. The cave was smooth and looked like it had been calved in some places. It angled down at a forty five degree angle.

"How far down does this thing go? He said.

“It can't be that far if Jorshean was climbing out of here every night," she said.

After about one hundred and fifty feet, the cave began to open up enough that Andra was able to stand upright. In the centre of this area Jorshean had placed a layer of leaves, animal skins, and clothing to form a bed. Against one of the walls stood a huge pile of weapons. Guns ranging from old muskets to modern handguns and rifles. There were swords, machetes, and an assortment of knives. Andra picked up a flintlock rifle.

"I remember these," she said.

She turned it in her hands, then looked down the sights only to find the barrel was bent. She held it out and noticed the patches of blood that had soaked into the wooden stock before drying.

"Ah, It's all fucked up. That's a shame," she said.

She lay it down on the floor and picked up a Smith and Wesson model 625. Aside from a few scuffs and scratches, it was still in good working order. With a clean it could be functional. She pushed out the cylinder and sniffed it.

"This was fired recently," she said.

"Must have belonged to one of those loggers I saw in the vision," said Alex.

Andra put the gun down and looked at some of the others on the pile. She picked up a knife and inspected the blade.

"I don't know. Some of these look a lot like the guns the vampires that attacked our base were carrying. This is a new knife. It's still sharp and looks lathe sharpened," she said.

"Jorshean did say that Ruhsarr had been sending vampires out here to try and bring her back," he said.

"That means he knew where she was all along. I said to you before that she has been missing for nearly four hundred years. I have plants in among the vampires. If they didn't know it means he's been keeping this close to his chest. Why is he running such deeply covert operations? He's up to something," she said.

"There might be more information in here. Let's see what we can find," he said.

On the other side of the cave stood a pile of clothing. Modern military uniforms and hiking clothing were sat among thread-bare centuries old Spanish soldier's uniforms and boots.

"There are modern materials and clothing here too. Clothing and belonging, but where are all the bodies?" said Alex.

"Check the back," she said.

"Yep," he said.

They walked away from the piles of items and deeper into the cave. There they found a pool of water that became darker the closer to the wall it got.

"I think that is a lot deeper than it looks. There may be more stuff down there," she said.

"One of us should go down there and check," he

said.

"I'll go," said Andra.

She put down her holdall and took off her boots. Emptied her pockets and put the content into the zip pocket of the holdall. She then took a length of rope from the main compartment and tied it around her waist. She handed the other end to Alex.

"I presume there is a tunnel down there. If there is, I'll see if it leads through to anything. If I pull on the rope tie it off around a rock or something and follow me. If not I'll be back in a few minutes," she said.

"Ok, be careful," he said.

"Don't worry. It's not like I'm going to drown or anything. On that note. Don't breathe underwater. It won't kill you but fuck it hurts," she said.

"Noted," he said.

She turned and wadded into the water for a few feet. Within those few steps she was in up to her waist. She dived down and disappeared under the surface. As she descended into the pool, Alex let the rope uncoil from his hands. She reached the bottom and followed it until she found a tunnel. She looked around for a moment and found some items. Two pairs of spectacles, an earring, and a ring set with ruby stone. She then followed the tunnel deeper. It curved and angled down for a few feet but soon began to raise again. She felt her face break the water's surface. She blinked the water from her eyes and scanned the area. It was even darker again in here. Completely devoid of light. She had to wait a moment for her eyes to adjust to the darkness.

Soon she could see she was in another large cave area. Over by one of the walls was a pile. Bones, hair, rotting flesh and mummified skin. This was the pile of bodies she had been expecting to see. She unfastened the rope from her waist, tied it around an outcrop of rock, and gave it a quick sharp pull.

On the other side of the pool Alex felt the tug and searched for a rock to tie the rope around. He took off his boots and backpack too. He waded into the water as Andra had done and let himself sink beneath the surface. He followed the rope through the tunnel and soon he emerged from the surface and joined Andrea in the other cave. He trudged out the water and stood next to her. She was examining one of the bodies. He knelt down next to her.

"What are you looking for?" he said.

"Bite marks," she said without looking at him. "I'm just curious about the cause of death."

"Some of these seem partially eaten," he said, as he examined some huge bite marks on one of the bodies.

"Some vampires have been documented eating the remains of their dead victims. Some seem to prefer not to," she said with a shrug.

They both examined more bodies. Checking the necks, wrist, chests and inner thighs.

"Aha! Found it. Here on the wrist of this guy," she said.

Alex came over and examined the body too.

"Jorshean didn't quit drinking human blood. She had just cut down the quantity she was taking. I mean, it's a significant cut but she hadn't quit entirely," she said.

"Probably explains why she kept healing. The dragon's blood helped her keep on changing but she still needed to be feeding," he said.

"That's true. We still need to find out why Ruhsarr kept sending his people to see her though," she said.

"Let's keep moving," said Andra.

They stood up and walked deeper into the cave. After a few minutes walking Andra looked down at the floor. She bent down and picked up a scrap of shredded paper. She looked down and saw more.

"Look at this?" she said.

Alex looked at the scrap and took it from her. It was covered in symbols that were obviously some form of writing that he didn't recognise.

"What language is that?" he said.

Andra had another piece in her hand and was reading it.

"It's Yargol. It's an ancient Germanic tribal dialect. It's not been used by humans for thousands of years. It's considered a dead language to most. Today it's only used by a few select vampires," she said.

"Ruhsarr and the children of the blood?" he said.

"Yep, and me," she said. "This is pretty much destroyed. We need to find more," she said.

They followed the scraps of paper for a few minutes until, in the centre of the cave, they found a pool of water.

"Ah shit!" she said.

The water was thick with the pulpy remnants of lots

of paper.

“Fuck. It’s all gone,” he said.

"We'll have to work with what we have," she said. She sorted through the scraps of paper for a minute.

"Mother fucker! I knew he was up to something," she said.

"What?" he said.

"There are a few discernible parts," she said and read all the parts aloud. "Demand your return...an assignment for you...has betrayed...intent of attacking me...you are to meet up with…chosen now to return...you are to assassinate."
She looked at him with anger in her eyes.

"Who do you think is this about?" He said.

"I don't know. Obviously, not us. It must be someone they both knew. But why would he need Jorshean to assassinate someone?" she said.
They both thought over this for a few moments.

"Maybe it's someone who wouldn't have trusted Ruhsarr himself," he said.

"Yeah. Or Ruhsarr showing up to kill someone himself would cause too much of a disturbance. I mean, who's not going to notice Ruhsarr? He needed someone who others would see but maybe not recognise. Who better than someone who hasn't been seen for four hundred years?" she said.

"Yeah. That is a good point," he said.

"I think she tried to disappear because Ruhsarr was trying to get her to kill other vampires," she said.

"You think that made her realise how corrupt she had become?" he said.

"Thankfully, yes. The world would have been a different place if she had continued her reign of terror. Let's see what else we can find," she said. They searched the cave but found nothing else more of interest.

"We should get going. We need to rendezvous with T.J." she said.

They returned to the pool and followed the rope to the other side. They collected their holdalls, returned to the hide, and gathered up the weapons and equipment. They packed them back into the holdalls and cases. It was 12.31 when they began to hike back. Alex was glad they brought the spare camouflage clothing as his other clothes were now shredded and lost among the trees from the chase. The hike was uneventful this time and when they reached the tree to which they had tied the canoes it was 01.39. They were happy to see they were still in place. They were not so happy about the four armed men who were stood talking among themselves just fifteen feet from the tree.

They both ducked down into the undergrowth.

"What's the plan?" whispered Alex.

"I think we should give them a scare," Andra said with a smile.

Alex smiled, "I like this plan," he said.

"Take your clothes off, you don't want to rip those too." He undressed while she continued to speak. "When we get to the canoes we'll travel downriver again. A friend of mine has a base thirty miles away. T.J. is waiting there for us, but first, this is what we will do..."

The four men were arguing among themselves in Spanish about how they were going to split the money for the animals they had captured. There was a rustling in the trees nearby and the men all turned to see what was causing it.

"Who's there? Come out or we'll shoot!" shouted one of them.

Andra stepped from behind the trees with her long wavy blonde hair obscuring her face and walked towards them.

"Oh…er… that's far enough. What are you doing all the way out here? Don't you know how dangerous it is out here?" said another.

"Yes, I know exactly how dangerous it is," said Andra as she flicked back her hair to reveal her elongated face. "We are the danger."

The hulking shape of Alex burst out from the trees roaring, saliva dripping from his gaping jaws. There was a flurry of movement from the men whose bodies reacted on instinct from the shock.

"Morrop! I told you he's real!" screamed one of the men.

They fell over each other in their attempt to run away.

Alex and Andra both roared as the men ran for their lives. Alex ran after them for a few minutes to keep them moving. He stayed on their tail but didn't actually catch up to them. Happy that they would probably never set foot in the forest again, he returned to Andra and they both laughed until they cried.

“That was brilliant. We are the danger,” he said.

“It just popped into my head,” she said through fits of laughter.

“Fuck, that’s funny,” he said, holding his sides. He walked into the undergrowth to change to his human form and put his on clothes while Andra untied the boats. She pulled them ashore and stowed their equipment. When he had laced up his boots he climbed into his boat.

“Ready?” she said.

“Ready,” he said.

## Chapter 22.

They used their oars to push themselves onto the water. Soon they were navigating their way down the river again. Clouds of insects buzzed as they flew back and forth overhead. They were caught and eaten by the bats who flitted almost silently through them.

Soon the river narrowed and the water began to flow fast as they descended into a gorge. Here the water quickly became a ferocious series of rapids. They struggled to keep their canoes upright as water forced its way over the sides and soaked them.

Andra's canoe bounced over the rapids, then crashed down deep into the water with a crack. The front end caught on the river bed. The water was relentless and the canoe flipped, throwing its content, including Andra, into the water. The ruined canoe continued to be dragged downstream. Andra was thrown around like a ragdoll as she was smashed against rocks and tree roots.

"Alex! Help!" she screamed as her head broke the surface.

She was swept over the falls and the current pulled her under. She held her beneath the surface as thousands of tons of water surged above her. She tried to push away from the riverbed but found she couldn't move. Alex rowed towards the spot she went under with all his strength. Although she didn't need to breathe and therefore couldn't drown, she was at the river's mercy. Without help she would be trapped there until it decided to let her go.

If it ever decided to let her go. A huge scaled hand was driven down through the water and wrapped around her chest. With herculean strength he pulled her free. She gulped down an enormous breath as Alex hauled to the surface and held her.

"You're ok just breathe," he said.

"Oh fuck! I'm ok, I'm ok," she gasped.

She took a few minutes to get over the panic and compose herself.

"Are you ok?" He asked.

She could see the concern in his eyes.

"Yes, I'm good. Thank you, Alex. I couldn't get out. I was properly stuck," she said.

Somehow, in her panic, she had managed to keep hold of her oar. Alex helped her into his canoe and then climbed after her. She moved towards the front and knelt down. Together they fought their way through the swell of fierce water for another mile before it calmed down. Soon the river widened again and the current became comparatively gentle. They heard voices from the shore and to be on the safe side they lay down and pulled the cover over them. Their bodies were pressed together in the confined space.

"I can feel you shivering, are you still cold?" said Alex.

"I'm ok. It's not like I'm gonna die," said Andra.

"Can you still get pneumonia though?" he said.

"No, I don't suffer from the cold in the same way humans do. But I still have to maintain my temperature. Wrap your arms around me," she said.

"This is awkward," he said as held her close.

"What's awkward? We're two friends sharing body heat in extreme conditions. You know would make it awkward?" she said.

"What?" he said.

She flicked out her forked tongue and licked his face.

"Behave," he whispered.

She put her hand to her lips to stifle her laughter. After five minutes had passed she looked out through the cover. Seeing there was no one on the banks she took the cover down and sat up. She unzipped a pocket on her trousers and took out her GPS tracker, which luckily was waterproof.

"Still another twenty miles to go. Let's start rowing, we need to cover more distance," she said.

Alex sat up and picked up his oar. For the next hour they rowed hard and fast. Easily travelling at twenty miles an hour. The river zipped by around them as they cut through it with ease. Andra took out the GPS again.

"Another mile until we reach our destination and then a short half mile hike," she said.

They carried on rowing and she kept checking the coordinates on the screen.

"Here we are. Head towards the bank," she said.

"Yes ma'am," said Alex.

As the canoe slid up onto the shore she stepped onto the dry land and pulled the canoe up out of the water. Alex stepped out then too. They let the air out of it, then folded up the canoe and the camouflage cover into rectangular blocks and put them both in the remaining holdall. The surrounding land beyond the river bank had been repurposed into agricultural land.

In the distance they could see the roof of a large old farmhouse.

“That the place?” said Alex.

“Yes,” she said.

The first signs of dawn were showing on the horizon as they approached the house. It was silent and all in darkness. As they got closer they could see T.J.’s plane, Phantom Lightening twenty feet from the farmhouse. They walked up onto the porch and knocked on the front door. For a moment the house was still and then an upstairs light came on. They could hear muffled voices of excitement and people moving through the house. The windows around the door lit up, a key twisted in the lock and the door opened. There in the doorway stood a tall, Caucasian man whose skin had been tanned by many years of working in the fields. His head was bald and he had a short trimmed beard. He wore a white shirt and a tattered dressing gown over the top of it. He stood and stared at them both for a moment, then his facial expression lightened up.

“Andra! I was not expecting you so soon!” he said.

“Hi Roger! I know. I expected that we would be later than this too. How are you, old friend?” she said with a big smile.

He stepped out onto the porch and gave her a strong hug.

“I am very good, thank you. It’s been so long,” he said.

He looked at Alex

"Alex, my boy. How are you? I shouldn't call you a boy. You're a full grown man now. Do you even remember me?" he said.

Alex was a bit taken aback by Roger's exuberance and then he realised who this man was.

"Yes, Yes, I do. I remember you. I remember Sarah, Andrew and Mary too. I remember staying at your house when I was young. I didn't know we were coming to see you," Alex said excitedly.

He stepped forward and they hugged.

"I know. I thought it would be a nice surprise for you. I told you we would meet Roger and Sarah again someday. When you said our target was in Peru I saw it as a chance for you all to meet up again," said Andra.

"Thank you, Andra. This is fantastic," said Alex.

"Yes. This is really great," said Roger.

"I'm happy you are both pleased to meet up again. I just wish it was under better circumstances," she said.

"Don't worry about it. I can't imagine it'll be any worse than some of the last few times we were in each other's company. We have guns here but hopefully we won't have to use them," said Roger with a smile. "Sarah will be wanting to see you too. Come in, come in, I know we have a lot to talk about," he continued as he let them in and showed them into a big sitting room with comfy chairs, a radio and magazines sat on a table, and a huge amount of books stacked on shelves that lined the room. "Your pilot T.J. is here too, he is asleep at the moment so it's probably best to let him sleep."

"Yes, it's for the best for now. We have a long flight back later today," said Andra.

As they were talking the upstairs floorboards squeaked, then the stairs, and Sarah stepped into the room

"Alex!" she screamed and came running over to him. She hugged him and squeezed him tight. "Oh, my boy. I honestly never thought I would see you again," she said.

"Me neither," he said and had to stoop a little so she could get her arm around his neck.

"How are Andrew and Mary?" said Alex.

"Oh yes. They are very well. Andrew is in the Army in England, we see him about twice a year, and Mary is a teacher in a local school here teaching English and French. She lives in the city with her husband our little granddaughter, Rita," said Sarah.

"Aww, that's wonderful. Good to know they are doing well," said Andra.

"I can't wait to tell them you've been here. We'll have to take a photo of us all together. So, how are you doing now?" said Sarah.

"You know. Ridding the world of vampires, one parasite at a time," said Alex.

"That is why we are here," said Andra. "Alex's special skills have got a lot more special recently. We have been here using those skills to eliminate a head vampire," said Andra.

"Ah yes. You're real bad news for the vampires, aren't you? You're something of a nemesis to them," said Roger.

"I am. Over the past week I've killed three of the Children of the Blood," said Alex.

"Oh shit, seriously? They are their hierarchy, aren't they? Which ones?" said Sarah.

"Saltorg, Gilad, and we just got Jorshean," said Alex.

"How the hell do you get close to them? I was posted in East Germany after the wall fell. We lost lots of good lads to Dienco and his soldiers in the two years I was there. He's an absolute monster. How do you do it?" said Roger.

"I bite them. I have an enzyme in my saliva that makes them solidify and die. Then I eat them" said Alex.

"You eat them, man. That really is turning the tables on them," said Roger.

"How do you get near them long enough to bite them? I mean, usually, if you get close it's them doing the biting," said Sarah.

"I think the easiest way to explain it is probably to show you," said Alex.

Three minutes later Roger and Sarah stood with their jaws hanging open in awe of what they had just seen.

"Well, if I was a vampire I'd be shitting myself right now," said Sarah.

"That was incredible. You are the most amazing and possibly the most terrifying thing I have ever seen. I'm glad you're on our side," said Roger.

"Thank you," said Alex with a smile.

"Can you do me a favour?" said Roger.

"Name it," said Alex.

"When you get your hand on Dienco tell him, this is for the 'Desert Rats' of the 7th armoured brigade, right before you bite him," said Roger.

"I will do," said Alex.

"So, umm. Are you all set to go as soon as possible or can you stay for breakfast first?" Sarah said.

"Breakfast sounds awesome. Can I have a shower first though?" said Alex.

"Of course you can," said Sarah. "Our home is your home."

"Yes, breakfast will be very much appreciated. We have a long flight ahead of us," said Andra.

"I was hoping you would say that. I wouldn't want to be flying on an empty stomach," said T.J. as he walked into the room rubbing the sleep from his eyes.

"Yes, I wouldn't let you fly on an empty stomach," said Andra.

"Come on. Let's go and find you something to eat," said Sarah.

She showed them to the kitchen.

"Go now, sit," said Sarah as she showed them all to the table. She and Roger then went into the kitchen and made a cooked breakfast.

"It's just past 5.00. I need to do a few pre-flight checks which will take us to around six. What time do you want to take off?" said T.J.

"Have your breakfast first. Do the checks at six and we can take off at seven. That will get us back to California for around 14.00. We don't have much to take on board. I lost most of my equipment. I got thrown out of my canoe on the river," said Andra.

"Oh, man. That sucks. Are you ok," said T.J.

"I'm fine. I have replacements for all the things I lost. It's just equipment," said Andra.

"As long as the personnel are ok that is what matters," said T.J.

"How are you? Did you sleep well?" said Andra.

"I'm good thank you, ma'am. Sarah and Roger are wonderful hosts. Their house is lovely and the room was amazing," he said.

"That's good to hear," she said.

Sarah and Roger came over with plates filled with food and pots of hot coffee. Alex walked into the room clean and showered and dressed in some clothes Roger had put out for him. They all sat down and talked while they ate. They spoke about the past twenty years and things that had happened. At six T.J. went to perform the pre-flight checks and Andra went for a shower.

Alex sat and talked with Roger and Sarah for a while longer. He told them about the fallout from Project Nomad, Vincent's life, and his death. At half six Andra came back.

"Are you ready to go?" she said.

"Yes, is T.J. ready?" he said.

"Nearly. He's done most of his checks. Take off is at seven," she said.

"I'm sorry we can't stay for longer but the mission is still ongoing," he said to Roger and Sarah.

"Don't worry, we understand. We are both ex-military," said Roger.

"Yes, of course," said Alex.

T.J. walked into the house.

"Hello, I've completed the checks. We can go when you are ready, ma'am," he said.

"Ok, it has been great to see you again," said Andra.

"The pleasure was all ours. If you ever have the time to come out this way again you are always welcome here," said Sarah.

They all hugged, shook hands and said their goodbyes. Andra, Alex and T.J. then boarded the plane. They waved from the cargo hold ramp as the plane taxied onto the runway and then took their seats. Roger and Sarah waved as the plane sped along and became airborne just before 7.00.

## Chapter 23.

The plane journey was long and gave them the chance to get some sleep. There was a sudden thud from the fuselage of the plane. The scream of tearing metal filled the space as long, black claws pierced the hull, then tore a hole in the side of the plane. The pressure inside dropped and anything that wasn't strapped down was sucked out of the hole. The hulking figure of Ruhsarr stepped into the plane and strode over to Alex baring his fanged teeth and growling. Andra just sat and did nothing as the scale covered, winged giant reached out a hand and gripped Alex around the throat. He screamed and fought as his nemesis tore off his seat belt and pulled him from his chair. He then lifted him to his face and opened his mouth. Inside was the decapitated head of Vincent. Alex woke with a jump and flailed his arms and legs in an attempt the fight off his enemy. Andra looked over the top of her book at him.

"You ok?" she said.

"Huh? Yes, I'm ok thanks. Just had a weird dream," he said.

"You look startled," she said.

"I was dreaming that Ruhsarr was attacking me," said Alex as he shielded his eyes with a forearm.

"Don't worry about him for now. I believe in you," said Andra as she reached out and placed a hand on his knee.

"I can't help it. I keep thinking, what if I can't beat him? What if I fight him and he gets the better of me? He's been alive for five thousand years. He might know techniques that I can't counter," he said.

"I'm not going to lie to you, he will be the toughest opponent you have ever faced. Yes, he is strong, but so are you. Believe in yourself. Beating your opponent in your mind is half the battle," she said.

"I've not even thought about how I'm going to attack him yet," said Alex as he rubbed his hands over his face.

"Isn't that how we go into every fight though? Who could have prepared for Saltorg having subdermal armour, Gilad being able to teleport, or that Jorshean would have not wanted to fight? All fights are improvisation and using our knowledge of martial arts to interpret our opposition's next move before they perform it. For now focus on Dienco. He will be an extremely tough opponent. He was a formidable warrior king before he even became a vampire. You can think about Ruhsarr when Dienco is dead," she said.

"Thank you, ma'am. How do you always know the right thing to say?"

"With age comes wisdom," she said with a straight face. "And during that time you have the chance to do a lot of stupid shit that you can learn from."

They both cracked up laughing.

They sat and talked for a while until T.J. shouted from the cockpit.

"Ma'am, Mr Donaldson is on the radio. He wants

to speak to you, says it's urgent."
It was one of the only times Alex had ever seen her look panicked as she ran to the cockpit. He followed close behind, curious to know what was going on.

"What's wrong?" he called after her.

"I've learnt many years ago if a member of the Donaldson family says something is urgent it's more than urgent," she said.

In the cockpit, T.J. handed her the radio handset. She looked at her watch. Its digital face showed 10.30. She clicked the button on its side and almost spat the words.

"This is Andra speaking, come back."

"Hello, Andra. This is Henry speaking, over."

"I'm listening. Go ahead, over." She said.

"There has been a development at a base in Newcastle, over," said Henry.

"What kind of development, over," she said.

"We've lost contact with them. The Glasgow base sent us a message saying Newcastle had sent out a distress signal, and have since gone dark. As of yet, the reason is unclear but we have to suspect it isn't a drill. All lines of communication are down. There has been no radio contact, no emails, and no phone calls coming out of the base. Nothing in the way of electrical communications either. No mobile communications, not even on a personal level either. Even social media has been silent, over," said Henry.

"Oh shit. This is bad Henry, this is really bad...over," she said.

"What are we going to do? We've been trying to

contact you for the last hour, over," he said

"The rainforest must have blocked the radio signal. Alex lost his radio in a fight with an anaconda and I lost mine early this morning in a canoeing accident. This is the first time your signal has got through to us, over," she said.

"Oh gosh, it sounds like you had a troublesome time. What are we going to do? Over," he said.

"We're in the air over Costa Rica on our way to you," she said.

She moved the mic from her mouth and spoke to T.J.

"Do we have enough charge to fly to England?"

"Yes, ma'am. Heck, we could make it halfway across Russia if we change direction now," he said.

She moved the mic back to her mouth.

"We'll change direction now. Round up my unit and put them onto a plane to Newcastle A.S.A.P. Contact the bases in Glasgow, Edinburgh, Carlisle, Manchester, Leeds and York. Tell them to rendezvous outside the Newcastle base but await my further instruction. It's going to take us at least another twelve hours to get there. No one goes in without my say so, over," she said.

"Yes, ma'am. I'll get a pilot and plane readied for take-off right away. I've already informed your unit of the situation. They are here awaiting your orders and are packed for the flight. Leave the rest to me. Over and out," he said

"Thank you, Henry," she said.

Andra passed the headset back to T.J. and he put it back on over his cap.

"Ma'am. I've been flying for over three hours now. If we are going to England I'm going to need to land somewhere to take a break at some point," he said.

"Don't worry. Alex and I can fly for a while. Just let us know when you're feeling tired. Alex can do five hours and I'll take the last five. If that's ok with you?" she said.

"Yes, Ma'am. That'll be just fine by me," he said.

*

Henry picked up the phone on his desk, keyed in the number for an internal line to the hanger and pressed it to his ear.

"Hello Sir," said the female voice deep with a southern drawl.

"Diane, I need a plane for six passengers going to Newcastle in England. I need it A.S.A.P. It's a matter of great urgency," said Henry.

"I have just what you need, sir. A Citation CJ3 small passenger jet. I just finished testing the electric engines myself yesterday. It will get your friends to England without a problem. We can have her fully charged, checked out and ready to fly within the hour, sir," she said.

"Thank you, Diane. That's perfect. See you in an hour," he said.

"See you then sir," she said.

Henry hung up the phone and went to inform the soldiers of their departure time.

An hour later they had taken their seats on the plane

and it took off without an issue.

It was now half twelve. Andra, Alex, and T.J. were over Puerto Rico. Alex tapped T.J. on the shoulder.

"You want me to take the wheel for a while?" he said.

"What have you flown?" said T.J.

"I've flown little four manner and had a few flights in a hurricane replica," said Alex.

"Ok. Exactly the same principle. This old girl will respond to any input of the controls but she ain't got the manoeuvrability of those little planes. However she is fast in a straight line, that's about the only difference. We ain't got no autopilot like some planes but luckily you've not learned to be reliant on that. Just maintain your altitude and keep your speed steady and we'll be just fine," said T.J.

"Ok. Go and get some shut eye," said Alex.

"No aerobatics, you hear," said T.J. with a warm grin.

"Yes, I hear you, sir," said Alex in a laugh.

"Carry on pilot," said T.J., patted him on the shoulder and walked away and out of the cockpit.

Alex flew for five hours before Andra came to take over from him.

"How's it going?" she said as she entered to cockpit.

"Good, really good. We're about halfway over the North Atlantic. I lost track of time there," he said as he looked up at her.

"Ready for me to take the wheel?" she said.

"Yes, ma'am," he said.

She sat down in the seat next to him, clipped in her seatbelt and placed her hands on the wheel. Alex unclipped his belt and stood up.

"Have fun. Not much to see at the moment, just a whole lot of ocean," he said.

"I will," she said.

Alex stepped out of the cockpit and into the cargo hold.

The rest of the flight went without a hitch.

## Chapter 24.

By 22.00. GMT the plane was approaching Newcastle.

"T.J. We're coming towards Newcastle. We're about twenty minutes away from the airfield," she shouted into the cargo hold.

T.J. and Alex looked from their cards.

"We'll pick this up later," said T.J. in an irritated tone.

"I'll still be winning," said Alex with a cheeky grin.

"Thought you didn't know how to play Rummy." Said T.J.

"I didn't. I did warn you I'm a quick learner though," said Alex.

"Whatever," said T.J.

"Why did that sound like fuck off?" said Alex.

"Practice," said T.J. with a grin as he walked to the cockpit.

"Hello ma'am?" he said.

"I need you to radio my private airfield, Northlands, and tell them we are coming in to land," said Andra.

"Yes, Ma'am," he said.

He moved the mic up to his mouth.

"Air traffic control for Northlands, this is Phantom Lightening. We need permission to land, over," he said.

"Phantom Lightening, this is Northlands. This is a private airfield, you need clearance to land here." said the air traffic control operative.

"One moment," said T.J. and passed the headset to Andra. "They said we need clearance."

"Hello Northlands, this is Lieutenant Colonel Andra Hudson, we have clearance. We need to land and we need to land now. It's a matter of utmost urgency," said Andra into the handset.

"Yes, Ma'am. You have permission to land as soon as you are ready," said the air traffic control operative.

She passed the headset back to T.J.

"Bring her in pilot," she said.

"With pleasure, Lieutenant Colonel," he said and looked up at her with a smile.

She put her hand on his shoulder and gave it a reaffirming squeeze. She walked into the cargo hold, sat down and clicked her seatbelt shut and Alex followed suit. The plane descended and touched down five minutes later.

"Come on you two. There's no time to lose," she said as soon as the plane was still.

"Ma'am, I have to park the plane and stay here to keep an eye on her," said T.J. as he stood in the cockpit doorway.

"What? Why?" she turned and stared at him.

"Mr Donaldson's orders ma'am," he said.

"Ok, I'm sure he has his reasons," she said with a frown.

"Come on soldier, let's go," she said to Alex.

"Ma'am," he said.

He slid the cocking lever of the M60 forward and passed it to her. They stepped out of the plane and set off running across the airfield at high speed.

"It's only five minutes away. We'll use to rooftops," she said.

"Ok, lead the way," he said.

Soon they were leaping from rooftop to rooftop and travelling across the city. They stopped on a rooftop across the road from a large group of warehouses.

"This is the place," she said.

They heard a lot of activity coming from the courtyard between the buildings. They approached the rooftop edge of the building and Andra put up her hand to stop Alex. In the large loading area of the central warehouse they were met by the sight of four hundred soldiers. All S.O.V.E.U. all awaiting their arrival.

"Wow. I wasn't expecting this many," said Alex.

"There aren't a lot of us S.O.V.E.U. but I can rally the troops when I need to," said Andra.

The building the soldiers were positioned in front of had the entire front door punched out. The reinforced concrete walls that surrounded it were blackened and smoke damaged. She stepped forward, dropped off the edge, landed on her feet and carried on walking without a single ripple in her composure. Alex stepped off the edge and landed but in a less elegant way. Both his fists hit the ground either side of his left knee and his right foot. The soldiers noticed them as they approached. Alex saluted them silently and they saluted in return. White and Mc'Ready approached them and stopped infront of them.

"Ma'am, Alex It's great to have you back. When did you land?" said White.

"Five minutes ago. We just ran here from Northlands Airfield," said Andra.

"You ran? Wow, well actually, that sounds kinda normal for you," he said.

"Did you all get here safe? What's happened here? Henry didn't tell me much," she said.

"The Glasgow base got a distress signal from this base. A unit had been on night patrol. They returned just before sunrise and found the base like this with the door breached. They went inside using their lowlight goggles and were attacked by something big. They engaged the target but it killed two of them. With the batteries on their goggles running low, the remaining soldiers were forced to retreat. That's when they contacted the commanding officer of the Glasgow base, she contacted Mr Donaldson, and he contacted you. They stayed and put up a restriction zone and kept watch over the base. The thing that attacked them was moving around in there all day. We suspect it left at sunset but they can't be sure. All our soldiers from the other bases you told Henry to contact got here within three hours. They have been here most of the day. We got here about two hours ago. Mc'Ready pulled up the blueprints and has been talking with the other commanding officers and thinking of possible infiltration plans. That brings you up to speed, ma'am," said White.

"Very well. Take me to the commanding officers, I need to talk to them. I want to get in there A.S.A.P." said Andra.

"Yes, Ma'am. This way," said White.

He walked her over to them while Alex talked to Mc'Ready and regaled her with stories about his mission in Peru.

"Excuse me, officers. Lieutenant Colonel Hudson is here and would appreciate your council," said White.

The officers stood to attention and saluted her and she saluted them.

"At ease, people. What plans have you come up with up to now?" said Andra

O'Brien, a tall woman with black hair tied back in a bun began to speak.

"We have whittled it down to three options. Firstly there is the option of sending in a couple of small teams with low light goggles to spot. When they give the all clear we move in the rest of the soldiers. It's risky for those going in but any move we make has its inherent risks. Second option is to all go in on mass. Safety in numbers but might get a bit crowded. The third option is to flood the entire facility with silver gas. We're all unsure of this one as it would make more work for us. We'd need respirators to go in there, and although it would eliminate the vampire threat, it might harm our soldiers who are still alive in there," she said.

Andra thought about these plans for a moment.

"They're all solid plans, O'Brien. I agree, the third option is the least safe. Option one get my vote on this. I'll go in with my attack team. We'll secure the first level and then move down to the second. How many of the Newcastle soldiers got out alive?" said Andra.

“Six of them, ma’am,” said Thomas.

“They know the layout of this base better than any of us, they stay on the surface and advise the next teams going in via radio. Alex will lead the next team. If anything gets past us the next team will hold them and we can contain them. O’Brien, Thomas and Edmund. You will each lead the subsequent teams of you and your soldiers. Hewson, Hendricks and Taylor, you stay out here with your soldiers. You’ll be our back up or our defence if anyone tries to attack the base and pin us all in down there. I want to get moving as soon as possible. Also, I’ll need another two soldiers to come with my team,” said Andra.

“Yes, Ma’am. Yates and Holt are the best soldiers I have. Yates is a fully trained electrician and Holt is a seasoned engineer. They have both done tours of Afghanistan and Iraq and have worked alongside each other for years. They’ll go with you into the base,” said Thomas.

“Good, that’ll make things easier. We stay in radio contact at all times. Go and give the soldiers orders. Ten minutes then we go,” said Andra.

“Yes Ma’am!” said the officers.

Andra gathered Alex, White, Davis, Mc’Ready, Hussain, Palmer and Hughes together.

“We have a plan put together. You are all coming with me.  We’re going in as a small spotting team. We’re taking an electrician, an engineer and another three soldiers in with us. We’ll have three units of soldiers staying outside. They’ll be our eyes and ears out here. Alex, you will lead the second group of soldiers into the base on my mark. You're my second in command now, I trust you to lead these soldiers in after us. If they get past us they will run right into you," she said.

"Yes, ma'am!" They all said.

Two soldiers walked over to them and saluted Andra. The soldier on the left spoke first.

"Sergeant Yates reporting for duty, ma'am."

She was a tall slim woman with a blonde, shaven head.

Then the soldier to her right spoke,

"Sergeant Holt reporting for duty, ma'am."

He was a short man with a stocky build and short grey hair. Both were in their late thirties.

"At ease soldiers," said Andra.

All the soldiers relaxed.

"Yates you're the electrician. Give me some quick background." Said Andra.

"Yes, Ma'am. I've been to Afghanistan and Iraq twice each. I was there trying to get power back to the cities and villages and maintaining allied bases. I was in the British army for twenty years now I'm part of the S.O.V.E.U." said Yates.

Andra looked her up and down.

"Good. When we get in there I need you to get the power back on. Can you work under pressure?" she said.

"That's when I'm at my best, ma'am," said Yates.

"Good to hear it," said Andra with a smile. "How about you Holt? Give me some insight."

"I was in Afghanistan three times then Iraq twice. Fixing and maintaining tanks, choppers and APVs.

Like corporeal Yates I too was in the army for twenty years, now I'm here," said Holt.

"We won't know what the damage is until we get down there. I may need you to fix blast doors, lifts and that sort of thing. Is there anything you have trouble fixing?" said Andra.

"If there is I haven't found it yet, ma'am," said Holt.

"Good," Andra said and smiled. "Ok, this is your brief: Yates, you're with Mc'Ready and White. Holt, you're with Davis and Hussain. Palmer and Hughes, you're with me. You stick with who you are assigned to. We move in slow and quiet. We have no idea what is going to be waiting for us down there. It could be an ambush or everyone in there could be dead. Alex go and brief your soldiers. The rest of you check and load your weapons and make sure your lowlight goggles have fresh batteries," she said.

There was a lot of movement as they checked their weapons and equipment.

"Rules of engagement, ma'am?" said Yates.

"Check your targets. I want absolutely no human collateral. If they're a vampire use whatever force necessary, guns, blades. Stomp their fucking head in if you need to. Let's move," said Andra.

"Yes ma'am," said Yates.

They all set off marching towards the door as Alex went to his post.

## Chapter 25.

Alex saluted O'Brien, Thomas and Edmund. They stood to attention and saluted him back.

"At ease Officers. I'm Alex Austin, Andra has just told me I'm her second in command. I'm going to lead the second group into the base on her command. I know this is the first time we have met but I don't want you to think I'm some young upstart who has pushed his way to the top. We need to work together as a team. There is a lot at stake and our actions will determine the outcome of the war," he noticed Thomas raising his hand. "Yes Thomas," he said.

Thomas was a big, barrel chested man, in his mid-fifties, with a bald head, a big grey moustache and constantly furrowed brow. He looked Alex right in the eye and he spoke in a highly educated manner.

"I think I speak on behalf of us all. Your reputation proceeds you. Word travels fast and we know of the battles you have fought, even before you gained your new abilities. Some of us have been waiting a long time for you to realise your potential. You have fought just as we have we have fought and we respect that. If Andra holds you in such high regard then we do too. Command us and we will follow you, sir," he said.
He and the other Officers stood to attention and saluted him. Alex stood to attention and saluted them back.

Andra and her team stood at the door of the base.

Despite the intense illumination from the floodlights the tunnel beyond the door was dark and ominous, like the mouth of some sleeping beast. She stepped forward into the dark and the team followed. They pulled down their lowlight goggles as the light dropped below their human field of vision. Everything they saw now was displayed in gradients of green. Andra saw everything with a blue hue to it.

The tunnel descended at a steady angle before turning to the right in a wide semicircle. An eerie silence and an unsettling sense of emptiness hung over the entire place.

"We've got blood splatter and bullet holes in the wall here, ma'am," said Hughes as he walked along the left side of the tunnel.

"Over here too, ma'am," said Davis from the right.

"No bodies?" said Andra.

"No ma'am," said all the soldiers.

"Ok. Keep your eyes peeled," said Andra.

They reached the bottom of the ramp and the tunnel opened out into a garage that was half the size of a football pitch. The walls were reinforced grey concrete, painted white. There were around thirty cars on this floor. Some were filled with bullet holes, some were flipped over and a few were torn open like tin cans.

"We've entered the garage," said Andra into her radio.

"Ma'am, the main electricity junction box is over to your left in a utility room," said one of the

Newcastle base soldiers.

"Thank you," she said. She then spoke to her team. "Yates and Mc'Ready, get the power back on. Stay in contact and watch each other's backs," she said.

"Yes, ma'am," they said.

The two of them split off from the group and approached the utility room. As Yates reached for the handle he noticed it was broken. She reached out and placed her hand on the door.

"On three. One…two...three."

She gave it a push and the door swung open. They both pointed their guns into the green darkness. Sparks hissed from torn wires in the junction box. They walked in and checked the room and ceiling. It was all clear. Yates propped her gun against the wall next to the junction box and rubbed her hands back and forth over her shaven head.

"Ah shit, what a mess. What a fucking mess," she said.

"This is bad," said Mc'Ready.

"Yep, it's gonna take a while but it's nothing we can't handle," said Yates.

She pressed the button on her radio.

"Andra this is Yates. The junction box is a mess. It's gonna take about half an hour to fix, over."

"Copy that. Work as fast as you can, over," said Andra.

"Yes, Ma'am. Over and out," said Yates.

She and Mc'Ready set to work switching off all breakers and repairing all the torn wires.

Andra and the others continued on into the base.

They swept the remainder of the garage and found more evidence of a firefight, discarded weapons and blood, but still no bodies. There were two ordinary lifts and a large maintenance lift, but with the electricity still out none were working.

"Looks like we're taking the stairs," said Andra.

"Yeah, I never liked elevators anyway," said Davis, her voice filled with sarcasm.

They descended to the next level, which was engineering, and began to sweep through it. There were mechanics bays filled with stripped down engines and partially repaired equipment. Everything remained as it had been when the attack happened.

"The attackers moved at an alarming rate. These weren't just your average vampires. Some of the soldiers here didn't ever get time to put up a fight. You can see from the blood splatter here, ma'am," said Hughes as he examined blood on a car's wing. Andra looked at the long sweeping streaks.

"You're right, Hughes. Some of their guns haven't even been fired," she said and showed him a magazine full of unspent bullets.

They moved across the floor checking every room, every cupboard and every work bay. They were nearly done and were looking for stairs or a lift. All they found was one blast door that was shut tight and jammed.

"Ma'am, there are no stairs to the next level. They must be behind this one door," said Davis.

"It's an attack door. If the base is attacked this door can be closed to turn the lower levels into a life preserve until help arrives," said Andra. "I had put plans in place to have these fitted to every base by the end of the year. This was the first one fitted three weeks ago."

"We have to open it now. They might still be alive down there," said Davis.

"We'll have to wait until Yates and Mc'Ready have the electric back on," said Andra.

Just as she ended the sentence her radio crackled.

"Andra, this is Yates. I think we're done up here. Just need to throw the breakers."

"Ok, do it," said Andra.

There was a moment of silence and then a buzz and all the strip lighting flickered momentarily and then came on. Some of them blew but the rest held out.

"Well done, good job," said Andra.

"Just get us a pint sometime," Yates said.

"Will do, now get your butts down here," she said. "Mr Holt, the door, please."

"Yes, ma'am," he said.

He opened his toolbox and got to work.

After twenty minutes of hammering an arm back into shape and prying debris from the opening mechanism he pressed the button next to the door marked 'Open'. There was a thud and some movement but nothing more. He looked at it with a puzzled expression for a second. The huge piston arm just sat there unmoved. Then he realised the problem.

"Ma'am, it's hydraulic. The brake is jammed in the on position. If I cut the brake fluid pipe it with allow it to be released. However, doing that could compromise the ability to reseal the door after. I just feel that I need your permission," he said.

"Yes, Holt, you have my permission," said Andra.

"Thank you, ma'am," he said.

He used a torque wrench to unbolt a panel on the door and lifted it away. Inside there was a series of pipes and wires. He took hold of one of the pipes and pulled it out a little then slipped the blade of a utility knife behind the pipe and sliced it. Highly pressurised, oily brake fluid squirted from the tube for a few seconds and then slowed to a trickle. There was a creaking sound as the brakes began to release their grip.

"Now, if I could have a little assistance," said Holt.

He took a crowbar, wedged it between the door and the wall and pulled. The others helped out using knives, claws and even fingers to pry at the door. It was Thick and heavy and took some doing but on the second attempt the door lurched open. A gust of air was sucked into the lower levels. They all heaved it open and pushed it back away until it retracted into its purpose built alcove. The doorway led to a descending flight of stairs.

"Let's get down there. This could still be a rescue mission," said Andra.

They reached the bottom of this flight and were stood in a stairwell. To their left another flight of stairs continued down. A sign above these read 'SCIENTIFIC RESEARCH' with an arrow that pointed down. Ahead of them stood a set of double doors. The sign above these read 'INFIRMARY'.

"We're at the infirmary," said Andra into her radio.

"Copy ma'am. Each floor is about the size of a football field. If there are casualties they will be in there," said the soldier.

"Copy that. We're going in, over," said Andra.

They walked through the double doors and above them were signs pointing to examination rooms, emergency rooms, ICU, wards, recovery rooms and the morgue.

"Mc'Ready, Yates, and White to the right. Holt, Davis, and Hussain to the left. Palmer, Hughes you're with me."

They all separated and began searching the floor. Davis, Holt and Hussain entered the infirmary. They walked through and bullet holes littered the walls, beds had been thrown over and the mattresses had been torn to shreds. Equipment had been smashed and thrown against walls. Partition windows were broken and doors had been torn off their hinges. More disturbingly, every desktop, every wall, all the floors, and even the ceiling were covered in blood.

"Ma'am, we're in the infirmary and making our way into the recovery room. It looks like a fucking tornado passed through here," said White into his radio.

"A tornado of blood by the looks of it," said Mc'Ready.

"Let me guess, no bodies, right?" said Andra.

"Not a single one, ma'am," said Mc'Ready.

"Ok, keep searching," said Andra.

"Yes Ma'am," said Mc'Ready.

Andra, Palmer and Hughes searched through the Emergency room and the examination rooms and only found more blood and destruction.

Davis, Hussain, and Holt were in ICU. It was a scene of similar devastation. They found a door marked 'MORGUE'.

"Fuck, do we have to?" said Holt.

"Unfortunately, yes. Let's just get it done," said Hussain and opened the door.

They walked in and the chilled air hit them and then the smell of decay.

"Ah, fuck," said Holt.

"I guess the cooling system went off with the electric," said Davis.

She and Holt both gagged on the malodorous air.

"Hoo-wee, that's a funk," said Hussain.

There were three banks of body freezers. They approached a bank each and began opening them. When all the doors had been opened they all looked at each other with confused expressions.

"This is getting weird," said Davis.

"I'm freaked out," said Holt.

"Me too," said Hussain as she clicked her radio. "Ma'am, we, erm…shits getting weird. We're in the morgue, and there are no bodies here. The one place you'd expect bodies, and there are no bodies."

"That is weird. Ok, get out of there. We'll meet back at the stairs," said Andra. "Mc'Ready, Yates, White that includes you."

Five minutes later they were all back together at the stairs.

"This is Andra. Alex, are you there?"
"Yes Ma'am," he said.
"We haven't found anything yet. We are moving down to the third floor. Move your team in," she said.
"Yes Ma'am," he said and turned to his team. "Here we go. Remember, just because the first team hasn't found anything doesn't mean we can relax. Keep your ears and eyes open. Vampires are sneaky fuckers, don't even give them an inch."
"Yes sir," they said and began their descent into the tunnel.

At the same time, Andra and her team were descending the flight of stairs into the scientific research floor. This floor, like the first two, was the size of a football pitch. It looked open plan with thick strengthening pillars about once every fifteen feet. It had, however, been separated by shatterproof glass partitions. These had been destroyed and now covered the entire floor in a layer of tiny glass squares. Along with these was an inch of water from the sprinkler system that had been triggered by a fire in the laboratory area. This gave the effect that the whole floor was moving as they trudged through it. Every piece of equipment had been smashed or broken. Bullet holes were concentrated around the door hole through which they had just entered the room but were also littered sporadically across the walls. Their random pattern showed the soldiers and doctors were shooting at the attackers but weren't fast enough to keep them in their sights.

Blood spatter gave away the areas where people had been killed, but again, there were no bodies. As they got nearer to the lifts there were large amounts of blood splattered across every surface. There were also deep grooves everywhere that showed a bladed weapon had been used with ferocious intent.

"Looks like whoever was here was a fan of swords like yourself, ma'am," said Palmer.

"Not swords, these are the marks left by a battle axe," said Andra as she ran a finger over one of the deep grooves in a wall. "I know whose handy work this is. He's old like me, but a vampire. Big and strong but not much of a brain in his big thick skull."

"You think this is the work of Dienco?" said Palmer.

"I don't think, I know. I've seen the carnage he leaves in his wake before. No finesse, just brute force and vampiric speed," she said.

Despite searching the floor from top to bottom they didn't find a single body.

"Ok, let's move on," said Andra.

She walked to the lifts and pressed the button between them. The sound of gears and cables moving emanated from above them. Red LED displays above each lift showed that they were all on the top floor and coming down. As they reached the third floor the doors shunted a little and then slid open. Andra and the others watched them, weapons ready. The walls of the two average sized lifts were covered with blood, viscera, and bullet holes. The large maintenance lift was clean as a whistle and in perfect working order.

"I'm, er, I'm gonna choose that one," said White.

"Me too," said Hughes.

"Good idea," said Andra.

Palmer got in last and pressed the button for the fourth floor. The doors closed and the lift descended. When the doors opened they were on the mess hall floor. The wall around the lifts was riddled with bullet holes. Three quarters of the room's floor space was open plan again with strengthening pillars. There were broken chairs and the splintered remains of tables everywhere. Some had been piled up as makeshift barriers but axe marks in the floor a trail of bullet holes made it possible to follow the trail the vampires had cut through the room. They all split up to search the room.

Holt, Davis, and Hussain stayed in the main room. Andra, Hughes and Palmer went to search the toilets. Mc'Ready, White and Yates made their way into the kitchen. They walked around the room switching off hobs with pans that had boiled dry and ovens that seeped smoke. Pans, utensils and cutlery were strewn across the floor.

"Ma'am, there is nothing here in the kitchen, just more blood and destruction. Still no survivors or bodies," said Mc'Ready into her radio.

"Nothing here either except blood and broken pipes. We're going to have to switch the water off. It's literally squirting out of the walls. Meet us at the lifts, we'll go down to the next level," said Andra.

"Yes, ma'am," said Mc'Ready.

"Hey, there's someone moving around in here," said Yates.

She lifted the latch and pulled the handle of the walk-in pantry door. It was struck from the other side by a tremendous force and swung open so fast that Yates didn't have time to move. She was hit by the door and crushed against the wall behind it, killing her instantly. Her blood splattered out across the wall, floor, and ceiling. An enraged vampire shot out of the pantry and grabbed White by the neck. Its flesh was burning off and regenerating at the same time. There were no features that could distinguish its gender of who it had been. White pushed his gun against its chest and let off a few rounds but the vampire didn't even flinch. It wrapped its arm around his neck in a headlock and dug its fingers under the base of his skull.

"Oh, fuck you!" White screamed.

The vampire pulled, and tore his head off his neck, then cast it aside. It lifted his body and bit deeply into the stump of his neck. His vertebrate crunched under the immense power of its jaws. It pulled away and swallowed down the slab of flesh and hungrily lapped at the blood that gushed from the wound.

"Contact!" Mc'Ready screamed into her radio as she raised her gun.

She shot at the monster but the wounds healed the instant to bullets passed through it. It threw White's headless corpse aside and ran at Mc'Ready.

Andra was running as fast as she could. She could hear Mc'Ready's voice screaming into her ear through the radio and echoing from the kitchen into the cavernous room of the mess hall. Despite all her speed she was too late. As she reached to door she saw the vampire holding Mc'Ready above its head. With a monstrous display of strength it tore her friend in two at the waist. Its tongue lapped wildly at the blood and viscera that showered down over it from her bisected torso. Andra ran and swung her sword at the blood soaked fiend too fast for any vampire to dodge but this thing dropped the now dead Mc'Ready and moved. It was so fast that even she could barely hit it. When she did it healed and grew back limbs so rapidly it was as if she hadn't even injured it. Hughes, Palmer, Hussain Davis and Holt stepped through the doorway and fired a hail of bullets. The majority hit their mark but nothing more than a slight direction to this vampire.

"Alex! Alex! I need you now. I need you right fucking now!" screamed Andra.

Alex was moving towards the stairs on the second floor when Andra's screams came over the radio.

"Andra? I'm on my way," he said.

He turned to his team.

"Radio the surface. Tell them to move in. I'm going on ahead. Follow me as fast as you can. I'll see you down there," he said.

The soldiers did as they were ordered and Alex ran down the stairs deeper into the building. As he did he tore off his shirt and trousers. His shoulders pulled back then grew and moved back bigger and stronger. As he made his way down the levels his head and back transformed. He followed the sounds of gunfire he grew in size and build. His skin thickened and his scales flattened down into armour.

"Move!" he roared to the soldiers as he ran into the mess hall. The soldiers lowered their guns and hurriedly stepped aside as Alex skidded and grabbed the kitchen door frame. He bound into the room but the sight of Mc'Ready torn apart and dead stopped him like a brick wall. He stood still and stared at her. The breath caught in his chest and, for him, time seemed to stop.

The vampire was pushing Andra back towards the corner of the room. She was fighting with all her might but the vampire was relentless.

"Alex! Help me!" she screamed.

Her words cut through his stupor and something deep down inside him pulled tight, then snapped. A roar burst from his jaws, the vampire turned its attention away from Andra and looked at him. Alex ran at them. Andra thrust her sword through its chest but it slapped her aside. The vampire tried to jump over Alex but he hit it like a train, grabbed it around the chest and slammed in into the floor. He lifted it by the ankles and threw it into a wall. It hit with such force that when it fell to the floor an imprint of it remained in the wall. Alex strode over to the thing as it began to stand up. It was on broken but rapidly healing limbs and despite being unsteady was already trying to run. He ran after it, slapped his hand down on top of its head, and knocked it down to the floor. He bent down and it flipped itself over. It slashed at his face and arms with talon-like claws. He knelt on its legs and pounded his fist down into its head. Its arms continued to flail and slash at his flesh. He slammed his other fist into its head. He did this over and over in more rapid succession until his arms were a blur. Andra walked over to his huge mass. The vampire's head was paste but its limbs continued to flail around. He grabbed an arm and bit off. Its flesh began to hiss and crackle at the stump like burning oil.

"Alex," Andra said.

He stood up and stamped his foot down into its torso, crushing its ribs and pelvis repeatedly.

"Alex, slow down," she placed her hand on his huge arm. He spun his head and locked eyes with her. His expression was one of pure, unadulterated rage, but upon recognising her, he stopped his attack. The vampire burst into an intense and violent blue flame. Alex instinctively pushed Andra behind him to shield her from the heat. Seconds later the vampire was nothing more than ash. He turned to her,

"Are you ok?" he growled.

"Yes, thank you, but Mc'Ready and white. Alex, I'm so sorry. I ran as fast as I could but there was nothing I could do," she said as tears ran down her face.

He walked hesitantly over to Mc'Ready's body knowing there was nothing he could do, even with all his power, to change this. He fell to his knees and reached out his hand to touch her, but his whole body shook, and he sobbed. His body transformed back into his human form. He ran his hand over her cheek and brushed blood soaked hair from her face. He leaned down and put his hands on his knees. Tears fell onto his bare legs and he tried to compose himself. When he finally did he looked back up at Andra the tears still ran tracks down his face. Andra wiped the tears from her face.

"Oh shit, White. Davis, I'm so sorry," said Hussain.

"No," Davis. She ran to White's body, then turned and looked at his head. For a moment she stepped towards it with a hand stretched out towards his face. Then she bent over where she was and vomited. Hussain ran over and held her as she sobbed. Palmer held his hand to his mouth, Hughes wiped tears from his eyes and Holt stood solemnly with tears in his eyes and saluted Yates. A mix of anger and sadness ran through the group. They all shared a burning rage that would further their pursuit deeper into the base. Alex moved his lips to speak but then stopped for a moment as even speaking broke his composure.

"What the fuck was that thing?" he said.

"It's clear that Dienco and his spawn attacked the base. He and Ruhsarr are the last two vampires who can change a person into a vampire with one bite now the other children of the blood are gone. The arsehole set a trap for us. It looks like he bit a group of our soldiers and then shut them in the pantry. They changed but with no other source of blood they were driven mad by the hunger and attacked each other out of desperation. Drinking vampire

blood is a double edged sword for vampires. It makes them immeasurably strong, as we witnessed. That thing was still healing when it should have been dead. However, their increased abilities use up their bodily resources at an accelerated rate and, ultimately, destroys them," said Andra.
She passed him a package of clothes from her backpack. He took them from her and began to dress half-heartedly.

"This is what happened to Vincent. He said he had let another vampire bite him. That's why he burned up the way he did," he said.

"That would make sense. Dr. Fletcher said it was as if all the cells in his body had died all at once. With him being a first generation vampire must have made him more resilient to the effects. There should be more ash around here," she said.
She walked over, looked into the pantry and found it coated with a thick layer of ash.

"There must have been five or six soldiers locked in there; poor guys. Can someone find some tablecloths or something? We can't just leave our own like this," she said.
Hughes and Palmer searched the room and found some chef's uniforms. They all worked together to spread them out over the bodies. The blood soaked through them in a matter of seconds but it was the best they could do in the moment.
Alex paced back and forth swinging his arms and flexing his shoulders.

"I'm gonna kill Dienco. For Mc'Ready and for…I'm gonna fucking kill him!" he said.

Andra grabbed him by the shoulders and stopped his pacing. She then moved her hand to the sides of his head.

"I know, Alex, but right now I need you to focus," she said.

"Focus? How the fuck am I supposed to focus? He killed Mc'Ready!" he said in a growl.

"You need to focus your rage and use it at the right time. Right now I need you here and controlled. You understand?" she said.

Tears began to roll down his cheeks again and he nodded. She pulled him into a hug and held him there until he regained his composure.

"Ok. I'm ok," he said.

She let him go and squeezed his shoulders then turned and talked to the whole group.

"I'm sorry that this must seem unsympathetic but we must continue with the mission. It's not over yet and there might still be soldiers who need our help," she looked them all in the face one by one. "I know Mc'Ready, White and Yates were special to us all. They were more than just soldiers and colleagues. They were our friends and to some of us more than that, but we have to move on. We have a mission, and to leave that mission incomplete would mean our friends died in vain. Besides that, we are the fucking S.O.V.E.U. we don't just walk away. Take a moment, get your thoughts together, reload your weapons and then we find our soldiers," said Andra.

Alex walked over to Davis and put his arm across her shoulders. She stood up straight and looked him in the face. There were still tears in her eyes but her expression was stern and resolute. She saw that her expression was mirrored in his face. They both turned and looked at Andra.

"Yes, ma'am!" the all said in unison.

"I'm gonna get him. He'll pay for this," Alex whispered to Davis.

She nodded and forced a smile.

A few minutes later they were all up and ready to go.

"Sadly we are going to have to leave the bodies where they are just for now. But we will treat them with the respect they deserve when this is all over. Right now we're gonna take the lift down to the next level and continue the sweeps until we find out what the fuck is going on here," she said.

At that moment the commanding officers and the soldiers started to arrive.

O'Brien, Thomas and Edmund walked over to Andra noting the bloody sheets.

"What happened here? Are those our soldiers, ma'am?" said Thomas.

"We were attacked by a soldier who had been turned and then locked in a walk-in pantry with other bitten soldiers, forcing them to drink vampire blood. Sadly, we lost Mc'Ready, White, and Yates. Why are you down here?" said Andra.

"Alex sent an order for us to come move in. Do you want us to return to the surface?" said Thomas.

"No. We need to continue the mission. This level is clear, we need to keep on and search the lower levels. The base seems to be completely empty of soldiers and we need to know why. I need you to stay here with five platoons and secure the top three levels. Alex and I will take the sixth platoon and search the lower levels. Stay alert for my signal to follow us down deeper," said Andra.

She turned to her unit.

"We're going down to the next level and we're taking a platoon with us," she said.

O'Brien turned to the commanding officers.

"I'll take platoons one and two and head to level one."

"I'll take platoons there and four and head to the second floor," said Thomas.

"Got it. Platoon five make yourselves comfortable. This is our post until further notice!" said Edmund.

Andra looked at platoon six. "Right, people. It's your lucky day. With me, let's go, let's go," she said.

She marched them across the room to the lifts at the far end of the room. Her attack unit were already stood at the open doors and the maintenance lift. Andra, the attack unit, and the platoon stepped inside. The doors closed and they descended down to the next level. The doors opened they looked out into what had been office space. There were knocked over cubical walls, upturned desks, smashed monitors, and broken computers. Everything was destroyed, even the water cooler bottles had been pulled from their dispensers and emptied all over the carpet. Again there was blood splattered all over everything.

"Fuck," said Palmer. "This is crazy. If we go look

at the printer are we going to find a printout of some vampire's ass?"

"Wouldn't fucking surprise me, mate," he said Hughes grimly.

They checked every bit of this floor and found nothing more, so they continued down to the next floor. This was the armoury, weapon development department and shooting range. The wall here had been torn apart by thousands of bullets but the firefight had not been won by the humans.

"Gather round. We are going to split into groups of ten Then sweep the entire floor. Keep your eyes open for traps. Maintain radio contact and don't open any doors without my permission. Are we clear?" said Andra.

"Yes ma'am," said all the soldiers.

"Ok. Move out," she said.

They swept the floor. Davis Radioed Andra.

"Ma'am, we've found the weapons vault. It's been torn open and every weapon has been bent, snapped, or pulled to pieces. There's weapon parts everywhere we look over here," she said.

"Ok. Make your way back to the lifts. We'll see you there soon," said Andra.

"Yes ma'am," said Davis.

The rest of the groups searched the remainder of the floor. Still, they found no one alive or dead, just more blood and destruction.

"What the actual fuck is going on? Where the fuck is everyone?!" said Palmer.

"I don't know but this is starting to scare me," said Hussain.

They all made their way back to the lift and stepped inside. The door shut and as the lift descended. This time it took a little longer than it had between all the other floors. As the doors opened they stepped out and found they were stood in the midpoint of a long, wide hallway with high ceilings. There were three pairs of double doors along the wall facing them. A pair at both ends of the corridor and one pair across from the lifts. The soldiers all eyed it with some trepidation. Andra and her attack team approached the door. Hughes stepped forward and pushed open the door. A gush of air swooped into the corridor, bringing with it the thick stench of death and decay.

Saliva wet his lips and his stomach tried to turn but he held it down.

“Heeeeww,” he said.

Some of the soldiers turned their heads and gagged as the smell of putrification swirled around them.

“Ok, soldiers, pull it together. Whatever is in here I’m sure we can deal with it,” said Andra as she stepped through the doors.

The words caught in her throat and she stopped in her tracks. What she saw filled her with horror and disgust.

Alex walked up beside her. They stood in a large sports and training hall with high ceilings. A stage stood three feet higher than the rest of the floor at one end of the room. Retractable seating stands were folded back against the other three walls. All the training equipment had been broken into scrap and lay in a pile on the stage. Above a crisscross reinforcement framework that spanned the entire room supported the ceiling. This was also the fixture point for all the lighting rigs. From this framework at a distance of five feet apart, hung by their necks with rope, and their hand tied behind were the soldiers and staff of the base. All one hundred and twenty five of them. Their feet swung five feet from the vinyl flooring. Some of them however were missing limbs, some were little more than a torso but every single one was there.

Andra stood with her mouth a gape.

"Oh...What the fuck on earth?" said Hughes as he moved towards Andra and Alex. "This is fucked up."

"I know, even by vampire standards it's fucked up," Andra whispered.

She looked at all the bodies and tears rolled down her face.

"Cut them down. We're not leaving our own like this. Cut them all down," she stopped and thought for a moment. "Check the ropes before you cut them though. We know now that Dienco has a fondness for traps."

She clicked her radio.

"O'Brien, we've found the missing soldiers. They're…They're, all dead. Over," she said.

"All of them?"…over," said O'Brien.

"Yes, every fucking one of them. We need your help, over," said Andra with a sigh.

"Yes ma'am. We're on our way, over and out," said O'Brien.

The platoon were ushered into the room. They

showed a range of emotions upon seeing the bodies. Some gasped in shock, others gagged, some bowed their heads, and others looked on with stoic expressions. They all worked together to bring the bodies down. Soon all the soldiers from the upper floors were in the training room.

After an hour Thomas walked over to Andra with a grim look on his face.

"Excuse me, Ma'am," he said.

"Yes, Thomas," she said as she was helping Hughes lower a body to the floor.

"I've been cutting the ropes from the necks of the soldiers. I'm too old to be climbing up the ladder, and well, I've er...I've noticed something disturbing. Some of the bodies were obviously dead when they were hung up but if you look around the noose on this body," he said, examining the neck of the body they had just laid down on the floor. "Here around the neck. There are no rope burns and no evidence of a sudden tightening of the rope, also the neck isn't broken."

Andra looked at the body for a second. Inspecting the wounds caused by the noose.

"You mean they were hauled up?" she said.

"That's what it looks like, Ma'am. The ones who survived the initial attack died slow deaths," he said.

"That's barbaric. This is just brutality for the sake of it. Even Dienco has never been this merciless," said Andra.

"Looks to me like he's sending a message. I hope I can be there when Alex kicks his ass," said Davis from close

"Yes, it does. Davis, gather my attack group and Alex. We need to make a plan. Thomas, tell the soldiers to continue cutting down the soldiers," she said.

A moment later Hussain walked over to Andra.

"Ma'am. We found Fletcher. There is a note attached to him. It's addressed to you specifically, ma'am," she said.

Andra looked at Hussain who had an uneasy expression on her face. She stood up from the body she had laid down.

"A note? What does it say?" she said.

"I think you better come and see it for yourself, ma'am," said Hussain.

"Ok. Lead the way," said Andra.

Hussain then led her to the far end of the room. Sat tied to a chair was the long limbed form of Fletcher. He was shirtless and his right arm dangled loose. The skin of the wrist and hand was ripped and covered with dried blood. He had worked it free from the zip tie that had held his arm to the chair. His phone was held loosely in his fingers. Blood had pooled and congealed around his now lifeless body. A large piece of paper was pinned to his chest with his own combat knife. Written on it in black marker were the words:

"You kill ours, we kill yours. Your husband is most displeased with you 'Andra'. Your little monster will die."

Andra looked at the words and felt a sensation like the ground was dropping out from beneath her. She had the sense that everyone was looking at her.

"Ah, shit," she said.

"Ma'am? You told us your husband died," said Davis.

"Why is your name in inverted commas?" said Palmer.

"I can explain, but please, don't let Alex see this," said Andra.

"Alex has already seen it," said Alex from behind her.

She closed her eyes tightly and mouthed the word: 'shit'. She turned around, opened her eyes and looked at him.

"Who is your husband? You told me he died. You said Ruhsarr killed him," said Alex.

"My husband is dead! Ruhsarr did kill him. There was nothing left of him after he changed. There was nothing left of my husband in those cold, hard eyes. I looked deep into them right before he attacked me. There was only that…thing," she said.

"Are you saying your husband is a vampire? Why not just tell us?" he said.

"No, Alex. No, he's not a vampire, not exactly. My husband tried to chase a dragon off our land. The dragon bit my husband causing him to transform. He then attacked me and transformed me into, this," said Andra holding out her hands.

"Andra, you told me Ruhsarr attacked you," said Alex.

"He did. Ruhsarr was my husband," she said sheepishly and lowered her eyes. "When he was human he was my husband. He was a great and generous man who was kind and sweet. That thing he became, that monster, is not the man I married," said Andra.

"I can't believe this. How can you have kept this from us?!" said Alex.

"Do you think this is easy for me? Do you think I like having this round my neck?!" she said.

"I trusted you, we all trusted you. You can't just keep things like that from people who rely on you," said Alex.

"And what would you have done? If I had told you, how many of you would have joined me? 'Hey come and help me kill this monster that has hurt you all in some way. Oh Yeah, by the way, I'm its wife'. You would have all said fuck that!" she said.

"That thing and the things it made killed my entire family! You could have at least had the decency to tell me the truth," said Alex.

"Alex, everyone here has a reason to be here. Did you think that I was any different?!" she said.

"I thought that he had turned you into what you are today. I didn't realise you had once been on his side," said Alex.

"I was never on that thing's side. I was married to the man, not the monster! Why the fuck do you think he attacked me?! I had attacked him first. I had slit open his belly and was covered in his blood. I was trying to kill him when he overpowered me. He tore my jaw off! He left me for dead!" she said.

"Why were you trying to kill him if he's your husband?" he said.

"Because I would rather he be dead as man, than

alive as a monster who still thinks it's my husband!" tears of both anger and sadness fell to her cheeks and zigzagged down her face between the scales. "My husband died thousands of years ago! That thing likes to use that to torture me by pretending it's still him!"

Alex backed down a little but then came back at her.

"Right well, we need to go for Dienco, now. Strike while the iron's hot. We can't just let him get away with all this," he said and gestured to the dead soldiers.

"No. We need to formulate a plan. All this proves is that they know we're coming. This is bait. They want you to go in hard. Remember what I taught you about using your anger but not letting it control you. I've tried to kill Ruhsarr twice before. I failed on both occasions and now he's stronger than he's ever been," she said.

"We need to do something!" said Alex.

"We will. We will, but we need to approach it calmly and have a plan in place. If you go rushing in and making rash decisions you could be walking right into their trap," said Andra.

"So, we just sit on our arses and let them get away with it?" he said.

"Alex, look around you. We're not sitting on our arses. We're reeling from an attack. All the S.O.V.E.U. we have here are all we have right now. We've just lost Mc'Ready, White and Yates and all these one hundred and twenty five soldiers. They have just put a huge dent in our forces and made it look easy. We need to plan our next move very carefully. We can't go into a fight with Dienco half cocked," she said and approached him.

"Ok, ok. Whatever," he said as he looked left and right avoiding her eyes.

"Hey! You show me the respect you owe me! I don't care how big or strong you are or what has happened to you today or in the past. I'm still your superior!" she said.

He looked her in the eyes.

"I'm sorry, ma'am. I apologise. I didn't mean to be rude. I just...I just need to get some air," he said.

He turned and walked away.

Andra turned to Palmer.

"My name is in inverted commas because I changed it in the hope that Ruhsarr would not be able to find me. The name my parents gave me was Theda. I didn't mean to mislead or betray you. All that I did, all I have ever done has been for the safety of the S.O.V.E.U. Is that understood?" she said.

"Yes, ma'am," said Palmer.

The rest of the group followed suit.

"Good. Now help me. We need to examine Fletcher's body," she said.

## Chapter 26.

A wall clock showed that it was 1.00. as Alex walked past all the other soldiers and made his way out of the building. He walked out of the front door avoiding as many people as possible. His mind raced as he formulated a plan of action.

'How can she think I can't handle this? Of all the soldiers here I'm the only one who can handle this. I have to do something, I have to do something right now,' He thought.

He used his speed to allude the soldiers, leapt up onto the roof, and disappeared into the night.

*

Andra, Palmer and Davis were examining Fletcher's body. His eyes were sunken and under the layers of dried blood his flesh was pale.

"He'd been dead roughly the same amount of time as the others," said Palmer.

"They tortured him. Look here, his toes are burned and broken," said Davis holding Fletcher's left foot.

"His legs are broken too, at the ankles, calves, knees and thighs," said Andra as she moved and examined his right leg.

She slipped the phone from his hand she saw the word 'watch' had been smeared across the screen in his blood. It was dried on and it was clear that he had written it with his thumb. There were three other thumbprints on the lower area of the screen.

She tried to turn it on but the battery was dead.

"Has anyone got a charger?" she called.

The word went out around the room and moments later she was handed a charger and promptly plugged the phone into a mains socket.

*

Alex ran across the rooftops of the city towards the airfield. He found Phantom Lightening and approached it. He could hear T.J. snoring inside. He walked around the plane and tried the door but found it was locked. He tried knocking twice but there was no answer. He put his hands on the fuselage and rocked the whole plane back and forth. He could hear movement and cursing coming inside. The door burst open and the look of fear on T.J. face was clear as day. He was about to jump when he noticed Alex stood below him. The look of fear turned to shock when he saw the young looking soldier.

"What the hell, Alex? I almost jumped on your head. You feel that quake? I didn't know y'all had quakes here," he spluttered.

"Quakes? It wasn't an earthquake, it was me. I tried knocking and you didn't wake up so I shook the plane," said Alex.

"You shook the plane! You crazy bastard, you scared the shit out of me!" said T.J.

"Sorry about that," said Alex. "I had to wake you somehow, I need your help."

T.J. took a few deep breaths and calmed himself.

"What do you need? Is it to do with the mission?" said T.J.

"No. This is a new mission. I have to go to Germany. Pass me your phone," said Alex.

T.J. handed his phone over. Alex took it, found the app and zoomed in on Germany. He zoomed in on the country the same way his vision had done. He could feel the connection he had made with Dienco and his fingers were drawn towards the west of the country, to a city named Trier, close to the border between Germany and Luxemburg. Then to an area northeast of Trier, to a large stone and brick fort. He showed T.J. the place on the screen and handed his phone back to him.

"Sure, I'll radio Andra and let her know we're going to set off," said T.J.

"No. That won't be necessary," said Alex and placed his hands on T.J.'s shoulders.

T.J. squinted his eyes in suspicion.

"What's going on Alex? Why does Andra not need to know?" said T.J.

"She's really busy at the base. So, I'm acting on her orders. Things are crazy are going on over there right now. We lost a lot of good people today. All the resident soldiers at the base are dead. Andra is pissed off, big time. Radioing her to confirm her orders will only piss her off more. You don't want to do that, man," said Alex.

"Ok, Ok. I'll take you. Come on, climb aboard," said T.J.

"Good man," said Alex.

He clapped T.J.'s shoulders and stepped onto the

plane. T.J. then made the preparations for take-off.

*

Andra held down the on/off button, after a few seconds the phone vibrated and lit up. The home screen showed a photo and Fletcher's two daughters. Andra looked at their faces. Sadness welled in her for a moment but then the hard stoicism fell back over her face. One of the three bloody thump prints on the screen was over the home button and another was over the camera button. She pressed the camera button and the screen showed her face. In the bottom left corner a circle showed the last picture he had taken was one of himself. She pressed the image and Fletcher's bruised and blood smeared face filled the screen. At the bottom was a triangular play symbol. She clicked play and the video began.

Blood oozed from Fletcher's mouth as he struggled for breath. He started to speak in laboured heaving gasps.

"This is a message…for Andra. I have managed to…engineer a weaponised …version of the pro…coagulant from Alex's saliva. Unfortunately, I only…managed to make sixty…hypodermic cartridges before…they attacked. They can be fired…from gas powered dart guns. I locked them in the…floor safe in the armoury. In the far right…corner of my office. You have to step…on the top cover panel…three times. It will slide away…to reveal a keypad. The code is…3725. All you need…is in there. I hope they help. I'm done…tell my wife…I love her."

The video ended. Andra had tears in her eyes.

"Follow me," she said sharply to her attack unit.

She led them to the lift, up to the armoury, and into what remained of Fletcher's office.

"What are we doing here, ma'am?" said Hughes.

"Did you not hear Fletcher's video?" said Davis.

"No, I was moving bodies," he said.

"Over here," said Andra and led them to the top right corner of the room. "Fletcher said to press down on this panel three times."

As she spoke she did as he had instructed. The floor tile lowered by an inch into the floor then slid aside, revealing the floor safe with a numerical keypad and a digital screen.

"Ok, that's pretty damn cool," said Hughes.

"Wait till you see what's inside it," she said.

She keyed in the code '3725' and the door opened upwards with a heavy electrical whine. Inside were six gun cases. Andra lifted them out and passed one to each of the soldiers. She lifted out the last one and opened it. Each case held high powered dart gun and two magazines with five darts in each.

"This is literally all we have of this weapon outside of Alex. We'll have to use them sparingly and with great accuracy," said Andra.

She looked at each one of her team.

"Where is Alex?" she said.

*

Phantom Lightning had been in the air and travelling over the North Sea for an hour. They hit another pocket of turbulence and the plane bobbed back and forth through the night air. Alex was thrown to his knees as he went around the cargo bay strapping down anything that was loose. He got to his feet and walked back towards the cockpit.

"That should do it. Everything out there is either strapped down or stuck to the fuselage with duct tape," he said.

"Thank you, Alex. I wouldn't want to lose anything in this crazy ass stunt," said T.J. as he shifted in his chair. "Look, Alex. Be Honest with me. Andra doesn't know we're heading out here, does she."

Alex looked down at his feet.

"No. Andra thinks we should plan the next step of this ongoing mission," he said.

"But you don't, right?" said T.J.

"I think we should hit them now and hit them hard. She thinks there might be a trap," said Alex.

"A trap? Who's going to catch you?" said T.J.

"Exactly, but she wants to do things by the book. The vampires don't do things by the book. They play by their own rules," said Alex.

"She may have a point though. She has been around a long time," said T.J.

"I know, but I'm sick of waiting around. Those fuckers have taken everything from me. My entire family and now the woman I love. I've had enough. This ends tonight," said Alex.

"Damn, you aren't playin' anymore are you?"

said T.J.
"No sir. No, I am not," said Alex.
T.J. slapped his hand onto Alex's shoulder and gave him a closed lipped half smile.
"I hope you know what you're doing," he said.
"I do. How long have we got?" he said.
"We're over The Netherlands. Another half an hour or so I'd say and we'll be over the western border of Germany."

*

Holt was the last to return after they had all been searching for Alex.
"Ma'am, we can't find him," he said.
"Where have you looked?" said Andra.
"We've looked everywhere. I can't find him. I've looked in on every level, in the kitchen, topside and even the khazis," said Holt
"He must be somewhere!" she said.
"I know Ma'am. We've had everyone looking for him but it's like he's just gone," said Holt.
"Where could he go? It's not like him to just wander off," she said.
"I wouldn't know Ma'am. I can't say I know him all that well," said Holt.
Andra stood and thought for a moment then a look of realisation grew on her face followed by an expression of terror. She had a sinking feeling in her stomach.
"Oh fuck," she whispered.
"What is it Ma'am?" said Holt.

"Oh fucking hell!" she yelled. "Has anyone checked the airfield?"

"No Ma'am. I didn't think to send anyone. I'll go now," said Hughes.

"No, I can get there quicker," she said.

"Why do you think he's gone there?" said Davis.

"I think the fucking idiot has taken the plane. He's going to fight Dienco by himself," said Andra.

"That's insane," said Hussain.

"Meet me there as soon as you can," said Andra. She ran up the stairs and out of the base. She ran so fast over she barely touched the rooftops on her way to the airfield.

The sky in the east was still dark. Another three hours and the sun would be rising. She stood where the plane had been placed with her hands on her hips shaking her head.

"Crazy fucker. Crazy fucking mother fucker," she said aloud.

*

As the plane flew over the German border and approached the city of Trier, T.J. looked over at Alex.

"Are you sure you're doing the right thing?" he said.

"Yes. I know I am," said Alex.

"Well, good luck to you and I'll be seeing you when all this is over," said T.J.

He extended his hand, Alex took hold of it and gave it a firm shake.

"Thanks, you too, man. The moment I jump out, you get the hell out of here. I don't know what type of defence system they have in this place," said Alex.

"In all honesty, I wasn't planning on hanging around," said T.J. with a laugh.

Alex laughed then stood up, put on his radio headset, and walked out of the cockpit. He closed the door as he stepped into the cargo bay.

"Two minutes to drop zone," T.J. said over the radio.

Alex put his parachute into the storage box, closed it, and took hold of the railing above his head.

"One minute," said T.J.

The cargo bay door began to open. The air swilled and pulled at Alex and his clothes but he held on tight to the rail. T.J. began the countdown.

"Thirty seconds......twenty…ten seconds...and five, four, three, two."

The door was fully open now and Alex sprinted towards the opening.

"The drop zone is green. Repeat. The drop zone is green," said T.J. barely audible over the roaring wind.

Alex leapt out into open air. The plane pulled up and he began free falling.

"I'm clear, repeat, I'm clear," he said into his headset.

He could see the cargo door beginning to close as the plane banked to the right.

"How's your descent?" said T.J. into the radio.

"All good," said Alex.

“Pull your chute at about thirteen thousand feet,” said T.J.

“I’ve not got a chute. You know when I said I’m going to hit ‘em hard, I meant it,” said Alex.

“Alex! What the fuck! You crazy son of a...” T.J.’s voice disappeared as Alex pulled off the headset and threw it. He got the fortress in his sights, and pointed himself at it head first. He tucked his arms in by his sides and squeezed his legs together. He began to fall faster and was reaching his terminal velocity. Soon he could feel Dienco and his children in the building beneath him, even at this height. He let the change come over him and felt his bones and muscles shudder and move inside him as he grew and shifted form.

*

Andra sat in the cockpit of the plane the rest of her team had flown to Newcastle in. While they were in the base the planes batteries had been charged to full capacity. It had taken half an hour to perform all the pre-flight checks before they took off. They had now been in the air now for just over half an hour. Holt, Davis, Hussain and Hughes were in the body of the plane and sleeping. Palmer walked in and sat next to her.

“How are we doing?” he said.

“Another forty-five minutes and we’ll be there,” she said.

“How are you?” he said.

“Pissed off. Pissed off is how I am. It’s

irresponsible of him to just go off like that. He needs to realise he's part of a team and under my command," she said.

"I understand. I'm sure he'll be ok. With all due respect, ma'am, you can never truly control someone like him. He's not a regular run of the mill soldier. He's a living weapon. How would you feel if someone tried to tell you what to do?" he said.

"Shut up," she said.

"Exactly." He chipped in before leaning over as far as he could in the chair so she couldn't reach him.

"Arsehole," she said quietly to him with a smile. "Yes, you have a point."

"You know it," he said. "Maybe this little slipping of the leash might teach him a lesson. You have to let him do his own thing from time to time. He's still a person."

"I know. He and Mc'Ready are going to…" her words trailed off and she looked over at Palmer as tears welled in her eyes.

"That is why he has gone. I think he has had enough. I wouldn't like to be Dienco right now," said Palmer.

"Me neither," said Andra.

*

Just outside of Trier city, inside the fortress, Dienco was celebrating with his children. The bodies of dead and broken humans lay strewn across the floor around them. More starving, pathetic looking humans were locked in small cages around the edges of the room.

"Shouldn't we be making preparation for that bitch and her little doggy?" said Sesire.

"Ha! There is no rush. If I know Andra she'll be planning their next move. We have a few days yet," said Dienco in a mocking tone. "We'll have a nice surprise waiting for them when they arrive, a very nice surprise."

He pulled his axe from where it was embedded in a wall and shook it in the air. He then swung it down into an oak table, where it embedded itself deep into the wood.

They all laughed.

"I need another drink," said Dienco as he opened another cage and dragged the bound and gagged man out of it.

On the roof a Blutesser soldier was doing his rounds. He watched the roads and smelt the air. He could sense something was coming but he couldn't figure out what it was or where it was coming from. He heard a faint whistling sound but thought nothing of it. It was similar to the sound of a plane descending but somehow different. Something passing through the air at high speed. Human ears couldn't have heard it but it was real. He ignored it for a while until he noticed it was getting louder. He looked up above him expecting to see a plane passing over. What he saw was the silhouette of something huge and curled up in a ball. The thought 'I should sound the alarm,' entered his mind but never went any further than a thought. He was obliterated by Alex who smashed through him and the roof he stood upon.

The roof gave way, collapsing into the floor below as Alex smashed through the floor and continued down through the next ten floors below it before his momentum completely dispersed. Screams of pain and alarm erupted throughout the building as shattered stone, splintered wood, and roof tiles fell inwards. The torn flesh and shattered bodies of vampires littered the debris. Alex uncurled and stood up. He flexed his neck and shoulders as debris fell onto and around him. Unaffected by the falling wreckage he looked up and at what remained of the fort above him. Vampires were standing up and trying to understand the devastation that had just ensued. Some of them had injuries that were beginning to heal. Others were slipping into death and as they burned up strange new air currents that moved through the building swirled their ash into little vortices. He strode through the rubble sensing Dienco's location and trying to figure out how to get to him.

The ancient vampire pushed up his huge body from the floor and stood up straight. He looked around and saw the destruction that had been inflicted on his fort. Anger and rage boiled inside him and was released as a roar from his huge lungs

"We are under attack! To battle! To battle!" he said.

He grabbed his enormous battle axe from where he had earlier driven it into the table and ran to the edge of the hole that had been punched through the floor.

"They are firing missiles at me?! They want war, they will have war!" he said.

He looked down into the crater and there five floors below him stood the gargantuan armoured frame of Alex looking back at him. For the first time in five millennia words eluded Dienco. Alex pointed a long clawed finger at him.

"Dienco! I am here for you!" he said.

"You did this? How did you throw yourself into my home?!" said Dienco.

"I jumped from a plane. Does your primitive mind understand what a plane is?" said Alex.

"Of course I know what a plane is, you disrespectful little shit. You're Alex I presume, Andra's pet. Go back to her and tell her the prophecy is a fairy tale. You have already failed by coming here," said Dienco.

"I am no pet, I am death to your bloodline. Your brother and sisters found that out. They didn't believe the prophecy either. Now they are part of it," said Alex.

A little smile played across the ancient vampire's face then he threw his head back and bellowed a hearty laugh.

"I have lived for over five thousand years. There is no one but Lord Ruhsarr himself who can outmatch me. Your little escapade to fulfil some idealised dream of a prophecy ends here, tonight. You are nothing more than Andra's little doggy. I'm going to send you back to her in a box," said

Dienco.

"Come down here and fight me. Or are you just as scared of me as Saltorg and Gilad were?" said Alex. Dienco took his sharpening stone from his pocket and ran it along the blade of his axe. He then fixed Alex with a stare as he returned it to his pocket.

"Death you say. I'm going to teach you all about death," he said.

He lined himself up with Alex, furrowed brow and he let out an almighty roar as he leapt from the edge of the hole. He swung the axe back over his head as he did so. He rapidly fell down through the hole. He then brought the axe down at Alex who quickly stepped aside. Dienco buried the head of the axe into the rubble. Alex then stepped towards Dienco in an attempt to kick him. The old vampire was nimble for his size and he grabbed Alex by the foot and flipped him onto his back. Before Alex realised what had happened Dienco was swinging the axe down towards him. He rolled to the left as the axe crashed its way through the rubble where his head had been. Dienco lifted the axe and swung it again. Alex pushed himself up from the ground with his arms and flipped over the axe as it parted the air under him. Dienco heaved it over his head and brought it down at Alex. This time though Alex blocked the blade by slamming his fist outwards against the flat side of the head. He punched Dienco square in the face. He felt the bones of Dienco's nose and jaws collapse beneath his fist with a sickening crunch. Dienco was knocked off his feet, thrown back and hit the ground hard. Alex tried to stomp on his chest but he rolled back and stood up wildly swinging his axe as his face reformed. Alex stepped back as the blade zipped past him, then ducked and ran under the axe. As it clattered across the scales of his back he rammed his shoulder into Dienco's stomach and kept on running. The two of them crashed into a brick wall and continued right through it. He continued running right through the room beyond, smashing desks, and scattering computers and other office equipment as they went. He forced Dienco's body right through a stone pillar and then through another wall. At that point he lost his footing and landed on top of Dienco. They slid across the floor of a room full of Blutesser soldiers. Alex opened his mouth in readiness to sink his teeth into the Dienco but the vampire pushed a hand under his jaw. Alex's head was pushed back and his mouth shut.

"Attack!" cried Dienco.

The troopers threw themselves at Alex, they rained down punches and kicks on him. Some of them were even trying to bite him. Then all of them grabbed hold of him wherever they could and began to pull. They were trying to drag him away from Dienco. He could feel himself beginning to move. They couldn't outmatch him in size and strength on their own but their numbers made up for what they lacked individually. They grabbed at his eyes and clawed at his face so he couldn't see. They were all over him. He felt hands reach into his mouth so he bit down hard. Bones shattered and crushed between his teeth. He could hear their screams as they fell away with their flesh solidifying. He stood up and thrashed his arms at them like a man swatting away flies. He tore apart the ones he caught. The others showed no decrease in the ferocity. Something solid hit him in the chest. He stumbled back and slammed his huge body against the wall. Soldiers cried out and fell away as the wall collapsed under his weight. Bricks showered down crushing them, but Alex stood up as the stone rained down around him. More soldiers ran and leapt at him and beyond them he saw Dienco coming at him readying his axe. Alex ran at him knocking soldiers aside like a bowling ball through pins. He blocked two downward swings from the axe and managed to grab the handle. The two huge warriors fought over the weapon each pulling in opposite directions. Alex then switched to pushing. Dienco lost his footing and Alex ran him into the wall behind him. The impact knocked the wind out of Dienco, Alex took the opportunity, grabbed him by the throat and slammed his head into the wall again. The wall crumbled and fell around them. The ceiling began to give way. Dienco put his foot on Alex's chest and pushed him away. His grip around Dienco's throat slipped and he fell back into the previous room. Wood and stone fell on him from the three floors above, burying him. Dienco smiled and then laughed. However, his amusement was short lived as the rubble began to move. Alex pushed up with his arms, chucks of stone and debris fell away as he stood up. He scooped up a handful of rubble and hurled it straight at Dienco's face. The vampire raised his hands to protect himself. The rubble hit him and Alex followed right behind it. They tumbled through the remains of the desks and computers. He grabbed Dienco by the beard and spun him around like a hammer then released his grip. Forty stones of vampire hurtled across the room, destroying everything in his path, before crashing through another wall. More soldiers flooded into the room through the hole he'd made in the wall. Dienco got to his feet feeling dazed. He stepped back through the hole. As he did he grabbed a handful of bricks and threw them in at the intruder. Alex tried batting them away but the soldiers were leaping and clambering all over him again. They tried to stab and cut him with knives and racked their claws across his flesh. Their efforts in honour of their Lord were in vain. He caught them and pulled them to limb from limb and smashed them into the floor with his fists. Dienco swung his axe at Alex's. The blade caught him in his left shoulder and the impact knocked him off his feet. He landed on his back and crushed more soldiers beneath his huge mass. He rolled and got to his feet then stepped aside as Dienco swung the axe down towards him. An unlucky soldier took the full impact of the blade and was split in two from skull to groin.

"Stand still you twat!" Roared Dienco.

Alex moved to attack when he was struck by something huge. He was sent sprawling across the floor. Tuhak charged into him grabbed Alex by the shoulders and lifted him with ease. He swung Alex around and threw him towards Dienco who was already swinging his axe. Alex hit the floor and rolled to Dienco's feet. The axe struck against the scales of Alex's back and the head shattered, shooting off splinters in all directions. Soldiers fell to the floor dead, their hearts had been pierced by shards of the weapon.

"No! My Axe!" cried Dienco.

Alex stood up and saw Tuhak charging at him. The vampire leapt at Alex but he spun and grabbed Tuhak in from the air and slammed him into the floor. It crumbled and shook and then gave way beneath them. The two of them fell through to the level below and landed in a corridor. Tuhak punched Alex's face repeatedly when they landed. He retaliated by smashing his elbow into Tuhak's head. The vampire managed to push himself to his feet and stumble around. Alex kicked his legs from underneath him. As Tuhak was flipped into the air Alex grabbed him by the foot, swung him at the wall of the corridor, and let go. The weight of Tuhak punched a hole in the wall. He crashed through the contents of the room beyond. A moment later he burst back into the corridor and hit Alex square in the chest. Alex held onto him and the two of them sprawled back and crashed through the wall behind them. As they fought on the floor Alex put a hand on either side of Tuhak's head and squeezed. There was a crack as his skull fractured. Alex opened his mouth and moved in for the bite. Tuhak struggled and put his hands on Alex's snout trying to keep himself as far from those teeth as he could. He was outmatched and despite his screams and struggles Alex leaned in and sunk his teeth into Tuhak's right shoulder. The vampire roared in pain as the pro-coagulant flowed into his blood and began to do its work. He struggled free leaving a chunk of muscle and bone in Alex's jaws. His right arm hung loose as he jumped up through the ceiling and landed on the floor on the level above. He looked down at his arm as it swung loose.

"Father," he whispered.

He stumbled forward as his flesh began to solidify. Dienco saw his son's eyes turn opaque. Before he could reach him Alex burst up through the floor and took hold of Tuhak's shambling frame.

"My son! What have you done to him?" cried Dienco.

Alex took another huge bite out of Tuhak's shoulder and the arm came away with it. Alex threw his head back, crunched the limb in his jaws, and swallowed it down whole.

"No! You fiend!" cried Dienco.

Alex bit into Tuhak's solidified head and the skull collapsed. Dienco ran towards them, jumped over the remains of his son and took hold of Alex's head.

"Let go of my boy!" he roared.

Alex threw Tuhak aside as he fell back. A wave of soldiers jumped on him and Dienco punched at his face. The hits were strong and heavy. Alex roared and thrashed his limbs around. He saw the tall, muscular form of Sesire. She swept the soldiers aside with her strong arms and grabbed his feet. He kicked out knocking her back then took Dienco by the hair and head butted him. He flipped himself up onto his feet and lunged at Sesire as she caught her balance. He caught her in the stomach with a flying shoulder charge. The impact sent her flying back and she crashed to the floor. Alex landed on her and pushed his knee into her chest. He raised his arm to punch her in the face when huge clawed hands grabbed him, threw him up through the ceiling and he landed on the floor above. Dienco burst up through the floor and landed next to him. Alex swung a fist in the vampire's direction but his arm was grabbed by Helden who smashed down from the level above. He gripped Alex's arm and twisted it. He roared and trashed around as his bones popped out of place. He threw his other fist at Helden and punched him in the face. The vampire fell back, reeling from the impact. As Alex's arm began to repair itself Dienco ran at him. Alex tried to block the attack but was sent tumbling across the floor by an almighty uppercut. He rolled, then flipped himself back onto his feet. He bared his teeth at Dienco as Helden swung a clawed hand at his head. Alex slammed his repaired arm down across the vampire's hand, grabbed him by the shoulders and spun him into a wall. They crashed through it and he hurled Helden across the room. Dienco ran in through the doorway, grabbed a block of stone from the wall and ran at Alex. He was inches away when Alex ducked and kicked his legs from under him. Dienco fell and bashed his head against the block as he hit the floor. Alex picked him up by the neck and lifted him off the floor. He opened his mouth and put his teeth on Dienco's face. Before he could bite down two hands broke through the floor, gripped his ankles and pulled him down. He lost his grip on Dienco as he fell to the floor below. It buckled under him and he fell through that floor too. He landed on the floor below and Sesire fell on him. She slashed her claws across his face, slicing his flesh. However, he healed almost instantly.

"You fucking cunt. You'll never kill my father, not while I'm around," she said.

She punched him in the face and gouged at his eyes. He blocked her next attacks and pushed her aside.

"You can fight me as hard as you like, but you can't stop me," He said as he got to his feet.

She leapt at him but he knocked her away with a strong swipe of his forearms. She crashed through tables and cabinets before she came to a stop fifteen feet away. Helden came crashing through the ceiling towards Alex but he quickly stepped aside and the vampire slammed both his fists into the floor. Sesire jumped on Alex's back, and dug her claws into his face, gouging out at his eyes, Helden stepped toward Alex and slashed open his stomach. His eyes and flesh healed almost as fast as they were damaged. He reached over his arms behind his head and grabbed for Sesire. The first few times she dodged his huge hands but then on the third attempt he got hold of her. She fought but it was no use. She was incredibly strong, but he was far stronger. He pulled her from his back and slammed her down head first onto Helden's head. The two vampires fell to the floor dazed. Alex took Helden by the arm and pulled him up. Helden threw punches at Alex with his free arm until he caught hold of that arm too.

"You're not going to make it out of here. We'll find a way to kill you," Growled Helden.

"No, I don't think you will," said Alex.

He pulled the vampire's arms in opposite directions. Helden screamed as his shoulders were yanked out of place. He continued to scream as the flesh of his left shoulder started to tear. Sinews and muscles tore as the arm ripped away. His knees buckled and swung limp from his right arm still in Alex's grip.

"Fuck!" Helden screamed in pain. "You fucking arsehole!"

Alex grabbed Helden by the back of the head and plunged his teeth into his face. As he pulled back most of Helden's face came away in his mouth. His body shook and his flesh and blood began to crystallise. Alex bit off more chunks and swallowed them down. Suddenly he was struck from behind. He fell forward and dropped what remained of Helden as he put his hands out. The wall couldn't support his weight and he crashed through it. He turned round and Sesire landed a two-footed drop kick squarely in his chest. He fell and landed on his back. Sesire jumped on his chest, screamed incoherently, and stomped on his face and broke his jaw. He caught her foot as she brought it down for another stamp and swung her like a rag doll and slammed her into the floor to his left. He then swung her up over him and she crashed against the floor to his right. He got to his feet still holding her by the foot. He swung her at a wall but Dienco crashed into him from his left, knocked him off his feet and Sesire slipped from his grasp. She hit the wall but not with as much force as Alex had intended. Dienco grasped hold of Alex around the waist, lifted him onto his shoulder and ran with him smashing him through wall after wall until they hit a solid outer wall. He pushed Alex against this wall, gripped him under his jaw and slammed his head against the wall. With every hit he roared a word.

"Stop! Killing! My! Children!"

Alex swung a balled up fist at Dienco's head that caught him under the chin. Dienco stumbled back and Alex grabbed him by the beard. He swung him around and threw him into the wall. Then took him by the neck and smashed his head into the wall. Stone blocks fell from the wall to the ground outside. Sesire landed on his back but he swung his elbow back and smashed her face. She fell from him, stumbled back and fell to the floor. He took Dienco by the head and moved along the wall smashing his head into it with every step. He continued this until there was a line of twenty holes along the wall. Alex lifted Dienco so they were face to face. He was a mess, his eyes were hanging out, his nose was crushed and his jaw was shattered. Alex bared his teeth to bite him again when Sesire jumped on his back. She put her hands into his mouth at the front, making sure they were in the gaps where his teeth didn't reach. She then put her knee at the base of his skull and pulled his head back. He couldn't believe he was so close and she was stopping him again. He let out a roar of anger that was so loud she had to resist putting her hands over her ears. He threw the barely conscious Dienco at the wall where he hit and slumped down to the floor. Alex shook his head violently trying to dislodge Sesire but she held on tight. He clawed at her but she moved to avoid his reach. He threw his head forward hard causing her to lose her grip and slide over his head. He jerked his snout upwards and buried his jaws into her thigh. She screamed as his teeth sliced through her muscles and bones. She landed in front of him and he bent down and roared in her face as her flesh began to crystallise. He grabbed her husk and threw her at the wall next to Dienco. Her body shattered on impact and there was a deep rumble as the whole building shook. The wall had already been weakened from Dienco's head being repeatedly smashed into it. This impact was all that was needed to loosen the few stones that held it together. The whole wall bowed out and then collapsed down on itself. Alex tried to drag Dienco away but the floors above them started to fall down onto each other. The whole building around this area concertinaed and began to fall. Dienco disappeared into the rubble as the building came down around them. Alex turned to run, steel beams screamed as they twisted and tore. Wood and stone fell like rain and he found himself tumbling down as the floors gave way beneath him. He was swallowed up by the debris, then he and everything fell for what felt like a long time. He landed heavily and tons of rubble landed on top of him. It built up layer after layer. He lay still and waited for it to stop. The world shook around him. Eventually, everything became silent. The screams of crushed and dying vampires made their way to him under the piles of stone, steel and wood.

He heard feet running around, individuals gathering together and orders being shouted. Rubble was being moved around by the vampires. Another sound then seeped down to him that forced him to move. It was the voice of Dienco, he was still alive.

"He must still be here. Find him. I want him. I want to make sure he's dead!" said the vampire.

Alex moved, forcing tons of rubble aside and dug his way upwards. He burst up from his rubble tomb sending stones and debris flying in every direction. Vampires were crushed under the huge lumps of stone that he threw off of himself.

Dienco ran at him, pulled a sword from its scabbard, and thrust it into him.

"Be silent!" he spat.

Alex looked down at himself and the roar died in his throat when he saw that it was stuck in his chest. He'd never been stabbed before. Anger bubbled up inside him and rage exploded into his muscles. Dienco tried to pull out the sword but Alex threw out a hand that knocked the vampire off his feet and across the rubble covered ground. He took hold of the sword by the handle and pulled it out of his chest. Soldiers ran at him but were sliced into chunks as he wielded the sword with ease. Dienco jumped up and dodged the blade as it sliced the air around him. This only served to spur on Alex's rage. Dienco caught his hand and tried to disarm him but Alex was too strong. They wrestled for the weapon until Alex took the blade with his other hand and snapped. Dienco looked on in shock.

"That blade was made for me over one thousand years ago!" he said.

But Alex was too incensed to talk. He threw the hilt aside, grabbed Dienco by the head, and drove the broken blade into his abdomen. As Dienco gasped Alex put both hands around his throat and ran at one of the two remaining fort walls. He smashed the vampire's head into the broken edge of the wall and ran through the entire length of it using Dienco's head as a battering ram. The building fell like dominos above them as they ploughed through the wall that supported it. The inner walls began to collapse and vampires scurried out like rats escaping a sinking ship. Dozens of them were crushed by the falling bricks and debris. Finally, Alex reached the end of the wall and ran out from it as it came down. Dienco's head resembled a mixture of mincemeat, jagged bones and brain matter. Even after this amount of damage Dienco was still alive, and his flesh and bones were already beginning to knit themselves back together. His arms twitched and the reforming jaw worked up and down. Finally, uninterrupted, Alex bit into these remains of the skull. Dienco jerked and twisted as he tried desperately to get away from the jaws. His body tried to resist the pro-coagulant but it was too late. He trashed a few final movements before his flesh hardened and crystallised. Alex tore into the husk as the building fell behind him and was completely raised to the ground. As he chomped and gulped down most of the huge body he felt thoughts and memories race into his mind. He winced and bent double as a long life shot through his mind.

He saw a young boy raised as a warrior. He felt the fear and exhilaration the boy felt in his first fight. Saw him battle against fully grown men and win at the age of sixteen. He saw him become the leader of his own settlement and tribe in his early 20s. He saw the warriors of this tribe make a journey to find the dragon slayer named Ruhsarr. He observed the final moments of Dienco's life as a man and his rebirth as a vampire at the hands of Ruhsarr. He felt the power of the dragon's blood rush through Dienco as he drank the liquid from his spooned hands. He saw this once respectable man gorge his thirst for blood from entire towns of people. Saw him destroy communities, then cities with blatant disregard for the lives he destroyed. All this devastation under the rule of Ruhsarr. Thousands of deaths and battles for thousands of years. Then he saw the warehouse he had been in just a few hours earlier. He saw Dienco and his spawn kill S.O.V.E.U. soldiers with smiles on their faces. This was fuel to the fire of Alex's rage. He saw what he had been seeking for so many years. Ruhsarr. The huge beast of a man was in a helicopter approaching what looked like a war zone. The dust and smoke bellowed from a fallen building. The rubble was piled up and there were burning bodies everywhere. He heard the unmistakable thump of the helicopter propellers.

He was pulled from the vision by the same sound and he could sense Ruhsarr was close by. He looked up and saw a helicopter approaching him. It was the exact same one from the vision. He bared his teeth and was about to launch himself at it when saw something zip towards him and hit him in the shoulder. He looked down and saw a large syringe digging into his flesh. At the moment the needle hit his skin four arms with hooked ends sprung over and buried themselves in his flesh. They had a screw mechanism where they met the syringe that pulled the needle tight against his skin. The needle itself was shaped like a thin drill bit. The screw mechanism in the arms began to turn as the needle spun and drilled a hole into his flesh. The liquid inside the syringe began to be injected into his body. Before it completed its task he grabbed it, tore it from his shoulder and threw it aside. He crouched down and launched himself at the helicopter and its occupants. As he got closer he could see a Blutesser soldier leaning out of the side door with what looked like a modified RPG launcher. There was an expulsion of gas from the rear of the gun and another syringe was shot at him. It hit him in the chest and began to drill into him. Another hit him a moment later, followed by another, and another. He swiped a clawed hand at the soldiers as he entered the helicopter but they jumped back. He landed where they had been stood but felt unsteady on his feet. He tore the empty syringes from his flesh. Stood right infront of him was Ruhsarr. His nemesis, the enemy he had sought for so long was right in front of him.

His nose was flat with long slit nostrils. The scales on his face were small, rough and covered in spines. Horns grew from the corners of his eyes, then around to the crown of his head. They were longer along the sides of his head and then reduced in length as they met at the crown. He was tall, muscular and covered from head to toe in the same spiny scales that covered his head. On his arms, legs, back and chest the scales were fused into plates. His wings were folded up against his back.

"I need him alive, but not awake and dangerous like this. Take him down!" said Ruhsarr.

More syringes were plunged into his flesh by soldiers he hadn't even noticed were right next to him. He knocked them aside and pulled out the syringes. He tried to go for Ruhsarr, but his legs were heavy, and he stumbled forwards. He was starting to feel dizzy and nauseous.

"You are determined to be a thorn in my side, aren't you," said Ruhsarr with a sigh.

He picked up a syringe, grabbed Alex by the back of his neck, and thrust it into his neck then held it there. Alex tried to push Ruhsarr away but he held on tight. So, Alex wrapped his arms around Ruhsarr's waist and stepped backward. Ruhsarr stumbled forward, pulled along by the increasingly unconscious weight of Alex. The two of them fell from the open door of the helicopter. Ruhsarr tried to open his wings but they were held to his body by Alex's arms. They rushed down towards the ground and landed with a heavy thud. Fortunately for Ruhsarr, he had kept the syringe held into Alex's neck and all the liquid had now been injected into him. Ruhsarr stood over Alex as his body jerked and twisted as the solution drained his strength and painfully changed him back to his human form.

"So, finally we meet. You are a formidable opponent. I would have liked to fight you but I need you for something bigger than the both of us. I suppose I need to thank you. I have been searching for you for the past three decades and sacrificed thousands of my soldiers to find you, even my own children. Now, here you are of your own accord," said Ruhsarr jovially.

"I'm going to kill you, you cunt," slurred Alex as he tried to sit up.

"How quaint," said Ruhsarr and pushed him back down to the ground with one finger.

Alex could no longer fight. The solution had done its work and he slipped into the comfortable dark of unconsciousness. Ruhsarr picked him up and jumped up from the ground, threw out his wings and flapped them once. He then pulled them back to his body just before he landed back in the helicopter. He lay Alex on the floor.

"Seefa, get him prepped. I don't want him to wake up until I need him. Message control, tell them to contact the attack teams in all countries. Tell them the bear is caged, it's time to initiate the Reclamation Protocol. Let's go, we have 24 hours,"

said Ruhsarr.
The pilot turned the helicopter around and flew away from the destroyed fortress.

## Chapter 27.

Fifteen minutes later a plane flew over the area where the fortress had stood.

"What am I supposed to be looking for?" said Palmer as he looked out of the window.

"There should be a building down there. A fortress with a brick tower. You should be able to see the lights from the windows," said Andra.

"No Ma'am. I can't see anything," said Palmer.

Andra looked out of the window and saw a huge dark gap in the lights of the outskirts of the city.

"What the fuck! My resources say that Dienco's headquarters are supposed to be right here," said Andra.

"I don't know what to tell you, ma'am," said Palmer.

"It's gone, the entire building has gone. There has been a fortress stood in that location for over one thousand years," he said.

Palmer squinted his eyes in thought for a moment.

"You think Alex has been here?" said Palmer.

"Damn right I do. It would be too strange a coincidence if he hadn't. I know a little airstrip close by. I'll set us down there and we'll go and have a look. Hopefully, the authorities haven't shown up yet.

*

A Hulington 20 was flying high over Washington DC. It was a similar design to the plane that had dropped the vampires on the Oxfordshire base but smaller and carried a maximum of twenty soldiers. The pilot clicked a button on his earpiece to answer a call on his radio.

"Kingdom to Hornet's nest," said the voice in his ear.

"This is Hornet's nest. Go ahead Kingdom," said the pilot.

"The king has caught the bear. Reclamation Protocol is go. I repeat Reclamation Protocol is go," said the voice.

"Thank you, Kingdom. The hornets are leaving the nest," said the pilot.

He clicked the earpiece and connected to all his passengers via their Bluetooth earpieces.

"Hornets, we have a green light. Two minutes to twenty thousand feet. Be ready on my mark," he said.

"Thank you, Nest," said Sergeant Errat. "You heard him. Two minutes and we help change the world. When drop keep the formation tight. Blane, no stunts. Be ready with the change guns. We want a clean entry."

"Yes sir," said the other nine members of his team.

They made the final checks on their equipment and stealth wingsuits. Two minutes later the pilot's voice spoke into their ears.

"Hornets, we're at twenty thousand feet, you are green," said the pilot.

"Here we go!" said Errat.

He pulled the release handle and all the individual

doors in the plane's hull slid open at once.

"Arrow formation!" he shouted as the air roared around them.

The soldiers quickly swarmed together and found their formation, then positioning their arms and legs to get optimum performance from their wingsuits they soared at high speed across the night sky.

*

Andra brought the plane down and made a bumpy landing along the old airstrip. It had not been used for many decades. The surface had become cracked by weather damage and the grass around it had grown wild and unkempt. At the end of the concrete strip sat an old fashioned but well maintained cargo plane. She instantly recognised it as Phantom Lightening. She taxied her plane up towards T.J.'s plane and brought it to a halt about twenty feet away. They all unfastened their safety belts and prepared to disembark. Andra opened the door and stepped out. A bullet zipped an inch over her head.

"T.J.?! What in all of fuck are you doing?!" she exclaimed.

He quickly stood up from where he was hiding with his hands held up. In one hand he held his gun up and the other hand was open.

"Sorry Ma'am. I didn't know it was you. We can't take any chances right now," he said sounding genuinely sorry.

She stormed towards him and he could tell by the way she strode across the concrete that she was angry.

"Come here, I want a word with you," she barked.

"Ma'am, I can explain," he said.

"You better start bloody explaining then. You can start with telling me why you are here. I want to know why you and Alex left without my permission. I want to know where Alex is and I want to know why you are shooting at me!?" she said.

T.J. wrung his hands nervously,

"I was sleeping in the plane when Alex woke me up and told me he needed to come here, to Germany," he said,

"Why did you act without my orders?" barked Andra.

"Ma'am, he said those were your orders. He said you were busy and didn't want to be disturbed further. He confessed after we had been in the air for about an hour that he was acting off his own back," said T.J.

"So what happened? Why did you not turn the plane around? Why are you here?" she said.

"Well, ma'am. I've been around a few years, not as many as you mind. But, in that time I have been in the presence of men who have, for whatever reason, been pushed beyond the brink. And, Alex, he's been pushed beyond the brink. I have seen what he is and what he can do. I wasn't about to tell him no. When we got over Trier he jumped out of the plane. It was only after he had exited the plane that he told me he had no chute. I then understood what he meant when he said he was gonna *hit 'em hard.* You see what he did to the building. I saw the thing fall, the noise was unbelievable. He told me to leave after he jumped out but I figured I'd stick around. Thought he might need a way out," he said.

"So, where is he now and why the fuck were you shooting at me?" she said.

"Begging you pardon Ma'am. I was getting to that. I decided to go and see what was happening. I didn't get too close as that fort was coming down all over the place. I saw Alex in his badass mode eating what looked like a body. Man, I almost threw up. When he was done this chopper that I'd never seen before flies over and they started shooting at him; hit him too. He jumped up into it while they were still shooting and disappears into the chopper. Then he falls back out fighting with, erm, fighting with this other big guy. From what I know about him it resembled Ruhsarr. Horns growin' out of his head and a pair of wings. I never been so frightened. I don't know what he did but Alex turned back human. Ruhsarr picked him up jumped back up to the chopper and they flew away. That's when I came back here and that's why I was shooting. I thought it might be him coming back for me. That's the truth, ma'am, I swear, "said T.J.

Andra could see the fear in T.J.'s eyes as he spoke. He had been a fighter pilot, he wasn't the type to scare easily. She eyed him up and down for a moment.

"Ok, I believe you. I'm still angry with you though," she said.

She turned to her team.

“We’re going to look at what’s left of the building,” she said.

Five minutes later Andra walked among the rubble of the fallen fortress. The police had evacuated all the local residents and had cordoned off the entire site. The bomb squad would soon be searching the area before letting the fire services in to search the rubble for survivors. She and her team only had a couple of minutes here at the most. They could see that the rubble was covered with ash. To the untrained eye it just looked like dust among the bricks, steel and stone, but they knew it was vampiric remains.

“Do you think the police will know what it is?” said Davis.

“No. They’ll just think that it’s ash and dust. They won’t even do any tests on it. Why would they? It’s not like they’ll be looking for vampire remains,” said Andra.

“Alex was definitely here. Who else could have done all this damage?” said Hughes.

They all looked at the site. Any remains of Dienco’s children had been crushed to powder and lost to the rubble and wreckage. Andra wrinkled her nose and sniffed the air.

“Ruhsarr was here, I can smell him. T.J. is telling the truth,” she said.

“How can you smell him over all this? All I can smell is dust and smoke,” said Hussain.

“I can smell at that. It’s there underneath it all. It’s too faint a scent for humans to detect, but he was here. We have to find out how he stopped Alex," said Andra.

She scanned the rubble as she walked and something caught her eye. She walked over and picked it up.

"What have you found?" said Hussain.

"It's some kind of modified syringe. It has a hollow drill bit instead of a needle. I've never seen anything like this," said Andra.

She pulled a strip of grey flesh from the drill needle.

"What the hell is that?" said Davis in disgust.

"It looks like Alex's flesh," said Andra.

"What?" said Hussain.

Andra held the drill tip to her finger and collected a drop of liquid. She smelt it and then touched it to the top of her tongue and quickly spat.

"Carfentanil. Fuck, this is the stuff they use to knock out elephants," said Andra.

"That's how Ruhsarr made Alex change back to his human form?" said Davis.

"It would seem so. This syringe must have drilled into his skin and administered the tranquiliser. We need to go. We have to find out where they took Alex," said Andra.

*

"Approaching the target," said Blane into the tiny radio mic built into his helmet.

"Copy that Blane. Things might get choppy. Single file," said Sergeant Errat.

They changed formation as they flew towards the target at high speed.
The guards who surrounded The White House and those inside had picked up on the group's radio chatter but couldn't locate the target on radar.

"Smoke," said Errat.

Three of the soldiers fired tear gas canisters on the lawn surrounding the building. They instantly began spewing out thick white smoke that burnt the eyes and throat of anyone who was unfortunate enough to be too close.

"Blane, it's a bit smoky, open a window," said Errat.

"Certainly," said Blane.

Strapped to Blane's chest was a weapon that resembled a quadruple barrelled harpoon gun. He pulled the trigger and the projectiles fired from it looked like mini javelins. They pierced each corner of a side window on the second floor of the presidential building and then exploded. The bulletproof glass was blown out of its frame and thrown into the room. Milliseconds later the soldiers flew into the building through the breached window. They landed one after the other then rolled before jumping up and positioning themselves against the wall on either side of the door against the wall.

"The silent alarm has been triggered, expect maximum resistance. Shoot as many as you can with the vamp darts. We need them on our side A.S.A.P. Kill anyone who doesn't begin to change immediately. The guards are highly trained but they are still only human. Keep that in mind. We take the president alive. That is non-negotiable," said Errat. He then opened the door and gave them the signal to go. The soldiers ran out into the corridor, scaling the walls and ceiling to give them the advantage.

The dart guns they all carried had been designed by Saltorg's scientists. They used electromagnetism to shoot steel pins coated in a small, highly concentrated amount of Ruhsarr's blood into their targets.

The security agents tried to defend the politicians and staff but right away it was a losing battle. Their bullets were almost useless against these attackers and when the darts hit them it didn't matter who they were. They fell to the floor writhing and foaming at the mouth as their DNA and bodies began to change.

The soldiers made their way down the corridors bursting into rooms and shooting everyone they found. They made no physical contact with the occupants of the building, they needed every humans they found to be turned into vampires. Eventually, they secured the top floors and descended a flight of stairs heading towards the Oval Office. The presidential guards back into the office and more tried to block the door. They were not fast enough for the vampires and by the time the call for automatic rifles got out the people who had been shot with pins were coming down the stairs in droves. The soldiers made short work of the remaining guards and flooded into the Oval Office. The guards inside were arranged in a circle around the president. He was stood in a lift that could carry him and two guards and they had begun to descend. The guards were panicking as they were emptying magazines into the soldiers and it made little to no difference. They on the other hand were dropping like flies. Bullets zipped and darts hissed until only the president and his two guards in the lift remained human. One of the soldiers lunged forward and grabbed the president by the lapels of his jacket. The guard in the cage to the president's left pushed the barrel of his gun against the soldier's head and pulled the trigger. The soldier fell to the floor with blood arching from the wound. A moment later the blood turned to ash and the soldier burned up. Seeing what he though was a human disintegrate before his eyes the guard screamed, "What the fuck are you?!"

He shot at the rest of the vampires in a trained fashion, but wasn't able to kill any more of them. Errat shot a pin into his screaming mouth. The guard coughed and reached into his mouth with fumbling fingers as he tried to dislodge it. He then slumped down into the cage and convulsed. The vampires grabbed the sides of the lift and pulled as hard as they could. It jerked and jumped as the electric engines whined as they tried to draw it downwards. Sparks then burst from it and there was the tortured sound of grinding gears. Something snapped and the lift stayed where it was. Errat opened the cage and grabbed the president. The remaining guard tried to stop him but was dragged from the lift and shot in the face with a dart. Errat spun the president around and ziptied his hands behind his back.

"You must be insane to think that taking me hostage will help your cause," said President Miller.

"You think of yourself too highly. You're just a little part of a great big picture," said Errat as he pushed the president down into a chair where two of the vampires zip tied his ankles to the chair's legs.

The guards were starting to stand up as newly turned vampires.

"What are our orders, sergeant?" said one of them.

"Defend the building. Kill anyone who tries to enter without my permission. Go and give these orders to everyone outside this room," said Errat. They opened the door to the horde of new vampires. They moved through the building giving the orders as they went. The clatter of assault rifles and the screams of injured humans drifted in from outside the building's front entrance.

"Hornets to Nest. Top Dog is in our possession," said Errat.

"Copy that, I'll pass the good news on to Kingdom," said the plane's pilot.

Errat then took a mobile phone from his pocket and held it up so President Miller could see the screen and tapped on a news app.

"Breaking news. The prime minister has been taken hostage in his office in Number Ten, Downing Street. The hostage takers are said to be heavily armed and wearing some kind of advanced body armour. Strangely, the other MPs and security agents present seem to be in some kind of alliance with the hostage takers. They are said to not be cooperating with the police or the armed forces," said the news reporter.

Errat clicked another link. A French news reporter was talking about the French president being taken hostage. He clicked another link. A Brazilian reporter was telling the same story about her president. Another link and a Swedish reporter was talking about their prime minister. Every link he clicked was another report of a premier politician being taken hostage and their government highjacked. Another link showed a reporter outside the White House. Beyond an army barricade.

"In scenes that are being mirrored around the world, President Miller has been taken hostage. The staff and security seem to be in alliance with the hostage takers. Police have now been replaced here by armed forces. Every attempt to gain entry has been thwarted by this mysterious group and the security staff. Reports are coming in that this could be the work of some shadowy organisation and they are the same organisation behind the other hostage situations across the globe," said the reporter.

"You see, Mr Miller. You're just another piece in the puzzle," said Errat.

*

Andra was in the passenger hold of her plane and heading back to England. They were all watching the same reports on a laptop as Palmer was upfront in the cockpit.

"What are we going to do, Ma'am?" said Davis.

"We're gonna go back to the base in Newcastle and wait for Ruhsarr to make his next move. Unfortunately, he's now holding all the cards, including our ace. I'm going to contact Henry and get his staff to put all their effort into searching the world for any clues as to where Ruhsarr might be holding Alex," said Andra.

"What then? I mean, this is Ruhsarr we're talking about. He's unopposed now. The entire vampire army is at his disposal." said Hughes.

"To be fair, they always were. None of the children of the blood would have dared say no to him. To answer your question though, here's what we're going to do. We're going to find him and wait for him to lower his guard, even for a moment. When he does we're going to get our Alex back, and then we're going to finish this once and for all," she said.

The unit all looked at her and saw the steely determination in her eyes. There was an unrelenting fire in her heart and they knew she would not stop until this was over. Any doubts they might have had about her past relationship with Ruhsarr were gone.

"Fuckin' A," said Davis.

"Fuckin' A," they all repeated.

*

Alex was in darkness. There was no up or down and he felt nothing. No sensation nor the passage of time. He had no limbs or body, his lips tingled then vanished. The tip of his nose and his eyebrow tingled. His eyes came into being and he became aware of a fluttering sensation. He also became aware of light like rays of sunlight through a pool of water. Outside of his drug induced stupor, his eyelids fluttered and opened ever so slightly as he roused to a level of semi-consciousness. His vision was blurred and watery but he began to recognise the grotesque collection of mismatched shapes as the face of Ruhsarr.

He was looking into Alex's face with his fiery orange and red eyes.

"How long will this take?" said Ruhsarr to someone Alex couldn't see.

"Just another ten minutes, sir," said a voice from somewhere nearby.

"Good, I can't have him breaking loose," said Ruhsarr.

Alex's vision cleared a little and he found he was able to move his eyes. He noticed the intravenous lines in his arms. His memory was coming back and he remembered the helicopter. He suddenly understood that they were flooding his body with drugs. He became aware of his limbs. They were there but too heavy to move. This gave him the sensation that he was floating. He could also feel something cold and solid holding his limbs in place. There was a loud crackling noise, it took him a few moment but he recognised it as a welding gun.

Ruhsarr stared at him and began to speak.

"I have waited an extremely long time for this moment and now everything is falling into place. You know the prophecy don't you Alex? Of course you do, you must have heard it many times. Apparently, you are going to destroy me. You probably began to believe it was true, yourself. You have been force fed this notion that you were the one who could destroy me. However, I have other plans, my own plans. You remember Gilad? Yes, well, she berated me when she found out that I had attacked your mother. Shouted at me, her Lord! Said that I had destroyed us all. She always was one for the dramatics. But I needed you. I became sick and tired of her, Jorshean, Saltorg and Dienco's interference. They were useful in the beginning. It was good having others to help build and control my army but, after five millennia, I have grown bored of their indolence. I wanted to push for more control over the human species before the rise of the Roman Empire but they all wanted to keep our existence a secret from the masses. It was those same Romans who later knocked me from my throne and pushed us further into the shadows. After their fall I began to regain some of my control but then the Genghis Khan attacked us. We were recovering from the Mongol decimation and rebuilding our numbers when the Templars and the Ottoman Empire drove me and my children into hiding once again. I kept on building my army under their noses and now I will rise to power once again for, I, am a living god. If you don't think so take a look at their depictions of the devil. He has horns, wings, scaly skin and the ability to transform all mankind. Remind you of anyone?" said Ruhsarr holding out his arms with a proud smirk on his face. "It's time for me to make my move, but I couldn't do it with my children holding me back. I could have destroyed them all myself, but I didn't want to make myself their enemy, and I didn't want them to think that it was I who had betrayed them. I simply decided to allow them to be released them from their vampire lives. I needed a nemesis, a common enemy, someone for us all to unite our forces against, and then there you were. It took thirty years of waiting for all the pieces to come together but that amount of time is merely a heartbeat to a true immortal like me. It also gave me time to plan this attack. I created you to destroy them and now, the time has come to destroy you."

Alex tried to move his arms but the restraints held him securely.

"Fuck. He's becoming resistant to the tranquiliser. Turn up the dosage," said Ruhsarr.

"But a higher dose could kill him. He's already on enough to kill four elephants," said a vampire from somewhere.

"He's damn near immortal. Drugs aren't going to kill him. Besides that, if he is already on that much what damage is a little more going to do," said Ruhsarr.

"Yes sir," said the vampire.

They turned up the dosage and Alex's eyelids closed again as he slipped back into the nothing of unconsciousness.

*

The sun had risen by the time the plane came down and landed on the airfield in Newcastle. Andra and the rest of the team departed the plane and made their way back to the base. The soldiers who had remained in the base were still busy repairing equipment, cleaning up the blood and destruction Dienco and his children had left in their wake, and fortifying the base as best they could with the supplies they had. All the bodies were now in body bags and had been placed in the cold storage unit on the medical level.

The soldiers at the main entrance let Andra and her team in. Andra made her way down to the Commanding Officer's personal office. She slumped down into the cushioned office chair and stared at the blank screen of the monitor. It was the only working computer left in the base. The deaths of Mc'Ready, White, Yates and all the soldiers who had been resident at this base had seriously knocked the morale of all the remaining members of the S.O.V.E.U. Though, it would take a lot more than this to break their spirit. Her determination would not let her give in. She nudged the mouse and the screen lit up. She logged in and made a video call to Henry. He answered the call and she saw his face appear in a box on the screen.

"Hello, my dear. What happened at the base?" said Henry.

"Dienco happened. He and his fucking children attacked the base. They killed everyone here including Fletcher, my head scientist," said Andra holding her head in her hands.

"Oh my! I am sorry to hear that. Words can't express the sadness I feel. All those good men and women lost," he said.

"I know. I wish there were something I could have done to save them. The fuckers laid a trap that got two of my team and another soldier killed. Mc'Ready, White, and a soldier named Yates who had just joined our team. Alex liked Mc'Ready and it pushed him over the edge. He went against my orders and had T.J. fly him to Germany where he avenged all their deaths. Dienco and his children have been eliminated. Despite that small victory we now have an even bigger problem on our hands," she said.

"I assume you are referring to the news? What a mess. These attacks must have been orchestrated right from the top of the vampire hierarchy. Straight from that bastard, Ruhsarr," he said.

"You're not alone in thinking that. I mean, who else could do this now? And that brings me to why I have contacted you. After Alex killed Dienco in his own base, Ruhsarr must have been waiting for him. He has managed to capture and sedate Alex and is now holding him somewhere. I need your help to find out where he has taken him. My hands are tied.

I can't do anything till I know his next move," she said.

"I'll start searching on Living World right away. What was his last known location?" he said.

"Just north of a city called Trier in Germany," she said.

"Ok. I'll start searching right away. I'll get everyone on this and contact you the moment we find something," he said.

"Thank you, Henry," she said.

"What else is on your mind, my dear?" he said.

"I'm just worried. What happens if Ruhsarr finds a way to kill Alex? I can't lose him not now, not after so many years. I know I shouldn't have put all the figurative eggs in one basket, but I have put all my hopes on him succeeding. What if he doesn't? Where will that leave us? I've made mistakes, I know I have, and too many people have died. I just expected things to be getting better for us," she said.

"We are at war, mistakes are made in wars. And yes, a lot of people have died but a lot more would have been killed if it wasn't for you. Don't worry, my dear, we are going to find him. Ruhsarr's days are numbered, you mark my words," he said.

"Thank you, Henry," she said.

"Now, you take your head out of your hands and work out what you are going to do when we find Alex. It'll be in your best interest to be ready to move at a moment's notice. I'll contact you as soon as we find anything. Ok?" he said.

"Yes, thank you so much, Henry. Speak to you soon," she said.

“Bye for now,” he said with a smile and ended the call.

She started searching through the intelligence files on the computer. Bringing up maps, and profiles on Ruhsarr, his known hideouts, and known locations. She was working out a plan in her mind of how to attack his most recently known hideout.

An hour passed and Henry called her back.

“I found the fortress. I’m going to stream you the footage,” he said.

An aerial image of the fortress filled Andra’s screen and Henry’s image was reduced to a small box in the corner. As the video began to play he commented on what they were watching.

“This was at a quarter past three, German time. You see here the plane flies over and Alex jumps out of the back. He then falls but doesn’t open his parachute. He begins to transform and impacts with the top of the fortress causing considerable damage as he punches through into the building itself,” he said.

“Bloody hell,” she said.

“Precisely. This isn’t the end though. The fight must have taken place inside. You see T.J. land the plane half a mile away. Here you can see the roof collapsing in and the windows exploding out. I assume that is due to the inner floors collapsing. Blocks begin to fall along North facing wall. Soon after that entire wall falls closely followed by one side of the building. You can see Alex and Dienco fighting while they are surrounded by vampires. Alex runs back into the building holding Dienco by the throat. You can see the East wall collapsing just before they emerge from the other side. Alex then really does eat Dienco. It's disgusting but quite fascinating too. A few minutes later this helicopter approaches the collapsed building. Alex jumps up at it and almost immediately flies back out brawling with Ruhsarr. Alex lies still on the floor while Ruhsarr stands over him, talking I assume. He then picks up Alex and flies back up and into the helicopter and they manoeuvre away. Now here is the part that matters, the helicopter heads east into the Hunsrück Mountains and lands at a remote base nestled in between three mountain peaks. It's still there now," he said

"That's great, Henry. Thank you, we'll get ready to deploy," she said.

"Don't be too eager. The base is almost inaccessible and highly defended. There is a lot of activity there. Helicopters are buzzing around it like flies. From what I can see I would assume they are getting ready to move again soon," he said.

"Hmm, ok, keep me informed. The second they step outside I want to know about it," she said.

"You will my dear," he said.

"Thank you," she said.

"I'll speak to you soon," he said.

Andra clicked an icon ending the call and the computer returned the display to the home screen. She looked out the office through the broken window, there were soldiers still clearing up destroyed equipment. There was still a lot of work to be done. She didn't know how much time they had until Ruhsarr made a move. She could feel her frustration rising. She had an idea. She searched the computer for Fletcher's files. There was nothing on this computer so she accessed the central hub. She used her password to access all of Fletcher's work. She clicked on the file named 'Alex Austin Physiology'. It opened and among the files within she found one named 'Procoagulant synth'. She smiled. If she could make more she could make more darts it might make attacking the vampires easier. She moved her mouse over it and clicked on the file. It opened but showed a message that read 'Damage File. Cannot be accessed.' She frowned and gritted her teeth. She stood up abruptly from the chair, sending it crashing into the wall.

"Fuck! For fuck sake! Fucking, cunting, shitting, fucking cunt!" she screamed. She grabbed the edge of the desk and was about to flip it but then realised how precious the computer that sat upon it now was. She released her grip and chose to turn instead and punch her fist through the wall. Davis approached her cautiously.

"Things are pretty crazy right now, huh?" she said.

"Things are pretty fucked," said Andra. "I have just found out Ruhsarr has Alex locked away in a mountainous base in Germany. The place is locked up tight so even if we could get there we can't sneak in. There isn't much we can do right now but wait for him to make his next move. As if that wasn't bad enough all the research Fletcher did to make the synthesised procoagulant has been destroyed so the darts we have are quite literally all we have."

"Ruhsarr and the vampires are planning something big, but as you said before, he's going to make a mistake at some point and when he does we'll hit him," said Davis.

"We don't have the resources or the manpower for a full scale assault. I don't want to mount an attack and find a deserted base by the time we get there," said Andra.

"Then we bide our time. If Henry is right and they move Alex somewhere more attainable we'll sneak in like we always have. We'll use the darts to get to Alex and free him, then let him do his thing," said Davis.

"Davis, you're a genius. We saw what he did to Dienco. We don't need to go in hard, we just need to get in. It seems we have the beginnings of a plan?"

"It seems so, ma'am," said Davis.

Andra felt her spirits lift a little but it was better than the anger she had felt a few moments before.

"We just have to wait. I feel I should sleep but even if I did I'm so bloody anxious right now even if I did try I don't think I'd be able to rest," said Andra.

"Well, ma'am, we could use your help out here clearing up if you want to lend a hand," said Davis.

"Of course," said Andra with a smile.

## Chapter 28.

The morning whiled away inside the mountain base in Germany. From the outside it looked like a two story high altitude army base. The next four floors were calved into the mountain behind it. Inside, soldiers in the armoury cleaned and checked their weapons and others trained in the huge assault course. In the mess hall captive humans were held in narrow cages with their arms held out to either side of them. These limbs were locked in structures that exposed only their forearms. The vampires only drank what they needed and never overfed as it would make them lethargic. In the basement a small number of humans at a time were released into the recreation of an urban setting. The vampires took turns to chase and attack this group to keep their hunting skills sharp. Outside, fifty soldiers stood guard. They were dressed from head to toe in UV protective clothing. Not a single area of skin was uncovered. No one and nothing was going to get near this base without being seen and Ruhsarr knew it.

He was sitting on a tall metal throne surrounded by human bodies he had drained. Some of them were beginning to turn into vampires. In one hand he held the end of a long iron chain. The other end was padlocked around the neck of a human woman. After seeing what he had done to the people lay around him she thrashed and pulled back against the chain. He slowly pulled her towards him, let her scuttle back a few feet, then pulled her forward again. He had been repeating this process for half an hour. He enjoyed the fear that seeped from her being.

A sergeant Hart walked into the large hall and stopped to Ruhsarr's right and stood to attention. He waited patiently until Ruhsarr looked at him.

"Yes, Hart," said Ruhsarr in an irate tone.

"Our, guest, is ready to be loaded onto the helicopter," said Hart.

"You don't appreciate him being here?" said Ruhsarr.

"No, sir. I'd prefer it if he was dead. He's..." Hart's words were cut by the woman's screams and cries as Ruhsarr pulled her close to him and bared his teeth, then opened his huge jaws.

"Surely you appreciate that he is extremely dangerous? Sir, must you play with your food like that?" he said.

Ruhsarr turned his attention away from the woman and fixed Hart with a cold, hard stare.

"Do you feel sympathy for this, thing?" he said.

"No sir. I just don't believe in prolonging her suffering," said Hart.

"If you feel so much for this human's suffering then kill it. Seeing as you consider yourself of a higher moral standing than I," said Ruhsarr in an angry tone.

"Sir, I did not mean to offend you," said Hart.

"You kill it," said Ruhsarr.

"I…I can't, sir, please forgive me," said Hart.

"Kill it!" roared Ruhsarr.

"She is yours, sir. She is not mine to kill, sir," said Hart as he stepped back shaking his head.
Ruhsarr stood up and grasped Hart by the throat in one sweeping motion.

"That was a direct order. Insubordination and humanists will not be tolerated in my army. Also, now you appreciate that I too am extremely dangerous," he said.
With that, he crushed Hart's neck, then twisted off his head. The woman screamed hysterically and dropped to her knees. Ruhsarr dropped the lifeless body to the floor. As it landed it shattered to dust. He dragged her across the floor and straight to his feet in one powerful pull of the chain. He pulled her up into his hands and plunged his teeth into her neck. She writhed in pain as he drained her then dropped her body to the floor too.

"Fucker, telling me what to do. Not enough discipline and respect anymore," he mumbled to himself with blood dripping from his jaws.
He looked around at all the bodies for a moment and at the pile of ash that had been Hart.

"Kerr, get in here," he said.
A tall woman with short dark red hair walked into the room.

"Yes, my Lord?" she said.

"Kerr. Do you have a problem with taking orders?" he said.

"No, my Lord," she said.

"Very good. You have just been promoted," said Ruhsarr.

*

13.21.

Andra and her team were nearly finished sweeping the sand they had put down to collect the glass and soak up the fuel from the cars into a pile. The whole building was as tidy as it was going to get. Most of the soldiers had been sent to the base in York at 9 am to eat and rest.

"How is it going?" said Palmer as he stepped out of the lift.

"About as good as it can be. I can't believe we're going to have to abandon another base. There won't be any left if this shit carries on," said Andra.

"Ma'am, Hughes and I have been watching all media sources. There is something you should see," said Palmer and handed her a tablet.

The screen showed a paused news site video. She tapped the triangular symbol in the middle of the screen and the video began to play.

The male news anchor, Bill Tonstone, an elderly reporter who seemed to have been on the news since the station began, spoke in a morose tone.

"In what has been a tense day for the entire world the United States of America have been placed into a state of emergency. President Miller is still being held hostage and every attempt to gain access to the White House has been thwarted by a group of, as of yet, nameless aggressors. No country or terrorist organisation has taken responsibility for the attacks as most are themselves victims in this crisis. We go now to Ted Smith at the scene as it unfolds outside the White House."

The screen then showed the reporter stood a quarter of a mile away from the presidential building. Between him and the building were soldiers, police officers, armoured personal vehicles and emergency response vehicles. Ted Smith, a reporter in his early 30s with an expression of genuine fear on his face began to speak.

"Thank you, Bill. I come to you from here in Washington DC. The scene is something none of us ever wanted to see or in fact, ever thought we would see. It's one of crisis and an unimaginable terror. Last night every occupant of the White House was taken hostage. The building is now under the control of a highly sophisticated but nameless terrorist organisation and the president is being held hostage. In a bizarre twist of event the security agents, guards and all other staff now seem to be working with the terrorists. The police and armed forces are still trying to gain entry to the white house but all attempts have been thwarted. We have had word that the hostage takers have made contact with the negotiators. We'll keep you informed on that as the situation progresses. In other parts of the world, in scenes that could easily have been taken from a movie script, every other president, prime minister and premier around the world has also been taken hostage. This is escalating to be the largest successful terrorist operation ever recorded."

The screen returned to the female news anchor, Debbie Warner, in the studio and Debbie, who was usually bubbly and all smiles, now looked like she was about to burst into tears.

"I've just heard that President Miller is going to address the nation. We take you now to the White House. We warn you, some viewers may find the following scenes upsetting," she said.

The president's podium appeared on the screen. President Miller was sat tied to a chair. Soldiers dressed from head to toe in black body armour and helmets with tinted visors stood one on either side of him, with another stood behind him. The soldier to the right prodded the president with his gun.

"Read," he demanded.

"My fellow Americans. Please do not worry. I am being held hostage but I am safe and well. My life and that of all the world leaders will, however, be in danger if you do not cooperate with these people. They are about to address you and the entire world. Please stay calm, cooperate and everything will be ok," said President Miller.

The soldier behind him raised their hands to reveal a roll of black duct tape. They peeled a length of it away from the roll, stuck it over the president's mouth and wrapped it around the back of his head and over his mouth again. They then tore it from the roll and pulled a black bag over his head. The soldier to the left then picked up the chair with the president sat in it and carried him away. The Soldier who had stood behind him then stepped forward and began to speak.

"I am Sergeant Errat. I am talking to you with the permission of, and on behalf of, the great and mighty, Lord Ruhsarr. Now that we have the world's attention I want to make a few things clear. There will be no negotiations. We will not kill your leaders if you follow these simple rules. All you have to do is listen and do as you are told. But if you continue to try and rescue your leaders every single one of them will die. Not just the one that you are attempting to rescue but all of them. So, if you try to save President Miller here, the Prime Minister of the U.K., the president of France, the president of India, the prime minister of Australia, etcetera, will die. And so on and so forth, you get the picture. If you attack the buildings they are being held in all of them will die. We are not asking for any form of ransom and they will not be released. Lord Ruhsarr has plans for them. This is a transfer of control over the world to your new leader, Lord Ruhsarr. Cooperate and comply and this will be as painless as possible."

The screen returned to Bill Tonstone whose expression of shock was plain to see on his face.

"We, we, have just heard the hostage takers terms. It would seem their terms are just to do as we are told. I hope as I am sure all of you do that President Miller is ok. He seemed well, though, I never thought I would see our President treated like that. There are a few questions that I think you and I are asking right now. Firstly: Who is this Lord Ruhsarr? What does this mean for the world?"

Andra pressed the pause symbol and the image froze. She stood for a moment in complete silence.

"What the fuck is he planning? When is he going to make a move? We've got to do something. He is threatening the global governmental system," said Palmer throwing his hands into the air.

"He has some fucked up notion that he has the right to be the ruler of all the lands. I know he's a megalomaniac but I never thought he would actually be crazy enough to try to take over the world," said Andra.

"What are we going to do?" said Palmer.

"We're going to be patient. I'm still waiting to hear from Henry," she said.

*

14.45.

The sun was low in the sky as Ruhsarr stepped into the Mil Mi-26 helicopter and looked around. There were vampires milling around, moving equipment and checking everything was present and correct. Seefa, a woman with short blonde hair, who was in her early 40s when she was turned, was checking on Alex.

"Seefa, how is he doing?" said Ruhsarr.

"He is doing well. All his vital signs are steady and holding," said Seefa.

"Good. We move in twenty minutes," he said.

"Yes sir," said Seefa.

Ruhsarr looked at Alex. His head was slumped forward. The only thing keeping him stood up was the steel restraints welded into a basic human shaped frame with his arms out horizontally from his sides and his feet shoulder width apart. Ruhsarr placed his hand on Alex's head and pushed it back. Alex's eyes moved slowly under his eyelids and his lips twitched as saliva seeped from the corner of his mouth.

"The great Alex Austin. You should be out cold but even now you fight. You would have been a formidable foe. I would have liked to beat you in a fair fight but I've got too much riding on your demise. You may have been a valuable ally, we could have done great things together, though I doubt that was ever an option for you. I'm afraid Andra's lies and the loss of your family and friends to this war have sullied your beliefs that we could ever be anything but enemies. To do anything but destroy you would be seen as a sign of weakness in the eyes of all vampires. And your humans have made me look a fool for far too long," said Ruhsarr. He let go of Alex's head and let it fall back to its slumped position. He made his own final checks, then the soldiers were rounded up onto the helicopters. When they were all on board he stepped into the helicopter and took his seat.

"When you are ready pilots," he said into the mic on his headset.

The rota blades picked up pace and the helicopters hovered upwards and manoeuvred away from the base.

*

15.05.

The computer screen pinged into life and Henry's face appeared in the large box.

"Andra! Andra!?" he said.

"Yes, Henry! I'm here, I'm here," she said as she ran to the office.

"Andra! He's moving! He's moving!" he said as she sat down on the chair.

"Does he have Alex with him?" she said.

"Yes, he's in some sort of restraint but he has him," said Henry.

"Where are they headed?" she said.

"I'm not sure. They're in seven Mi-26 helicopters. Hundreds of the bastards. They're headed west so possibly France, Belgium, Netherlands, or the U.K. I'll keep you informed," he said.

"Thank you, Henry. If I was there with you I'd kiss you right now," she said.

"I suppose I'm rather awesome," he said with a smile.

"More than that my friend. A lot more than that," she said and smiled back at him.

She ran out of the room and to her team.

"Ok guys, listen up. Ruhsarr is moving. I don't care what you are doing, drop it we are going to York Right now," she said.

"Let's go," said Hughes.

"Fuckin' A," said Palmer.

They all ran out of the building and climbed into the last van in the car park and sped to the airfield. Once there they made some checks to the plane, boarded and took off within twenty minutes. Twenty minutes later they landed at the S.O.V.E.U.

base in York. It was one of the only bases with a small airfield.

They all departed the plane and walked into the base. There they were greeted by Commanding Officer Thomas.

"Hello. I got your message, ma'am. Anything you need we'll do our best to provide. We have a lot of soldiers on base right now so things are hectic," he said.

"I need to speak to everyone here. Can you arrange a meeting in the next half hour?" said Andra.

"Yes, of course, ma'am. I can do that," said Thomas.

He took them down to his office and made an announcement over the base intercom.

"This is a message to everyone. Lieutenant Colonel Andra Hudson has called an urgent meeting on the training level. I want you all up and dressed in half an hour," he said.

The whole building came to life as the sleeping soldiers got out of bed and others dropped what they were doing.

Half an hour later everyone in the base was together on the training level. Andra stepped up to the microphone, she looked out at them and they looked back at her. They all looked tired and dejected.

"Ruhsarr is on the move. My associate, Henry Donaldson, is monitoring his movements as we speak. But as of yet we don't know where he is going. As soon as we do there will be a more definite plan. What I do know is that they outnumber us about three to one. I know those numbers are daunting but we have been sneaking under the noses of not only the vampires but also the vast majority of the human race for years. The strategy I have devised accounts for that. If anyone wants to leave I understand. You may leave and go to your families but Ruhsarr is planning some kind of power grab. If we do not act the lives you know will no longer exist. Would you want your family to live in a world where vampires rule? No, I do not think you would. Everything would change, they would enslave us all. We stand together, we can stop this. We might be the human species' last hope. I personally will never stop until this is over and I hope you feel the same. I'm asking you to stand and fight with me, to never give up, to never stand down until this monster and all his spawn are dead. So, are you with me?" she said.

All the soldiers, every last one of them, threw their fists into the air and cheered.

"Ruhsarr has his army, we are yours. Lead us and we will follow," said Hussain close enough for the microphone to pick up her voice.

"Then let's get prepared and be ready. This is going to be one hell of a fight," said Andra.

## Chapter 29.

16.45.

"We're coming in for the final approach, sir," said the pilot of the lead Mi-26 helicopter.

"Good, bring us in steep and fast. I want them to see us, I want them to panic," said Ruhsarr.

A sharp toothed grip splayed across his face. The pilot brought the helicopter down fast in a high arc over the walls of the castle. The Blutesser soldiers were dropping and running across the lawn before the helicopter even touched down. The guards on patrol in the Tower of London had no choice but to take cover as these vampires launched their attack. They readied their weapons as the colonel in charge gave orders over the radio.

"Open fire!" barked a sergeant.

The vampires zipped across the courtyard towards them. Gunshots rang from both sides as the last tourists of the day screamed and scrabbled away like rats trying to evade fire. Well aimed bullets tore at vampire flesh but didn't stop them advancing. The vampires were killing the soldiers with their bare hands but the soldiers never gave up. Ten of the vampires were killed by the human resistance was ineffective. With no cover that could shield them and no door that could withstand the vampire hordes the battle lasted only nine minutes.

Ruhsarr stood in the middle of the courtyard and shouted orders.

"Close and barricade the gates. Restrain the humans, then divide them up into groups and spread them among our numbers. Their armed forces will resist bombing us if they know that there is a chance they will kill their own," he said.

The vampires rounded up the tourists, ziptied their hands and moved them into different parts of the castle grounds.

*

Thomas had allowed Andra to stay in his quarters to rest while he worked. The intercom on the wall near the door beeped and his voice came through the speaker.

"Andra, I'm in my office. Henry Donaldson is on a video call for you," he said.

Andra was sat watching the news unfold on the TV. She ran over to the intercom and pressed the button.

"I'll be there in two minutes," she said.

She ran out of the door and dodged soldiers and staff as she made her way from the quarters on the fifth floor to Thomas' office on the third floor.

"I'm here, I'm here," she said as she ran into the room.

Thomas stepped away from the computer and she bent down and looked into the camera at the top border of the monitor.

"He's in London, Andra! He's in the tower of London. The vampires are eliminating the armed guard. You have to get there as fast as you can!" said Henry.

"Thank you, Henry. We're ready to go. We've been waiting on your word. We're going to get as many soldiers down there as possible. I'll message all the other bases now and tell them to get there as soon as possible," she said.

"Andra. I won't say good luck because this isn't down to luck. You have trained for this. I feel that this will be the last push. Save Alex and he will save us all," said Henry.

"Thank you, Henry. I'll see you soon," she said. She smiled at the camera and ended the call.

She ran over to the intercom and began to give out orders.

"T.J. go and ready the planes. If any of you need ammo and weapons go to the armoury right now. You won't have another chance. Davis, Hussain, Palmer, Hughes and Holt. Meet me upstairs in the garage. Captains, commanders, sergeants. Have the soldiers ready and lead them to the airstrip. I'll tell you my plan on the way. Those fuckers are attacking the Tower of London. This is it, this is the last push! Let's go! Let's go! Let's go!" said Andra. The base burst into a flurry of action. The anticipation was so thick in the air it was tangible.

*

Three Apache attack helicopters approached the Tower of London. Ruhsarr spotted them approaching but decided to let them get close. He watched as they moved into formation overhead and hovered high above him.

The pilot of the lead helicopter radioed his base.
"We are above the target. Awaiting orders," she said.
A monitor back at their base showed the commander exactly what the pilot was seeing via a camera mounted on the pilot's helmet.
"What the fuck is that? The big guy man near the tower, some sort of body armour?" said the commander.
"I'm not sure, sir. I think it might be," said the pilot.
"Take him out. Re-enforcements are arriving now. They can deal with the others. Fire at will," said the commander.
"Yes sir," said the pilot.
She squeezed the trigger on her controls and the barrels of the mini-gun began to spin. Ruhsarr squatted down, then with tremendous power, he jumped upwards. He headed straight towards the helicopter and smashed right through the cockpit. The pilot and co-pilot were crushed and he then tore into the helicopter. Some of the re-enforcement soldiers started shooting in his direction. He threw out his wings, spun the body of the helicopter in the air then threw it at them. It landed right in the centre of their group and burst into flames killing and injuring most of the group. The other two helicopters aimed their guns at Ruhsarr and fired. He flapped his wings, soared towards the next one and held out a hand. As his fingers dug into the body of the vehicle he rammed his other hand into the engine compartment and pulled out chunks of

hot, oil soaked metal. The pilots screamed at him as the remains of the engine tore itself apart. Red hot components were thrown in every direction. There was a burst of flames and the helicopter began to fall. He pushed off from it and flew at the remaining helicopter. Bullets burned hot as they hit his flesh. Most ricocheted off his scales or missed, but some found a home in his skin. These bullets didn't bother him. They would be pushed out over time like nothing more harmful than splinters. The gun was fast, he was faster. He flew past the stream of bullets and smashed the propeller to pieces. Shards of metal were hurled in every direction. The vehicle fell from the sky spinning uncontrollably. Ruhsarr hung in the air flapping his wings and watching as it crashed into the soldiers below. The tail rota killed at least thirty of them as it spun wildly through the crowd and eventually fell to its side and came to rest. News vans were already turning up. Ruhsarr could see they were pointing cameras up at him. This is exactly what he wanted and he smiled to himself.

*

While Ruhsarr was taking control of the Tower of London a helicopter hovered above the BBC television centre in London. Vampire soldiers poured out from it onto the roof. With a motion of the Captain's hand twenty of the soldiers split from the group and jumped over the side of the building in unison. They landed on the ground, killed all the security guards and quickly blocked all the entrances and exits.

The soldiers on the roof quickly located the roof access doors and flooded inside. They made their way through all the floors in sweeps from the top of the down. As they went they gathered up all the employees and moved them into the news broadcasting rooms. Within a few minutes they had the entire building secured and locked down.

All the staff were crying and screaming until the tall vampire captain stepped infront of them all and shot a bullet into the ceiling.

"Silence, all of you! My name is Captain Rhodes. We are high jacking this television station. Get down on the floor and remain calm. The more you cooperate the easier this will be for all of us, also, you'll be more likely to survive," he said.

The people did as they were told and lay face down on the floor. The soldiers went around and zip tied their hands behind their backs. With one hundred vampires tactically positioning themselves throughout the building most of the staff were quick to comply. One older male employee stood up. He thrashed his hands away from the soldier who was trying to cuff him.

"Get off me, you brainwashed idiot!" he said. "This is preposterous. You think you can just come in here waving your guns around and expect us to do what you say because you're armed. Well, no. I'm not lying down."

"Get on the floor, old man," said Rhodes.

"Go fuck yourselves," the man said in a sneer.

"Ok, you mean old bastard. You've won a prize. I'm gonna make an example of you. Soldiers, grab him," said Rhodes

Five soldiers stalked around him in a circle, then pulled off their masks to reveal their long, sharp teeth. As they glared at him they each let out a low, rumbling hiss.

"What is this?!" said the man.

"Break him," said Rhodes.

The vampires jumped on the man and sunk their teeth into his flesh. They fought over their meal and he screamed as they pulled him in all directions. They dug their claws into him and tore the flesh from his bones. His left arm came away first followed by his right leg. The employees screamed and cried out in horror. He was pulled and wrenched until his right arm tore away and just his left leg was attached to his quivering torso. The vampires then discarded his dying body and licked the blood from their hands. When they were finished they pulled their masks back on like nothing had happened. The hostages however screamed and cried and some vomited.

"Shut the fuck up all of you!" roared Rhodes. The hostages fell silent. "Now you know who and what you are dealing with! Do any of you want to argue with us?" The room was silent. "No? Good. Listen to me, this is the most important thing you will ever hear. I will not hesitate to kill you all myself if needed. It is as simple as that. Do as I say and you will live. Do anything other than specifically what you have been told and you will die, today, right here. Is that clear?"

The hostages sat in silence as shock made them twitch and sob silently.

"Is that crystal fucking clear?" said Rhodes.

There were some whispers and sobs of "yes" from the humans.

"Good," said Rhodes.

The people were mostly quiet but some sobbed as the soldier tied their hands.

"Now I need the news crews to make yourselves known. I have a feeling you will be getting a very important live feed coming in very soon," said Rhodes.

The news crew members raised their bound hands as well as they could and tried to wave. They were pulled from the crowd and marched to the area infront of the cameras.

"Boon, Yarhnock," said Rhodes. Two vampires turned to face him. "Your time to shine. Get on the network, install the program and be ready to broadcast on my word," said Rhodes.

*

Ruhsarr flew down and landed on the ground outside of the Tower of London right infront of the BBC News Team. While they were filming him he grabbed them and bundled them into their van.

"Congratulations. You're getting the exclusive," he said as he slid the door shut. He then climbed up onto the van, dug his claws into the sides of the vehicle and flew back over the wall into the castle grounds.

*

In the skies above Yorkshire the S.O.V.E.U. chinook helicopters were gaining altitude. Andra sat in the cockpit of their lead helicopter, she was speaking over the radio to T.J. who was flying the one behind.

"How long will it take you to get down to London?" she said.

"A little over Forty five minutes, Ma'am. We'll be about five minutes behind you," he said.

"Ok, can you put this through the speaker so that I can talk to everyone," she said.

"As you wish, ma'am," he said and clicked the intercom switch. "Everyone's listening."

"Listen up. I said I would tell you the plan when we were in the air, so, here we go. The main body of you will led by Commanding Officers Thomas and O'Brien. You will split into two groups. These two groups will attack the tower of London from the East and West sides causing a diversion. You will be aided by the traditional army who are already in position. Their numbers are low because the rest are already occupied surrounding Westminster. There the prime minister is being held hostage along with the rest of the political cabinet. They have underestimated the magnitude of the current situation at the Tower of London. You will bolster their numbers with both training and knowledge. You know how vampires engage in combat, they don't so you will guide them. Try to keep the vampires at a distance. While you are doing that, my small attack team and I will sneak in, find Alex, and evacuate him. Then we will regroup and take on Ruhsarr with the help of the army. This might just be the day we beat the vampires. It will also be the last time I address some of you directly. This is not going to be an easy fight but it might just be the most important in human history. Whatever the outcome it has been a pleasure serving with you. But you're not going to get killed are you?" she said.

"No Ma'am," said every one of the soldiers in unison.

"Good. That is what I like to hear. Keep your focus, work together, and remember your training. This is as real as this shit gets," she said.

The helicopters continued on their journey with only the sound being that of the engines. All the members of the S.O.V.E.U. sat in silent readiness.

## Chapter 30.

In a room on the top floor of the White Tower Ruhsarr stood behind the news reporter Michael Arnold. He had his hand wrapped entirely around Michael's neck.

"Tell your camera operator to point the camera at me!" said Ruhsarr.

"Josh, please point the camera at us," said Micheal.

"I...I'm scared. If I point the camera at you that thing will kill you," said Josh.

"He won't. If he does he won't have anyone to introduce him," said Micheal in his best reassuring voice.

"You will refer to me as Lord Ruhsarr, and I will kill him if you don't point the camera at us!" growled Ruhsarr and tightened his grip on Michael's neck.

"Please, do as Lord Ruhsarr says," croaked Michael.

"Ok, ok, Lord Ruhsarr. I…I have you in frame, my Lord," said Josh.

"Rhodes, can you hear me?" said Ruhsarr into his radio handset.

"Loud and clear, my Lord. And we can see you perfectly too," said Rhodes.

"How do I look?" said Ruhsarr.

"Like the true ruler that you are, my Lord," said Rhodes.

"Very good, very good. Are you ready to go there?" said Ruhsarr.

"We just need to launch the program, my Lord," said Rhodes.

"Good, let's get this started," said Ruhsarr.

In the news studio the news presenter's were sat behind their desk with vampires operating the cameras. Under the desk where the cameras couldn't see, the presenters lower bodies and legs were tied to their chairs. Another lay dead out of shot after not cooperating with Rhodes' commands. He pressed the barrel of his rifle to the presenter's chest.

"Just remember, don't fuck this up and I'll let you live," he said.

He walked over to Boon and Yarhnock who were busily working on the network control computers.

"Lord Ruhsarr is ready. Is the program installed?" he said.

"Yes sir. It's installed and ready to launch?" said Boon.

"Ok, do it," said Rhodes.

Boon moved the cursor over a button labelled 'Launch' and clicked it.

"The program is launching and going global. It may take a few minutes, sir," said Boon.

Around the planet the program bypassed firewalls, security systems and VPNs. It uploaded itself onto computers, mobile phones, tablets, smart TVs and all internet connected devices. Simultaneously, they started to show a blank, white screen, the devices wouldn't respond to the user's input and couldn't be switched off.

*

As the chinooks flew over London air space they were hailed by the military defence.

"Helicopter, identify yourself there is a state of emergency declared over London following the attack on the houses of parliament and the tower of London," said a voice over the radio.

"This is Lieutenant Colonel Andra Hudson of the S.O.V.E.U. We're transporting additional soldiers to the tower to aid the Armed Forces surrounding the area."

"Affirmative, Lieutenant Colonel Andra Hudson. You have permission to enter the zone," said the voice.

"Thank you," said Andra.

She flew the helicopter towards the centre of London and brought it down a mile to the East of the tower in Swedenborg Gardens. They were followed soon after by the second helicopter. The third and fourth were not far behind. As the soldiers disembarked Andra barked orders.

"Fall in!" she said.

The soldiers arranged themselves into an orderly formation twenty soldiers long by ten soldiers deep.

"Attention!" said Andra.

The soldiers stood to attention on the runway.

"Present arms!" she said.

The soldiers moved their guns and stood still as statues.

"Ok soldiers, the tower is a gentle jog in that direction," she said pointing west. "However, we do

not have the option of doing anything gently, so let's move our fucking arses,"
They all began to run as a unit.

*

"The program is live, sir," said Boon.

"Very well," said Rhodes. "Are we ready to broadcast, Yarhnock?"

"Affirmative, sir," said Yarhnock.

Rhodes turned on his heels and pointed at the dishevelled looking news presenter, Joe Cartwright.

"Ok, we are live. Do what you do. This is the most important broadcast of your life. Your time to shine," he said.

Joe's scared and tear streaked face was broadcast into every home and to every screen around the world. He had always dreamed of being seen worldwide. He thought that if this had ever happened to him he would be nervous and excited. Now it was actually happening, but in this current situation, it was the most terrifying thing he had ever experienced.

"We, erm. We, erm...come to you. I, we, we come to you live now with a very special report from London to you wherever you are on the planet. I'm Joe Cartwright. Our Lord, Ruhsarr, wishes to address us all. We are all his subjects. We will take you live to the Tower of London where our highly honoured reporter Mike Arnold is with Lord Ruhsarr himself."

The camera then cut to Mike Arnold who still had Ruhsarr's hand wrapped around his throat.

"Thank you, Joe. Yes, I'm here with Lord Ruhsarr, live from London. Please do not try to adjust your viewing device. This is a very important report and deserves your full attention. Your public is listening, Lord. What do you have to say?" said Mike as calmly as he could.

*

Outside the tower the S.OV.E.U. soldiers ran towards what appeared to be a sea of soldiers and military vehicles.

Injured soldiers screamed and moaned as they were being stretchered away from the scene by medics. The dead were being put into body bags and put onto the back of trucks. It was already a war zone.

The S.O.V.E.U. came to a standstill to the North of the tower. Andra gave the order to stand to attention and they responded without a flinch. As they did, a tall, well-built man with a war hardened face and huge moustache approached them.

"You've arrived just right on time. We need more soldiers. I am Sergeant Major Leigh. Who's in charge?" he said.

Andra walked over to him with an outstretched hand. He looked taken aback for a moment and then stepped forward and shook her hand.

"Ma'am, please forgive my reaction," he said.

"Don't worry about it. I get that reaction all the time. I understand. Not many people who look like me. I am Andra Hudson," she said.

"Indeed. Sorry, all the same. Ok, I need your soldiers to..." Leigh began.

"Excuse me, Leigh, but you seem to be mistaken. We are not here to assist you. You are here to assist us," she said.

"I have been waiting here for backup for an hour. You finally arrive and think that you can order me around?!" said Leigh.

"With all due respect, Sergeant Major Leigh, you have no idea of the capabilities of the enemy you are dealing with here. Now I'm sorry you have suffered casualties but you need to listen and listen well. You do as I say without question or more of your soldiers will die. We are not backup. We are Special Operation: Vampire Elimination unit!" she said.

"Special Operations: Vampire Elimination unit?" scoffed Leigh.

"Are you just going to repeat everything I say, Sergeant Major? You should know my full title is Lieutenant Colonel Andra Hudson."

"Ma'am. I apologise, I'm just under a lot of pressure here. I recall hearing about your unit now but in very hushed tones. Your work is extremely covert," said Leigh back peddling.

"I understand, Leigh. There has never been an attack like this. There is a lot of pressure on everyone. My unit is very real and our main objective is to hunt and kill vampires. The fiend who has managed to get himself all over the TV and internet is Ruhsarr Miehyelzah. He's the lead vampire. The first of their kind. We're here to fuck up his plans. Is that understood?" said Andra.

"Yes, Ma'am. Loud and clear," said Leigh.

"Good, you're going to help me get in there. Their holding one of my soldiers hostage. We're going to go in and free him," she said.

"Are you not going to kill this Ruhsarr?" said Leigh.

"That comes later. Firstly this is what we do," She pulled out a floor plan of the tower and surrounding area and laid it across the front of a nearby Land Rover. As she spoke she pointed to areas on it. "I need you to command your soldiers and mine. You will attack from the East and the West points, here and here, causing a diversion. That's when I'll make my move. My team and I will go in through this small access door in the Legg's mount. Your soldiers will work with mine. The enemy are fast and incredibly hard to kill, so keep them at a distance. Kill them if you can but the main thing is to keep them off my arse for long enough to free my guy. Is that clear?"

"Yes Ma'am?" said Leigh.

"Good. Give your soldiers these new orders. Mine have already been briefed," said Andra.

*

In the tower, Ruhsarr began to speak while still holding Mike.

"Humans, I am addressing you all entirely as a race. Do not try to adjust your viewing device. We have taken over everything. All your devices are under our control. You do not need to know how but you do need to know why. I am Ruhsarr. My army has taken your leaders hostage because the time has come for things to change," he said.

*

Outside the tower walls, Commanding Officers Thomas and O'Brien ordered the soldiers into position. There were two hundred soldiers in each group. They took position behind armoured cars, heaped up sandbags behind walls, and on top of nearby buildings.

"Ok, soldiers. You've got your orders, teamwork is key. When you're ready, fire at will," said Thomas into his radio headset.

They fired upon the vampires who quickly began to return fire. There was a shout of orders and excitement among them. Soon they had the vampire's full attention. Both armies were simultaneously forced to take defensive positions.

Andra spoke to her attack team.

"Time to move in. No risk taking. Keep your heads down and only engage targets who pose a direct threat. Move in," she said.

She ran towards the building with a rope over her shoulder. When she got close she leapt up onto the battlements and threw the end of the rope over the side. One by one she quickly pulled each member of her team up. The air around them was filled with the sound of gunfire from the diversion. It drowned out any sound they were making but it also made it more difficult for them to hear approaching vampires. They moved across the rooftop towards and down a staircase, stopping at the bottom. A group of vampires ran past them. Hussain aimed her gun at them but Andra placed her hand on her shoulder and shook her head. The group passed and the team continued on to Devereux Tower. They found a door and entered onto the ground floor. They were moved in an organized pattern. Holt and Hussain were on point. Holt moved forward and checked the path was clear then took cover. Hussain then did the same. Checking and moving until they reached a door that led out to a small courtyard between the Devereux Tower and St Peter Ad Vincula Royal Chapel. They signalled for Andra and the others to follow. Hussain opened the door just enough that she could see out. Seeing that way was clear she opened the door and turned to look across the courtyard. That way was clear too so she stepped out and crouched down with one knee on the ground. Holt and the others followed her and they ran east across the courtyard towards another wall with a doorway. Just before they reached it two vampires stepped out from the other side. As the soldiers took position behind the wall one of the vampires saw Andra. He opened his mouth to sound the alarm and a dart hit him in the throat. He coughed once before he began to solidify. The remaining vampire turned and looked at his colleague, as he did he saw Palmer pointing a gun at him. He raised his own gun and there was a light hiss. A dart hit his forearm. He looked at this dart in shock and lifted his foot to step back, but the procoagulant was already beginning to solidify his limbs. With only one foot on the ground and now statue like the vampire fell and shattered like stone across the ground.

"Fuck yeah," whispered Andra.

She then signalled for them to move and they silently pass through the doorway into the passage between St Peter Ad Vincula and Waterloo Barracks. From here they had an almost clear view of the White Tower.

*

Inside the White Tower Ruhsarr continued to address the world.

"You're governments have failed you. They are besieged by corruption and greed. Politicians with no interest in anything but their own personal wellbeing and positions of power. Your religions have failed you for much the same reasons, giving the leaders more power and status than they deserve. You have been fed a lie all your lives that you are the top species on the planet. The top of the food chain. You are sadly mistaken, and it's time you were told the truth. I am going to tell you that truth. I am going to show you where you stand. I was the first vampire to ever walk this earth and for five thousand years I have grown in strength and power. Now I am ready to take my place as your one true Lord and master."

*

In the courtyard Andra and her team were approaching the tower. They darted three more vampires on their approach. They reached the North wall of the White Tower and flattened themselves against it, then followed it in single file until they came to a security door.

"This is our entry point. Davis, you're up," said Andra.

"Yes Ma'am," said Davis with a smile.

She made her way up the line to the door. She reached into her utility belt and pulled out what looked like two thin white strips of card. She slid the end of both these into the gap between to door and its frame at the points where the bolts were situated. She pulled a thin cotton-like fuse from the end of each and twisted them together. Reached into her belt, and took out a lighter.

"Look away," she said as she lit them.

There was a quick flash and the door popped open. Andra slipped through the doorway and drew her monk staff from her back. The air hissed as the blades sliced the limbs and heads from three vampires inside. They crumbled to ash as they hit the floor. She signalled for the others to enter. As they did they saw the room was brightly lit with walls adorned with breastplates and mannequins dressed in full suits of armour. They turned left with

Hussain leading the way up a spiral staircase. At the same moment a vampire came down the stairs. She saw them and opened her mouth but there was a hiss from Hussain's gun. The dart hit the vampire in the chest and she toppled forwards. Hughes caught her solid body, rested it against a wall and covered it with a tapestry. A vampire approached them from behind, raised his gun and pointed it at Andra. Before he could pull the trigger she thrust the monk staff out behind her and the half-moon blade separated his head and right shoulder from his body. As he fell apart she quickly shoved his disintegrating corpse behind a display case. With Hussain and Holt were on point again they climbed the stairs.

*

"As with all animals we too need to eat, and that is your place. We gain nutrition from the blood of living beings, primarily humans. Your lives are no longer your own. You now belong entirely, as a race, to us. In exchange for our kindness of letting you live on our planet, you will give us your blood willingly. If you resist we will take what we need by force. These are the terms of our supremacy and rule. Do as I say or be destroyed. There is no alternative. Now you all know where you stand. I know some of you will be angered by this. You are not the first. There are some who have been trying to kill me since my creation," Ruhsarr continued.

*

Hussain stepped through the door to the first floor and Holt followed her. They were in a narrow, cold corridor. Along one wall of the corridor were three small windows. Along the other were three arched doorways that all lead to the same large room. A vampire stepped out from the first of the three archways and turned to face them. His eyebrows raised as a dart hit him in the left eye and grey skin rapidly blossomed out over his face within a moment he was a statue.

"Hey Jones? Jones, what are you doing?" said another vampire walking towards them. She pulled up her balaclava as Hussain ran up to the husk of Jones and gave the head of the darted vampire a quick punch. As it cracked from the body and fell, she shot the next vampire before they realised what was happening. A look of shock was frozen across their solid face and Holt caught Jones' head before it hit the floor. Palmer lifted the headless husk and moved it.

Hussain sneaked towards the door the vampires had come from. It was a large room the same size as the one they had been in on the floor below. It was again adorned with display cases but this time they contained mannequins on horseback, weapons and military uniforms. There were five archways on the wall opposite him. All but one were covered with tapestries and display cases. She also counted twenty five vampires in the room. Another vampire walked in from the open door in the opposite room and shouted orders. All the vampires but for a few who were crowded around something at the far end of the room filed out into the other room. There was shouting and commotion and it sounded like they were moving into the lower floors. She focused on the vampires at the far end of the room. Two of who were studying something while another four stood guard. The something that held their attention was some sort of frame with a mannequin held within it. She almost passed it off as some sort of torture display. She was curious as to why the vampires were so interested in it. She then noticed a monitor and wires. She looked at the mannequin and realised it wasn't a display. She looked at Andra and mouthed 'Alex'. Andra smiled with relief. Hussain mouthed 'Vampires' and held up six fingers. Andra, made a hand for three of the soldiers to branch off to the next doorway. When they were in place she signalled for them all to pick a target and fire in unison.

*

"They think that I am evil. That I need to be destroyed. But every attack they have tried on me has been fruitless. Every time they have tried, they have failed. I am still here and they have nothing that can hurt me, until recently. There are some who believe in a curse, a prophecy that speaks of one who will destroy me," continued Ruhsarr.

*

The six vampires were each hit with a dart simultaneously. As they solidified Andra and her attack team silently moved across to the far end of the room where their friend was situated.

In this large, cold room Alex was trapped in a standing position by a thick custom made metal restraint. Around him stood six husks. They had been monitoring his vitals and had been doing a good job. He was alive and heavily sedated but still not fully unconscious. Andra approached him.

"Alex, can you hear me?" she whispered.

He groaned and moved his head in an almost imperceptible nod.

"Hold on. We're going to get you out of here," she said.

She took hold of two sides of the restraint around his left hand and pulled. The metal barely moved. She tried again with all her strength and the metal moved a little more but ring around his wrist stayed welded shut.

Davis and Hughes stepped forwards, each with a set of bolt cutters. They tried to cut through the metal but it was too dense and too hard. Andra took the cutters from Hughes and tried again but ended up only bending the handles. She threw them aside and went to take Davis' set.

"It's no use, Andra. It's too strong. We could try the grinder," she said.

"Do it," said Andra.

Davis opened her bag and took out a cordless angle grinder. She was about to switch it on when

Hussain came running over shaking her head and waving her hands.

"Ruhsarr is in the next room. I can hear him talking," she said pointing to the door at the opposite end of the corridor.

"Try to lift him," Davis said to Andra.

Andra looped her arms under the frame and tried to lift it but could barely move it. She adjusted her grip and tried again but it was no use.

"Fuck. Fucking bastarding fuck," she whispered.

She slammed her hand against the metal restraint, as she did something swung loose from the corner above Alex's shoulder. As she looked at the bag of intravenous fluids a plan formed in her head. She followed the giving set with her eyes, down along the tubes that were attached to needles going into the veins of his left arm. She reached up and switched off the drip.

"What are we going to do?" said Davis.

Andra pulled out the needles from his arm and snapped them off. She then taped the lines back onto his arm.

"We going to hope that this works," said Andra.

*

"This prophesied hero is named Alex Austin. He is no hero though. He is a wild beast. He murdered my offspring, Saltorg, Gilad, Jorshean and Dienco. He killed all of these brothers and sisters in cold blood. All because he believes it is his destiny. He is driven by the words of the psychopathic cult leader, Andra Hudson. She has driven him to believe he is also prophesied to murder me. But I don't believe in curses or prophecies. I believe I make my own fate. Tonight I will show you why. If I was destined to fall before him and to die by his hand how would it have been possible for me to capture him? He will never prevent my reign as Lord of this Earth because tonight I am to going kill him right before your eyes," he threw the reporter aside and gestured towards the doorway behind him and said. "Bring him in."

*

In the other room the attack team hid the solidified vampires behind some of the displays. Andra pressed her hand to Alex's cheek and kissed his lips.

"I'm sorry, Alex," she said.

Davis took her other hand and pulled her away.

"Time to go," she said.

Andra reluctantly followed her and the others and hid.

Four vampires walked out from the chapel, down the corridor and into the room. They walked up to Alex and moved into position to lift him up.

"Shouldn't there be someone watching him, you know, making sure he's still alive?" said one of them looking around the seemingly empty room.

"Do you really want to spoil Lord Ruhsarr's big moment?" said another whilst he was finding a handhold on the restraint frame.

"Well, no, obviously," said the first vampire.
"Come on then. Let's move the shithead," said the second vampire.
With a lot of straining they lifted Alex up in the frame and began to carry him towards the corridor.
"Dead man walking. We got a dead man walking here," said one of them.
"Shut up," the other three said.
"He's about to die, you know, like on death row," he said.
"Yeah, but we're the only ones who are walking, you dickhead," said another.
"Both of you shut up. This is serious shit. If Ruhsarr hears us this guy won't be the only one dying today," said another.
They continued down the corridor and into the Chapel in silence.
Andra stood up from her hiding place.
"What are you doing?" said Davis in a strained whisper.
"I can't just let them take him. In that room is one of the only beings who can truly kill him. I'm not just gonna sit here. You all should get out of here. If we lose Ruhsarr will hunt us all down," said Andra.
"With all due respect, Ma'am. We ain't going nowhere," said Palmer.
"Fucking A," said Hughes.
Andra gave them a warm smile.
"Ok, stay here though. It's defendable from all entrances," she said.
Here radio then crackled into life. Thomas' voice carried in the air like a lost soul.

"Ma'am...Ma'am. The vampires. They're...they're overrunning us. They're shooting us with...with...needles. The soldiers who have been shot are turning. They're turning into... I'm sorry, Andra. I'm so sorry. We tried, we really did. There are only about fifty of us left. It's over. It's all over. We've lost."

There was pop and a hiss and the radio went dead. Andra pressed the radio button on her collar.

"Thomas? Thomas. Come back... O'Brien...O'Brien? Come back... Leigh? Leigh? Answer me. Anyone?" she said.

From the lower levels of the building they could hear the crashing of glass and armour as raging hordes of vampires searched for them. They were getting closer by the second. It was only a matter of time before they climbed the stairs and found them.

"Be ready. We are the last resistance," said Andra

*

In the chapel the vampires put Alex down infront of Ruhsarr and moved aside. Ruhsarr walked up to the pathetic restrained figure. He put his elbow on the shoulder of the restraint frame and rested against it. He slapped Alex on his bare chest.

"This is the mighty Alex Austin. This is the one they say will destroy me, destroy all of us. See how big he is. See how strong he is. Just look at him destroying me. Too sarcastic?" he said and blurted out a huge deep laugh. The other vampires in the room laughed along. "I killed the dragon that made me by tearing out his heart. Now watch ladies and gentlemen, boys, girls and all people of my Earth. My fellow vampires, watch as I do the same to this man and bring this human reign over the Earth to a close," he said.

He pressed the claws of his fingers against Alex's chest. The skin broke and blood began to slide down his chest towards his navel. Ruhsarr worked his fingers through the flesh till they touched the ribs underneath. Alex moved his head slowly from side to side. Ruhsarr applied more pressure. The bones cracked and splintered as his fingers cut deeper. Alex let out a wail like an injured beast. The other vampires in the room rushed forward carrying the cameraman with them.

"He's doing it. He's really doing it," said one of the vampires excitedly.

Ruhsarr opened his hand and could feel Alex's heart beating as he closed his hand around it. Alex thrashed around but still wasn't quite conscious.

"All I have to do is pull," said Ruhsarr as he revelled in the moment.

The vampires laughed and howled like a pack of hyenas. So much so that they didn't see Andra push open the door and run into the room. They only noticed when burning ashes flew around them, and by then it was too late. Three more of them were dead before they moved to respond. A vampire drew his gun and shot six bullets at Andra. They tore through her but nothing was going to stop her. She sliced the shooter balls to brain with one fluid movement and kept going. She cut her way through the group skilfully avoiding the human cameraman. Soon only Ruhsarr stood infront of her, his hand still in Alex's chest.

"Watch your dog die," he snarled.

Andra did not answer but the blade of her monk staff did. She swung hard. The blade bit into the scales of his forearm and stopped. They both looked at the blade and then at each other. Ruhsarr released Alex's heart and slid the hand from his chest. As ever, he couldn't miss the chance to gloat. He moved his arm and the weapon moved with it. The blade was wedged tight. With a flick of his elbow he pulled it from Andra's grasp. With his other hand he threw a heavy punch that smashed her arms which she held in a guard position into her head and pulverized her skull. She was thrown across the room and her bones smashed against the stone wall. She fell to the floor in a heap.

"I'm a lot stronger than last time we fought, wife, and my scales are too thick for your little blade," he said as he pulled the weapon from his arm as he walked over to her and picked her up by the throat. "I want to see the last moments of your pet's pathetic life."

The punch had been devastating but her bones were healing. She felt dizzy and nauseous as the room spun. Ruhsarr raised her up and looked into her eyes. He thrust the crescent blade of the monk staff into the stone floor so the weapon stood upright. He then thrust Andra down onto the long blade. It slid in beneath her ribs and into her chest so she was held in an upright position with her feet dangling above the floor.

"Watch," said Ruhsarr.

He turned to reach into Alex's chest but found that his hostage was now fully conscious and fully aware.

"Fucking cunt!" spat Alex.

There was so much hate and rage in his words that it even permeated the saliva that dripped from his lips and the air that rushed from his lungs.

"How are you awake? Don't worry, I'll have to make this quick," said Ruhsarr.

He plunged his hand into Alex's chest. Alex screamed and thrashed in pain as he fought to free his hands. However, the restraints at his elbows and shoulders prevented him from bending his arms. He felt Ruhsarr's hand squeeze around his heart. He knew his life depended on his next move. Whatever happened was going to be painful. He bent his arms at the elbow. The Ulna and Radius in his forearms snapped like twigs. He cried out and pulled, forcing his thumbs to break and the skin of his hands to tear as they slid out from the restraints. His arms flopped around and then the bones moved and clicked back into place and healed. He grabbed Ruhsarr's arm with both hands in a vice-like grip. Ruhsarr tried to pull away but Alex held his arm in position.

"You...you're not going to stop me!" said Ruhsarr.

He squeezed the heart trying to crush it. Alex looked him right in the eye and roared. His irises cracked and black spider webs spread out from his of pupils and throughout his eyes until they were as black as coal. The muscles in his arms bulged and his hands grew. He squeezed one hand into a fist around Ruhsarr's arm and punched his other hand through the broken arm. Ruhsarr fell back looking at the stump where his hand had been.

"No...No!" he roared.

"Yes, Alex. Do it!" said Andra.

The arm in Alex's chest turned to ash and fell away and the wound closed up. His muscles expanded and his limbs stretched as his bones grew. As the pressure from his limbs forced against the restraint the welds burst open around his shoulders and arms. The metal screamed as it bent and tore apart as the figure of Alex transformed. He shook his legs and pulled at the metal until it broke away from his limbs. Grey scales burst from his skin and flattened down all over his body. The mangled remains of the restraint fell to the floor with a heavy ringing thud. Ruhsarr looked up at Alex who now stood a foot taller than him. He raised his newly regrown hand and punched this beast across the face. Alex's head snapped to the side but he brought it back to the forward position and glared at Ruhsarr. He rocked his jaw from side to side as his face began to change shape. The bones of his skull reformed themselves, his nose and maxillary jaw slid forwards under his eyes becoming his snout and his eyes slid wider apart on his head. His mandibular jaw grew and elongated. While this happened his huge teeth broke out through his gums and his bones crunched into their final positions.

"Did you think this was going to be easy for you?" said Alex.

"You've ruined my plans you fucking animal. I should have pulled your heart out when I had the chance," said Ruhsarr.

"Bullshit. You want this fight just as much as I do. Let's stop wasting time," said Alex.

Before Ruhsarr could reply Alex punched him in the chest sending him sprawling across the room.

*

In the next room the team were hunkered down behind displays and waiting for the inevitable arrival of the horde of vampires. Fraught screams of anger came echoing up the stairs.

"Stay down. I'm going to see if we could find another way out," said Holt

"I already told Andra that we're staying here," said Palmer.

"No disrespect but I have only been part of this team since last night. You heard Thomas. It's over. We need to look after ourselves now. I'm not going to sit here and wait to die. You can all stay here but I'm going," he said.

With that, Holt jumped up and ran down the corridor. A moment later he came running back into the room. Just as he made it through the doorway a vampire pounced on him and took him down to the floor. It tore into his back while he screamed and writhed around. He managed to pull his sidearm and roll onto his back. He pushed the pistol to the vampire's temple and pulled the trigger, but the vampire was too quick. It pulled its head out of the way before the bullet left the chamber. It screamed at him and rammed his head into the floor destroying the back of his skull with a wet crunch. It then tore into his neck and gorged itself as the blood gushed from the wound.

It happened so fast that all the team could do is watch in horror. Hussain pointed her gun and shot a dart at the fiendish thing just as it looked up at her. The dart hit its mark and solidified the fiend like some hideous blood soaked gargoyle.

"Holy fuck!" she said as she lowered her gun. The vampires scream alerted more vampires to their location. A reply scream echoed from the floor below and a group of them began to climb the stairs in a run.

"Conserve your ammo. Use the darts first. Try and make a barrier from their bodies," said Hughes.

As the vampires climbed the last few steps and rounded the corner the team shot at them. Soon the statue-like bodies began to build up and blocked the doorway. This barricade held for a few minutes. The vampires behind it looked in shock at the husks that had been colleagues just moments before. They began to hammer at the bodies with their guns and fists. Soon they broke through and the team had no choice but to open fire again. The first few vampires were cut down by well-placed bullets but soon they were approaching on mass.

*

Ruhsarr caught his balance then ran at Alex and threw punches at him. Alex had the agility to dodge the first few but Ruhsarr moved so fast that he then caught him right across the face with the next two and one to the chest. He felt his jaw and ribs crack but they began to heal immediately. He snarled and smashed his fist down across Ruhsarr's head. As he slumped to the floor Alex grabbed him by the throat and lifted him off his feet. He then spun and slammed Ruhsarr into a wall. Ruhsarr punched his fist into Alex's arm shattering the bones. He cried out and dropped him. As his arm was healing he was hit with an uppercut to the Jaw. As his head snapped back Ruhsarr kicked him in the chest. Alex crashed into the wall and several bricks moved but stayed in the wall. He quickly regained his composure and leapt at Ruhsarr landing a fist heavily across his face. Ruhsarr stumbled away but swung his claws and caught Alex across the face, ripping open his lips. Alex jerked away from the blade-like fingers then leaned back in and grabbed Ruhsarr by the face digging his own claws deep into the socket of his left eye. Ruhsarr roared in pain and slashed at Alex's neck. They grappled for control of the fight and smashed their fists into each other faces. Ruhsarr dug his claws into Alex's neck until blood poured over his arm. Alex brought his fist down onto Ruhsarr's head until the bones cracked and his forehead began to cave in. They beat and tore at each other and in the confusion stumbled into the wall that Alex had weakened. The bricks gave way this time and they both burst through the wall. They fell to the courtyard below that now swarmed with vampires.

They jumped on Alex stabbing and clawing at him. As he fought them off Ruhsarr grabbed him, dug his claws into his flesh and lifted him off the ground. He threw him back into the building via a window. Alex slid across the floor, then rolled and got back on his feet. Ruhsarr burst in through another window and ran at him. Before he could make contact Alex drove his fist down into the top of his head. His forehead had just healed but now his face smashed against the floor. He took hold of Alex's ankle and pulled the legs out from under him. He then jumped up to his feet, pushed his jaw back into place, and held it until the bones fixed themselves as his face clicked back into shape. He was just about healed when Alex took him by the arm and swung him like a hammer before letting him go. He sailed through the air and crashed through a display of artefacts. He crashed into the floor and the stone slabs cracked under his weight. As he stood up Alex roundhouse kicked him in the chest. He stumbled back and the huge bulk of his body crashed through a window and out of the tower again. He landed on his back but quickly stood up, leapt away and opened his huge wings. Alex jumped out through the same hole and fell towards the ground. Ruhsarr was nowhere to be seen. Vampires ran at him from all angles. He fought with them but was crushed down to the ground when Ruhsarr landed on him from a huge height. He felt multiple points of horrendous pain as Ruhsarr sunk the talons of his feet into his back.

"You want to fight I'll give you a fucking fight!" said Ruhsarr.

He flapped his wings with enough force to lift them both high into the air. He then flew out across the city forcefully smashing Alex down into the roofs of every building they passed. Alex fought to free himself from Ruhsarr's talons but they were buried deep into the muscles of his back. He put out his hands and grabbed at the rooftops trying to find something strong enough to hold on to. Finally, his fingers caught hold of a huge girder and he held on tight. Ruhsarr flapped his wings with all his strength trying to break Alex's grip but try as he might Alex could not be moved and he had to release him. He flew away then turned back and rapidly flew at Alex. As he got closer Alex crouched down on the girder and then launched himself at Ruhsarr. They slammed into each other in mid-air tumbling, throwing punches, breaking bones and tearing flesh.

They crashed into the road below, shattering the tarmac. Cars screeched to a halt around them. Ruhsarr got to his feet as Alex got to his hands and knees. He raised his foot and stomped Alex's head back down into the tarmac. Alex took hold of his leg, and threw him down onto the bonnet of a car. The driver quickly opened the door, leapt out, and ran to safety. Ruhsarr kicked out at Alex freeing himself from his clawed grip, rolled off the bonnet and onto his feet. He walked the side of the car, hooked his fingers into the front and rear wheel arches and lifted the entire vehicle. As Alex stood up Ruhsarr brought the car down onto his back. It smashed against him, and knocked him back down to the road. Ruhsarr raised the car again but before he could swing it back down Alex jumped up and gouged a chunk of tarmac up and threw it into Ruhsarr's face. He fell back and people on the street scattered away as he fell towards them. He landed on his back and the car crashed onto other vehicles. He rolled and got onto his knees as a police officer squirted pepper spray at his eyes.

"You are joking, right?" he said.

He grabbed the man by the throat and began to close his fist. Alex strode over to Ruhsarr, grabbed him by the back of his head, and smashed his elbow into his face. Teeth flew from his mouth as his nose and jaws collapsed inwards. Ruhsarr's hold on the officer's neck relaxed and the man fell to the ground. He coughed and took in lungfuls of air. Alex took hold of Ruhsarr, lifted him over his head and threw him into a concrete wall of a building. He crashed against it, then fell to the ground. The wall was damaged but it held. He got to his feet, launched himself head first at Alex, caught him square in the chest, and knocked him off his feet. As they hit the ground Ruhsarr grabbed Alex by the head and slammed it into the tarmac twice. He then stood up on his chest, dug his talons into his flesh, and hauled him into the air again. As they flew up and over the buildings Ruhsarr punched Alex in the face. Alex tried to block them and threw a few of his own back at Ruhsarr. He blocked a left hook and sunk his claws into Ruhsarr's scalp. As he drew his hand towards him the flesh tore away from Ruhsarr's skull and he screamed. Blood ran down his face into his eyes. As he tried to wipe it away Alex reached his hands out over Ruhsarr's shoulder and grabbed his wings as they came in on the down stroke. Ruhsarr felt the hands on the strong limbs and pulled them away, but Alex's claws punctured the stretched skin, splitting it open. He flapped his wings again but Alex caught the damaged limbs again and pulled with all his strength. Ruhsarr screamed as the bones popped from their sockets and the flesh tore. A sheet of searing pain shot down his side as the left wing was torn from his body. He screamed a line of garbled rage and took hold of Alex by the throat. He pushed his head away as gravity and momentum pulled heavily on them both. His intention being that Alex's head would take the brunt of the impact.

"Die, you fucker! Die!" he roared.

Alex looked over his shoulder and saw they had crossed the river Thames and were headed directly towards The Shard. He struggled and punched at Ruhsarr but it was no use. Glass exploded all around them as they burst through the outer structures of the building. They smashed through the twenty fifth floor and two more after that. The twenty second floor cracked under their weight but managed to hold.

They both lay next to each other among a pile of shattered glass, cement, and splintered office furniture. They were both heavily injured but healing at an equal rate. Ruhsarr managed to get up first as his right wing popped back into place and the left wing began to regrow. He lifted Alex by the throat and slammed him down onto the already weakened tiled floor. The floor rumbled and a crash came from below as it gave way and they fell again to the twenty first floor. Desks, chairs and computers rained down on them. Alex grabbed Ruhsarr by the head and punched him in the neck and body then smashed his fist up into his jaw. Ruhsarr saw stars as his teeth smashed again. Alex saw the opportunity and opened his mouth to go in for the bite, but Ruhsarr ducked down out of his grasp. He then spun, leapt up, and smashed his elbow into Alex's head. Alex dropped to one knee, but when Ruhsarr came in with another punch, he jumped back and landed on his feet. Ruhsarr rushed at Alex still throwing punches which he blocked. Ruhsarr then jumped on him clamped a hand on either side of his head and squeezed. Alex felt the bones in his skull start to crack. He tried to pull Ruhsarr's hands away but his strength was unrelenting. He wrapped his arms around Ruhsarr and squeezed until he heard ribs snap. Still, Ruhsarr held on and the pressure on Alex's head grew. Alex then set off running through the building. They crashed through desks and partition walls but Ruhsarr still wouldn't let go. Alex ran as fast and as hard as he could at the glass windows. He could barely see where he was going and the pain in his head increased with every stride. They hit the window and Alex kept running. He felt Ruhsarr's chest crush and heard him scream as his ribs burst through his flesh. They shot out from the side of the building like a cannonball. As they fell Alex smashed his fists into Ruhsarr's body. They hit the ground with a boom and their flesh crumpled together.

They both lay still for a moment. Ruhsarr struggled to breathe. A moment later Alex's arms snapped back into shape and he pushed himself up. He tilted his head from side to side and the bones in his neck crunched and slid back into place as his skull reformed. Ruhsarr coughed and tried to move but Alex hammered both fists down into his destroyed chest. Ruhsarr threw a still broken fist across Alex's head which knocked him away and then using both feet he kicked him back. He landed ten feet away before he rolled to a stop. Ruhsarr stood up and tried to speak but his lungs were still regaining their form. He pushed his hand against the sides of his chest. The flesh and bones moved back into shape and helped to speed up his recovery. Alex ran at him but he dodged aside.

"Alex! Alex, listen to me! It's clear neither of us is going to win. We can keep beating each other until we smash this city to the ground, or we could join forces. The age of humans is over. It's over, Alex. But you and I, we are not just immortal beasts. We're better than that. We're the immortals that the elders of my village use to depict in their hieroglyphs. We should rule the people of this world. We should be their gods. We are their gods. Don't you see, Alex? Two titans, two gods, two

Lords of immortality, side by side for eternity. Imagine it, Alex. It could be glorious," he said.

Alex stared at him as if the words angered him even more than Ruhsarr himself.

"Do you really think that I would ever consider joining you? Because of you my mother and father are dead. Because of you my brother is dead. Because of you Mc'Ready is dead. Everyone that I have known who has died has died because of you. I would rather spend the rest of eternity locked in a battle with you than spend one second in any sort of alliance with you. I will not stop, not until you are dead!" said Alex.

"Very well. Then you choose death," said Ruhsarr.

"I choose your death," said Alex.

They ran at each other and as they collided they reigned fists down upon each other. Alex caught Ruhsarr's arm and pulled him towards him and his opened jaws but Ruhsarr uppercutted him shattering his face. Alex swung Ruhsarr around by his arm and let go. As he tumbled through the air he righted himself and flew high above Alex. He then flew straight down and hit Alex at high speed smashing him into the ground. He stood over Alex who lay motionless then slammed his fists down into Alex's chest over and over again until blood poured from his mouth. He clawed his way through his chest and was reaching again for his heart. Alex's hand shot up and grabbed Ruhsarr by his face. He opened his eyes, got to his feet and smashed Ruhsarr's head down into the ground in one movement. He then ran down St Thomas Street ploughing up the concrete with Ruhsarr's skull. Ruhsarr smashed his hands down into the ground gaining some purchase. Alex fell forward and let go of him. He caught his balance and turned to look at Ruhsarr who was getting to his feet. The flesh of his face hung from his skull in ribbons. He ran at Alex, grabbed him by the head, spun him around like a hammer and let go. As Alex hurtled over the buildings Ruhsarr leapt into the air and flew after him with his fully healed wings. He hit Alex with both fists held out infront of him. This sent Alex into a spin. He did this twice then flew at him again. This time Alex bounced over his back and snatched hold of his wings. He snapped the bones of the limbs and they fell. Ruhsarr screamed, turned, and clawed at the flesh of Alex's face. They crashed down onto the train tracks headed towards Southwark train station.

Under the impact the rails bucked and popped from their huge bolts. The sleepers burst into splinters and they left a shallow crater in the ground. People stood on the nearby train platforms stared in shock as the two beasts got to their feet and continued to exchange attack. Ruhsarr gripped the sides of Alex's head, quickly pulled it down and brought a knee up into his face. The people screamed in terror and all tried to run from the platform and down the stairs as Ruhsarr ran towards them. Alex shook his head and chased Ruhsarr. He leapt onto his back and as they both fell he rammed Ruhsarr's head into the tracks. He then lifted him and smashed his face down again into the sleepers.

Ruhsarr grabbed the tracks and held on tight. Alex lifted Ruhsarr up for a third time and he pulled up the tracks with him. A piece broke free and Ruhsarr swung it toward Alex's feet, knocking them from under him. As he hit the ground Ruhsarr stood up and brought the piece of track down onto Alex's head three times. He lay spitting out teeth for a moment, then Ruhsarr lifted him over his head and slammed his head down onto the platform edge. Ruhsarr jumped up then came straight down stomping his feet into Alex's face, cracking his skull, and shattering the concrete platform. He stamped on Alex's head repeatedly until he stopped moving. He lifted him and threw him into the wall on the platform. The few people left scurried away, pushing into the herd as they all tried to run down the stairs, desperate to be out of the warpath of the two monsters. Ruhsarr then picked up the motionless body of Alex and threw him into the wall on the opposite side of the tracks. As Alex lay on the platform Ruhsarr landed on his back and dug his talon into him. He then jumped into the air, flapped his wings, and headed west.

*

In the Tower of London Andra's hands and arms had healed enough for her to grip the shaft of the monk staff. She held onto it with both hands and forced herself upwards. The blade slid out for her torso. She then pushed herself away and fell to the floor. Her legs were still not quite healed enough to hold her weight. Her skull had knitted itself back together and she worked her jaw up and down. It clicked a couple of times but then moved freely. She pushed herself up and got her aching legs beneath her. Gingerly she got to her feet. There was pain in her first few steps but it quickly subsided. She took hold of her monk staff and rocked it back and forth in an attempt to free it but the crescent blade snapped off and stayed embedded in the stone floor.

"Fuck, that was my favourite weapon," she said. She threw it aside, reached to her back and pulled the two short swords free.

*

In the next room the team were trying to hold their ground but the vampires just kept coming. They had been pushed to the back of the room where Alex had been held and were still being pushed even further.

"We should have tried to move towards the doors," said Hussain.

"Too late for that," said Hughes.

"Fuck! Last dart!" said Palmer.

"Make it count," said Davis.

Palmer scanned the sea of vampires as they flooded over every surface. A huge seven foot tall vampire barged through the crowd pushing other vampires aside as he went. He was halfway across the room when the dart hit him square in the nose. His legs collapsed as his hardening body fell back onto some of the others. Palmer swung the M16 from his shoulder and shot into the horde at chest and head height. There were vampires among them in S.O.V.E.U. uniforms and civilian clothing.

"This ain't right," said Hussain as she shot at them in short bursts.

"Make every shot matter. Ignore how they are dressed. Keep them back," shouted Hughes over the gunfire.

Vampires were being torn apart by bullets but there were so many of them it seemed like they would never stop coming. These small band of soldiers were all that were left of Andra's Army and they had now reached the far wall of room. The vampires continued to pour into the room.

"I'm out," said Hussain.

Palmer handed her another full magazine.

Vampires swarmed towards them like ants defending their nest. The soldiers shot into the crowd putting down their targets but only made a small dent in their numbers.

There were only six feet between them and the vampire when the wall burst open and Andra stepped out. She positioned herself in between the soldiers and the horde and swung her short swords at the vampires. Limbs and body parts flew in all directions as her blades separated them from their owners. The vampires at the front hissed and roared at her as they tried to back away but the ones behind kept pushing forward.

"Go through into the chapel!" she said.

The soldiers stepped through into the room beyond as Andra kept swinging the swords and making quick precise cuts. When all the soldiers were through the hole in the wall she took a few paces back as her nose and jaws grew outward into a snout. She took a deep breath and lowered her swords. A few vampires lunged forward in an attempt to attack her but were engulfed in the huge fireball that erupted from her throat. They burned up in seconds and their ashes were blown apart. The vampires behind were too crammed in to turn and run. The flames sweep over, around and through them in a wave. They burned with the ferocity of a wind fuelled forest fire. The vampires on the stairs turned and ran. The ones closest to the stairwell forced themselves into it until the sheer amount of bodies caused a blockage. The ones stuck in the room were all set ablaze. They threw themselves against this wall of bodies and set them on fire too. The ones closest to Andrea broke apart and fell onto the growing pile of ash. Soon all the vampires in the room and on the stairs were burned up. Despite the danger vampires began to turn and run back up the stairs and back into the room. Outside vampires were jumping up to the hole in the chapel wall that Alex and Ruhsarr had fallen from. Andra and her soldiers cut them down as they moved in closer but the numbers continued to increase.

They were all driven by the need to be the one to tell Lord Ruhsarr they had slain Andra and her murderous followers.

The soldiers were shooting at the ones Andra missed but they were quickly being overrun and from both sides now. Davis' gun began the hollow clack that signified her last mag was empty. She threw her rifle aside, and pulled her desert eagle from its holster. She picked her targets wisely but her bullets were running down too fast.

"Is this one of those situation you see on TV where someone says save one for yourselves?" said Hussain.

"Fuck that shit! I have a pound of plastic explosive on me. If we go we're taking the whole fucking lot of these fuckers with us," said Davis.

"Fuckin' A," said Hughes.

"Fuckin' A," Agreed Palmer.

*

With Alex still in his talons, Ruhsarr flew over Westminster Bridge. His wings had fully regrown and Alex was bordering on consciousness as his head was almost healed. People watched from the bridge as they passed over. He could hear their cries and screams.

Soldiers and police were in position around The Palace of Westminster. News camera crews were nearby waiting for someone give them and update about the members of parliament. Some of them spotted Alex and Ruhsarr as they approached. The soldiers took aim and fired shots at the pair but the bullets only served to annoy Ruhsarr.

Alex began to come round as they flew closer to the building. He clawed at Ruhsarr but the vampire lord punched him in the head repeatedly. They flew right towards to clock tower.

"What are you doing?!" said Alex.

"You're out of time," said Ruhsarr with a smirk.

He let go of Alex and banked hard to the left. His wing narrowly missed the tower. Alex hit the eastern clock face and crashed through it. Destroying the mechanisms within.

Ruhsarr laughed to himself as he flew round to the west side expecting to see Alex falling out through that clock face but it was still mostly intact. The lights that illuminated the clock faces flickered and he saw a silhouette projected from the other side. He barely got chance to react as Alex burst through the clock face brandishing the Big Ben bell. He brought it down heavily on Ruhsarr's head knocking him out of the air. He plummeted to the road below and crashed into the ground. Alex landed on his feet next to him. Ruhsarr was trying to get to his feet when Alex swung the bell at him. The impact knocked him off his feet and rolled across the ground. He had barely got to his feet when Alex swung the bell again. The impact pulverised the left side of his head. He hit Ruhsarr relentlessly over and over again. Eventually, he stopped for a moment and Ruhsarr lay sprawled out on the ground. He lifted his head and spat out his teeth. He then sat up. The bones of his shattered skull had punctured his flesh. Blood poured from his eyes and ears. He got to his feet and stumbled from side to side. Alex brought down the bell down for another blow, smashing Ruhsarr back to the floor. He lay twitching and his arms moved just before Alex hit him once more before he cast the bell aside. He grabbed Ruhsarr and hauled him from the floor so they were face to face.

"I do this for everyone you have ever killed. Everyone you have ever betrayed. Every life you have ever destroyed. Most of all though, I do this for my family," said Alex.

"Oh do go and fuck yourself," slurred Ruhsarr from his broken mouth.

Alex bared his teeth, opened his jaws as wide as he could, pulled Ruhsarr close, and sunk his teeth deep into his shoulder. Ruhsarr cried out and clawed at Alex's neck and head but it was too late. He put his hands on Alex and pushed him away with all his strength. The huge chunk of flesh between Alex's teeth tore from his shoulder. He crunched and swallowed it down. Ruhsarr had a sudden boost of strength and fought his way from Alex's grip. He fell to the floor and his eyes bulged with fear. He pushed himself to his feet as blood poured from his mouth and let out a horrendous pained howl. He raked his hands over his flesh as he writhed and stumbled around. New flesh grew from the wound in his shoulder but then fell away and turned to ash. Alex wrapped his arms around his waist and bit him again deep into his other shoulder. Ruhsarr pushed him away and uppercutted him with enough strength to knock him back. Ruhsarr's body tried to resist but it was no use, the chemical reaction was already in motion. The venom rushed through his arteries and veins. His internal organs began to crystallise and solidify. His muscles and limbs stiffened and despite his best efforts he found he couldn't move. A layer of white crystals spread outward from his chest. His breath became laboured as he panicked. Finally, he breathed out one last time and the crystals spread over his face. With his arch-nemesis finally dead, there was one last thing for Alex to do.

*

In the tower of London, the vampires closed in on the soldiers. One leapt on Davis but she quickly pushed her knife through its neck and just about held it back. Andra was hacking vampires down but for every one she killed another took its place. Hughes was dragged into the horde. Before he was overrun he smashed the face of a vampire with the butt of his gun and stabbed his Knife down into the skull of another. He was then bitten multiple times and dragged to the floor. He screamed and fell silent.

"No!" screamed Palmer.

He rushed forward shooting with his sidearm and hacking wildly with his machete, but his friend was gone. The hammer in his pistol clicked an empty chamber. The vampire facing down the barrel snatched his hand and pulled him into the horde. He felt multiple sets of teeth sink deep into his arm. A wail of anger and pain burst from his mouth.

"Fuck you all!" said Davis.
She reached for the detonator on her belt that would trigger the plastic explosive and held her thumb over the button. All at once every vampire stopped moving. They all stood completely still, and then burst into flames. They screamed and howled as their flesh burned. Twisting and contorting their bodies. Their flesh contracted and pulled from their bones.

The people of the world watched as the vampires holding the presidents, prime ministers, kings and premiers hostage burst into flames. Across the world vampires hiding in society as politicians, musicians, TV celebrities, news reporters, religious leaders, motorbike gangs and drug dealers burst into flames. The flesh burned from their bones and their skeletons fell to ash.

A moment of confusion fell across the remaining members of the S.O.V.E.U.
Andra swung her swords through the ash that hung in the air. Palmer was hacking at nothing with his machete. Hussain put her hand on Davis' shoulder, whose eyes were tightly shut and gripped her thumb tight.

"They're gone, Davis. Release the detonator. They're gone, they're gone," she said.
Davis opened one eye and looked around before opening the other.

"They're gone? They're gone," she said.
She released the detonator and hugged Hussain. Palmer stepped forwards.

"Hughes, Hughes?!" he said.

There was a movement in the piles of ash where he had fallen. Palmer stepped towards it with caution. A cough and a splutter blew up a plume of dust and Hughes sat upright. Palmer reached out and took his hand and helped him to stand up. He then wrapped his arms around him and hugged him tight.

"You're alive. Oh, man. I thought they got you!" he cried.

"I thought they got me too. When they started burning I thought Davis had blown us all up," said Hughes.

"I nearly just did," said Davis. "Thankfully Hussain stopped me."

Palmer stepped back as Davis walked over to them. She brushed the ash away from Hughes' shoulder and hugged him. Hussain took hold of Palmer's wrist.

"You're bleeding," she said.

Palmer looked down at the bite marks in his arm. His arm was covered in blood and wisps of smoke drifted from the puncture marks. He took a first aid kit from his trouser pocket and wiped his arm with an antiseptic wipe. The wounds had been cauterised.

"How do you feel?" said Hussain.

"I feel fine. It's a little sore but ok," said Palmer.

"You two are fucking lucky. You were nearly toast. You got off with some cool scars," said Hussain.

Palmer laughed and pulled her into a hug
His huge frame swallowed her.

"I fucking love you guys," he said.

“Love you too, big guy,” said Hussain.

“Ma’am, Is it over? Does this mean Alex beat Ruhsarr?” said Hughes.

“I think he did,” said Andra.

“What do we do now?” said Hussain.

“We can rest,” said Andra with a smile.

“We can grieve,” said Davis.

Hussain put her arm around Davis’ waist.

“I need to find Alex,” said Andra.

She turned and ran to the hole in the wall and jumped out. She landed in a deep pile of ash, stood up and brushed herself off. She pulled her smartphone from her belt and turned the volume up. It was still showing news coverage. Police were cautiously approaching the huge shape of Alex outside the palace of Westminster. She slipped the phone back in her belt and set off running.

## Chapter 31.

Alex strode towards the solidified body of Ruhsarr and took hold of it. He bit into the head. He tore off a chunk, crunched it in his teeth and swallowed it. A group of armed police officers and soldiers approached but kept their distance from him.

"What the hell is that thing, Serg?" said one of the police officers.

"It's that guy from the News who transformed," said the Sergeant.

Alex tore another bite from Ruhsarr's husk.

"What are we gonna do, serge?" said another.

"Maintain a parameter until the Army can control this situation. That thing just used the Big Ben bell as a weapon against the other. I ain't going anywhere near it," said the sergeant.

They watched as a dark blur sailed high over their heads and then came down and landed next to the tall scaled beast.

"What the fuck," said the Sergeant.

Andra stepped closer to Alex with a look of astonishment on her face.

"Alex, you did it. You saved us, you saved everyone. It's over," she said.

He was still tearing into the remains of Ruhsarr and currently biting a chunk away from the chest of his nemesis.

"Alex, did you hear me? It's over," Andra repeated.

“I know, I can’t help myself. I must eat his heart,” he said.

Andra could do nothing but watch and wait. As she did it dawned on her that Ruhsarr was gone. After all these years, he was finally dead. He could no longer torture her by pretending to be the man he once was. Tears rolled down her face for the husband she had lost a long time ago. There was also a smile on her face because he was no longer the monster.

News crews were closing in and getting a little bit braver but still had no intention of getting too close. The reports started talking into their microphones as Alex tore mouthful after mouthful from what was left of Ruhsarr. When he had eaten all the chest and the heart he was able to stop. Ruhsarr’s arms and wings lay on the floor. His lower torso and legs were still stood up like a destroyed statue. Alex turned around to face Andra.

“Now it’s over, Andra,” he said.

She stepped towards him and threw her arms around him.

“At last,” she said.

He hugged her tight and he looked down at her.

“We did it. He’s dead. Mission complete,” he said.

She stood on her tiptoes, kissed the end of his snout and smiled.

“Mission complete, soldier. Dismissed,” she said.

“Yes, Ma’am.”

He hugged her again.

“I’m sorry,” he said.

"Sorry for what?" She said leaning back and looking up at his strong face.

"For all this. If I had just waited and planned like you told me to we would have gone in smart and quiet. I went in all big and angry and caused all this destruction, all this death," he said.

"Alex, this was going to happen even if we had planned everything out. Ruhsarr was waiting for us to make our move. He had planned to capture you in one way or another a long time ago. He was a lot stronger than I had anticipated and he knew that you were literally the only one who could stop him. All the death and destruction was his fault and his alone. Without you, things would have been a lot worse," she said.

"Thank you, Andra. I mean Ma'am," he said.

"You don't have to call me Ma'am anymore. You just saved the entire human race. We should all be calling you sir," she said.

"Just Alex will do," he said with a smile. "You'll always be my leader. You're the brains. I'm just the brawn."

"You're a lot more than just brawn," she said and rubbed her hand on the side of his jaw and pulled him close.

"This is weird," he said.

"Why is this weird?" she said.

"Not the hug. Usually after eating one of these vampires I get an insight into all their past, all their thoughts and feelings. It's not happened yet. Maybe it won't happen now that their all," he said

He stumbled back away from her and fell to his knees.

"Alex, what's wrong?" Andra cried.

He couldn't reply. All the muscles in his body contracted then convulsed. He fell forward and put his hands palm down on the ground. He opened his mouth and wretched. A clear slime poured from his open mouth. Andra jumped aside as it began to form into a shape. It continued to pour from Alex's mouth and the shape started to form into a huge body. A long neck formed, then a head that stood sixteen feet above the ground. A huge pair of wings spread from its back and a long tail swung to and fro behind it. Its form became more detailed. Finally, the liquid stopped flowing from Alex's mouth. He got to his feet and looked in awe at the dragon-shaped figure. The huge figure then spoke in a voice so deep everyone around could feel it resonate in their chests.

"The curse is over, the prophecy is complete. I am the spirit form of the dragon Azangor and finally, I am free," It looked down at Alex. "You must be the destroyer of the abomination who called himself Ruhsarr."

Alex could only nod his head.

"I can only apologise for all that has transpired since my passing. I am the one who accidentally turned Ruhsarr into the beast he became. If I had known what a tyrant he would become I would have just eaten him when he came to attack me as a man. When he pulled out my heart my spirit was forced into my blood so that it would run free from my body. That fiend caught my blood in a mead vase of all things. When he and his little monsters started drinking my blood my soul was divided between the five of them. You have reunited all the shards of my soul, and for that I thank you. You have freed me so that I may take my place amongst my family in the Afterworld. We dragons used to be the protectors of this world. When I cursed Ruhsarr I was the last of my kind. I hoped that the nemesis he created for himself would be worthy of the title. I am pleased to see you have stepped into the role with ease. I intended that when the task of destroying Ruhsarr was complete you should return to your human form, but I feel the world may still have need of you. Do you want to remain in your form as the protector?" said Azangor.

"Yes, please, but just one thing. My bite kills vampires, but now there are none of them left. I need it to adapt to enemies," said Alex.

"Very well. You have shown courage and strength even when outnumbered and outmatched. You shall remain as protector of this world and you bite will be deadly to all your enemies," said Azangor.

"Thank you. Can I ask one question?" said Alex.

"Of course," said Azangor.

"A lot of people have lost friends and family because of Ruhsarr. Is it possible that you could return those people?" said Alex.

The dragon placed a hand on Alex's shoulder.

"Sadly the ability to return the dead to a state of living is one I do not possess. Keep them in your heart and remember them fondly. That way they will always be with you. I am sorry for those you have lost," said Azangor.

"I understand. Thank you," said Alex.

Azangor then turned his attention to Andra.

"Ah, Andra. The player in this game that neither I nor Ruhsarr foresaw. If he was the joker in the pack, and Alex the royal flush, you have definitely been the ace up my sleeve. You too have freed me and I want to reward you too, but what would you want the most?"

"Can I just have a moment to think about it," she said.

"Of course," said Azangor.

"You could become human again. You said you used to dream of being buried near your parents. Would you still like that after your life has ended?" said Alex.

"That was a long time ago, Alex, when I was still human. The place where my parents were buried has changed so much that I have no idea where they are now. Besides that, they would be little more than dust now. Also, what use would death be to me? I have been alive so long I no longer want for death or all the ceremony that goes along with it. And besides that, someone has to stick around to look after you," she said the last sentence with a smile.

She took Alex's hand in hers and winked at him. After a few moments she looked back at the dragon.

"I have decided," she said.

"What will it be?" said Azangor.

“I want to be able to breathe fire whenever I have the need for it. Also, as much as I love my body as it is I would like to be able to return to my human form at will,” she said.

“Very well. The two of you are my gift to the world. I leave it in your capable hands. Thanks to you I am now free. My family have awaited my arrival for far too long. I cannot make them wait any longer,” said Azangor.

“Goodbye,” said Alex and Andra.

“Farewell,” he said.

His figure became clear again as the camera crews drew closer. His body began to dissipate and turn to a vapour. It rose high into the air and vanished. Andra turned and looked at all the reporters. They all came closer but still kept their distance from Alex.

“It looks like we’re not so secret anymore,” said Andra.

“Yep, we certainly have made quite an impact tonight,” said Alex as he looked up at the damaged clock face.

Andra looked and glared at him but struggled to hide her smile as the corners of her lips turned up.

“Behave,” she said.

The reporters started shouting questions.

“I’m sorry, I’m sorry,” said Andra holding up her hands. “We can’t answer any questions right now.”

At that moment five black SUVs with blacked out windows pulled up. Fifteen special ops agents jumped out and ran towards them. They stopped and saluted.

“Lieutenant Colonel Andra, Alex. I am Captain Hawkins. Would you please come with us?” said one of them.

“Where to?” she said.

“The government requires your council,” said Captain Hawkins.

“Very well,” said Andra.

They started to follow them when one of the reporters said,

“Please, Ma’am. Did I hear that, erm, that dragon, correctly? Will you defend us if any attacks like this should happen in the future?”

Alex leaned down towards the microphone that the reporter was holding out with the hope of getting an answer.

“Damn right we will,” he said with a toothy grin.

They then followed the agents to the cars.

“And who are you?” said the reporter.

“We’re the S.O.V.E.U.” said Andra.

Alex opened the boot of the second vehicle and climbed in. Andra opened the rear door and got into one of the back seats. As the cars whisked them across London Alex let his limbs, and muscles return to their human size and his face and jaws became human again.

“Where are we going?” he said.

“The Mi5 building. I suspect someone wants a word with us,” said Andra.

## Chapter 32.

The cars drove right up to the building and through a set of gates. Alex was given a set of clothes which he promptly put on. They were escorted into the building and then into a lift. It ascended to the fourth floor, the doors opened and they were then escorted down a corridor that led to a large conference room. The doors were opened and they were ushered inside. Sat at the table were Hughes, Palmer, Hussain, and Davis. When Andra and Alex walked in they all looked at each other and smiled tired and wearily. They stood up and hugged each other.

"You, my friend, you are fucking awesome," said Hughes as he grabbed Alex, hugged him and slapped his hand on the back.

Davis hugged him and kissed his cheek.

"You saved us all, man. We fucking love you," she said

"Thank you, Alex. I love you," said Hussain as she squeezed him tight.

"You put on a good show. We've just been watching the video in the car. Thank you on behalf of, like, everyone," said Palmer, shaking his hand and then pulling him in for a hug.

"Thank you. All of you, really. If it hadn't been for you Ruhsarr would have killed me live on TV. I have learned that I am part of this team. I'm lucky to have you as friends. The world could have been a very different place," said Alex.

"The world is a different place now. No more vampires. What are we going to do?" said Hussain.

"Well, we'll have to change our name. We can't go around calling ourselves the Vampire Elimination Unit if we aren't hunting vampires anymore," said Hughes.

The door opened, and a short woman in her fifties walked in. Her hair was blonde, cut in a bob, and she was wearing a green trouser suit.

"Please, sit down, sit down, you've all earned a rest," she said with a kind smile. "I am Sheila Johnson. I am a correspondent for the Prime Minister, Anthony Dean. Thanks to you he is safe and well if not a little shaken. He also would like to address you personally but due to the nature of the crisis that has just been averted, he can only correspond with you via a video link. Hence the laptop."

She gestured to the computer tucked under her arm. She walked round to the other side of the table and placed it down on the table top. She opened it took a small mouse from her jacket pocket and plugged it into a USB port in the side.

"Sorry. I can't get to grips with these touch surface mouse things. I just find a desk mouse easier to use," she said.

"I know what you mean. Technology is changing so fast," said Andra with a smile.

"Not the same as when we were young, is it?" said Sheila.

"It's like a different world," said Andra with a smile.

Sheila moved the mouse around and clicked it a few times.

The strangely familiar voice of the Prime Minister emanated from the computer.

"Hello, Sheila. Are they all present?" he said.

"Hello, sir. There are some of them here. They like a lot of us have suffered heavy losses," she said.

"Ok. Thank you. I will address them now, please," said Anthony.

"Yes Ma'am," she said.

Sheila turned the computer around so the screen faced Andra and the others. The weary but smiling face of Anthony Dean filled the screen.

"Ah, hello to you all. I have been informed as to who you are, and what you have done for the people of the world tonight; myself included. I'm so glad to see you. You all have performed an incredible act and a gesture of the utmost selflessness. I'll ensure that you will all be rewarded for saving us as a species. It's a hard thing to imagine. Our entire species was under threat. But you save us and we are extremely grateful. I understand that unfortunately, you have suffered heavy losses. Are there many more of you?" he said with a sombre expression.

"Mr Prime Minister. I am Lieutenant Colonel Andra Hudson. The leader of this team. All you see here are what remains of my personal team. There are a few more remaining in our UK based companies but we have lost roughly ninety percent of our soldiers. There are others in the Americas and Europe but as this country, we are all that remain. We have lost not only soldiers and colleagues but friends and family," said Andra.

"I am sorry, please accept my deepest condolences for all those who were lost. I didn't understand the severity of your situation," he said. He seemed to shift awkwardly in his chair.

"Thank you, sir," said Andra.

The group hung their heads and some fought back tears as the depth of their loss became apparent.

"Those who were lost, will their families be financially compensated?" he said.

"Yes Sir. I have a pension and compensation scheme set up. Their families knew what they were getting into. Some of them were with us because they had no family remaining due to vampire attacks," she said.

"You have my deepest sympathies. Would you accept financial help to compensate for their loss?" he said.

"My financial position is stable enough to cover the compensation without any downfall or need for aid. I appreciate your offer but decline to accept it," said Andra.

"Please if not financial aid we would like to reward you and want to accept the gift of a base right here in London. It's ready for you to use and there will be soldiers assigned to your company at your disposal," said Anthony Dean.

She looked at the others and Alex smiled at her. A smile that said 'impressive.'

"We would be happy to accept your gift of a base. A lot of ours have been severely damaged and need to be repaired before they will be functional again. The soldiers though I don't know if we can accept. We are mercenaries and ex-military," she said.

"I know that you work alongside our British military but I would like to make your unit a part of our military. Then you could recruit soldiers at the start of their careers," he said.

"Thank you for the offer sir but we can't be part of the British military exclusively. We will work with you but we can't work for you. We defend you all as a species, not as nations. I also need seasoned soldiers who have seen combat. What we do isn't for new recruits as we aren't fighting a human enemy. I also like to vet each soldier I recruit personally. After many years of experience I know what qualities make a good soldier," she said.

"I thought you would say something like that and I understand. There is the matter of the damage caused in the altercation with the vampire's leader, Ruhsarr. It will cost millions to repair. We will foot some of the bill but we do have a budget as to how much money we can make available," he said.

"I know. That won't be a problem. I can help cover the costs," she said.

"Thank you. The subject of people and companies having to raise funds and pull money together usually causes a lot more arguments," he said.

"With all due respect sir, I'm not most people. I have been doing what I do for a very long time. I'm also extremely good at saving money," she said.

The Prime Minister smiled. He seemed impressed that Andra was so in control of the situation.

"There will be cars at the front of the building to take you to your new base. Will you be taking some time off now? A little R&R now that this is over?" he said.

"The thought had crossed my mind and a few weeks is definitely in order. But this isn't over. All we have done is remove the vampires from a power struggle that has spanned thousands of years. There are others, entities, who have been trying to take control of this Earth for millennia and only my team and a handful of others have stood in their way. This is not over Prime Minister. This has just begun," said Andra.

The End.

**Author bio**

Paul J. Kearns is an author from Bolton, Northwest England. He lives there with his wife and two children.

From a young age Paul has had an interest in writing. He is also a fan of all things dark and horrifying.

After leaving school he started working as a dental technician and earned a B-Tec National diploma and a UCHE in Dental Technology from the Manchester Metropolitan University. He still works as a Dental Technician today.

In his spare time he loves to spend time with his family and friends, writing, watching movies, gaming, and drawing.

He started writing this novel series in 2010. Before that, he had written a few short stories but had no experience in the art of novel writing. So what you hold in your hands is many years of learning and honing the skills needed.

Dear reader,

I hope you enjoyed reading this book. I hope you enjoyed the story, and love them or hate them I hope you were drawn in by the characters.

If you were inspired in any way to write that story you have been thinking of, I would encourage you to go ahead with it.

And remember, you aren't afraid of the dark, you're afraid of the things that use it as camouflage.

Printed in Great Britain
by Amazon

43952596R00253